HER IMMORTAL MONSTERS

PREMONITION OF PEACE

KEL CARPENTER & AURELIA JANE

Premonition of Peace

Aurelia Jane and Kel Carpenter

Published by Raging Hippo LLC

Copyright © 2024, Raging Hippo LLC

Cover by Okay Creations

About the Authors

Kel Carpenter and Aurelia Jane are the hilarious team behind the international bestselling series, A Demon's Guide to the Afterlife.

They pride themselves in being absolute weirdos, spending hours on the phone coming up with detailed worlds, and laughing about crazy ideas for torturing characters. While they believe they each have the personality of a rabid badger, people still seem to like them okay.

They share a love of coffee, snarky t-shirts, and tacos. Best friends and work wives, Kel has the audacity to live in Maryland while Aurelia lives in Texas, but they try to see each other as much as possible.

You can subscribe to our newsletter at https://kelandaurelia.kit.com/subscribe.

instagram.com/Kelandaureliabooks

patreon.com/kelandaureliabooks

tiktok.com/@kelandaureliabooks

"When you feel like you have been hit, dig deep and hit back. Rock bottom is not your end' it is your beginning."

~Christine Evangelou

For everyone who has been with us since the beginning.
Thank you.

I

NATHALIE

THIS WHOLE SITUATION WAS FUCKED SIX WAYS TO SUNDAY.

"Sasha?" Mist bolted across the room to hug Sasha, wrapping her lithe arms around her body, and squeezing tight. It took Sasha a good second to respond, hugging her in kind. It was short and quick, as I would expect. Neither of them were much for hugging.

If anyone was, it was me, but I couldn't bring myself to move. Not with the state of uproar going on inside me. Ann was focused on Sasha's appearance. The Warden wanted to defend Mist from Lucifer. Peace wanted to go back to bed with him, which wasn't a surprise. Caretaker was trying to get them all to settle. The only one who was silent was Bad Nat.

She sat with a completely neutral expression, waiting to see what I would do.

"Nathalie?" Mist asked hesitantly, clearly holding on to her calm by a thread. She moved a fraction closer to Sasha and eyed Lucifer, who stood stark naked in the living room with an arm wrapped around me. Clearing my throat, I stepped out of his embrace. Or I tried to. He moved with me, as if we were dance partners in a choreographed routine. Lucifer had watched me for nearly a year. He knew me to my core. He also knew, apparently, that I would try to put space between us.

"This isn't the time," I said quietly, not taking my eyes off Sasha.

"I didn't ask about the time," he replied with a slight shrug.

"You know what I mean."

"No, actually, I can't say that I do—"

"Oh for fuck's sake," I said, finally tearing my eyes away to stare at him. "I don't have time for this. Go wait in the bedroom until I can figure out some clothes for you."

"You'll have to forgive me, love, but I'm not comfortable leaving you with—"

"Lucifer. Bedroom." When he didn't move, I added a demanding, "*Now.*"

"I wasn't aware that caring was a crime," he said, using a deep timbre that made me want him to do unspeakable things to me.

I sighed, rolling my eyes. "Stop it. I know what you're doing."

His only response was to tip his head at us. "Ladies," he said.

A sense of guilt nagged at me. I knew he was trying to manipulate me, but that didn't change the fact that we needed to talk. That conversation would have to wait. Sasha's return trumped everything.

As he left the room, I turned back to Mist and Sasha, both of whom were watching him with expressions that couldn't be more different. When the sound of a door closing echoed, Sasha spoke again.

"You didn't have to send him away."

"You're back, and he's a distraction right now." I kept my tone warm and sincere. I felt anything but.

"He's the devil; you don't say?" she replied with a wry smirk while she followed him with her gaze. Her expression was so familiar, it caused an ache in my chest . . . right up until the moment her green cat-eyes pulled away, coming to focus on me.

"Is Señora Rosara on her way up?" I asked lightly, glancing at the door.

She shook her head. "No, she wasn't in the shop when I woke up. Everything was closed, lights off."

"Have you gone to see Sienna yet?" I forced a smile, but it kept it smooth.

"No, I wanted to come see you first. After all, I know what you did for me . . . with the lure . . ." Her response felt like it was meant to have emotion, but the delivery was just off somehow.

"Well, that's not important now." I waved it off. "Sienna is going to be beside herself. We have to get her." I looped my arm through Sasha's, laying my palm against her forearm.

"I can do it," Mist volunteered, playing into my hand.

"That would be great," I responded, and she was out the door within seconds.

"Is everyone seeing what I see?" Ann asked, her voice strained as she looked to the others who wordlessly nodded. They were all in agreement now that Lucifer was gone. *"This takes precedence over everything."*

Pulling her away from my front door, I headed toward the couch.

"Shouldn't we be concerned about Lucifer too?" Her eyes darted to the door where he had exited the room. "We're both back from the dead. Seems newsworthy."

"She's awfully interested in him," The Warden noted.

I grimaced as I slid my hands out from under her arms, taking a seat and patting the cushion next to me. "I can only deal with one thing at time, so for now, let's pretend he's not." I gave her a concerned look as she sat down. "How did you finally make it back?"

Sasha stared for a moment before shrugging apathetically. "It wasn't that hard once you told me what to look for."

"Right," I pushed out a chuckle. "Was Señora's human Ouija board really what did it?"

"It was," she answered. "That and the lure. It helped, but it also made things tricky."

"Tricky?"

She nodded slowly. "Think of the room where my body was being kept as a fence. The lure acted as a hole in that fence, but not a very big hole. And when I was in the veil . . ."

I narrowed my eyes a fraction, leaning forward with rapt interest. "What happened in the veil?"

"I wasn't alone. Someone, or something, is there too. Hunting."

The very notion of it rocked my foundation. I swallowed, considering my words. "What do you mean by 'hunting'? Hunting other souls?"

She lifted a delicate shoulder, her tank top drawing attention to her perfectly smooth skin. It practically glowed beneath the soft lighting of my apartment. "I don't know," she answered. "But it made it difficult to work my way past the lure. I needed a long enough gap where they were gone so I could push myself through it."

I sat back, hands folded over my lap as I took in what she was saying. "Do you think they were trying to prevent you from coming back?"

She thought about it for a moment. "I really don't know. It's all a bit of a haze. Like a bad dream that lingers after you wake up. I remember things in fragments."

That was when I should have comforted her and said it was all okay. That's what a good friend did. Instead, I skipped over false assurances and said, "You should see Señora."

"What for?" Sasha asked sharply.

"You've basically been to hell and back. I just want her to look you over. Make sure everything's okay." I shrugged. All things considering, it wasn't an odd request.

"I'm fine. It wasn't that bad." She waved away my concern.

"I mean, just to be sure—"

My front door opened, interrupting us. "Sasha?"

Sienna stood in shock with Mist, Piper, Ronan, Anders, and all of the kids in tow. Sasha jumped up from her seat beside me.

My eyes found Ronan as his brow furrowed. *"Don't say anything,"* I mentally said to him. His features smoothed and nothing but the hands he placed on Honor and Orson's shoulders gave him away.

"Sienna," Sasha said with the most emotion she'd shown since coming to my apartment. Sienna rushed into her twin's arms, wrapping herself around Sasha and holding her tight—as if she feared she would vanish at any moment.

"I thought you were going to die. I didn't know what I was going to do," Sienna said between sobs. Sasha patted her back, shushing her cries, and if I didn't see it with my own eyes, I'd question if I'd overthought things only moments ago.

"I missed you too," Sasha said, wrapping one arm around her sister's shoulder in a hug.

"I'm glad you made it back from the veil okay," Piper chimed in, her violet eyes meeting mine. "Did you find the spirits we were looking for?"

"I . . . I can't remember," Sasha answered, seeming flustered.

Piper smothered the moment of disappointment with a half-smile that didn't meet her eyes. "It's okay, we'll just have to find another way to contact them."

I grimaced. Our window for a proper séance had

passed with Samhain and there weren't enough of the bodies left for a resurrection.

"Are we going to talk about Lucifer?" Sasha's question broke through the brief peace that existed in the room, and her words hit like an anvil in a pond.

"What the hell does that mean?" Piper bit out. Her eyes found mine and she arched an eyebrow. "Nathalie, what does she mean by 'talk about Lucifer'? Is there something I need to know about your not-so-friendly neighborhood poltergeist?"

I cringed and opened my mouth to speak, but of course, bad had to become *worse* and Lucifer appeared beside me out of thin air. He was dressed in a three-piece suit and adjusting his cufflinks. I craned my neck to look at his face, but his ineffable mask of pleasantness was firmly in place.

"Not a poltergeist, thank you," he said, "I'm her familiar, or didn't she tell you? Either way, I like to think I'm quite friendly these days."

My elbow shot out, nailing him in the side. The asshole didn't even do me the service of pretending it hurt. I absently rubbed my arm where I was sure to bruise.

"I thought you were dead," Piper said, appraising him like she would a bug that dared crawl beneath her boot.

"So, things progressed . . . unexpectedly." I winced but held my hands up in surrender. "I'm handling it. I promise."

"Yes, I was dead, thanks to the lot of you. What? No

celebratory hug? Not even a high five?" Lucifer grinned like he wasn't perturbed. If I thought it would make me feel better, I'd elbow him again. "Tough crowd."

Piper lifted an eyebrow as if to question how well I was "handling it."

"How exactly are we handling him?" Peace asked, poking her head out of the greenhouse.

"Trust Prime, she's got it," Caretaker said with a soft smile.

"I have this under control. Mostly." I met her gaze and pleaded with my eyes.

"If your concern is 'what will Lucifer do now,' I can share my plans and put you at ease." His words earned an eyeroll from both me and Piper. Ronan's eyes were more focused on Sasha than Lucifer, which was telling given he and his brother hadn't parted on the best of terms. It seemed they wouldn't reunite on them either.

"Okay," Piper said, putting her hands on her hips. "Lay it on me. What are these 'plans' of yours and do they involve me sending your ass back to the spirit realm?" She jutted her chin toward Lucifer, taking a not-so-subtle step in between him and Mist, who was pulling at her sleeves in discomfort.

"For starters, I have no intentions to usurp you from your metaphorical throne," Lucifer replied with a disinterested look. "In fact, I have no desire to rule again at all."

"As if you could," Piper muttered in response. "So what, you just expect us to believe you have no purpose coming back? Just happy to be alive, huh?"

"Oh, I have a purpose." Lucifer's eyes locked on mine. "I've been given a second chance, and I intend to use it wisely."

I swallowed under the weight of his gaze. Looking away, I noticed a coolness in Sasha's features as she watched our interaction.

Anders moved forward and clapped Lucifer on the back. I wasn't surprised he was the first to accept his return. They'd worked together for years and always got along well. "Glad to have you back, man," he said with a crooked smile.

"Nice to see you in the flesh," Sienna added, giving him a fierce one-armed hug while holding onto Sasha's hand with her other. I could only imagine what she was feeling; her long-dead lover and almost-dead sister back in one day.

Sasha stepped forward; her eyes bright. "I'm so glad you found your way back to me," she said, moving closer to him in a way that made my stomach twist with an emotion I refused to admit was jealousy. "We have much catching up to do."

"Hmm." Lucifer looked her over before flashing another half-smile.

His noncommittal response was not lost on Sasha, and it clearly didn't please her. She pulled away and looked at her sister.

"I'm tired. I want to go home," she declared.

"Of course," Sienna said, nodding. "Hallie, come on—"

"Wait." I jumped in. The room snapped to attention. I

internally cursed and told myself to tone it down. "I was going to offer for me or Piper to keep Hallie for the night, so you and Sasha could spend time together and she can get her rest."

"Hallie, stay with me," Orson added, instantly keen on the idea.

"We can have a sleepover," Hallie agreed, holding hands with Orson in the pure way that only small children could.

I forced a smile again. "Is that okay with you?" I asked Piper.

"Oh yeah, for sure." She frowned. "We're skipping over some of the finer details of the whole Lucifer-is-back-in-the-flesh thing, but I'll entrust this one to you."

I mouthed "thank you" to her and Sienna pulled Hallie into a hug, saying goodbye.

"Can I sleep over with you guys?" Mist asked, not hiding her wariness of Lucifer. I couldn't blame her given he compelled her to not compel him.

"My Angel sleepover too?" Hallie beamed, staring up at her with absolute adoration on her face.

"Of course, Mist. You're always welcome," Piper answered easily.

"Great, all settled. Ready to go, Sienna?" Sasha pushed, heading toward the door.

"I'm coming. Bye, baby." Sienna blew Hallie one more kiss and gave us all a wave. A second later, the door slammed shut behind them.

"Mist, why don't you take the kiddos into your room to hang out?" I suggested as soon as they were out of the apartment. Mist looked at me curiously but followed directions.

Everyone but me had super hearing, so sending the kids to the other room didn't do much. Hopefully Mist would be enough of a distraction. They were all at an age where secrets were hard to keep.

As the door closed to Mist's bedroom, silence fell over the group. I took a deep breath before finally speaking the dreaded words that had been swirling in my head.

"That wasn't Sasha."

2

NATHALIE

The silence hung over us like a guillotine. Everyone stared at me for one beat...two...and then the blade fell.

"What do you mean it's not Sasha?" Piper demanded, sounding upset. Knowing her, it was probably at least partially due to irritation that she hadn't noticed as well.

"I'm telling you something else slipped through and has taken up residence in her body," I stressed, making the situation bare. "The real Sasha—our Sasha—is still in the veil."

"I noticed something was weird," Anders admitted slowly. "I couldn't quite put my finger on it, but the energy around her was not what it used to be."

"She did seem kind of off, sure," Piper agreed, crossing her arms, "but I guess I just chalked it up to the effects of the veil. Who wouldn't feel off after something like that?"

"The magic surrounding her wasn't death magic,"

Ronan confirmed as his brow furrowed in deep thought. "It was chaos."

"Who the hell would come back with chaos magic?" Piper asked, brushing her thumb over her bottom lip in contemplation.

"Well, to answer that, we should ask ourselves *who* in the veil has chaos magic. Then go from there," Lucifer interjected as he crossed the room. I avoided his unsettling, gold gaze as he seated himself in the center of my sofa and spread both arms across the back—like the king of the apartment. *As if.*

"That's a rare magic, and there aren't many supernaturals that have it," Anders said, rubbing at his jaw thoughtfully. "Even in the veil."

"It has to be someone that also knows us," I added.

"Why would you say that?" he asked.

I looked between each of them as if it were obvious.

"That entity knew about us, well enough to blend in. While she seemed off, no one would have thought that wasn't Sasha, if not for the change in magic. We would have assumed she was just different after coming out of the veil. That goes beyond watching us for a short time and implies they've been at it a while." I glanced over at Lucifer before moving my eyes back to the group. "She was also very excited to see *him.*"

"Little witch, are you jealous?" Lucifer asked, his tone dripping with satisfaction. I didn't answer. I didn't even look at him, choosing instead to roll my eyes to the ceiling and then train them back on the group as a whole.

"So, we're sifting through people who know us, know Lucifer, and have chaos magic." I ached to disappear in my memory loci and pull some files. There must be something in there that could narrow it down.

"That does give us a better starting point to work from." Piper sighed as she shifted her stance, crossing one ankle over the other.

"It does," I paused, thinking carefully how to phrase my next thought. "But I also feel like that makes things worse. Any of the people we know that would have had chaos magic . . . it could be a disaster if they were back."

Lucifer's eyes narrowed, his eyes scanning my face. "Do you have a suspect in mind?"

I ignored him and pushed forward.

"Whoever this is," I continued, my mind still racing through the possibilities, none of them reassuring, "they know enough to mimic Sasha well. They definitely know more than we'd like and that makes them infinitely more dangerous."

"We need to act," Ronan growled, his face crumpling with anger.

Anders shared his agreement. "While we still have the upper hand and the element of surprise."

"What about the real Sasha?" Piper hissed. "If we attack and things go wrong, we could damage or even kill her physical body. Then how would we get her back?"

"Which is why we're not going to act or do something rash," I said, trying to be the voice of reason. "We should act normal. Don't give them any cause to suspect that we're onto them. Buy time."

"What exactly is buying time going to do for us?" Ronan asked. "If that's not Sasha, then the real Sasha is lost to us. She has been in the veil for so long—"

"That doesn't mean she's gone," I said, hardening my tone. Ronan was a realist by most people's definition, and usually, so was I. "Sasha is strong. She'd never abandon Sienna willingly."

"Nat . . ." Piper interjected kindly; her voice soft.

"If we jump too quickly here, we end up with nothing. We'd have no idea what her impersonator is here for, or why they're choosing her body," I countered. "If they managed to get past the Señora's lure, then whoever this is, they're powerful. We need to know who and *what* we're dealing with. If we send them back to the veil immediately, what's to stop them from doing this again?"

No one spoke. I had a point, and they knew it.

The group nodded in agreement, the plan falling into place like the pieces of a puzzle. It was risky, but we had to play our cards right. Lives were on the line, including Sasha's, trapped as she was in the veil. I tried not to dwell on what might happen if we failed. Or the fact that Real-Sasha was still wandering alone out there. There was a very real possibility that Ronan was right, and Sasha was lost to us forever.

The odds were stacked against us in every way. But I just couldn't let myself believe this was it. Until I had no other choice, I refused to accept failure.

I wasn't going to stop trying and I wouldn't give up on Sasha.

"So we just let this body snatcher continue walking around the city? Let it near the kids?" Ronan questioned. "I'm not okay by that."

"We do need to act," I agreed, but followed it with a pointed look. "Just not right now. They didn't attack right out of the gate, and they could have. They chose to pretend instead and go along with us which makes me think that they may have a bigger plan, and things are going to be relatively safe while we play along."

"We need to move quickly, though," Anders countered. "If you really think Sasha is out there and trying to come back, every second matters."

Piper's jaw clenched. "Whoever it is was around the twins. Around Hallie. If you hadn't stepped in, we'd have sent her home with *something* . . ."

"No." I shook my head firmly. "Ronan knew something was wrong too, and I'd never send Hallie home knowing a spirit was impersonating Sasha."

"I'm going to go check on the kids," Ronan interrupted, even more broody and overprotective than usual. He walked toward Mist's room, Anders on his heels, and knocked gently on the door before pushing it open.

Turning back to Piper and Lucifer, I gave the latter a look of irritation before I moved closer to Piper. Angling my back to him, I tried to have a semblance of a private conversation. I still didn't know what to do with him.

"We need to tell Sienna." Piper nodded her head in

agreement, strands of her blonde hair moving around her face.

"I know, but it's going to suck," she replied with a long sigh. "She was so excited. This has all been so hard on her. How do we tell her that her sister is actually *not* back and is instead still floating in the void with no way out, and also, hey! –there's something wicked using her body?"

"Yeah. . ." I let out a long breath and ran a hand through my hair. "Her emotions are already fragile. Someone needs to break this to her discreetly."

"I can handle that. When I go to pick up Hallie's stuff, I can find a way to tell her. That's the easy part. The aftermath? Not so much."

"We'll also have to come up with an excuse for Hallie to stay with you until we figure out who this is and what their motives are. I don't think they'll attack, but I'm not risking any of the kids' safety on a maybe."

She glanced down the hallway before returning her gaze to me. "Mist will need to stay with us too while you sort out your *situation*," Piper said, thrusting her chin toward Lucifer. "I'll tell Sasha—or Not-Sasha—that Mist just really wanted to spend extra time with Hallie."

"That'll work, and as far as everything else, we'll figure it out," I said, more to convince myself than anyone else. I wondered internally if we'd be okay.

Ann, The Warden, and Bad Nat were suspiciously quiet in my loci, and that wasn't comforting.

3

MARCEL

THE WATER FROM THE SHOWERHEAD POUNDED AGAINST MY skin, the hot spray doing little to alleviate the deep, relentless ache in my bones. I leaned heavily against the cool tile, letting the water run over me, trying to will the pain away. Gods, it hurt like hell. Everything did at this point.

I tried hard not to show it, especially around Nat, but this shit was breaking me. Had been for a long time now. She had enough to worry about without adding my suffering to the list. In moments like this though, when I was alone, it was impossible to ignore. The mask I wore for her and for the world dissipated, leaving me vulnerable and exposed. It was getting harder and harder to push through the pain.

I loved Nat more than anything. She believed she could find a solution, but I knew better than to pin a single hope on that. She wasn't the first to try and so far, luck was never on my side. This affliction—this curse—had no cure. My magic was eating my body alive from the inside out. I was dying, closer and closer to crossing the veil every day and I was trying like mad to accept it. But it was hard. So damn hard.

There was still so much I felt needed to be done, especially with Nathalie. She finally knew about my past, my sickness, about her mother's manipulations. She knew about the way I had been forced into situations against my will. She knew the *truth* now. Which meant I finally could move past it with her. But to do that I needed time, and time was the one thing I didn't have.

Letting out a slow, shaky breath, I braced my hands against the walls and steadied myself before I was ready to get out. Turning off the water, I stepped out of the shower, wrapping a towel around my waist. My reflection in the mirror caught my eye, and I pressed my teeth together, pointedly ignoring the man in the mirror. I barely recognized him.

A knock at the door pulled me from my thoughts.

I pulled on a pair of gray sweatpants that hung a little looser around my waist than normal. The knocking continued fiercely, and I sighed as I pulled my glamour around me, letting it settle over me like a sheen of oil. Uncomfortable, for certain, but familiar at this point. I'd worn it for so long, I didn't even know how to fully feel like myself without it.

"Coming," I called, lumbering for the door with stiff joints. When I peeped through the eyehole, I saw

Nathalie standing there wearing dark jeans and a tightly fitted Nine Inch Nails t-shirt. I wasn't familiar with the band, but that didn't mean much. She enjoyed every genre of music, and I couldn't keep up.

"Nat, hey," I greeted, trying to sound less out of breath. "What can I do for you?" I lifted an arm to lean against the doorframe. My glamour shifted, showing the muscle I should have had in my biceps. Nat's light brown eyes flicked toward it for a fraction of a second then back down, her cheeks turning a shade pink.

"Hey, Marcel, um . . . is August here?"

"No," I said, my voice a little harder than intended. I fixed my tone before I continued. "I can tell him you came by—"

She shook her head, a slight look of relief crossing her face when she cut me off. "No, I'm here to see you. I was just, uh, curious if he was around. There's a lot going on with Sasha right now."

"Oh . . ." I tried not to let the fact that she wasn't here to see him please me too much. I wasn't dumb. I knew I had a hill to climb, greater than the other guys vying for her attention. But I would be damned if I gave up before the grave took me.

She looked at me with an amused expression. "You gonna let me in or . . .?"

I stepped to the side, and she moved past me, giving me a hint of her jasmine and lilac scent. Closing the door, I followed behind her, unable to stop myself from watching the sway of her hips. It was impossible to forget what that ass felt like clutched in my hands as I pinned her to the shelves in her parents' library, fucking her like I owned her. I did. Past tense.

The thought bothered me more than almost anything because I would give anything to own her again.

"What's up?" I asked as we sat on the cushions across from each other. "Not that I'm not happy you're here, but you look tense."

And she did. There was a stiff set to her shoulders and a stormy look to her gaze that I couldn't make sense of. She looked at me, guarded, as we sat across from each other on the couch. Repressing a groan, I uncomfortably adjusted in the seat.

"Nothing that we need to get into right now," she said quickly, changing topics before I could speak. "We need to talk about your condition."

"I'd rather not and say we did," I retorted sarcastically, before sobering.

"You're wearing a glamour," she said.

I shrugged, running a hand through my hair. "I always wear a glamour." Especially around her.

"I need you to drop it so I can see how you really are."

I stiffened. "I don't think that's necessary—"

"If I don't know how you're progressing, I can't help you, Marcel."

My lips pressed together. I fought internally over whether I should drop it. She had a point, but . . .

"Please," Nat whispered softly. "Let me in. I won't judge—"

"I'm not worried about your judgement." I was

worried about her pity. The way she looked at me the first time I'd dropped my glamour was burned into my memory, and I hated it. My sunbeam had a bleeding heart, even if she'd learned to encase it in steel. I didn't want her to see me this weak. A mere shadow of my former self. A husk.

"Then what? I've already seen you . . ." She stopped as understanding crossed her features. "Marcel . . . it's okay."

"I don't want a caretaker, Nat. And I don't want you to see me as some broken thing you need to take pity on." I wanted her to see me as a man. Her man, specifically.

"I'm not going to pity you, for fuck's sake. Since when did giving a shit about someone equate to pity?"

"When I saw how you looked at me without my glamour." There it was. Out in the open.

She got to her feet and crossed the space between us, taking the seat beside me. My body hummed at the close proximity.

"Look. It was a surprise. You can't blame me for having a reaction," she said, pausing for a moment. "I don't look at you like you're broken. That's not what this is."

"You sure about that?" The bitterness in my voice was thinly veiled.

Nathalie pinched the bridge of her nose, inhaling deeply. I waited for her retort, but it never came. Instead, she softened. "Does everything have to be a fight between us? I don't want to do that anymore. It's so fucking taxing and I don't have it in me. I'm on your side. Why can't you see that?"

All the resistance I had built up began to crumble. I didn't have it in me either. "I know you are. Maybe it just feels like old times when we argue. When things weren't as complicated yet. We were always pretty good at it," I said softly, a slight smirk appearing. I winked at her, and I could see her frustration with me dissipating.

"You know," she said, taking my hands in her, "you also used to let me have my way quite a bit too."

I sighed deeply, knowing she was going to win this one. It was little more than a thought to drop the glamour. I tensed, waiting for her expression to change. For my heart to crack open and bleed all over us both.

"Well?" I prompted.

Nathalie leaned in close, lifting a hand to cup my cheek. Gently, she brushed her thumb beneath one eye—no doubt tracing the dark circles lining my face. "You look exhausted."

"That's not a very nice thing to say to someone who's dying."

She chuckled, accepting my attempt to lighten the mood. "You want me to be honest, or do you want me to coddle you?"

"Fair enough," I said, taking a strand of her hair and twirling it around my finger.

"I won't, you know."

"Won't what?"

"I won't coddle you." A small smile graced her lips.

"You're a pain in the ass, Marcel. I know you don't want a caretaker, but you can't stop me from trying to help."

"Who's the pain in the ass now?" I shot back, raising a brow. "Not taking no for an answer. So very like you."

"You're right," she huffed, laughing lightly. "Arguing does feel like old times. Maybe that's why we can barely be in a room together without fighting about something. Anything, really."

"Remember what else we used to do?" She raised her brows in question. "*After* we'd argue . . ."

It was a long shot. Not one I really expected to turn into anything. Just something to make her smile or playfully smack my arm. I wanted to feel a sense of normalcy with her. She shocked me by leaning forward, closing the gap between us. I'd wanted to feel her again for so long, but for some reason, I froze, not believing this was real. Soft lips brushed mine before she whispered, "You going to kiss me back or what?"

That's all it took to snap me out of it. I groaned, leaning into the kiss. My free hand came up to knot in her hair. I fisted it tightly as I pulled her closer, expertly parting her lips with my tongue. Nathalie opened up, letting me in.

"Fucking finally," I growled. Our hands unraveled and I reached for her hip, pulling her to me. Nat gave in, throwing one leg across my waist to straddle me. Her heat enveloped me. Home. I was *finally* home.

Our mouths clashed as we came together, unable to get close enough, to breathe in enough, to devour enough—I nipped her bottom lip. She pulled my top

one between hers then sucked on my tongue. I
groaned.

Nathalie's hands cupped my face, sliding backwards
to run through my hair. She pulled at the strands, giving
me a bite of pain. I didn't complain. It was a different
kind of pain than what I was used to. A kind I welcomed.

Our lips broke apart, but I continued sliding my lips
over her jaw, down her neck. I inhaled her deeply, my
hand on her hip tightening.

"Do you have any idea how much I've missed you?
Missed this?" I whispered. Then, before she could
respond, I sucked on that patch of flesh just below her
ear that drove her wild. My sunbeam moaned, her body
going taut against me.

"Yes," she breathed.

"No, I don't think you do." I bit her neck, making her
jerk in my lap. Her center pressed against my cock—
seeking friction. Times may have changed. I may be
worse than ever before, but I knew all her buttons to
press. "If you did, you would have caved to me sooner."

"I almost did," she sighed, swaying her hips back and
forth. "But I was so . . . hurt? Angry? All of the above."

"And now?" I licked that spot on her neck, and she
shivered.

Nat sighed and leaned back, putting her weight on
my legs as she created enough distance between us to
look at me. "I'm tired," she admitted. "Tired of fighting,
of pushing you away. I don't want our last moments
together to be angry words and—"

And there it was. The mood killer. Nathalie had

already pulled herself away, physically and emotionally, working on how to fix things. Preparing for the worst. My hand slipped out of her hair. I put a finger to her lips, shushing her. "I'm still fighting. There's still time."

Her face crumpled into a grimace. "We're running out of time, Marcel. There's no amount of glamour or witty remarks that can change that."

"There really aren't any options, Nat," I told her without an ounce of hesitation. "I've lived with this for so long now that I've thought through everything more than once. But I'm open to suggestion."

I was dying and I was fucking screwed.

But I would fight that losing battle till the end. For life. *For her.*

"I thought about trying to turn you into something else," she said, her eyes straying from mine. "But turning into a vampire or a werewolf is out of the question now. And taking blood from a demon would likely kill you too. You're too weak."

I tried not to react like I'd just been punched. No guy wanted to hear how weak he was, especially not from the woman he loved. Even if it were true.

Not that I believed that idea would have worked to begin with, but there was no need to say it. "So that can be marked off the list. Any other ideas?"

"Not really," she admitted, her voice barely above a whisper. "I'm still digging for an answer. If you had told me earlier . . ." She let her voice trail.

Should've, would've, could've—none of it helped us

now. But I knew my sunbeam, and her inability to separate what could have been from where we were.

I shook my head. "You'd have been sacrificed by your
mother and none of this would've mattered in the first
place," I said, my tone firm. "I don't regret what I did to
protect you. I just want the chance to make it up before . .
. just before."

I couldn't say it. Not yet. Not to Nathalie.

Silence settled in the room and Nathalie tried, but
ultimately failed, to hide her terror. It would have
warmed my heart if it weren't so very real for us both.

Try as I might, my hourglass was nearing its end.

"I visited Carissa the other day," she said suddenly,
breaking the quiet, "and she attacked me. Not in a
Carissa way either. It was super weird, honestly."

I stiffened as concern and frustration mingled within
me. "You should've taken me with you," I said, my jaw
clenching. "I could've—"

Nathalie cut me off, smoothing away my concern
tracing my lips with her finger. "It's fine. I had August
with me. We left before it got too bad."

My jaw clenched. I knew she was involved with him.
I didn't like it, but I understood it. That he was there for
her, protecting her, helping her—it hurt. It should have
been me. Maybe I should be happy that she'd have
someone when I left, but all I could bring myself to feel
was bitterness. I wasn't that good or kind or pure.
Nathalie was mine, but banging on my chest and making
my displeasure known would only make her shut down
more. "I'm happy you had him with you."

"Are you?" she asked, raising her brow in question.

"No. But I can concede it's better than going alone."

Nat snorted. "I suppose I should give you points for trying."

"I'll take what I can get when it comes to you," I said, squeezing her hip. The warmth of her beneath my palm calmed my soul.

"Will you, though?" she asked quietly. "You know I'm with him and—"

"It fucking kills me to say this, so know that now. I love you more than anything in this world or the next. You are the reason I'm fighting. I would give anything for a future with you, even a future where that other fucker exists in your life too. I know he makes you happy, and as much as I loathe that you need more than just me, your happiness matters more. I recognize that you're trying to move past what broke us, and it's about damn time—"

"Marcel," she said flatly.

"My point is, I fucked up. I broke us. You put the pieces back together without me, so I don't get to say how they should go. I wasn't there. I wanted to be. My heart always was. But your reality was that you were alone, and if this is the consequence of that—so be it."

"I'm not doing it to punish you."

"I know," I answered with a smile I didn't feel. "You're a lot of things, but you're not vindictive."

We were quiet for a minute, but it wasn't awkward. It was easy, it always had been between us. In many ways I missed this just as much as every other part of Nat. What I felt went far beyond fucking her. It was a little dark and dangerous and obsessive. I wanted her body. Her thoughts. Her silence. Everything. She was my peace, and so I'd give anything to have even a part of her.

It was more than I deserved after all I'd done, but I wasn't the noble sort. If she wanted me, I was hers. Period.

"What did you really come here for?" I asked, rubbing circles with my thumb into her side. "While I won't complain, I know it wasn't for this," I added, giving her a squeeze.

She heaved a deep sigh. "I have a question for you, and I need an honest answer. Please."

Her tone was serious, and I brought my eyes back to hers. My eyebrow raised expectantly.

"Why did Kat try to contact Morgan Le Fay?" she asked, her gaze steady, seeing straight through me. "And don't lie again. I know you did last time."

Her question was unexpected. Enough so that I paused stroking her skin, having to consider my answer.

"Nat, that's not my story to tell. I'm sorry."

As much as I loved Nat, I loved Katherine too. In a totally different way, but I wouldn't betray her trust if I could avoid it. In the viper's den, she had become my best friend. For as long as I could, I'd protect her, and I'd guard what she entrusted me to know.

"Marcel, something bad is going on. I know it," she said, her voice firm. "And I have a hunch that Kat's efforts with The Morrigan is why." When I didn't say anything she continued. "People are dying. I need to know what she's gotten herself into."

"Nat, I swore I wouldn't tell a soul. What kind of man does that make me if I break my word?"

Nathalie pressed her lips together, understanding but not letting it go either. "If I'm right, either Kat's next on the hit list, or I am."

Her words dropped deep into my stomach, weighty and overwhelming. I'd protect Kat as my best friend and I'd fucking kill for Nat, die for her. Anything. I grabbed my bottom lip between my teeth and bit punishingly hard. *Fuck.* It felt like betrayal, but for this?

If what she said was the truth, then vows be damned.

I wouldn't put either of them at risk.

"She wanted to find out how to bring back Prudence," I confessed, and Nathalie reeled back in surprise.

"What?" Her brows puckered in surprise. "Why would she want to do that?"

"Prudence wasn't just her best friend, Nat," I said, slowly. "Prudence and Katherine were together."

"Together?" It took a second before understanding crossed her features. "Oh . . . *oh* . . ."

"She was the love of her life. Still is, really."

A long moment passed as Nathalie processed what I'd told her. A brief look of sadness appeared before she covered it up. "Gods. No wonder she never forgave me."

"What has she gotten herself into?" I pressed. "Why did you ask about that? And why do you think you might be targeted next?"

Nathalie sighed heavily, her shoulders slumping

further. "You're better off not knowing. It's just going to stress you out."

"Are you serious right now? No. Don't do that," I demanded, my voice hardening. "I just spilled Kat's most deeply guarded secret, and I did it to protect you both. I deserve to know."

Nathalie measured me with her gaze, then nodded. She shifted her body, and moved to stand, offering me a hand up. "Fine, but you're going to need to put some pants on. Nothing about what I'm going to tell you leads to sexy time."

4

NATHALIE

Sitting in my car, I gripped the wheel, turning my knuckles white as I stared ahead at the unmoving scenery around me. I'm glad I couldn't find a parking spot closer to August's apartment. I didn't want to risk Marcel seeing this happen.

I didn't want him to see me break down.

Muffling a sob and a groan, I let my head fall heavily onto the wheel with a thud. My shoulders started to shake with the effort to repress the cries itching to push out of me. *Gods, he looked worse than I've ever seen him.* The exhaustion was etched into every curve and groove of Marcel's face. The pallor of his skin against the dark lines of magic threatening to break through was heart-breaking to see.

I felt like everything was weighing on me and I was crumbling beneath the pressure. I promised Marcel I'd find a cure for him, but I was no closer to that than when I started.

Now I got to add fucking *Not*-Sasha to my never-ending list. New Chicago took a lot to run, and god knows it would fall to shit if I didn't do everything I did underground and behind the scenes.

Banging my fists against the wheel, I let out a strangled scream of frustration. It all felt like too much to carry sometimes.

"But who else could carry it?" Caretaker asked kindly. "Who else could bear it?"

I nodded to myself because truly, who else could? It wasn't just that I had the money to make things happen. I had the resources, the knowledge, and my eidetic memory that never let me forget a single thing. I knew I was capable of more than the average person because of my memory loci. Multiple versions of myself existed, researched, had conversions, all at the same time. My blessing might also be a curse, but it was one that I bore for the greater of the whole.

Taking a shuddering, barely steadying breath, I leaned back against the headrest and closed my eyes, pushing down the tears once again. Working to calm myself, I finally turned the ignition on, a blast of hot air hitting my skin. Putting the car into reverse, I pulled out. The drive back to my place passed in a blur. Soon enough I was tramping through Señora Rosara's shop, stepping around one of her cats that was peering up at me with creepily human emotion.

Turning the key in the lock, the weight of exhaustion practically dragged me down as I stumbled my way into my apartment. I pushed the door closed carefully considering the bomb still planted on it, courtesy of Piper. Immediately veering for the kitchen, tea on the brain, I couldn't help the yawn that pulled out of me.

I was already struggling to sleep with everything that we've had to face. Lucifer. The Morrigan. Bree. Lorcan. The literal hell hole that opened up in New Chicago . . . I shook my head as I pulled out the loose-leaf jasmine tea mix. Hopefully it would calm my nerves and maybe allow me to get a couple of hours in before the anxiety nightmares started.

A few minutes later, I was swirling honey into a cup of jasmine tea, toast with brown spread over it sitting next to me. When I turned around holding a treat in each hand, my heart nearly leapt into my throat.

"Fuck, Lucifer," I exclaimed, steadying my cup, glad my startling didn't slosh its contents over the sides. Lucifer stood there, shirtless, leaning effortlessly against the fridge.

"The last time I heard you say that it was a lot breathier." He looked away with a wistful, fond smile. "Maybe we can try to mimic that experience again."

"Not likely." I shot him a scowl, my heart still pounding as I scrambled for a way out of this conversation.

"You look like you've seen a ghost," he said, a hint of amusement dancing in his eyes. He crossed his arms over his chest and his biceps flexed in a way that really just *did* it for me, though I wished it wouldn't.

For a moment, I forgot how to breathe properly. My eyes skimmed over the hard planes of his chest, across his arms, and down, down, down to the sharp Vee at his waist. Shaking it off, I forced myself to focus on his unearthly gorgeous face, ignoring the knowing smirk he wore.

"Why are you still here?" I set my food and tea on the counter and ran a hand through my hair, attempting to regain composure.

"Where else would I be?" he asked, quirking an eyebrow as if my question was just the most ridiculous thing he had ever heard.

"You got what you wanted. You're back. Don't you have devil things to do?"

"I'm exactly where I should be," he answered without hesitation. "As for 'devil things' . . ." He paused for a second before dragging his eyes over me lazily. "You look even more tired than usual."

"You're part of the reason I look like this," I retorted, my voice a mix of weariness and irritation.

"Part, not whole." He grinned in satisfaction, then looked at me with a more serious expression. "You're under a lot of stress and not sleeping. You need to let your body rest, little witch."

"I'll sleep when the world isn't falling apart," I snapped. "*Again.*"

He stepped closer, the air suddenly thick with his presence. "Fuck the world. You need to take care of yourself more."

"Not all of us can be as selfish as you," I mutter to myself, sidestepping him and moving toward the living room.

"Don't start with me."

"Can we not?"

"Can we not *what* exactly, little witch?"

"Can we not *do this*." I motioned toward him with the hand holding my toast. "I'm tired. I'm cranky. And if you don't leave me alone, I'm not responsible for the things I say."

Lucifer chuckled. "Give me your anger. It may not taste as sweet as your lies, but I want it all the same."

Internally, I felt a pang of betrayal mixed with a strong pull of attraction. I would love to relieve some stress with him. Damn, would I love it. But things didn't feel the same anymore. After finding out he basically tricked me into fucking him back to life, I wasn't in the mood for more games.

I was the idiot that fell for it once.

And as Piper would say, fool me once—shame on you. Fool me twice—eat lead.

"I like him," Peace interjected, looking up from her latest smutty romance. "He's refreshing." She thumbed the page of her book, toying with the corner. "Lucifer doesn't expect us to be perfect. He loves us as we are—even if it's unconventional."

"He's not a stable variable in our lives," Ann countered. "He's unpredictable and utterly impulsive."

"Not to mention manipulative," The Warden chimed in.

Bad Nat cocked her head and crossed her arms. "And yet, the Prime still fell for him."

"Fell. Past tense."

Bad Nat snorted. "Save the lies for Lucifer. You're not capable of moving on because of this memory of yours. Every moment exists in the present. There is no past. You fell for him, and you are still falling. You want to talk of blessings and curses? That's the real one you're afflicted with. You can't let go."

I shuddered.

The silence was damning.

The truth couldn't hide.

But that didn't mean I was going to address it right now. Shaking off their commentary, I focused back on Lucifer as I settled on the couch, sipping at my tea. "Circling back, why are you still here, Lucifer? Isn't there literally anywhere else for you to be? I have a hard time believing you want to spend your second chance hanging out in my little apartment."

His expression darkened briefly before he masked it with an easy smile. "I've lived all over this world. I've seen the great wonders. I've watched empires rise and fall. In truth, I find the world a bit boring after all this time," he said. I swallowed hard on my toast. "But let's not beat around the bush. You don't really think I want to be anywhere else. You're simply upset about being left out of the plan for my return."

My anger spiked, running through my chest. "Gee, I wonder why being *used* would have that effect on me," I replied caustically.

The muscles in his jaw tightened. "I didn't use you."

"Bullshit."

"Okay, fine, in the strictest sense I used you. Answer me this, would you have done it if you knew it would bring me back? Would you have still fucked the devil knowing I'd no longer be your dirty little secret in the light of day?"

"I'm not doing this with you—" Lucifer disappeared and reappeared directly in front of me. He squatted down, putting us face to face. "How did you do that?"

"We'll get to that. First, we're going to address my question. You have a choice, little witch. Answer or kiss me."

I leaned in close, the scent of blood and sex filling my nostrils. "Read my lips, devil. Fuck. Off."

"So be it," he murmured. Lucifer closed the gap between us. His mouth conquering my own. I stayed frozen for all of a second. That's how long my willpower lasted.

Right as I gave in and softened to him, Lucifer pulled away. I chased him, too late to stop myself. He smirked like the devil he was. "Now, let's try this again. Would you have helped me come back? The truth, Nathalie."

I sighed, setting my toast and tea on the coffee table. "I don't owe you anything now. Not until I ask you a question."

"Oh, but you did. You asked me how I moved from the kitchen to here. To answer your question, I can travel between the veil and the living realm now." That was handy. Also inconvenient because it meant he could still spy on me all he wanted. "Now, stop playing games—"

"How dare you," I snarled.

"Answer the fucking question, Nathalie. If you want me to fuck you, I will gladly take you on this couch and every other surface in your home, but for once, be honest with me. Be honest with yourself." The darkness in his tone didn't scare me, but it did make me pause.

All at once the exhaustion crashed down, leaving me tired. Just like with Marcel, I didn't want to fight.

"I don't know," I said. "I hadn't thought about it, so I'm not sure where I'd stand."

Lucifer hummed. "If I asked you, either you'd tell me yes—in which case you were directly responsible for my return. Or you'd say no. And let me tell you a secret, Nathalie." He leaned in close, our lips so close that they brushed just the tiniest bit as he spoke. "I never bought your lie that you wouldn't bring me back because you didn't want to play god, but if given the choice—when no one would get hurt—if you said no . . ." His eyes closed and when they reopened, they glowed with power. "To say I'd be angry is an understatement. I want you. I desire you. I would do anything for you. It may not be love in the traditional sense, but it's as close to it as a demon can feel. I *chose* you. And whether you want to admit it or not, you chose me too, little witch. The day you took my blood you made your choice. That decision set us on this path, to which there is no return. So, I will be patient. I'll take all parts of you that you won't even give to the men you admittedly love—but eventually, I'm going to have the rest of you too. *That* is my purpose now."

My breath stalled in my lungs.

"Why not simply say that and give me the choice? If you'd been honest with me—"

"You weren't ready to hear it. I still don't know that

you are, but my patience grows thin. I'm not a creature that is accustomed to hurting and when I do . . ." He looked away, the sharp planes of his face taking on a darker edge. "I care for you enough to want to be better and spare you my wrath."

"Lucifer . . ." I sighed. Unable to help myself, I wrapped my arms around his shoulders. He grabbed me by the waist, pulling me into his embrace. "I wasn't lying when I said I'm too tired to deal with this. I need time to process. To think things through."

"We have nothing but time."

"And with that," I started, more cautious in my approach now that I understood where he was coming from. The way he'd gone about it might be screwed up, but the motivation was from a good place. For better or worse, I trusted that, and him. "I need space."

"I don't like that."

Under different circumstances I would have chuckled. Instead, I pulled back to look him in the eyes. "I didn't think you would. But if you really want me, then give me a second to catch my breath."

"What exactly does 'space' look like? I'm not leaving this apartment unless you are too, so don't ask it of me."

"There are going to be ground rules."

"Rules?" He repeated the word like it tasted bad. "I've never been a fan of confinements, little witch. You don't cage a demon."

"Be caged or sleep elsewhere."

"Hard bargain." He flashed me a seductive smile. "Tell me more."

I hold up one finger. "First, you sleep in the guest room."

"The guest room is for guests," he responded with distaste. "Anyone who has had you in the positions I have is not a guest."

"Second," I said loudly, shooting him a glare as I held up a second finger, "you can't follow me everywhere anymore. Even in the veil. I need to have my own privacy. The ability to choose what I share with you."

He glared at me, and I stared right back, daring him to protest. "And what if something happens and I'm not there to stop it?"

I snorted. "You mean like you stopped 'it' all those times as a ghost?" I cocked an eyebrow.

"I couldn't then. I can now."

"Is this coming from a place of worrying about me or wanting to stalk me?"

The thread between us pulsed. Begrudgingly, Lucifer said, "Both."

I shook my head, a smile threatening to bloom. "Time," I repeated. "And space. That's what I need right now. With Not-Sasha and Marcel's ailing health, I have a lot on my mind, and I can't just set that aside to deal with *us*."

"Baggage hardly deserves your time," Lucifer griped.

"Lucifer."

"Fine, but only because it's a matter of time before you want me back in your room and in your bed."

"Yeah, right," I scoffed, but the sound died in my

throat as he kissed my forehead. It was oddly sweet and protective, not at all what I associated with Lucifer.

"Oh, I know I'm right," he said as his breath fanned over my face. "What we share is not so easily ignored, little witch."

And with those words, he retreated to the guest room. I sat there for a minute, my heart racing and sending pulses to places that were better left unexplored for now. Food forgotten, I drained my cup of tea and tossed my toast into the compost pail, then went to my room.

Centering myself, I slipped into the relief of my own internal thoughts. Instead of the peace and organization I was hoping for, entering my memory loci was like entering a war zone.

Inside, everything was in complete disarray, but I supposed I couldn't be mad. My memory loci was a reflection of my scattered thoughts. All of the versions of me that existed were agitated, which just made things worse.

Peace was stubbornly refusing to leave the greenhouse, and she kept yelling insults at the others through the door. Meanwhile, Caretaker tried in vain to coax her out. The Warden and Bad Nat were engaged in their usual heated arguments. Ann was flipping through books like mad, tossing them aside when they didn't have what she was looking for.

It appeared that whether it was inside or outside, I couldn't find a moment of peace.

"We can't rush into anything. Are you stupid or just

insane?" The Warden insisted, her voice edged with anger. She was glaring harshly at Bad Nat.

"No, but you are if you think that we can just ignore this." Bad Nat picked at her nail, the picture of indifference, and the nonchalance grated on The Warden's nerves.

"We're not equipped to handle another being with chaos magic, especially if we want even a slim chance of Sasha returning," Ann called from across the library.

"Look," Bad Nat snapped, her eyes flaring, "we can't sit around waiting for Not-Sasha to do some damage. Everyone is acting like Prime doesn't know who's in the body. Meanwhile, she's wasting time trying to convince herself it's someone else."

All eyes turned to me for a second and I gritted my teeth.

"We can't be sure," I said firmly, my eyes narrowed into slits. "I have no concrete evidence for anything. I'm literally just guessing, and the worst thing I can be right now is wrong."

Bad Nat scoffed. "You know you're right and you're still sitting on it. Do you really want to let *her* get more power?"

"Yes, because I refuse to make a mistake because I rushed impulsively into something." I stood my ground, holding my chin up firmly. "Sasha doesn't deserve our mistakes."

"Sasha doesn't deserve our hesitation either." Bad Nat rolled her eyes, but didn't argue further. "But whatever, you do that. I'll be anywhere else but here."

With that, she stormed off like a petulant child and dropped into to her favorite chair, slamming the heel of her boots on the table after she sat. I shook my head. "I swear. Sometimes . . ." I muttered, and Ann and The Warden knew exactly where my sentence ended.

"You're right, Prime," Ann said, pushing her glasses up her nose. "We need to be one hundred percent positive before we consider acting in any way."

"Agreed." The Warden nodded as she spoke.

"First things first, we need to shelve everything else and start sifting through our childhood memories," I instructed. "There's likely to be something there that would help. We're looking for anyone we knew that had chaos magic, any conversation we overhead about chaos magic, and how they would have a connection to Lucifer," I continued. "If we can just—"

"What the hell is this?"

All three of us jumped at the sound of a smooth voice. *No fucking way.*

The three of us looked at each other in shock as the appearance rippled through the loci, drawing both Peace and Caretaker to turn away from the greenhouse. The only one that didn't seem the least bit surprised and simply wore a sadistic little smile, was Bad Nat.

"Lucifer? What the fuck are you doing in my head?"

5

LUCIFER

I felt a sharp zinging jolt, like being yanked backward through a narrow tunnel. My eyes snapped open, and the library I had been in had vanished, replaced now by the familiar confines of her bedroom. I wasn't sure how to make sense of what I'd seen. It was her, but multiple. Each dressed differently and they were talking to each other.

Nathalie's light brown eyes swirled with a mix of confusion and rage. I looked at her and she stared at me like animals caught in a challenge of who would move first, neither of us wanting to be the one to do it.

"What was that?" she finally asked, her voice tight with defensiveness. I had clearly struck a chord. One I didn't even know existed.

"I'm not even sure," I admitted. I'd been sitting on the guest bed, mourning my intended role as her guardian-stalker when I was suddenly transported else-

45

where. To a library so large it rivaled The Library of Alexandria.

Nathalie's eyes narrowed, her arms crossing over her chest as it heaved in angry breaths. "How did you do that? How did you enter my mind?"

Her mind? It made sense. In a completely insane way. But if I wasn't in her mind, where else would I see multiple versions of my little witch, all dressed like caricatures of her personality? I'd been there for a few moments, stunned into silence, as I listened to them debate.

"I'm telling you, little witch, I truly don't know." I held my hands up in surrender under the power of her angry, wild glare. "I was sitting in the guest room one minute, and in that library the next."

She looked away and muttered, seemingly to herself. "This makes no sense. I created the loci. He shouldn't be able to enter it. Something's not right."

I wanted badly to ask questions, but it didn't take a genius to know she was deeply unhappy about this turn of events. I could see the vulnerability in her face, the rawness of having her most private sanctuary invaded. After we just had a conversation about privacy and space, I can only guess how thoroughly I'd crossed a boundary I hadn't known about.

"Little witch," I said softly, getting her to look at me. "I'm sorry for startling you. I didn't mean to do that."

"What exactly did you see?" she asked, still on edge.

"Versions of you," I said slowly, not wanting to spook

her even more. "A library. Some back and forth about searching through childhood memories." The whole thing was unexpected to say the least.

She muttered some more to herself, looking away once again. Weighing my options, I decided to push just a little bit. See if I could get even a few answers.

"May I ask," I proceeded cautiously, "what it was that I found myself in?"

"No, you may not," she said with a glare. I wanted to fight it. To snatch her up and demand answers because my obsession with her knew no bounds. But she wasn't in a place to share, and I wasn't jeopardizing anything. I would learn all about this place in her mind soon enough.

"Understood." I dipped my chin, making a show of washing my hands of it. "I will let it be."

She scoffed. "That's it? You're just going to magically drop it?"

I nodded. "I just told you we had nothing but time. It's clear you need it. I'm not pushing this." I turned to leave her room.

"Wait." Nathalie sighed, running a hand through her hair.

"Yes?"

"I call it my memory loci," she said reluctantly, wrapping her arms defensively around her body.

"And what purpose does it serve?" I asked, keeping my tone gentle. Well, gentle for me.

"I have an eidetic memory, and that can be overwhelming at times. All the time, really." She watched me carefully, monitoring my reaction. "I never forget a single thing I see, hear, or experience. I needed a way to organize my thoughts, or I'd go insane. That's where the memory loci came to exist. This is my way of organizing."

"And the different versions of you?" I prodded, encouraging her to keep talking. I had Nathalie when it came to her body. She came undone for me in the sweetest ways, but I wanted more. I wanted to know her inside and out and I had a feeling this new discovery was something close to who she was at her core.

And I wanted it. *Bad.*

She shot me a sharp look. "What about them?"

"Where do they come from?"

"Why? Hoping you can fuck them?"

"Nathalie." I fixed her with a look. "I'm your familiar —like it or not—and there's a reason our psyches were close enough to push me into your mind in the first place. Is it such a far reach to be curious about these other versions of you?"

"Maybe that speaks more to how pushy you are than to how close we are."

I sighed, leveling her with a stare that begged her to be honest.

"Look at me like that all you want. You still didn't answer my question."

"I wasn't thinking about fucking them," I answered. *But I am now.* Nope, not going to say that. I could only imagine how poorly that would go. Which is why even if the thought now occurred to me, I wouldn't be acting on it.

"Fine," she grumbled, glancing away as she explained. "Each version of me represents a different aspect of my personality. I'm known as the Prime because I'm the main self and the one calling the shots. Ann is the analytical side of me. The Warden is the protector. Peace is the part of me that wants to bury my head in the sand and just live—without taking care of everyone else. Caretaker is her opposite. She's the nurturer. Bad Nat is the uninhibited one, and . . . that's it."

"So, when you disappear into your head, you're quite literally inside this memory loci, and what? Discussing things with them?" She seemed embarrassed but gave me confirmation with a single nod.

"I know it's weird that I talk with myself but . . . yeah."

"I wouldn't call it weird." I gave her an appraising look, seeing her more clearly. "I wouldn't know what having a photographic memory is like, but I have lived for a very long time. Existence like that . . . you have to forget in order to keep moving. I can't imagine remembering every facet of life in perfect clarity."

She flashed me an almost grateful look. As I absorbed her words, the pieces clicked together in my mind.

"So, that's where you go when you stare off into space," I said, more to myself than to her.

She pressed her lips together, a slight blush coloring her cheeks. "It helps me process everything. But it's supposed to be private."

I stepped closer, my expression softening. "I won't tell anyone, little witch. Your secret is safe with me."

Nathalie's eyes searched mine, looking for any hint of deception. Finding none, she finally nodded, a small, relieved smile tugging at the corners of her mouth. "Thank you, Luci."

"What were you doing in there just now?" Cocking my head, I reached out and rubbed a tense spot in her shoulder. "If you tell me, maybe I can help too."

She groaned as I worked at the tense spots, but didn't say anything for a bit. I kept massaging, hoping that she would let me in. Breaking through her walls was not going to be easy. It seemed since being back in the flesh, it might have actually gotten harder. Finally though, she spoke.

"I need everyone to go through my childhood memories to find anyone with chaos magic. I won't say more than that," she admitted before giving a shake of her head. "I'm not planting a seed in anyone's head."

"You have a suspect."

"It's speculation."

"Is it? You can see their magic. What color was it?"

She pressed her lips together tightly, nostrils flaring. "I don't know. Not-Sasha camouflaged it." It was clear from the worry lines between her brows that she'd been thinking about this from the moment she realized it.

"That's . . . unfortunate." And cause for considerably more concern.

"Isn't it?" She sighed and shook her head again. "If I'm wrong, people could die."

"People might die either way. You can't take that on yourself."

"Sure, but if I'm wrong and we make certain assumptions, it could kill a lot of people. Besides, that's not the only thing we were going to discuss. We're still trying to figure out these murders, and where Katherine is now. Also a way to save Marcel . . ." Her face twisted in phantom pain for a moment before clearing. "It's a lot I'm trying to sort through, honestly."

"You know that you don't have to be the only one who figures out the plan to save the world," I reminded her, moving my hand to cup the back of her neck. I pulled her closer and her breath caught in her throat.

"Maybe not, but in this case, it feels like a personal attack that I need to defend," she confessed, eyes flittering away from mine for a split second, seemingly needing an escape from the intensity of my gaze.

"Let others help you," I urged softly, my eyes flickering from hers to her lips and back again. "Let me help you."

"Luci," she murmured, her voice trailing off. I leaned forward and brushed my lips against her. I told myself I just wanted a little taste. But as it always was when it came to this woman, a little wasn't nearly enough to satiate me. Still, I held back, not wanting to push her any further tonight.

I might be the devil, but I wasn't stupid. I could recognize she was pushed to her metaphorical edge.

Pulling back, I added, "Also, you need to get some actual sleep. You can't save the world if you crash. Go get some rest. Not just retreat into the loci. Everything will still be there when you wake up in the morning."

She made a sound of agreement and began to leave. Unable to help it, I gripped her tighter for a second longer and then I let go, allowing her to walk away. Reluctantly, I might add—but I knew my place with her was fragile right now. Everything was happening quickly, between Samhain and somehow entering her most private space—she was bound to run if I pushed too hard or pushed too far. My little witch was not the kind of woman you could force into a position she did not want to be in. Out of the bedroom, anyway. I bit back a smile at the thought.

I turned to leave her room heading back to the guest room that might as well be a doghouse.

"Goodnight, Lucifer." Her soft whisper broke the silence, and it took everything for me not to go back to her.

"Goodnight, Nathalie," I said, inhaling her heady juniper and lilac scent as I closed the door behind me.

For a moment, I stood there, gathering my thoughts. Already I could hear her tiny, soft snore and even breathing as she fell into an immediate sleep.

I groaned, wishing I could turn around and go back to her. Nathalie was my only weakness. I'd give her anything she wanted, just to be near her for the rest of my life. She could ask me to relinquish my title as the devil, and if that is what her heart desired, I would do it. For her. She truly didn't understand the pull she had over me.

That simple fact put us both in danger. Probably more than I was willing to admit.

6

NATHALIE

I slept like shit, but as they say, there's no rest for the wicked.

Despite my world imploding, the earth kept on spinning. I had no choice but to roll with it. At least one thing was going well. I adjusted my grip on my phone, tucking it between my ear and my shoulder as I made a cup of tea. My contractor, Mick, had called to report on the progress of my new house that was being built. With everything else going on, updates had been on the back-burner for a while.

"We're putting the finishing touches on now. Everything should be done by Friday," Mick said.

"Thanks," I replied. "I'll schedule the designer to come in over the weekend and start furnishing the place."

"Sounds like a plan, boss."

He was about to hang up when I stopped him. "Before you go, there's something we need to discuss."

"Hit me."

"I'm implementing a new protocol going forward."

"A new protocol?" he echoed, sounding confused.

"Yes," I said, lowering my voice. "From now on, all communications over phone or in person need to start with a code word. Yours is 'dandelion'."

"Dandelion?" He chuckled lightly, but didn't argue.

"Yes. It's essential that before getting into any details with me, I need to provide you with this code word *without you prompting*. That bit is important. You can't ask me for it."

"Is, uh, everything okay?" Mick asked hesitantly.

"Someone has been impersonating me," I admitted, but rushed to add, "I don't think they mean harm, but I can't tip them off that I know. If it happens, just notify me via text and you can relay fake information if necessary."

There was a pause on the other end, and then Mick said, "Understood, Ms. Le Fay. I'll make sure everyone on the team is aware that any calls must come through me."

"Thanks, Mick. Have a good one." I hung up the phone and picked up my tea, taking a sip. Turning around, I nearly jumped out of my skin. Lucifer was standing shirtless, watching me *again* as he leaned casually against the fridge, a bemused expression on his face.

"Code words?"

"What is *with* you and creeping around shirtless?" I placed a calming hand to my heart and gave him a miffed look.

"It's not my fault your hearing is subpar compared to

other supernaturals, little witch." He shrugged, reminding me of one of my many 'failings' by nature of being a witch. Our lack of superhuman qualities was a bit of a sore spot for me, particularly in the immortality department, but I wasn't getting into that right now. "Now, what is this with the code words?"

I rolled my eyes. "Katherine is still impersonating me, and I need to find her."

"Again?" he replied, arching an eyebrow. "What do you need to find her for?"

I gnawed on my bottom lip, toying with how much to tell him. "You won't tell anyone else?" I asked.

The look he gave me had a flush spreading across my cheeks in seconds. Lucifer leaned forward, his abs flexing as he slowly stalked toward me.

"What do you think?"

I pressed my lips together. "That I need an answer."

His arms came down on either side of me, caging my body between them. The heat radiating from him was smoldering. "I care little to nothing for most creatures, the singular exception being you. Your secrets are safe with me and have *always* been safe with me."

I swallowed hard. "And you won't try to interfere?"

A smirk lifted one corner of his mouth. "Me? Interfere?"

"Yes, you. The pushy demon who doesn't know how to take no for an answer. I need you to promise me you won't get involved."

"It involves you. I can't promise that."

"Lucifer."

"Little witch."

I pinched the bridge of my nose to calm my slightly erratic breathing.

"Tell me why you need to find her," he whispered, lips ghosting my neck. I arched involuntarily and Lucifer chuckled.

"No. Not if you won't promise to stay out of it."

"You're in it. I am your familiar. By extension it affects me, whether I choose for it to or not. You're not asking something I'm capable of doing."

I opened my mouth to argue with him, except . . . he had a point.

Crap.

"Fine, but I still want you to promise you won't tell *anyone* anything. Okay?"

"Done." The gold tether between us flared with his promise, his magic enforcing that he keep his word.

I sighed, wondering how much to divulge. "I need to know if my hunch about Not-Sasha is correct. Katherine is the only one who can answer my questions."

"That wasn't so hard, now was it?"

I hid a smile by ducking my head and swatted at his chest. "You got your way, now let me by. I have work to get to."

"You haven't eaten today." I pulled my eyes back to him, startled that not only was he right, but he was calling me on it.

"I'll grab food on my way."

"Get lunch with me. Work after."

I hesitated, taken aback by the sudden invitation. Or demand, depending on your perspective. With Lucifer they were often one and the same. "Lunch? You want to get lunch together?" I squinted at him.

"I didn't stutter, and your hearing isn't *that* bad."

I opened and closed my mouth, having nothing to say in response. It wasn't that I was opposed to eating with him. It was a normal thing. But maybe that was the problem. Lucifer wasn't normal. He didn't do normal things, like dates.

"He also doesn't love, and yet your name is branded over his heart," Ann said.

"Seriously?"

She shrugged. *"Just pointing out the facts. He may not be the most logical creature, but even a broken clock is right twice a day. If he really is intent on spending his second life with you, then it stands to reason he would want to date."*

She was right, and I wasn't sure how I felt about it.

"You're doing it again," he said quietly, pulling me from my thoughts. "Retreating into your memory loci." I flushed again, this time for a different reason.

Lucifer gave me a devilish smile and said, "Come. There's no need to overthink this. We'll go to the place on the corner you like, and I can finally try their chocolate cake."

"That . . . sounds really nice, actually."

Lucifer lifted an eyebrow. "What did you expect?"

"I'm not sure. Maybe for you to make some crude

joke about eating me for lunch. That seems more like you."

He snorted. "I am driven by desire, both mine and yours. I told you, I want more than your body, little witch. I want your thoughts. Your opinions. Your attention. I want to be as integral in your world as you are in mine. While taking you to bed might be a nice place to start, it isn't enough."

Without even trying, he stole the breath from my lungs.

I couldn't help myself from asking, "Will it ever be? Enough, that is?"

He studied my face, considering his answer. "Probably not. The way that I feel about you . . ." He shook his head, but I wasn't letting him stop there. After a lifetime of being mistreated, I was hungry for his proclamations. Starving for his truths.

It was wrong on every level to want this man, and yet I did. And I was getting tired of fighting it, no matter what he'd done.

"Tell me," I said.

His eyes flashed, glowing gold as they bore into me. "I want to possess every inch of your skin. To own your thoughts. To consume your dreams. I want everything from you, Nathalie. And I'll never stop wanting it. Demons are selfish creatures by nature, and I am nothing if not a model example of my species. I know you need the incubus and Baggage in your life—"

"Must you call him that?"

He placed a finger to my lips. "I know you need them, but I'm not giving up my spot. I'm not going anywhere, and if the day comes that they fuck up bad enough—I can't say I'll be sad. I'm selfish enough to want all of you, but I *will* put your needs first."

"If you had all of me, theoretically, don't you worry you'd get bored?"

Amusement flittered across his features. He palmed my neck with one hand and cupped my cheek with the other. "You are the most fascinating creature I've ever met. I can say with certainty, I will never be bored of you."

I wanted to doubt his every word, even when he spoke with conviction. I guess that was the part of relationships that scared me. It was my baggage. Marcel made me so certain before he broke my heart. A small part of me would always doubt because of it.

That didn't mean I couldn't take the chance. I could choose to be brave and open my heart again.

Bad Nat snorted. *"You act like you haven't already. You're gone for him. Stop lying to yourself."*

"Go to lunch," Peace encouraged. *"Spend time with him. He's good for us."*

"I don't know about that," Ann said. *"But he does seem to put us first and leash himself in some respects because of it. Our moral compass is fairly set. I'd say the odds of him dragging us down are low, but perhaps we can raise him up."*

Bad Nat rolled her eyes. *"I'd say we should go to the dark side, but I'd be wasting my breath."*

"Yes, you would," The Warden responded. *"I'm with*

Ann on this. We treat him like he's worthy of this relationship, and he will become that. His past is long, and mostly fucked up, but he's made a point to do better for us. That's worth a great deal."

"I can feel the pull when you do that," Lucifer said quietly. "I'm resisting it, but whenever you disappear, it's like my body wants to follow."

That yanked me firmly from my mind to stare at him. "Thank you for resisting."

He gave me a tight smile. "Let's just say I hope the day comes that you invite me in."

"I . . . don't know about that."

"I'm aware. I can be patient."

I wasn't sure how to respond, so I redirected our conversation. "Let's get lunch, shall we?"

Lucifer kissed me lightly and let me go. I stepped away, gripping the counter to center myself. There was going to be a lot of that in my future, I imagined.

We walked down the street in comfortable silence. Me wearing my low-heeled boots and black jeans with one of my favorite off-the-shoulder sheer blouses. Lucifer in one of his infamous suits. I'd be lying if I said I wasn't envious of the way he could pop into the spirit realm and pop out dressed to the nines. There aren't many powers I truly felt jealousy over, but that one was one.

When he got to the restaurant, heads turned. They weren't looking at me. They were staring at Lucifer.

It only occurred to me then that I should have glamoured him. Not because I was embarrassed, but because the sheer amount of attention we were drawing made me uncomfortable. Lucifer had been around a long time, and he ruled New Chicago for many years. Most supernaturals knew what he looked like, and many had dealt with him in some capacity over the years. Dressed in his classic white suit with gold cufflinks, he looked like every part the devil he used to be.

"We'll have to glamour you in the future," I murmured as we were being led away to our table.

"Why?" He glanced sideways at me.

"Everyone's staring."

"And?"

We took our seats, but the menus remained untouched as we continued our conversation.

"I'm not used to the attention. I prefer to operate discreetly."

Lucifer snorted. "There's nothing discreet about you. From the clothes you wear, to the car you drive, to the literal mansion you have just built. You're private, but you're no wallflower." I wasn't sure if I should be complimented or insulted by his statement. "Besides, it's not you they're staring at. It's me."

"Because that's so much better?" I arched an eyebrow.

"People are ants. They're going to scurry across the pavement to avoid a boot. You can't blame them for taking notice."

I sighed. Our waitress approached, halting our

discussion. We quickly put in our order and handed her our menus, but the young woman idled for a second longer. One tanned arm wrapped around the menus, one hand loosely resting over her heart. Blonde hair framed her face and deep brown eyes stared back with no small amount of fear. Or was that reverence? It seemed to be a bit of both.

"Can we help you?" I asked, voice polite despite the internal discomfort I was feeling.

"Is it true?" She asked quietly. "Are you *him*?"

"In the flesh."

"I'm so sorry, sir. It's just that we thought—"

"He's not the king of New Chicago anymore, Toni. You don't have to grovel to him."

Her mouth popped open and closed, floundering like a fish. Lucifer smiled, playing the part of a gentleman. "Nathalie is correct. I'm just a man, like anyone else. Well, a demon of desire, but you understand."

"Right. Of course . . ." Toni trailed off, backing away.

"Everything else may be gone, but at least my reputation still outlived me," Lucifer quipped, training his mesmerizing gaze on me.

"Hard to forget the cruel king of New Chicago," I retorted, truthfully.

"This again?" he countered. "You want to pin me to my old self. Does pretending you don't care about me because of my past make you feel less guilty for the feelings growing between us, little witch?"

Lucifer had a way of targeting my deepest thoughts.

He knew how to strip me open and lay me bare with his words as much as his hands.

"I can have feelings and still recognize the truth. You aren't that anymore, but you were," I said, my cheeks flushing, a mix of embarrassment and warmth flooding through me.

"Were, I'll give you. Might I also remind you of the atrocities committed in my absence before your demon queen came to power. I was who I needed to be at the time, but the past aside, are you not the one that believes in second chances?"

"Yes, but—"

"You gave everyone else a second chance," he pointed out, gesturing his hands in the air. "Baggage. August. Ronan, who has done as much if not more than I have, I might add. Even your best friend started your relationship as the killer of witch-kind, *and* your captor. Yet you give them all second chances."

"I did," I admitted quietly.

"Why not me? What have I done that is worse than them? What makes me so unforgivable?" He sounded almost *vulnerable* and the twinge to his voice melted my heart just a bit.

"I . . . you . . ." I took a breath and tried again. "It's complicated."

"Uncomplicate it."

I glared at him. "Gee. I wish it was that simple."

Lucifer shrugged. "It is, you just have to choose to say it. So tell me, Nathalie, what is really holding you back from this? Is it how the world will perceive you? Because

I know better than anyone that you don't give a shit what other people think. If anything, you welcome it so you can use it against them."

"I—" A groan slid from between my lips.

"Order up," Toni said, appearing with two plates in hand. I smiled and nodded even though I wanted to tug at my hair in frustration, but there were too many eyes still watching us.

"It's not that," I said when she left.

"Then what?"

"I'm not as sure you have changed as much as you profess." I finally said. "You tricked me to get back. Whatever your reasons, you used what was an intimate moment between us for your own gain and that doesn't feel like change to me. It's not putting me first, no matter what you claim. It's manipulation."

There was a long silence before he spoke again. "Little witch, I told you already that I knew that you would have had issues being directly and knowingly involved. And regardless, I've made plenty of mistakes and done terrible things and never in my nine thousand years have I regretted them. But, for you, I came back to life willing to change. Willing to do what I haven't done in nine thousand years. *Be better*. For you, Nathalie. The plan to get back, Samhain, all of it was my effort to get back to you. To be seen in your world and to be seen by you. To be so physical you couldn't send me away, salt me, or ignore me—or us."

My lips parted in awe as my heart raced and my

blood soared. Peace came out of the greenhouse during his speech and clasped her hands to her heart.

"*I knew it,*" she said dreamily, stars in her eyes.

Caretaker nodded in agreement. "*He's a charmer, that's for sure.*"

Bad Nat simply cocked her head in my direction, as if calling out checkmate. I gnawed at my lower lip, looking askance, trying to grab onto my swirling thoughts.

"Luci, I—"

"Lucifer. Nathalie," an all too familiar voice called. We both snapped up to see Not-Sasha heading toward us, a grin on her lips. She was wearing a flowy black dress that Sasha would never have chosen for herself. Lucifer and I shared a look.

"*What the fuck now?*" Bad Nat groaned. "*We were finally going to get somewhere here.*"

"*Why is she here?*" The Warden asked. Peace cringed and headed back for her safe place, Caretaker close behind.

"*There's no way she could have known we would be here unless she's following us somehow,*" Ann noted, pushing her glasses back into place. "*That's going to be a problem. We need to figure out how.*"

I pulled a smile to my lips. "Sasha, what are you doing here? Where's Sienna?"

"I left Sienna to shower," she replied nonchalantly, pulling a seat up in between Lucifer and I. "Decided I needed a walk, when I saw you two in here. I've been meaning to talk to you, but you're a hard woman to catch."

I made a noncommittal noise. "I've been busy with work and whatnot."

"Can't be too busy," she said, her gaze flicking to Lucifer. "You're having lunch with him, but it's fine. What I wanted to say can wait." She leaned into Lucifer, practically purring. Her cat tail swished like she had prey in her sights. "How are you, Luci?"

"Hey, Sasha," he said, pointedly leaning back. "You know I don't like it when people call me that."

Sasha pouted, shooting a look my way. "I know, but you let *her* use it. Why can't I? We were such good friends in life, after all. More than friends, really."

Lucifer lifted an eyebrow. "I helped you through your transition into immortality, Sasha. That was all. There's no need to make it out like something it wasn't."

She pursed her lips. "Hm. If you say so."

"I do," he repeated, a harder edge in his tone threatening violence. A shiver ran down my spine, but not out of fear.

It was *desire*.

"Well," she said, giving a fake smile and twining a lock of midnight hair around her index finger. "That's unfortunate. I wasn't aware the veil changed so much for you."

I choked on my sip of water, not liking where this conversation was going.

"Yes," he said, keeping his expression neutral. "It has a way of doing that, don't you think?"

"Well, Sasha," I cut in, before this conversation could get any more out of hand, "while we're happy to see you,

you caught us at a bad time. We were actually just heading out."

She cocked an eyebrow and shot a look at our untouched food. "Really? Seems like you just started."

"Business, what can you do?" I shrugged. I lifted a hand to flag down Toni. She approached our table with wary eyes and a polite, stiff smile.

"Can we get boxes and the check?"

"Of course, let me get those."

While our waitress flitted back to the counter, Not-Sasha continued her abrasive intrusion. "You seem to have a lot of business going on, huh?" She gave me a cool cursory look. "But fine, you can do that. Lucifer and I should catch up. Don't you think so?"

She trailed a finger up his arm seductively and even though he moved it, part of me wanted to hit something watching her touch him that way. I took a deep breath, reminding myself that this is most definitely *not* Sasha, and there is absolutely no reason to be jealous. Moreover, fighting an unknown entity in my friend's body was a big no-no.

"No," he answered bluntly. "What would we need to catch up on?"

My phone buzzed and I looked down, seeing August's name flash over the screen. My heart jumped, but I clicked the device off and looked back up. Toni appeared with those boxes, and I quickly paid the check.

"You're shaking," Not-Sasha noted.

I brushed a stray lock of hair back from my face and forced a smile. "Low blood sugar. You know how it is for us witches. Stuck with all the problems of humans when it comes to our bodies.

"Yes . . . I do know that very well."

That made me pause.

"Thank you, Toni. Take care, will you?" I murmured quietly as I boxed up my food and handed her the empty dish. Lucifer did the same, following suit.

"Sorry, Sasha, I'm actually her business partner now, so where she goes, I go."

I blinked up at Lucifer, tempted to lift a brow and ask him "is that so?" But that would have been too obvious. I settled for a noncommittal hum.

"Shall we?" Lucifer said, offering his hand to help me stand. I took it, ignoring the frost in Not-Sasha's glare.

"I'll walk you out." Sasha popped up, falling in line behind Lucifer. *Oh my gods, take a hint.* It would be sad under different circumstances, especially considering the real Sasha was still pining for a mate she couldn't have. As it was, the identity of our mysterious Not-Sasha was quickly becoming obvious.

If I was right, and at this point I was fairly certain I was, then that made Not-Sasha incredibly dangerous, and also a certifiable psychopath.

One I didn't want to be left alone with.

As we made our way out of the café, Sasha said, "I have some—"

Her words were cut off by yelling across the street.

"I'm sick of this shit," one of two figures bellowed. "You supernaturals are always taking more than your fair fucking share. I won't be put down any more by the likes of you people."

Before anyone could respond, he pulled a gun. The other figure took off running.

Straight toward us.

Lucifer pushed me behind him. A second later, several rounds fired. Lucifer jerked. It all happened so fast I could barely comprehend what was happening as gold exploded out from me.

7

NATHALIE

Magic saturated my pores. It poured off me in waves. Gold particles overtook everything in sight, but amidst it all—Lucifer hit the ground with a sickening thud.

My heart dropped into my stomach. I felt bile rise to my throat, but I had to get a grip. Now wasn't the time to break.

"Lucifer," I shrieked, falling to my knees at his side. Red bloomed across his shirt where three small holes glared back at me. His eyes were closed, his chest moving rapidly.

"*Is it a magic bullet?*" Peace cried, already pulling memory files about magical weapons. "*Oh gods, he can't die again. He just came back to life. What if he dies for real this time?*"

My chest hurt from how hard my heart pounded. I couldn't breathe past the lump in my throat. My lungs refused to expand. Black dots started to dance in my vision alongside the gold. So much gold.

71

"Luci?" I asked again, desperation bleeding into my voice. "Please answer me." Urgently, my fingers brushed against his face.

"I'm here, little witch," he coughed. Blood stained his lips. Cold filled my veins, spreading through every part of me.

A warm hand pressed against my chest. "You need to breathe," he rasped.

But how could I?

I was losing him, and I was powerless to stop it. If I were a healer I could close his wounds, but I was no white witch. I wasn't even sure I was gray; all I knew was that my magic was busted. Broken.

I could steal the magic of others, but I couldn't generate that kind of power on my own.

And he was going to die because of it.

His golden eyes held mine, steady despite the blood oozing from his wounds. He watched me with an intensity that should have scared me.

Instead, I was scared I'd never feel it again because somewhere along the way, my ghostly stalker had gotten beneath my skin. He'd become a staple in my life. A fixed presence that I wasn't willing to let go of.

"Lucifer . . ." I whispered. "I lo—"

"No!" Sasha yelled, falling to her knees on his other side. Warm brown hands cupped his cheeks. "You don't get to die, devil. Not now."

Her green eyes flared. A colorless magic skated down her skin, but before it could touch him, Lucifer brushed her hand away.

"I'm fine," he said stiffly.

The holes in his chest began to shift. Silver peaked out of each one and a half-second later, the bullets popped out, tinkling to the ground.

"Let me—"

"I said, I'm fine," he repeated, a hard edge to his tone. Lucifer sat up, brushing off his suit. "What was it you were saying, little witch?" A twinkle entered his eye.

"You're impossible," I muttered, shaking my head as my chest finally expanded.

He's okay. He's okay. He's okay—

"We get the fucking point, Prime," Bad Nat said, rolling her eyes. *"He's the devil, and a demon. He was never in any danger."*

Peace stopped searching, collapsing in on herself and crying. Caretaker wrapped her arms around my sensitive side, holding her tight as she fell apart in relief.

I'd barely noticed that the gold stopped pouring.

It settled on my skin like a fine sheen before sinking beneath the surface.

Lucifer watched intently, missing nothing as he stood up. He offered me his hand, and Bad Nat snorted. *"See? He's helping us. Not the other way around. Chill with the theatrics."*

"Are you sure you're okay?" I asked, eyes scanning every inch of his for further damage. It was hard to tell beneath the bloodied clothes.

"I promise," he assured me, motioning with his hand for me to take it. "But I will need a change of clothes before we go anywhere."

I gave him my hand and he pulled me to my feet, settling me against his hard body as he scanned the area. I followed suit looking around to see if the assailant or person running were still there, but they'd both up and disappeared while I had been having a panic attack over Lucifer.

"Needlessly," Bad Nat added.

"We get it," The Warden yelled down the hall. *"Keep the comments to yourself."*

"I should hunt that imbecile down to give him my cleaning bill, though." Lucifer touched one of the holes in his suit.

"I just don't understand," Not-Sasha murmured quietly from where she still kneeled on the pavement. "You loved me in your last life."

"Much has changed. Me. You. Our relationships. I thought you wanted to solidify things with your mate? You told Nathalie as much when you warned her away."

"After my ordeal in the veil," Sasha began in a clipped tone, "I decided that I don't want him anymore. He's not worthy of me and clearly, you make each other happy. She looked in my direction. "You should explore that. Just that."

"Wow, okay." I cocked my head at her, trying to see through her mask. "Thanks for the memo, I guess."

"Hmm," Lucifer hummed. "Quite some timing there. The veil must have really done a number on you."

I elbowed him sharply, casting him a warning look. He was straying too close to the truth, and Not-Sasha didn't need to know we suspected anything.

My phone buzzed. It was August calling again. That's the second time in a row, which was odd for him. I sent it to voicemail, but looked at Lucifer, giving him a look that clearly said, *"Behave."* He quirked an eyebrow at my phone but turned his attention back to Not-Sasha, crossing his arms over his chest.

I stepped away but wasn't willing to go far after recent events. Color me concerned, but seeing Lucifer bleeding out did something to me. It made me realize I was unwilling to lose him. I slid up on my screen to check my messages when it lit up showing a text from August.

August: So we're ignoring each other now?

Nat: No one's ignoring, just busy.

August: Well, if you are too busy to take my calls, will you at least put me on your schedule and meet me for dinner tonight?

Nat: Last time we did that, we ended up fucking like wild animals.

August: Okay so maybe not dinner. Or somewhere with a back room…How about that little diner off South Canal? It's busy there. Breakfast tomorrow?

Nat: Sure, 9.

Leaving it at that, I exited out of his messages and clicked into the group chat that included everyone except Not-Sasha. I shot off a text, letting them know Not-Sasha was here and on the move. Sienna was the first to respond cursing herself for showering. A few short texts later Anders has been elected to "find" Not-Sasha and keep her busy after Lucifer and I left the café. I put my phone away and walked back over.

Sasha said something and lifted a hand to his sculpted bicep, fingers brushing over him with familiarity. He stepped back and her face crumpled into a glare before smoothing over.

"Don't touch me," he said firmly.

Sasha brushed it off like it was nothing, though I could see the flicker of anger still in her eyes. "You're such a spoilsport, Lucifer," she said with a forced laugh. "I was just trying to help."

Lucifer shot her a look. "Help by not touching me."

"Things have changed," Sasha said, seeming to finally understand. Her eyes lifted for a second, and in their depths I could have sworn I saw a flash of something *other*.

Something dangerous.

"You no longer care for me, do you?" An odd note permeated her tone, something I couldn't quite put a finger on.

Lucifer sighed, as if not picking up on the change. "Must we do this? I don't know how to make my disinterest any clearer. Furthermore, I'm in a relationship. One that won't be ending *ever*."

A dark chuckle slid from between her lips. The hairs on the back of my neck lifted.

"All right, Lucifer. We'll do this your way."

The threat seemed to finally register with him, as he lifted an eyebrow.

The gold of his eyes swirled with a chaotic sort of energy, and I just knew he was seconds away from challenging her. That couldn't happen.

"We'll see you around, Sasha." I grabbed his arm and tugged him toward my apartment building. Slowly, Lucifer followed but not without a backwards glance at the imposter.

Her words hung in the air as we retreated, and I couldn't hide my confusion or my dread. What would Not-Sasha gain by pushing me toward August? And what did she mean by *we'll do this your way*?

"We need to move faster to get the real Sasha back," Lucifer said, a hint of irritation in his voice. "This imposter is . . . unsettling."

"There's more than just that reason to get her back," I replied, my thoughts spinning with the implications of Not-Sasha's behavior. "But, agreed." We entered the Señora's shop, jingling the bell on the door. An orange tabby cat lifted its head from the book it was resting on to peer down at me, then closed its eyes and went back to sleep.

"Do you actually have some business you need to attend to, or was that just an excuse?"

"I do have some things to take care of," I admitted. "I was planning to walk you back to the apartment before heading out again."

One of my food pantries had been raided and trashed, and I needed to go do damage control so we could get the doors back open. We catered to supes and humans alike, and that had put us at odds with some groups.

"Why can't I come to take care of this business?"

"Because I don't think the people at my food bank would take kindly to seeing the devil back to life."

"So glamour me?"

"Not this time. Maybe later. Trust me, word has already traveled that you're back."

Lucifer raised an eyebrow in challenge. "You wouldn't happen to be avoiding me, would you, little witch?"

"I'm not avoiding you. I came to lunch, didn't I?"

"Which was cut short. We didn't even finish our food thanks to the imposter, then I got shot. You're still hungry and I never got my time with you."

"We can have lunch again, no distractions."

"Stay," he hummed. "Just for a little while. You need to eat. Can't have you losing even an inch of that delectable ass."

"Lucifer!" I choked, smacking his side.

"What? I'm just being honest."

I sighed as we stepped into the elevator. "I can't with you sometimes."

"Oh, but you can, don't think I missed what you were about to tell me before Not-Sasha interfered. You're not fooling anyone."

"See?" Bad Nat said.

Before I could say anything, he leaned over and kissed me thoroughly. His soft lips pressed against mine with a heat that left me breathless. Despite all, he was right.

I'd fallen for the devil.

And there was no going back for either of us.

8

LUCIFER

It was late. Past midnight.

After lunch, Nathalie disappeared to flit around the city tending to her business. Despite the massive problems going on in her personal life, the woman was determined to keep up her presence in New Chicago. It was funny, when I ruled New Chicago, I didn't do half what Nathalie managed for the people here.

Granted, I didn't care quite as much.

But still, my power over New Chicago had done something I hadn't realized I would miss—fill my time. I was working hard to respect this inane need for "space" from my little witch. What I hadn't expected was to actually experience true boredom for the first time in my nine thousand years. While Nathalie spent the day fulfilling her purpose, I moved around this apartment coming to the realization that having a person who didn't want to be around me all the time meant that I had nothing to do apart from them.

That was a problem I didn't even know how to solve.

I was serious when I said I was not going to return for my throne. Not only did I not want to face a demon conduit as powerful as Piper, but I genuinely had no desire. Ruling didn't fulfill me. It's part of why I'd grown complacent. Something greater was now leaching into my existence. Anhedonia.

Nathalie saved me from that.

But it appeared she could not save me from boredom. Not when she had a life of her own she was hellbent on living. So what the fuck was I supposed to do?

Nathalie's teasing voice from weeks ago telling me to pick up a hobby came to mind, but I didn't have the first idea of what I'd want to do.

Thinking about the things I enjoyed in life . . . there were very few. Fucking. Punishing. That was it.

The only person I was interested in fucking was my little witch. So that left punishing.

Maybe I could take to hunting down scum and making them pay for their crimes. It's not like Piper could be everywhere. Surely she could use the help . . .

My thoughts were interrupted by the distinct sounds of Nathalie's nightly routine wrapping up. I shifted on the couch, glancing toward the hallway as I waited for her to emerge. When the bathroom door opened, Nathalie stood with wet strands of brown hair clinging to her face and shoulders. She was dressed in silk shorts and a tank top.

"What are you doing?" She walked into the living room, stalling in surprise.

I gestured towards the TV that was playing some random show.

"Just hanging out here, catching up on some of your shows," I replied, trying to keep my tone light.

Nathalie raised an eyebrow, a playful smirk on her lips. "Oh really? You always refused to watch any of the shows I had." She dropped her voice a few octaves, mimicking me. "'TV is mind-numbingly dull.' Remember?"

I flashed a smile that didn't quite reach my eyes. "True, but I'm finding that it's strange being so alone after spending months attached to one person," I admitted, a hint of vulnerability creeping into my voice, despite myself.

There was a pause, a moment where the air seemed charged with unspoken words. Then Nathalie surprised me. She hesitated just for a moment before she spoke again.

"Do you want to sleep in my room?" she suggested softly.

I met her gaze, searching for any hint of hesitation, but all I found was warmth and a flicker of something else, something that made my body buzz with awareness.

"Obviously," I answered. "But are you sure?" I asked, wanting to be absolutely certain.

She nodded, her eyes steady. "Yeah," she said with a small smile. "Second chances, right?"

I got up slowly, crossing the room to where she stood. Without another word, she turned and led the way. The soft glow of lamplight spilled into the hallway as we entered her bedroom. It was true. I'd grown used to this room, used to her presence most of all. The quiet and stillness without her was something I didn't care for.

Nathalie climbed into bed, and I followed, slipping under the covers beside her. She twisted to face me, and I reached out, looping an arm around her slender waist to pull her close. Her head came to rest where my bicep met my shoulder. I lowered my face to her hair, inhaling her scent.

"Today with Sasha was disconcerting," I commented after a long moment of silence, my hand sliding up and down her side.

"Yeah, well, it's not Sasha," Nathalie retorted with a snort. "Disconcerting is an understatement. You weren't helping, though."

"Who is Not-Sasha?" I asked point blank. She tilted her head back to look at me, taken aback by the directness of my question.

"I told you; I don't know for sure," she said with a sigh.

I gave her a look, not backing down. "You do," I replied evenly. "I can tell."

Nathalie groaned and sat up, pulling away from me. She ran a hand through her chestnut hair, the wet silky strands sliding seamlessly. "Why are we doing this again?"

"I can help," I offered. "I'm on your side, Nathalie. You have to know this."

"Oddly, I do." She shook her head, eyes softening.

"But you have a hard time containing your tongue. Today was bad enough. I don't want it to get worse."

"He's just trying to help. He wants to fix it for us, isn't that romantic?"

The voice I heard in my head was Nathalie, but her lips weren't moving, and her eyes had a slight haze to them. She was in her memory loci.

"He's not exactly good at fixing things, Peace." Another Nathalie, this one sounded less breathy and more like the Nat I knew.

"His choices are what led to the Magic Wars, followed by his own death, which need I remind you triggered the death of millions." This Nathalie sounded stern and calculated. The pull of the voices was unreal. They were like a siren's call.

One moment I was laying in Nathalie's bed, the next I was staring at an ebony round table of variously dressed Nathalie's. Every pair of brown eyes turned to me.

"That wasn't very kind," I said to the one I'm guessing spoke. She wore glasses and a designer suit. Her hair was pulled back in a sleek ponytail that swished when her head turned. "That was a low blow, blaming a guy for his own death, especially when a certain someone held the knife."

She narrowed her sharp eyes, adjusting her glasses. "Was it low, or was it truthful? I didn't have a choice in the hand I played. Your choices—pursuing Piper, punishing the witches for starting the Magic Wars—

those led you there. I thought I was rescuing someone dear to me at the time."

"Dear to you?" I asked, an edge entering my tone. By the way she described them, it wasn't Baggage or the Incubus. No, this was someone else. "Dear to you *how* exactly?"

"Unimportant." She waved her hand dismissively.

I turned to the Nat dressed like mine in the real world. The one I knew her others called Prime. "What's she talking about?"

Prime sighed. "There was a boy . . . I was close to him. I thought we were friends. I was wrong."

Jealousy licked at my skin, but I didn't let it show. Boy or girl, it wouldn't have mattered. Someone was close to my witch. As if that wasn't bad enough, they hurt her.

Perhaps if I took up punishing as a hobby, I would pay this person a visit.

"Ann is right," Prime continued after an extended silence. "He's unimportant. What I'd really like to know is why *you're* here. Again."

"I have no idea. One minute I was hearing different versions of your voice in my head, next I'm here. Somehow you're pulling me into your head with you."

"Hmm," the Prime hummed.

"I'm starting to think you're doing this on purpose," another Nat countered. This one wore jeans and an eighties band t-shirt, and she watched me with guarded eyes. The Warden, surely.

"He can't lie," another Nat scoffed. This Nat had her

feet kicked up on the table, a cigarette dangling between her fingers as she pointed at me. Bad Nat. Fitting.

"Okay," Prime cut in, "so you're not doing it on purpose."

"Nope, but since I'm here, can a demon get a chair?" I tutted at them. "Where are your manners, little witches?"

A chair appeared in between two Nats who hadn't spoken. One wore comfy clothes and a shawl with her hair tied back in a messy bun, the other dressed in shorts and a feminine blouse with her hair down—the way I liked it best.

"I've got it, Luci," a soft-spoken Nat said.

I strolled over and folded myself in the chair. Leaning on the table facing her, I used my free hand to lift her chin toward me. "You have to be the sweetest one, aren't you?"

"I'm Peace." She blushed and giggled, holding a romance novel to her chest. My eyes skimmed the cover, and I suppressed a chuckle at the shirtless man embracing a woman half-spilling out of a corset. I heard a gagging sound and turned to look at Bad Nat.

"Why are you flirting, Peace?" The Warden sighed, pinching the bridge of her nose. "You know he can't *do* anything with us."

"We should ignore them," Ann said. "Peace isn't useful most of the time anyway, and Lucifer . . ." Her sharp gaze raked over me.

"And Lucifer what?" I prompted.

She turned her chin, the slightest blush rising to her

cheeks. My, my. Even my analytical Nat wasn't unaffected by me.

"Is too interested in toying with me and my others to be of any real help," Prime said firmly. Her gaze settled on me, unamused but not upset. She saw me and accepted my hedonistic nature for what it was.

"I disagree." My hand dropped from Peace's chin as I settled back and crossed one ankle over my knee. "But I do love games, and I find I'm quite good at them. I could be an asset—if you let me."

"Out of the question," Ann muttered.

"He's been respectful of our wishes even though it goes against his nature." Caretaker Nat said, setting her tea aside. "I think we should give him a chance."

The Prime closed her eyes and took a deep breath. When she opened them, it wasn't me she was looking at. It was The Warden. "And you? What do you think?"

"We can handle this. It's not outside our power, and if it were, Piper is the one we should be going to."

"Exactly," Ann cut in. "So we're in agreement."

Bad Nat scoffed. "I wouldn't exactly call that a consensus. You never asked my opinion."

"Or mine," Peace muttered.

"Do you actually care?" Bad Nat asked her, hiking a brow.

"Well, no—"

Bad Nat snorted.

"Do you?" The Warden shot back, side-eyeing Bad Nat.

Bad Nat lifted a shoulder and rolled her eyes.

And a door in the house rattled violently.

"What's that?" I asked, lifting my gaze to the ceiling.

The Prime tensed, her expression guarded. "No one."

Ah, so not a what, but a *who.*

"Why must you insist on hiding things and lying? You know I can taste your dishonesty, little witch, even here." My voice was coaxing and smooth. "Who is it?"

She sighed, narrowing her eyes slightly in irritation. "It' . . . she's my rage," she admitted, albeit reluctantly.

"Prime keeps her locked away," Bad Nathalie cut in, clearly disapproving. "Even when we could use her help."

"She unpredictable," The Warden sighed, as if they'd been over this a hundred times. "And inevitably makes most situations worse."

"We've been over this," Ann spoke up. "We can't let her out. She isn't in the right mental space to be an actual asset."

"I'm going to have to agree with 'Bad Nat' over there," I began, using air quotations around her name. "I don't think that's very healthy. Naming a subset of your-self as bad because it's not logical, or protective, or taking care of everyone else"—I looked at each version of her as I spoke—"or wants to just enjoy life and be at peace, isn't exactly good for you, either." Bad Nat looked at me sharply, her expression shocked, though there was a hint of interest.

"I don't recall asking your opinion," Prime said, lifting a brow. "Or wanting it."

Ah. The situation was becoming clearer. For as well

rounded and strong as Nathalie was, she was also breaking apart at the seams. Her personality was fracturing under the weight of the world.

"Who are you, exactly?" I asked Bad Nat. "What's your purpose? Are you simply the rebel?"

She smiled, and it wasn't soft or kind, neither was it cruel or caustic—but something hid behind it. A sadness of a sort.

"I'm the truth."

"Enough." Prime held up her hand ending the conflict. She shot a glare at her rebellious alter ego before turning back to me. "You can stay, or you can go, but I've got work to do."

"Come on, little witch, don't ice me out," I murmured, trying to keep the pleading out of my voice. "I was just trying to—"

"You can stay and hang out with Peace if you want to, but leave me alone."

And with that, Prime, Ann, and The Warden stood and filed out of the meeting room. Peace turned to me and smiled sheepishly.

"Want to see my greenhouse?"

9

NATHALIE

I STOOD IN FRONT OF THE MIRROR, TURNING THIS WAY AND that, adjusting my crew neck sweater. I'd curled my hair and even went through the effort of putting on some very light makeup. You could clearly still see the dark circles under my eyes, but at least I looked a little further from exhaustion. I hated to admit it, but I slept like a baby in Lucifer's arms last night.

Our encounter in the memory loci had been a little awkward, but when we'd both come out of it, the tension had mostly dissipated. Thankfully he hadn't asked me any more about Rage. Lucifer had a lot of good qualities, but his impulsivity wasn't on that list. He didn't know the extent of the damage Rage could cause, and to push for her release was something I didn't tolerate, even from my others.

"You're putting more effort into August's breakfast than when I took you to lunch," Lucifer remarked casually from his spot on my bed. He was naked with only a sheet draped across his waist, displaying his body. I was pretty sure he had been the inspiration for some marble statues thousands of years ago. Lucifer had abs without needing to try, toned leg muscles, and smooth unblemished skin—apart from his white brands. His perfectly chiseled jawline and hooded golden eyes made him otherworldly, even amongst supernaturals.

My demon of desire was physically perfect in every sense.

I turned my eyes to him in the mirror and tried not to be distracted.

"Stop being jealous, Lucifer. It's not a good look on you," I retorted.

Lucifer said nothing but continued watching me as I finished getting ready in silence. I repressed a sigh and decided to just let him sulk.

When I moved toward the bedroom door to leave, Lucifer intercepted, appearing in front of me, blocking my path. He reached out, pulling me close for a deep kiss that took me off guard.

"Have fun," he murmured against my lips before releasing me.

I blinked, slightly dazed by his sudden intensity, then composed myself. "Uh, yeah, thanks."

With those stumbled words, I headed out of the door. Despite the fact that the diner wasn't far away, I decided to drive. It was chilly outside, and I just didn't feel like showing up with a runny nose and red cheeks.

In my short commute, I mulled over how to broach the subject of Sasha and Not-Sasha with him. There was still a lot that had been left unresolved regarding us. Things like their mate bond, my own bond with August, and what that meant for all parties involved.

The bell above the door tinkled softly as I walked into the upscale diner. There was a hum of conversation in the air, and the entire room was full of supernaturals— as was obvious to me because I could see the many shades of swirling magic. Unsurprising, honestly. It was hard to come across nice restaurants like this since the Magic Wars, but of the ones that did exist, it was generally only supes that could afford them.

Soft, ambient lighting streamed through large, arched windows adorned with lace curtains, casting a warm glow over the whole place. I spotted August sitting at a corner booth, giving him an unobstructed view of the entire room. As I approached, his face lit up with a warm smile.

August was always handsome, with curly black hair, glamoured slate blue eyes, and earthy brown skin. I found myself breathing easier in his vicinity, as if my body recognized a safe harbor.

"Hey," he greeted, rising slightly to kiss me. Our lips met and sparks ignited. I had to hold back a groan as his tongue slid against mine. The kiss was over too fast, and it left me breathless.

"Hey yourself," I breathed, sliding into the seat opposite him.

"You look beautiful, as always."

"Beautiful *and* tired," I added, trying not to scoff at his compliment. I didn't mean to be dismissive of his flattery. Around August, I just felt like I could be more honest about these things.

"Okay. And tired, though it's not something I would have said," he amended, placating me. "How are you holding up?"

"Fine," I replied, trying to muster up a smile, but I knew it fell flat. August's eyes narrowed slightly, seeing through the noncommittal answer easily.

"Did you just use the vague female go-to? '*Fine*?' he said, tilting his head. My cheeks flushed. I had indeed. He tsked. "Try again."

"Things are less than fine. Happy?"

"Have you slept?"

"I've slept." I winced and picked at my nails. I slept great with Lucifer, but it felt like fatigue was a shadow, clinging to me. I couldn't seem to escape it, and ultimately I didn't have the time. "Have you?"

I wasn't the only one showing signs of being tired. August was sporting a five o'clock shadow despite it being nine in the morning. The corners around his eyes crinkled more, making him look years older despite the fact he couldn't age.

"Like absolute shit," he said, reaching across the table to link our fingers together. He squeezed my hand when I looked at him with concern. "I sleep better when you're next to me."

That feeling was mutual. I felt heat creep over my skin as memories flooded me. All the things we do before we sleep. I mentally chastised myself. That was the exact reason we were meeting in public. We were far less likely to start fucking on top of the table in a crowded diner. The chances were slim, but they still weren't none.

"Enough about me, though. Your thinly veiled attempt to turn this around won't work. You said you're less than fine. What's going on?" he asked.

"What's *not* going on feels like a safer question these days," I murmured.

"Are you going to tell me what that means, or did you want me to ask you what's not going on?"

There was no reason to drag this out with small talk. Whether I wanted to or not, I had to tell him about it. I sighed. Taking a deep breath, I let it out, telling him that someone came back in Sasha's body, catching him up on every detail that had happened since then.

"That's a hell of a lot to process," he admitted a few moments after I'd finished, his hand still holding mine.

"Yeah, it is," I agreed, leaning forward in my seat, "That's why I haven't been around. I'm not avoiding you. I'm truly just busy."

"What does this mean for Sasha? The real one."

I bristled slightly, instantly feeling annoyed at myself for the hint of jealousy his question stirred up. I had no reason to be jealous. I knew that. It wasn't even my place to be jealous. He wasn't mine. Finally, I shook my head. "I don't know. Honestly, that's the answer to just about everything right now, but I don't know if she's capable of coming back."

I waited, thinking he was going to turn this into a conversation about the aurae bond.

He nodded a few times, thinking about what I'd said. "Is there anything I can do to help?"

Before I could respond, we both lifted our heads to the obnoxious sound of a chair dragging across the floor. My mouth hung slightly open as Lucifer plopped down between us in a chair stolen from the occupied table behind us.

"I think it's time we officially met," he said, holding out his hand to August. "Lucifer Morningstar."

August didn't move, just looked between Lucifer and me. I'd caught him up on every detail . . . except one.

"He was dead," he said flatly. His jaw sharpened like he was clenching his teeth, and the hand holding mine squeezed a fraction tighter.

"*Was*. I'm not anymore," Lucifer replied smoothly, tucking his hand away.

"Did you bring him back?" August asked, his voice laced with surprise and a hint of accusation.

"No—well, yes? Sort of, but not on purpose, and not in the way you think," I explained quickly.

"How many ways are there to bring someone back from the dead?" August asked. "I thought the only way a witch could is through resurrection."

Running my free hand through my hair, I pulled at the tangles that had managed to appear in the last half an hour since brushing it. "Um, usually, yes. This situation is a little different, though. Lucifer is a demon and feeds off desire. He used Samhain to cross the veil."

"She's shortening the story," Lucifer butted in. "Leaving out all the best parts aren't we, little witch?"

I cut my eyes to him in a way that absolutely screamed, *"Shut the hell up."* Lucifer looked completely unbothered in the face of my ire and August's irritation. Of course he would. Fucking devil.

August's thumb brushed over my hand gently in a calming manner. Lucifer leaned forward, his eyes locking onto August's.

"We need to have a talk," he said, ignoring my death glare. "Since we're both going to be with Nathalie, everyone should be on the same page." He said it like it was the most normal thing in the world, and I wished the booth cushion would just swallow me whole. August looked at me, my face undoubtedly red.

"This is *not*," I emphasized in a lowered hiss, "what I had in mind for how to tell August."

Lucifer shrugged. "I'm saving you the stress of the conversation and ripping the band-aid off."

August didn't react outwardly. He kept stroking my hand as if Lucifer didn't drop a bomb on him. "What's there to get on board with? We're both with her—well all three of us, if we're including the kid." I lifted my eyebrow at the way he addressed Marcel.

"You do realize he's three years older than me, right?"

"Physically. You're an old soul and wise beyond your years," August responded.

"Sharing isn't in my nature. My little witch is quite attached to you, though, so for her, I'll make this work." Lucifer pointedly ignored me until he tacked on, "So long as things are kept fair."

"What the hell does that mean?" I demanded, feeling my face heat up even more.

"I'm not sure yet. It can look many ways. We could always trade off days or nights with you," Lucifer replied.

"No," I said firmly, pulling my hand gently from August's so I could get my point across. "I'm not a toy you can schedule time with. That's not how this is going to go. I still have free will, and if I'm pissed at someone" —I shot a pointed look at Lucifer"—then I'm not spending time with him just to suit a stupid schedule. This also *isn't a priority right now.*"

Lucifer's expression softened slightly. "It's my priority," he said, then turned to August. "What about you?"

August met Lucifer's gaze, his resolve clear. "Nathalie is my priority," he said simply. "Which brings us back to my original question: can I help you at all, Nat?"

Lucifer scoffed. "She doesn't want help. She thinks she should go it alone."

"I was speaking to the lady," August said, keeping his cool as he spoke curtly to the devil. "When I address you, you'll know it."

I gritted my teeth, not liking Lucifer's tone, or his presence. Before he could respond to August, I laid into him. "That is not what I said. I said don't want *your* help because you have a tendency to act without thinking."

"Actually," he protested, "I put the perfect amount of thought in."

"Really? So you put thought into how you were going to approach all of this, and somehow you still managed to come across rude?"

Lucifer raised an eyebrow. "I'm being rude?"

I sighed, turning back to August. "I appreciate the offer, but right now, I want to keep you away from Not-Sasha. Your mate bond with Real-Sasha complicates things. She claims to have gotten over it in the veil, but she would know that you would immediately recognize it wasn't her, which means whoever is inside her would know the jig is up. Right now, they think they're getting away with it. We don't know who it is yet, or what they want, so we need to keep it that way."

August nodded, though he clearly didn't like it. "I can understand your reasoning, but if you won't accept help, who's going to keep you safe?"

"I—"

My phone buzzed with a text from an anonymous number. I opened it and my blood ran cold. It was a picture of Carissa.

Dead.

IO

NATHALIE

WHO WOULD KEEP ME SAFE?

That was a great question. Someone wanted to kill the Le Fays. My family was horrible, so it could be for any number of reasons. Maybe I was next.

Dead. The word echoed in my mind as I stared at the picture. I knew I couldn't answer why. Instead I focused on what I saw. The facts.

She was murdered. Her limbs were bent at odd angles, suggesting someone tortured her. Whoever sent me the text was either first on the scene, or more likely, the killer.

I looked up from my phone, my heart racing. "Carissa is dead."

Both August and Lucifer stiffened immediately, their expressions darkening. I didn't say anything else, just slid my phone on the table between us. Lucifer picked it up, and his lips set in a thin line before he passed it to August who blinked at the picture disbelieving. They started asking me questions, none of which I could answer. I couldn't focus on them right now.

"I'm going to go over there."

"Over where, exactly?" Lucifer asked, lifting a brow.

"The Le Fay mansion. She's in the front room. I recognize the scuffed wood floors." I stood up suddenly, ready to leave. They both rose with me. "What are you doing?"

Lucifer and August looked between themselves and then to me. "We're coming with you, sunling."

"Oh no," I shook my head firmly. "You guys aren't going."

"And why not? An anonymous text of your dead sister doesn't scream 'safe' to me," August said, seemingly on Lucifer's side in this.

"You are both a liability," I retorted, my eyes narrowing.

"How so?" Lucifer demanded, his jaw tensing.

"August, you need to stay behind just in case Sasha is around. She can't see you remember?" I chose not to tell Lucifer his impulsiveness was a risk. He would just get defensive. "Lucifer, if you really wanted to help, you'll find where Sasha and Sienna are. I don't know who else got this text. Keep a low profile, but make sure they stay away from the Le Fay mansion. Try not to engage with her, but if you have to, just distract them. *Don't* make this worse."

Both men opened their mouths to argue, but I cut them off with a pleading look. I was wasting time that I didn't have. Clues and evidence. I needed to get there before anyone interfered.

"Please. It's important."

Lucifer crossed his arms, his eyes narrowing. "Fine. I'll go," he muttered.

"If he's distracting Sasha, then me coming with you isn't an issue. I won't see her." August raised a brow, knowing he had a point.

Shit.

"Please, August. I have to do this alone. I need you to trust me."

His nostrils flared, and a moment later he nodded, disappointed but resigned.

"Thank you," I breathed in relief. "We'll raincheck breakfast." I shot a pointed look at Lucifer. "Alone, next time."

August pulled me into a tight hug and planted a kiss on the top of my head. "Be careful."

"I will," I promised, before heading out the door with a stormy and silent Lucifer in tow.

As we got to the car, I rounded on him. "I don't have time for this right now, but please know that I'm mad at you for what you just pulled with August," I said bluntly. "That wasn't how I wanted to do that. It wasn't your place."

Lucifer raised an eyebrow, his expression unreadable. "Noted." I ground my teeth and took a deep breath.

" And even though I'm pissed at you, thank you for doing as I asked and actually helping me the way I need."

He just hummed in understanding. "Consider it

done, little witch," he said, his tone serious. He pulled me into his arms for a brief, but strong hug. "Be safe, and don't do anything crazy. You don't have to face every choice alone. Remember that."

He let me go with a lingering kiss to the forehead and I slid into my car without another word. He held the door open for me, letting me climb in. I drove away watching him in my rearview mirror as he walked the opposite way, pulling out his phone as he went.

Driving to my family home, my mind raced with thoughts about this new development. Carissa was dead. It felt surreal. She had been a constant tormentor in my life, a presence that was more malignant than familial. Despite this, her death definitely disturbed me —not because I felt a loss, but because I was sure it was connected to everything else that had been happening.

As I drove, I felt the pull of my memory loci, but I kept my focus on the road. My different selves were arguing. As usual. The best I could do was let them talk. I could listen, but I couldn't allow myself time to retreat into my mind.

The Warden was the first to speak. *"Carissa's death can't be a coincidence. It's too neatly aligned with everything else going on."*

Ann agreed. *"We need to consider the possibility that her death is part of a larger plan. With everything going on with Sasha and the other murders, Carissa's death could be a strategic move."*

"But what if we're missing something?" Peace asked.

"What if her death was a warning or a message? What if it's a trap?"

Caretaker hummed. *"Carissa may have been awful, but she was still family. Her death means something. We have to be careful."*

Bad Nat scoffed. *"Who cares about the why? The point is she's dead, and it's connected to everything else. We need to focus on the bigger picture and figure out our next move against Not-Sasha."*

"We know her behavior was strange last time. It's possible she was influenced or controlled by something—someone," Ann suggested.

"You think it's connected to Sasha? Er, Not-Sasha? Or whatever it is that's in her?" Caretaker asked.

"That could make sense," I mumbled, glancing at the clock and then back at the road. "The question is what's the connection? All of this is intertwined in something bigger; I can feel it."

Peace spoke up, her voice steady. *"All of this is just saying we don't know exactly what we're facing here. We can't rush into this blindly. Maybe we should have let one of our guys help us."*

Bad Nat's annoyance was barely contained. *"Of course you want to play damsel and let the men do all the work. This is our problem, we fix it."*

I cut through all of the arguments, speaking out loud. "We're going to Carissa's body, and we face what we face when we get there. We can't hide out and we're not letting the guys handle our business. We'll gather information and be prepared for whatever comes next."

The Warden and Ann hummed in agreement, satisfied with the plan. Peace and Caretaker didn't argue, but they were clearly worried. They knew the decision had been made.

Pulling in front of the massive estate, my stomach churned with anxiety.

The front door creak echoed ominously as I pushed it open. The house was eerily quiet and every step I took seemed louder than normal. I found Carissa where the picture indicated, in the living room, her lifeless body sprawled on the floor. Her skin was pale, and there was a vacant look in her eyes.

What I didn't expect was to find another person in the room. Kneeling beside the body, her hands in her lap was none other than my twin sister.

"Kat?"

With her head hung low, she didn't look up as I moved further into the room. The chestnut brown hair that we shared covered her face. Her shoulders were hunched over and the whole scene was fucking bizarre.

What the hell is she doing here? Part of me wondered if this was something she did, like some of the other victims. I knew she hadn't been the cause of all of those deaths, but her explanation had been shaky at best.

"Kat? What are you doing here?" I asked again.

"Same as you," she said flatly, not bothering to meet my gaze.

My eyes flicked to Carissa, and back to Kat. I didn't want to ask, but I had to know. "Did you do this? Did you kill her?"

She scoffed softly. "No."

She couldn't lie to me. She could give sketchy, round-about answers, but she couldn't outright lie. And this? She answered as plainly as she could.

"Then who?" I whispered to myself. "And why the text to both of us?"

"It means our time is up," she said, clearing her throat slightly. I waited for her to give some extra clarification to that statement, but when silence was her answer, I pressed again.

"What are you talking about?"

"With Carissa dead, our time is up."

"I don't understand," I said, moving closer to her. "Do you know what caused this? Or who? Why?"

She sighed. "For what it's worth, I'm sorry I didn't find another way."

I was starting to get frustrated with the crazy mutterings and vague answers. "Another way for what?"

Kat tilted her head to look at me and her eyes were dead. "To save you."

II

NATHALIE

I stared at her for a long moment, waiting for an explanation or some kind of expansion as to what she was actually talking about.

"What the hell is that supposed to mean?" I put my hands on my hips, glaring at her.

My sister barely seemed to hear me, her eyes turned back to Carissa, her hands shaking as they lay in her lap. Instead of answering, she muttered to herself, whispering quietly about how hard she tried, how everything was over now, how she would never find "her" again, and so much more. I huffed roughly and looked away, running my hands through my hair.

"*Katherine*." She didn't answer. "Fuck, Kat, answer me."

Her eyes lifted to mine, and she frowned. "I tried to save us, Nat. I really did. I tried so hard."

She blinked back tears, and my mouth nearly

dropped open. The last time I saw Kat cry was the day Prudence died.

"I don't understand. You're not explaining anything."

"What is there to explain? Everything is over." She gave a mirthless laugh. "Might as well pack it up and start our goodbyes."

I was struggling, my anger rising until it was barely contained. With everything happening around me, with all of the people depending on me, I didn't have fucking time for this. I felt like she was wasting what little moments I had, and it was driving me up the wall.

"For fuck's sake! Enough with the cryptic words," I demanded, my voice shaking. "I need answers, Katherine. *Now*."

"Nat, it's not that simple."

I crossed my arms over my chest, refusing to back down. I was getting answers today if it killed me. Too many things counted on me being right. Too many people counted on me being successful, and I couldn't afford to let any one of them down. I hadn't failed before, and I wasn't ready to start now. At least not with this.

"Katherine, I swear to the gods if you don't start talking . . ." I stopped myself, taking a deep breath before I began throwing out haphazard threats. Slapping the shit out of her crossed my mind. Maybe it would knock some sense into her.

She sighed deeply and looked away. For a second I thought she wasn't going to answer and that would have probably sent me over the edge. But she did answer, finally.

"How much do you actually know about our family history?" she asked in a somber tone.

"What are you even talking about?" I felt like this whole conversation had been nothing more than rambling nonsense, leaving me confused over her refusal to answer my questions in a way that made any sense at all. Why was she making this difficult?

"I am talking about the fact that there is so much more to the Le Fays than you could ever imagine."

"Yeah, all of us are fucked up and we all have some serious family of origin issues. What else is there to know?"

She rolled her eyes, a bit of the normal Kat peeking through. "You think you knew everything when you ran off and left us all behind? There are more secrets than you could ever imagine."

"Well, enlighten me. Our whole family's dead now besides us, so what's the leftover secrecy for?"

"Really nice, Nat."

I shrugged but didn't defend my words. Sure they sounded harsh, but it was the truth, and more importantly, I didn't give a fuck. My whole family. Their beliefs. Their actions. Death didn't change who they'd been in life, nor did it change the pain it caused me. At this point, all I wanted was answers so I could go back to ignoring my family name and their fucked-up legacies.

"Look, just answer me this, were you and the coven stupid enough to bring back Morgan Le Fay?"

"What are you—"

"Yes or no?" I bit out, my eyes never leaving her.

Again, I didn't have time for the ambiguity. I glared at her with a hard expression.

"No."

I felt myself deflate at her words as my hands dropped to my side and my shoulders hunched over.

"That changes everything," Ann said from the loci, pushing her glasses higher up on her nose. *"I will have to change all of the plans. Every calculation."*

"We can't calculate shit until we know who the hell is in Sasha's body," Bad Nat seethed, leaning over the files Ann had spread out.

"Move," Ann muttered, batting her away.

"You're telling me The Morrigan has nothing to do with this?" I asked Kat, trying to ignore the input from the loci. I needed to focus, especially because if that was the case, it was hard to believe. Actually, believing it fucked up all of my assumptions. And that was why I had been hesitant to speak my thoughts aloud.

"I didn't say that." Kat weighed her words before adding, "Technically, no one can bring her back to life. She can't die in the first place."

"Huh?" I blinked, not understanding.

"The Morrigan," she drew out her words like she was talking to a toddler, "can't die."

"Thanks for repeating yourself. That really cleared it up for me. *Oh, wait,*" I said sarcastically, shooting her a dirty look. "How about you elaborate here? Witches aren't immortal. Even her. We can all die."

"Our bodies can die, but our souls can be immortal," she said as she rose to her feet. Katherine cast one last look at Carissa. Her face was hard to read. Her expression wasn't filled with sadness. More like a dejected acceptance. Kat took a deep breath. "This is a long story, and it involves the two of us, but I need a fucking drink for this."

She walked away from me, heading for the kitchen. Giving a groan, I followed behind, trying not to stomp my feet like a petulant child, and failing miserably.

"God, Kat just speak plainly." She ignored me and ruffled through cabinets and the pantry before she finally pulled out an old bottle of whiskey and two glasses. " I don't have time for the riddles."

"Look, you'll need this shot when we're done here." She poured out two fingers in each glass and slid one across the counter. It sloshed as it came to a halt at the end of the counter, close to me.

"I think I am good. Talk."

"Your choice." She shrugged and threw back the shot. Grimacing and shivering from the taste, she took a steadying breath.

"The Morrigan spent her entire mortal existence facing the reality of death," she began, her voice solemn and echoing through the quiet room. "She came up with a solution, and it was us."

She paused for effect, but I waited. I had asked enough times already and I was done playing games. So, I continued to eye her expectantly.

"Dolores was never our mother, Nathalie."

Now I understood why she'd paused.

"The fuck? Not that I am sad about this, but how

could she not be our mother? Who is?" Horror overtook me as I had another, disturbing thought. "Oh gods, is The Morrigan our real mom?"

"Gods! No," she exclaimed, reeling back at the very thought. "No, our mother is just some no-name witch."

"Bloodlines are everything in our family. Dad fathering children with someone they'd consider a random nobody doesn't sound like something Dolores would be okay with."

She snorted. "As if she had a choice. Our matrilineal line is through our birth mother, but our magic line isn't. Morgan Le Fay needed the perfect vessel—a *Le Fay* vessel. So, one blood sacrifice later combining her magic with our father's, and here we are."

"Why?" I managed to ask. "What's the purpose of this?"

"Like I said, our bodies can die, but our soul can be immortal. Her spirit can just keep getting passed on to the next Le Fay in line when one dies." Kat gestured to Carissa. "Morgan Le Fay left Carissa and went into your friend Sasha. But that's a temporary stop."

"Was Carissa . . . made? Like us?" I asked, the shock and hesitation leaking into my voice.

Kat nodded. "Her too, amongst others."

I inhaled, long and deep, trying to absorb what my sister was telling me. "How long has she been doing this?"

She poured another shot into her glass, tilting it back and swallowing before she spoke again. "It's no secret she's old as dirt. She's been trying to find a way to become immortal, and she's been doing that for centuries. She finds temporary solutions in the vessels she creates, but none of them can hold and match her magic."

"So she, what? Takes the body and then . . ." As I paused, the pieces clicked together in my head, thinking about the string of dead in New Chicago that fit the bill. "She drains them of their magic, doesn't she?"

Kat pressed her lips together and inclined her head. "That about sums it up. When they're sucked dry, she moves on to the next vessel."

"How many?"

"Vessels?" Kat asked, and I nodded. "Countless. And she's killed them all."

My mind was absolutely reeling. I felt like the ground had been ripped out from under me.

"I'll take that drink now," I said hoarsely, reaching for the whiskey she'd poured.

"Thought you'd change your mind."

I slammed it back in one gulp, feeling the burn splinter through my chest, grounding me in reality as more questions ran through my mind.

"Now that she's done with Carissa . . . what now?"

"All spells—even blood sacrifices—have rules. Birth order is one of them. I'm next."

"Kat, we have to get you somewhere safe. We have to—"

"She won't stop at me, Nat. It's not me she truly wants." Kat peered at me with heavy eyes as the realization dawned on me.

"The perfect vessel," I said, horror-stricken. "My magic. Morgan needs my magic doesn't she?"

"Yeah, Nat, you're the end goal." She looked at me with pity. "She needed a vessel with chaos magic. None of us knew it was you until after the ritual with Lucifer. No one knew you were chaos. That pushed her into action."

I clenched my fists, feeling a surge of anger and fear. "And you couldn't have told me this, I don't know, forever ago? Before she landed on my doorstep in my friend's body, maybe? Or, I don't know, before Carissa died too?"

"Say something to do what? End my own life prematurely for revealing family secrets?"

"This family and their fucking secrets. They're all dead, Kat! Who gives a shit! You could have told me about our lineage after the coven fell apart. You could have given us an actual fighting chance here," I yelled, my hands fisting at my side.

"There is no fighting chance when it comes to Morgan Le Fay." Kat looked down, her expression one of defeat. "The Morrigan is tied to each member of the Le Fay house. Those ties can't be altered, especially not for us. We didn't merely accept the tie. She helped create us."

"So, what are we supposed to do?" I asked, my voice rising. "Just wait for her to take over our bodies? There has to be something we can do."

"It's a soul tie, Nat, similar to mate bonds. Nothing can undo it."

Her words hit me like a ton of bricks. My loci was already in a state of chaos, each one of my selves scrambling for a solution, trying to find a way out of this nightmare. I rubbed at my temples, feeling a throbbing ache settle behind my eyes. Just what I needed. I wouldn't be able to see things clearly if it turned into a migraine.

Then, suddenly, something clicked.

See.

The Eye.

"There might be something that can," I whispered, shifting my gaze as my thoughts raced.

"What did you think of?" Kat demanded, her brows furrowing.

I shook my head at her and kept walking for the front door. "No offense, but not only do I not trust you, there is no way I am going to give The Morrigan a chance to figure me out if she gets to you first."

The words were harsh, but the situation called for blunt honesty.

"Right." She rolled her eyes and huffed.

"Look, I have to go. Stay safe and out of the way," I told her firmly.

"If The Morrigan wants me, she'll find me," Kat replied, her tone flat and resigned. There was no hint of self-pity, just a stark acceptance of the reality we faced.

"Then I will have to fix this quickly, won't I?" I sighed as I stopped at the door, pulling it open. "Just . . . don't do anything rash until then. I will handle this. I promise."

She didn't respond, only giving me a nod that conveyed a lack of faith in my vow. It stung, but I couldn't blame her. We were in this mess partly because of our family's secrets—secrets Kat had kept, thinking she was protecting us. I felt a mixture of frustration and sadness as my sister placed a hand on my shoulder, a silent farewell, before retreating back into the house.

As I turned to leave, a pang of sympathy struck me. Despite everything, she was still my twin, my psychic bondmate, and in this moment, she was just as trapped in this nightmare as I was. And she was next to die.

12

NATHALIE

Leaving Katherine behind felt like shedding some weight, but it was only a temporary relief. As I drove away, the familiar pressure began to build again, like I was Atlas, struggling to hold up a world I wasn't sure I could bear. The past few months had been a relentless barrage of challenges, each one adding to the burden until I felt like I might collapse under the strain.

My hands gripped the steering wheel tightly, the leather cool and smooth against my palms. The road stretched out before me, a seemingly endless ribbon of asphalt leading me back to the chaos I had left behind. I couldn't shake the conversation with Kat from my mind. The revelation that our mother wasn't actually our mother was already a devastating blow. Part of me felt a grim relief that a woman as vile as Dolores wasn't truly my blood, but that small comfort was overshadowed by the tidal wave of new questions and problems. To learn that my existence was intended to house my evil ancestor who just wouldn't stay dead? It was enough to make anyone spiral into madness.

Each revelation raised the stakes in this deadly game. I had been almost positive I was contending with The Morrigan, but I had thought it was a simple matter of exorcising her from Sasha's body. I had hoped the solution would be straightforward. But now, with the knowledge that The Morrigan was destined to pass from host to host, inevitably targeting me, I realized how wrong I'd been. Removing her from Sasha wouldn't end this. It would only bring her closer to me. Everything felt so irrevocably screwed up, like a puzzle where none of the pieces fit together anymore.

One thing was clear: I had to get The Morrigan out of Sasha's body before she could do any more harm. Then handle her before she reached Kat. And long before she got to me. The question was how. I had an answer, but part of me bucked against it. The implications weighed heavily on me. I wasn't just considering the risk to myself; I was contemplating the broader consequences of wielding such power.

Inside, I was torn between the necessity of action and the paralyzing fear of making things worse. The stakes were incredibly high, and I couldn't afford to falter now. But was I truly prepared to wield such power? The pressure of my choices felt suffocating, and the thought of making a mistake weighed heavily on me. What if the solution I was clinging to wasn't enough? What if it only led to more chaos and suffering?

My mind raced as I tried to piece together a timeline.

How long had Carissa been dead? Had The Morrigan killed her as soon as Sasha's body became available? A knot of guilt tightened in my chest as I remembered how I had unwittingly given The Morrigan directions to Sasha.

I needed to think, to strategize.

A small café I knew about was nearby, so I pulled into their lot and put the car in park. I slipped into my memory loci. Normally it was a place of comfort. A mental sanctuary where different facets of myself gathered around a table to debate and plan. Today, the atmosphere was tense. The arguments hadn't stopped since I had left Katherine.

The Warden sat back in her seat, arms crossed, her expression resolute. "We need to use the Eye. It's our best chance to sever The Morrigan's tie."

Peace, always the voice of caution, shook her head, her legs folded beneath her in a posture of anxious energy. "But the Eye is unpredictable, and the way we use it is risky," she countered. "It could cause more harm than good."

"It is a risk." Ann tilted her head side to side, her analytical mind weighing the options. "But it's a calculated one. The Eye is the only thing powerful enough to disrupt a soul tie."

"Without it, we'll be sitting ducks," The Warden emphasized, her eyes hard. "We'll be waiting for The Morrigan to kill her host bodies and jump to ours. We need to be prepared. Using the Eye is not just about severing the bond. It's about survival."

"She's right," Analytical Nat agreed. "We don't get second chances with Morgan Le Fay. This is it. The Eye has the power to do what we need."

Caretaker, ever the nurturer, looked pained. "But using the Eye could hurt us too," she said softly. "We have to consider our well-being."

The arguments bounced back and forth, the four versions of me usually in sync now on completely opposing sides. I stood at the head of the table, too agitated to sit. The debate mirrored the internal conflict tearing at me—a tug-of-war between options and risks, each one carrying potentially devastating consequences.

As the voices rose in intensity, Bad Nat sauntered in, her presence commanding attention. She crossed her arms over her chest, a smirk playing on her lips as she surveyed the discord. Finally, she turned to me, her eyes gleaming with a rare clarity.

"You already know what to do," she said, gesturing to the others. "Having us discuss it is wasting time we don't have, and you know it. Do what you need to, Prime."

For once, I found myself agreeing with her, without question. Deep down, I knew what had to be done. The risks were immense, but so were the stakes. If we didn't act, The Morrigan would continue her reign of terror, moving from one host to the next, leaving destruction in her wake. I had to protect everyone, even if it meant putting myself in danger.

"I am using the Eye," I said, my voice firm and unwavering. "The decision has been made."

The room fell silent, the weight of my words settling

over us like a heavy fog. The Warden nodded, her expression approving. Analytical Nat looked relieved, while Peace and Caretaker exchanged worried glances. But even they knew there was no other choice. The Eye was our only hope.

As I left the memory loci, my resolve hardened. I didn't *want* to do this. In fact, I hated the entire idea, and I wished anybody but me could be responsible for this particular solution. But this was caused by my family, my ancestor, and because of the pull of my magic. I had to be the one to do this. I had to be the one to act, to take control of this situation before it consumed us all.

Between leaving the parking lot and driving back to my apartment, I felt eerily calm, a stark contrast to the storm brewing inside the loci. New Chicago was cold and dreary, not unusual for a November day, and it reflected the emotion within me. My mind buzzed with plans and contingencies, each scenario more terrifying than the last. The Eye was as powerful as it was dangerous. The potential for backlash, for unintended consequences, loomed large in my mind.

But there was no turning back now.

When I pulled in front of my apartment, I didn't bother wasting time. I also didn't want to give myself the chance to back out or overthink it. I darted out of my car and jogged up to the building. My whole body felt like it was buzzing with nervous energy, but it was now or never.

I guessed Señora was of the same mindset because the moment I stormed into the shop, calling her name, she came out with a knowing look on her face. Hopping out of the way of one of her cats, I opened my mouth to talk, but she beat me to it.

"You've made your choice, haven't you?" It wasn't a question so much as a statement of fact, and I knew at that moment she must have seen me coming already.

Still, I nodded, feeling a mix of determination and anxiety swirling in my chest.

"Yes, I am sure," I replied, my voice steadier than I felt. "I am ready for the Eye."

For a moment, she simply stared at me, her expression inscrutable. Then, she sighed, her shoulders sagging slightly.

"You understand what you're asking for, right? This cannot be undone, Nathalie. The Eye will change you in ways you cannot foresee."

"I know," I said, meeting her gaze, "but I need its power to stop The Morrigan."

"The Eye will not do the work of defeating that witch for you," she warned, her voice harsh.

"I know, but with the Eye, I can manipulate the objects of fate, right?"

The objects of fate were largely unheard of, but I needed them—the spindle that creates the threads, the loom that forms bonds, and the shears that can cut those threads and break bonds. Those would do what I needed to ensure that The Morrigan couldn't get her hands on me. It was the only way.

Señora Rosara studied me instead of answering, her eyes searching mine. "And you're prepared for the consequences? The Eye is not just a tool; it's a living entity with its own will and desires. It will change how you see the world; how you interact with it."

"I'm prepared," I said, though the knot of fear in my stomach tightened. I knew there were many unknowns that could result from taking an ancient artifact into myself, and there was no way for us to predict the outcome. But what choice did I have? The Morrigan was too powerful to confront with ordinary means. "I have to do this. For everyone."

Señora sighed again, a weary sound. "Very well. But I will need time to gather the necessary supplies."

"What supplies?" I asked, a flicker of impatience creeping into my voice. I hated to be rude, but the longer we waited, the more time it gave The Morrigan to strengthen her hold on Sasha—or worse, kill her and move on to Kat.

Señora chuckled softly, shaking her head. "You're asking me to remove and replace your literal eye, Nathalie. It's not a simple process. I have surgical tools, and herbs for healing and protection. But I will need anesthesia. This isn't something I can do on a whim."

I swallowed hard, my mouth suddenly dry. The reality of what I was asking for hit me with full force. This wasn't just a magical ritual; it was a major surgery. I would do it regardless. I knew I had to for everyone's sake.

"We may not have that much time," I said, the urgency in my voice unmistakable. "How long will it take to get what you need?"

Señora regarded me for a moment, her expression unreadable. Then, she nodded, her demeanor shifting from casual to serious. "I have some herbs that will knock you out. It's not as precise as anesthesia . . . I assume you understand what that means?"

I swallowed thickly and nodded.

"Go and prepare yourself, then. I will get everything ready."

As she turned to gather her supplies, I felt a strange mix of relief and terror wash over me. This was it.

There was no turning back now.

13

LUCIFER

New Chicago was cold and brisk as I walked with my hands in my pockets down the street. I had just managed to extract myself from Not-Sasha's relentless clutches after what could only be described as the single most exasperating hour of my existence.

The woman's incessant need for physical proximity and her probing questions had tested every ounce of my patience, but I did as my little witch had asked. I didn't make it worse. I only intervened when I overheard Not-Sasha tell her sister that they should find Nat for something "business related" so they could meet up, insisting they call her. My presence did as expected. I was a distraction. Not-Sasha's interest in Nathalie suddenly gone.

I had barely managed to slip away when Nathalie's text had come through, letting me know that she was on her way home. I'd found an excuse to get out of it, and Sienna played into it well.

I could have simply moved through the veil to get back to Nathalie's apartment, but I needed the time to clear my head. I didn't get much of a chance when a sudden, sharp pang of distress sliced through me.

It was so intense that I stumbled for a moment, gripping the nearest lamppost for support. My breath hitched, and my heart pounded with a fierce urgency. The sensation wasn't mine and I knew that as certainly as I knew whose it was—Nathalie was in trouble.

My instincts screamed at me to protect Nathalie, to tear apart anyone who dared to harm her.

Without a second thought, I plunged into the veil, the familiar swirl of energy enveloping me as I blinked out of existence and reappeared at Nathalie's apartment. I knew instantly that she wasn't inside the apartment, but was in the building, meaning she had to be with Señora. Flashing out and back in again, I found myself in Señora's side room, a bright light glaring where a large table stood.

My eyes were immediately drawn to the sight of Nathalie lying on the operating table, her face smeared with blood. The air was thick with tension, and I could feel it knotting in my stomach. Standing over her was Señora, her hands were steady as she held a scalpel. I was seized by an overwhelming surge of rage, fear, and confusion. Señora's calm, unperturbed gaze met mine, and I registered the gleaming gold object she held in her other hand.

"Hold the Eye."

Her words pierced through my emotional turmoil,

and for a moment, I stood frozen. My primal urge to protect what was mine was tempered by the reality that was slowly sinking in. Without question, this was Nathalie's plan. Yet another thing I was left out of. I clenched my fists, feeling the sharp bite of my claws digging into my palms as I fought to steady myself.

Taking a deep breath, I extended my hand, accepting the Eye.

THE RHYTHMIC TAPPING OF MY FINGERS ON THE ARMREST OF THE chair was the only sound in Nathalie's bedroom as I sat by her. The room was dimly lit, with only the faint glow from the city filtering through the curtains. Nathalie had been out for hours, and I tried not to let that worry me. It was hard considering the old witch downstairs couldn't even give me an estimate for how long a magical eye surgery took to heal from.

My little witch had rushed headlong into danger, determined to save the world as always. She'd told no one else, of course. Why would she seek help from the people who cared for her? She was the most infuriating, stubborn, and wonderful person I had ever known.

And she was mine.

I pulled a seat into the operating room, and I watched the Señora work for over two hours. Afterwards, I helped the witch clean Nathalie up and clear out the space. I moved her body upstairs to her own bed, changing her into comfortable sleepwear. I had a cup of tea in my hands, being warmed every few minutes by magic flowing from my palms. I had a cool compress laying over Nathalie's closed eyes.

And now my job was sitting. Sitting and waiting and watching as she lay there unconscious. Just sit and go mad with the feeling of helplessness. I stared down at her in frustration.

She didn't know how deeply she'd ensnared me, how her every action, every glance, every breath pulled me deeper into her orbit. It wasn't just about the bond we shared as familiar and witch; it was more. It was everything. And it was terrifying.

Demons don't feel love, not in the way humans do. We're not built for it. Our emotions are twisted, dark, and driven by desire, possession, and power. But what I felt for Nathalie was an all-consuming need to make her mine, to be claimed by her in return. It was the closest thing to love a demon could experience; this relentless hunger that gnawed at my insides constantly.

When would I be trusted enough to be included in her plans before they happened? Was I truly so reckless that she felt she couldn't trust me with anything?

I supposed yes, considering a large part of me wanted to storm into Sasha's home and rip her apart myself. Of course that would result in Real-Sasha's death, which I knew was what we were all trying to avoid.

The memory of finding Nathalie, her face pale and bloodied, would likely haunt me forever. The raw, primal fear that had gripped me in that moment was unlike anything I had ever felt. It was a reminder of my own vulnerability; of how much I stood to lose. And I hated it. I hated feeling so powerless, so out of control.

But for Nathalie, I would endure it. I would endure anything.

I watched her chest rise and fall with each breath, my eyes tracing the delicate lines of her face. She looked so peaceful, so fragile. And yet, I knew better. Nathalie was stronger than anyone gave her credit for. She was brave, determined, and fiercely independent. It was one of the things I loved most about her.

I reached out and gently brushed a strand of hair away from her face, my fingers lingering for a moment on her soft skin. "You're not alone in this, little witch," I murmured, though I knew she couldn't hear me. "I am with you. Always."

As the night wore on, I continued to sit by her side, until finally, as the sun set and night came, Nathalie finally stirred.

She made a soft moaning sound in her sleep, and I leaned forward watching her shift. Her body twitched as she returned to consciousness. A groan fell from her lips as she put her hand to the cool compress on her eyes. I leaned forward, my heart pounding.

"Hey there, little witch," I said softly, trying to keep my voice steady. "Welcome back."

Her eyes remained covered, but a faint smile curved her lips. "Lucifer," she said softly, though it came out slurred and drowsy.

"The one and only," I replied, relief flooding through me.

"World couldn't handle more than one," she murmured under her breath.

I chuckled lightly. "How do you feel?"

"Like a truck ran over my face." She tried to move to a sitting position and stopped with a groan. "Twice."

"Sounds about right when you undergo a surgery at the last minute." I gave a huff, shaking my head despite the fact that she couldn't see me. "You always did have a flair for the self-sacrificing dramatics."

She shifted slightly, her hand reaching out blindly. "Come closer. I won't hit. Hard."

That makes me throw my head back with a laugh. "You know I like it rough. Don't tempt me with a good time."

"Where am I?" She tilted her head this way and that, trying to hear, still leaving the compress on.

"In your room." I frowned and continued, unable to help myself. "I brought you up here after the eye surgery you didn't bother to tell anyone about."

She gave a shrug. "Had to be done. Didn't want to worry anyone."

I shook my head, even though she couldn't see it. "You're impossible, you know that?"

"Yep," she said, the faint smile still on her lips.

"Here," I began, reaching for her hand and putting a pill in it. "Señora said to take this when you woke up."

"What is it?" She sniffed it, finding there was no scent. I had already done the same.

"A pain pill of her own creation, or so she says."

She twisted her lips, indicating she wasn't interested. "No, I don't want to be out of it. I'll manage."

"Señora said there are no loopy side effects. Just takes away the pain." I tipped the teacup to her lips, allowing her to drink and swallow the medicine.

After some time passed, the effects of the herbs began to wear off, and the pain did its job as she became more coherent. She pulled the compress off her face and her eyes slowly opened. She blinked a few times, trying to focus.

"There you are," I said softly, schooling my features against seeing the sharp gold reflected back at me, the one orb contrasting the light brown of her regular eye. "Welcome back to the land of the living."

She didn't answer me, her face going slack as she looked at her surroundings. Her gaze darted from me to every corner and crevice of the room. There was a strange intensity in her eyes, a focus I hadn't seen before.

"What do you see?" I asked, both curious and anxious at what she might say.

"*Everything.*"

I4

NATHALIE

Hundreds of golden threads overwhelmed my vision. Each one pulsed with a faint glow. My eyes fluttered rapidly as I tried to blink away the chaos surrounding me, but the gold threads weren't going anywhere. They connected everything, passing through walls, layered over one another, between us. They were the bonds that tie. Some thick. Some thin.

Theoretically, I knew I would see them. That's what the Eye did. Its purpose. There was just no way to accurately imagine how many there truly were. It was staggering. A small whimper slipped through my lips as I squeezed my eyes shut.

I tried to sit up, wincing slightly at the effort. The pill dulled the pain, but it didn't take away all of it. Lucifer put an arm behind me and helped push me into a sitting position.

"Easy there," Lucifer murmured, his tone unusually gentle. "You're okay. Just focus on me."

My eyes flickered open cautiously and I trained my gaze on him for a solid moment. But I couldn't help but see it—our connection. A thick, golden thread stretched between us, shimmering with an intensity that was impossible to ignore. It moved almost like it had a heartbeat, anchoring me to him in a way that was undeniable and unnerving.

I reached out, as if to touch the thread. "There's a thread connecting us."

Lucifer nodded and smoothed my hair back from my face. "I'm your familiar. Of course there is."

"Ours is so thick compared to the rest of them." I plucked my finger over the thread and almost felt the echoes of its vibrations in my core. A blush touched my cheeks as heat rose within me.

Note to self: don't touch the threads on purpose.

It would be impossible to avoid it entirely. There were simply too many.

"That's because it's permanent," he said with a self-satisfied grin. "I told you, little witch, you're stuck with me."

I couldn't help but smile at his words because I didn't feel stuck with him. Not really. I chose him. He chose me. It soothed something in my damaged heart to know he wouldn't leave me. "I'm tied to you. There's a difference."

His wasn't the only string that connected to me either. There was another bond, just as thick and vibrant. I focused on it, trying to feel who was on the other end to no avail. A third bond was forming, hundreds of individual strands twining together. Another piece, no bigger than a hair was settling over it, creating a rope of sorts. The last bond was smaller. Thinner. Dimmer. Something in my chest panged because I had a good idea who that one belonged to.

I closed my eyes again, this time for a very different reason. Lucifer smoothed a hand up and down my back, trying to comfort me.

"All the threads you see are the ties that bind us." His words echoed my earlier thoughts. "Eventually, you'll learn how to see around them easily."

"How do you know?" I asked, trying to focus on something else; anything.

"Because the Eye originally belonged to my father."

I peered up at him and realized that despite being down an eye, I wasn't missing peripheral vision. The Eye of Parcae was truly acting as a replacement and letting me see not only what was natural, but what was not.

"You don't talk about him much."

"There's not much to talk about," he replied, hand settling on the small of my back. "I was the second born son to Erebus and Gaia. Erebus was the Harvester of the Otherworld—before Ronan. He ran his family the same way he did the world. Ruthlessly."

I frowned, picking up what he was saying. "He wasn't a good father to you."

Lucifer hesitated. "He wasn't much of a father to me at all. Ronan was the first born. He had chaos magic. He was the heir Erebus wanted."

"And you?"

"I existed," he said quietly. "He wasn't necessarily unkind to me. I simply wasn't a priority."

I cupped his cheek, sliding my hand down and around to fist in the hairs at the nape of his neck.

"You were neglected."

Lucifer tilted his head. "Some might say that."

"What do you think?"

Lucifer sighed. His golden eyes dimming a fraction. "I think my father was a brutal man. When I was young I wanted his attention, but after all that's happened, I think I was, perhaps, better off being left alone most of the time."

My chest squeezed. "I understand that. Quite well, actually." Gods did I. My own family had done the same. We were alike in that way. "Carissa was the eldest. Katherine was the prodigy. I was simply the spare. It didn't help that my magic was broken and didn't behave like theirs . . ." I trailed off, not willing to let myself get lost in thoughts of the past. "So your dad sucked. Tell me about your mom. Gaia."

Lucifer smiled, slight and a little sad. "She was beautiful. Kind. She saw the best in everything, even me."

"You loved her."

"Greatly," he responded with a nod. "She was my safe harbor for a long time."

I narrowed my eyes. "What happened?"

"Aeshma."

Ah. His old atma. While Lucifer was my familiar now, every demon was born with an atma, or soulmate. The being whose magic was most complimentary to theirs. Over time, magic corrupts. It decays. It spreads. Bonding to one's atma stopped the growth, but it also stopped the decay. It ensured they never lost their minds to their magic—just like witches and their psychic bondmates.

"She rejected you."

"She did," he nodded. "To say I was angry was an understatement. I went to my mother about it, and do you know what she told me?" I waited, not bothering to respond to his rhetorical question. "If she rejected me, then that meant I was not worthy of Aeshma's love. She said I needed to prove myself. To earn Aeshma's affection and make myself worthwhile in her eyes by showing her I was more than a demon of desire."

Ouch.

There's advice and then there's that.

"That's honestly really shitty."

He chuckled. "I thought so too. Her response was the final straw that broke me."

"It's why you left."

He nodded again. "In my rage, I ripped open a portal between worlds and came to Earth. The rest, well, you know how it ended." He smiled ruefully, but I saw it for what it was. A mask to hide the pain.

"Your mother loved you in her own way."

"I know." He sighed. "It took me a few thousand years to come around, but I did eventually realize that she was trying to help. You only get one atma, and without them you risk going insane. She didn't want that for me, so she tried to convince me to win over Aeshma."

"And in doing so invalidated you," I said quietly. "She pushed you away without meaning to."

Lucifer inclined his head in agreement. "You know what I regret most out of everything?"

My lips parted. A small, unkind voice told me it would be Aeshma. That he regretted leaving and letting her slip away. Aeshma was long gone. Piper ended her. But it would kill a part of me if he wished for that future instead of the one he was now living with me.

I wasn't sure if I could stomach that answer. All I did was shake my head.

"Never saying goodbye." Anguish crept into his voice and my heart nearly cracked open and bled for him. "I stormed out and never went back. Demons can't die. Not without being harvested, so she would have known I'd left, but not where to or what became of me."

I squeezed a little tighter where my hand fisted his hair. Leaning forward, I pressed my forehead against his. I didn't have words to make it better. There was nothing I could say that would fix it or reframe the situation. It sucked, because he made a choice when angry and has had to live with it for thousands of years.

The door creaked open. I planted a quick peck on his lips before pulling away. I had to take a deep breath to steady myself for what I would see. Señora swept into the room, her arms clutching a wicker basket full of various herbs and stones. The number of threads and connections multiplied. Señora had a lot of bonds. Far more than I would have thought for a hermitess who had locked herself in her shop with several cats.

She set her basket of things down and turned back around, her gaze lingering on me. "How are you feeling, child?"

"I'm fine, just . . . overwhelmed by it all."

"Seeing the fabric of the universe will do that," Señora deadpanned. I pressed my lips together instead of saying something snarky in reply. I didn't get by this long without knowing when to keep my mouth shut. She might adore me, but the woman was terrifying and lacked morals. It's the reason I'd chosen to move in with her years ago, but still. Caution was *always* warranted.

"I've got the Eye. I can see the threads. Now how do I use it?"

She shrugged. "I don't know. Seeing as I've never worn it myself, I can't speak on the matter. Perhaps you should be asking him." She thrust her chin toward Lucifer who lifted his hands, palms forward.

"It was my father's. That doesn't mean I know how to use it."

Frustration bubbled up in me. Bad Nat kissed her teeth and said, *"It's almost like someone didn't read the manual before deciding to add it as a part of her permanent aesthetic."*

"There is no manual," The Warden replied.

"You were the one on board with her putting in the Eye," Peace argued at the same time.

Bad Nat shrugged. *"Never said whether I was or wasn't. I said she'd already made her decision. It didn't matter what we thought either way."*

I pulled away from them, my teeth grinding under my annoyance.

Señora approached slowly; her gaze trained on the Eye. I felt it shift to follow her, just like a real eyeball would. It was weird. "We do not learn a new skill from sheer force of will. It takes practice and discovery."

"How do I practice when I don't know what I'm supposed to be doing?"

"Discovering this new power will be much like wielding your own power." She rubbed a thumb under the edge of my eye, pulling the lower lid down slightly and inspecting my eyeball. "You didn't learn to control the magic of others overnight. It took trial and error. This is much the same."

"I don't have time to figure things out the long way around." I sighed deeply, raking my hands over my face. "I need to know how to wield the objects of fate."

"Your emotions are the most powerful tool you have right now," Señora added. "They will help you tap into the Eye's power and find the way to the objects."

I frowned, feeling a surge of irritation. "So, what? I just wait until I am really angry or scared and hope it works?"

"Perhaps. That is one way."

A growl threatened to pass my lips, and I clamped my mouth shut. "Is there another way?" I tried to be neutral when asking, but some of the impertinence leaked into my voice.

The Señora lifted an eyebrow. "There's always another way, child."

Lucifer squeezed my hand gently, drawing my attention back to him. "You've always been good at learning quickly, Nat. This will be no different."

I changed tactics and rephrased my question to the Señora. "Do *you* know of another way?"

One corner of her mouth turned up. "Know with certainty? No, but I might suggest that you consider not just your own power, but that of others."

With that, she turned on her heel and exited the room. I sighed, thinking about her turn of phrase. *Consider not just your own power, but that of others.*

Who else had power that affected their eyes?

A new sensation tugged at my insides, and I looked at the bond threads that connected to me. A thick, golden rope thrummed and pulsed in response, its power glowing like a beacon, leading me to the answer.

15

AUGUST

I hadn't heard a word from her.

Not a text, not a call, nothing. That left me alone with my thoughts, and that was a dangerous place to be.

I had tried to think about the surprising, and rather unwelcoming news of Lucifer's return. On any other day, that would be enough to distract me from most things. The implications of his return could be devastating. I needed more information, and not a detailed explanation of his proposed schedule with Nathalie. There was much I didn't know about their dynamics—and questions I planned on asking—but I was certainly pleased by her response, not only his suggestion but also his interruption.

She was not an animal that could be caged. Why did no one see that about her? Fucking fools, all of them.

It's why I left. It's why I fought my magic and my instinct and listened to what she wanted. Nathalie had made up her mind. If I pushed her to do what I wanted, all it would do was push her away. I tried to convince myself that I'd made the right choice. Now I questioned that decision. Maybe I was the fucking fool.

The silence of the room was deafening. Time was different when you'd lived as long as I had. It moved at a faster pace, and that passage had become barely noticeable. Now? The exact opposite. I felt each excruciating second pass, understanding time more than I had in my entire existence.

My fingers drummed on my thigh as I stared at the black screen of my phone, willing it to light up with her name. Estrid rested next to me, one paw on my other leg, purring softly in an attempt to soothe my anxieties. She was especially observant when someone was upset. She spent most of her time next to Baggage. I sensed it was because his condition had worsened, and while he meant nothing to me, he meant something to Nathalie, and she was my everything. I didn't want her hurting, which meant Estrid didn't either.

Unease clawed at me, and it was only the presence of the aurae bond that kept me seated in my apartment instead of heading back to the Le Fay mansion. Feeling the connection meant she was alive.

I wanted so desperately to honor Nathalie's wishes, but my magic was a different story. It didn't care that she was an independent woman who could make her own choices, and I'd be damned if I let the magic override my respect for her boundaries. She trusted me, and I wouldn't betray that, even if the desire to be near her would drive me to madness.

That madness would be here sooner than I wanted to admit.

The bond was getting stronger between us, and there was nothing I could do to slow it down. It had taken every ounce of me to walk away.

A familiar uneven gate sounded in the hallway just as her scent reached me, snapping me out of me thoughts. That delicious chord in my chest, the one that connected me to my sunling, pulled taut.

My heart sped up, and raced for the door, yanking it open before she had a chance to knock. She wore a sweater dress and thigh-high boots. Her dark brown hair was pulled into a delicate bun, but curls fell loose from it, framing her face. Fashionable sunglasses with blackout lenses covered her light brown eyes, making me think she'd been crying and wanted to cover up the evidence.

She held no love for her sister, so I couldn't guess what the cause would be, but what mattered most was that she was here, unharmed, and it eased the tension that had consumed my entire body. I scooped my arm around her waist, drawing her closer to me and holding her tight as I rested my chin on her head. She returned the hug, taking a deep breath that almost began to stutter.

"Come in," I whispered, letting her go as soon as she'd begun to release me.

She shook her head slightly, jutting her chin toward the apartment. I turned slightly, seeing Estrid walking down the hall toward Marcel's room. She pressed her lips together and brushed a hand over her jaw, a nervous tic

I'd noticed in the short time we'd known each other. "We need to be alone. Take a walk with me?"

"Whatever you want." As I stepped forward, and closed the door behind me, Nathalie stepped back, reaching for my hand, and lacing her fingers through mine. The touch of her warm skin soothed me, and I grazed my thumb over her while we walked in silence.

The chill of the fall air hit us. The sky was gray and cloudy, and moisture sat heavy in the air. A hard lake wind raked through my hair, slapping me in the face. New Chicago had changed in many ways, but the weather had not. She veered us toward a nearby park, but she hadn't spoken a word the entire time. I kept glancing at her, trying to read her expression, but the damned sunglasses covered half her face.

"What's with the sunglasses?" I finally asked.

She gave a small, tight-lipped smile. "I . . . need them today."

Grunting, I gave no response to her vague answer. Leaves crunched underfoot as we rounded a corner and approached Lincoln Park. In the time since the Demon Queen had taken over, the city had gotten somewhat better. There was a dedicated task force that cleaned up public spaces and worked on restoring them to their former glory.

Nat took a seat on one of the benches and I followed suit, sitting beside her. She held me hand still, resting it on her thigh after she'd crossed her legs.

"Penny for your thoughts?" I asked, mirroring a conversation we'd had after a night spent together.

A small smile curled up one side of her lips, and I felt satisfied with my success. "A penny is all you have to offer?" she said, playing along.

"Oh, I have much more to offer." Leaning over, I grazed my lips along her jawline, toward her ear, inhaling every pheromone that escaped her skin. She angled her head slightly and shuddered.

"August," she breathed out, squeezing my hand.

Heat shot through my body. The things I wanted to do to her now were not meant for a park bench. Well, not in broad daylight anyway. Despite my cock straining against my pants, and the desire to take her anywhere but here and ravage her, I pulled it together, kissing her earlobe softly before sitting back.

"For another time," I said, angling my head toward people walking on a trail in the distance. "Which I suppose is why you brought me here?"

She smiled. "We have a tendency to . . ."

"Enjoy our time together?"

"I was going to go with 'get distracted,' but sure."

"No more distractions. Promise." I brought her hand to my mouth and pressed a kiss on top before I gently rubbed circles with my thumb. "What's on your mind?"

She sighed. "Can I ask you something?"

I nodded. "Anything."

She hesitated for a moment, then said, "Your eyes. The glamour. Why do you wear it?"

Caught off guard by her question, all I could do was blink as her words registered and then repeated in my mind. "I . . . how did you know?"

She turned, looking out at the park, taking her time before answering. "I suppose you deserve an answer to that before you'd be willing to trust me with your secret." She returned her attention to me. "I can see when someone wears a glamour, but I can't see beneath it."

"You've known the entire time, then?" I asked, and she nodded in confirmation. "You've never asked about it before. Why now?" I did my best to keep my voice neutral, but the truth was that she'd rattled me.

"Because I need your help." With slow, hesitant movements, she reached up and removed her sunglasses.

My breath instantly caught in the back of my throat.

One eye was the palest brown I'd ever seen.

The other wasn't an eye at all.

"What—when—" I broke off, struggling to find the words. My hand reached for her face, toward the golden orb that stared back at me. She flinched away and my fingers closed midair, my hand resettling at my side.

Guilt and rage consumed me. I never should have let her go to Carissa's by herself. This is what happened. My magic whispered that we should have been there. That this is what happens when we're not with her. The demon couldn't protect her. Marcel had one foot in the grave. Someone had hurt her, and even though I struggled as my emotions warred for control, I had to know so I could kill them slowly. "Who did this to you?"

"I did it to myself, August," she said quietly. I felt like I'd been slapped.

"Why?" I demanded, and the moment the question

came out of my mouth, I realized what she'd done. I narrowed my gaze in understanding. "That's the Eye."

"I need to find the objects of fate," she said simply, even though there was nothing simple about it. "The only was to use the Eye is to, well"—she pointed at her face—"see with it."

"I can't believe you did this without talking to me." The words unintentionally came out in a low, rumbling tone . "We could have discussed it and figured out if there was another way—"

"I don't need your permission, August," she retorted, her tone defensive. She pushed away from me, rising from the bench. Nathalie walked away while I dragged my hands through my hair. I got to my feet and ran after her, my legs eating up twice the distance hers could. I caught her by the wrist, pulling her back to me.

"Listen to me. No, you don't need my permission. Not for anything you do. You know this. Never once have I held you back in any decision you've made."

The tension in her jaw released. "I know."

"Then why did you hide this from me? I could have helped you weigh your options. Talked through it first. This is irreversible, Nathalie."

"I wasn't trying to hide it from you. I just had to act fast and get it done. You're the first person I came to."

"No one else knows?"

"Señora Rosara did the procedure. Lucifer took care of me afterward."

Jealousy burned in my chest, but I kept that beast on a tight leash, refusing to let it show. Those feelings might be natural in this situation, but it wasn't what Nathalie needed.

This time when I reached up to cup her cheek she didn't shy away. "Tell me what happened with Carissa and how it led to this."

Nat sighed but leaned into me as she filled me in on what led up to her surgery. Every detail seemed to get worse. In all reality, the Eye was the least concerning out of everything she'd said. When she got to the end, my chest constricted.

"What do you mean she's coming for you? She can't—"

"She can," Nat whispered. "It's not Kat she wants. It's me."

"Why?" I cupped both her cheeks, my thumb brushing under the Eye.

Nat pressed her lips together. I wasn't going to like this next part.

"My magic. We're both chaos witches. That's apparently what she's been trying to create the entire time."

I closed my eyes, pulling her close to me in a comforting embrace. I could smell magic's signature, but I couldn't identify it. I had no way of knowing what kind of magic Nat carried, until she told me.

"Why chaos?" I asked, keeping my features as neutral as possible.

She shook her head. "I don't know what would happen if she was able to consume my magic, but obviously nothing good could come of it. That's why I had the Eye put in me. It's the only way to use it, and I need the objects of fate to break the bonds between Morgan Le Fay and me."

"What's your plan?"

"She can't kill a body she occupies. So right now, I'm assuming she killed Carissa, so that makes me think she's using Sasha's body to hunt Kat and kill her too, thereby skipping over next in line and jumping straight to me. If I can knock her out of Sasha, I can trap her in Kat's body. Temporarily. She can only make the jump into whoever is next in line by order of birth. Kat's next, which buys me time, but only as long as my sister is alive."

"What's the contingency?"

"There isn't one." She pulled away from my arms and shook like a leaf in the wind. Her words were so quiet, I barely heard them. "My body is forfeit. Like every Le Fay before me, I'll be pushed out of the driver's seat, and she'll take over, except this time, she has her coveted vessel."

"Fuck," I growled, stepping back and running my hands through my hair roughly before settling them on my hips.

Nathalie crossed her arms as a cold gust of wind cut through the park. "I need to cut the bonds so that she can't body jump again, then find a way to separate her from Kat so we can end her. For good."

"What's to stop her from jumping to someone else once she's in Kat?"

"I'm going to use transfiguration to turn her into something else—some animal maybe. Once she's there, I trap her permanently and turn Kat back to herself." She bit her lip, staring at me with hesitation.

I blinked, processing the complexity of her one and only plan.

"That's," I scrambled for the right words, "ambitious."

Risky. The word was risky.

Her plan was detailed and clearly well thought out, but there were too many moving parts. I didn't want to tell her that I hated it. That I hated this entire fucking situation.

Except there was no way out if she didn't cut the bond between her and that crazy bitch.

I understood why she replaced her eye without waiting. The consequences if she didn't move fast enough were deadly.

Which is exactly what led to this threadbare plan that was strung together with hope and her sheer force of will, something I usually loved. This time, the stakes were too high.

"It will work." She sounded confident, but I caught the flicker of uncertainty across her face. "It has to," she repeated.

As if on cue, raindrops began to fall from the sky, pattering softly against the leaf-covered ground around us. Nat glanced up at the darkening clouds, then came back at me.

"We can go back to my place," I offered. With everything she just told me I wasn't willing to part from her yet.

"Marcel might be awake." A look I couldn't quite decipher flickered over her face. "Let's go to my car. It's parked nearby."

I had to assume she wanted to keep this from him at all costs. It was hard enough for me to absorb. The kid was deteriorating something fierce, and he damn sure couldn't deal with this level of shit. The rain started to come down harder, soaking us both as we hurried to shelter. We climbed inside her car as the soft hum of the rain against the roof filled the silence between us. The tension hung in the air, palpable and thick.

"So now you know everything about my eye," Nathalie eventually said, turning in her seat to lock her searching eyes with mine. "Your turn."

I swallowed. "It's not exactly a happy story," I grumbled.

"I didn't imagine it would be," she said, leaning her head against the headrest.

"I guess now's as good a time as any," I muttered, adjusting uncomfortably in my seat. "Technically, I'm blind." The announcement dangled in the air for a moment.

She looked at me skeptically. "How can you be blind when you can . . . see?"

"Magic, of course."

"You glamour your eyes because you're blind? There's no shame in that, August." Nathalie placed her hand on my knee reassuringly.

"Not for that reason, no. They're glamoured because . . . Look, for as dark as humanity is now, it doesn't hold a candle to the middle ages. History books don't scratch the surface." I rested my hand on hers, enjoying the warmth she offered. "My mother was a terrible woman. She used her magic to lure and ensnare anyone she could, taking their money and any valuables they had. She feasted on thousands of men, just to get what she needed."

"What did she need?"

"There was magic drug back then—azmarsk—which was far more potent than the drugs on the streets now. She loved it. Craved it. The way humans fell into a liquor bottle or opium in the middle ages, she fell into a bottle of her own." I sighed deeply. I hadn't said these words out loud in ages. "Eventually she owed more than she could afford. So, she traded my eyes to pay her debts and get her fix."

Nathalie gasped at this revelation, but she kept her thoughts to herself, and her gaze trained expectantly on me. So, I continued, clearing my throat.

"I was just a small boy. I grew up blind and experienced the world alone in darkness for most of my childhood." Reaching up, I toyed with a lock of hair that framed her face. "Until, one day, my older brother—Rafael—tracked me down." I let her sit with that information for a second before I continued. "Rafael couldn't stand what had happened to me. He took me away from her and searched high and low for a solution. One day, he found one." I thought back to those years when all was dark. "Stones, similar to your Eye of Parcae, and through them I could see the world again."

Nathalie listened intently, her expression a mixture of sympathy and curiosity. "How did you do it? Go from having sight to having your vision stolen, and just left alone to fend for yourself?"

I smiled faintly. "My other senses became enhanced. I managed to get around just fine. Eyes just help you see what's already there. I was able to visualize what I knew was real. What things looked like when I had my sight. Once I could see again, it was just a matter of correcting my picture of the world."

After a moment of silence, she said, "Show me."

"No." The words came out of my mouth before I'd even considered her request.

"I want to see you without the glamour, August. You don't have to hide from me."

I hesitated, uncertainty igniting in my chest as I pulled my hand away from her. "It's not pretty, sunling."

"Let me be the judge of that." She pulled my hand back to her, pressing her lips to my upturned palm.

"You're sure?"

She nodded sternly.

With a sigh, I lifted the glamour, the magic sliding away from my face like fabric slipping over my skin. Her eyes took me in, and I knew what she saw. The stones themselves were a deep, shimmering blue, nestled securely within the hollows of my eye sockets. The bumpy scarred skin where my eyes once existed peeked out behind the stones. I braced myself for her reaction, expecting shock or revulsion.

Instead, Nathalie leaned forward and kissed me

softly, her lips warm as she pressed them against mine. Her kiss was soft and tender, and completely took me by surprise. I pulled back my hand moving up to cup her face.

"You continuously surprise me," I murmured.

She grinned. "I like variety," she quipped echoing her words from the first time we slept together.

I pulled her back toward me, and she met me halfway, her fingers curling into my hair, her body pressing against mine over the console. There was no urgency between us, even though there was a distinct need that had been simmering as we dealt with the fallout of everything around us. Instead, our movements were intentional and slow, as if we were both savoring the time we were able to steal together.

Fire licked at my skin, and I groaned into her mouth. It wasn't the fervor, not quite. But I know that moment was building, and this was just the appetizer. One of her hands left my hair and a second later, she leaned into me before she braced her hands on my shoulders and slid herself over my lap.

"I have this distinct feeling of déjà vu," I said, recalling a similar position in her car once.

"Me too." She smiled, warmth heating her cheeks to a light shade of pink. Toying with a button on my shirt, she added, "I also remember we didn't finish what we started."

I paused. We didn't. We had things to talk about. Discussions we hadn't yet made the time for.

"Nathalie . . ."

"Leave it. Not now." She placed my hands on her bare thighs, and leaned in, kissing me deeply and murmuring, "Touch me, August."

A growl rumbled in my chest, and I dragged my fingertips over her delicious body, memorizing every inch of her as I shoved her sweater dress up and over her thighs, letting it pool at her waist. My mouth still moving against hers, I put a finger between us and began teasing her clit through the lace of her underwear.

She moaned, moving against my hand for friction, grinding with abandon. I could feel how wet she was. A jolt of pleasure shot through me, settling over my skin. Her scent was suddenly stronger, and I froze, pulling my hand away.

"Nathalie, wait," I said through gritted teeth, trying to regain my composure. "The bond . . ."

"I know," she breathed against my lips, nodding her head.

Gods, I wanted her, but I needed to know she truly understood. We were on the cusp of the fervor as it was. This could push her straight in.

"What do you remember?"

Taking my hands in hers, she brought them down her body slowly, then she leaned into me. "It strength-ens. If you feed from me"—she bit her bottom lip, glancing down at my mouth before returning her gaze to meet mine. "If you fuck me"—she rocked her hips, grinding against me, then pushed my hand to cup her heated center. "Anything we do will strengthen it."

"Is that what you want?" I looked at her intently, needing to hear the words.

"I know what I'm doing. Stop talking and fuck me, August."

This woman. Gods. That was all it took to undo me. I reached between us, forcefully ripping the lacey underwear.

She gasped, pulling back, and raising a brow. "Those were my favorite."

"It's cute when you pretend to by angry." Weaving my fingers in her hair, I tugged sharply at the strands, just enough to make her eyes glaze over. I was going to take my moment with her however I could get it.

She lifted enough to unbutton with my pants, making quick work of lowering my zipper and pulling my cock free.

I grasped her hips, positioning myself at her entrance.

I groaned as she lowered herself, slowly inching down my length. "I want you to take all of me, sunling." Bracing my feet on the floor, I angled my hips, thrusting upward while pulling her down, burying my cock inside her in one swift motion. Her inner walls stretched to accommodate me. She cried out, arching her back and clutching at my shoulders as we began to move. "So fucking tight," I ground out, pumping slowly as she whimpered. "So wet."

Sweet, little moans filled the car, and her fingernails bit into my shoulders as she anchored herself. We found our rhythm, moving against each other in the seat.

"Fucking perfect." With one hand gripping her hip, I cupped the back of her neck with the other, pulling her mouth to mine. A rumble vibrated in her throat as she slammed her hand into the ceiling of the car, giving herself leverage to press against me harder while she rocked her hips.

"Fuck, yes," I growled, pumping faster. The tension built between us, coiling tighter and tighter with each powerful thrust. The sounds she made, the way she whispered my name, begging me to make her come, only pushed me closer to the edge.

Her scent, her magic, her lust: it permeated the air, and I drank it in, feeling the rush in my veins. Steam coated the windows, and sweat dripped down her neck, disappearing into the collar of her sweater. Tilting her head back, she moaned again.

"Eyes on me, sunling," I said, reaching between us to find her clit, pressing into it as I fucked her more vigorously than should be possible in the passenger seat of a car.

Gasping, her gaze focused on me, and she bit her bottom lip. Her brows furrowed, quivering as her tight cunt rippled around me. Her movements came faster and faster until we lost all rhythm, both seeking the release we desperately needed.

"I'm close," she whispered, and I thrusted harder. When she tilted her head back, exposing her tender neck, I wrapped my hand around it, squeezing and restricting her air as she built up.

"Come for me," I growled, my fingertips digging into her hip to hold her against me.

Nathalie's body seized up around me, her mouth falling open as her pussy clenched around my cock so tightly I saw stars. I released my hold, and she sucked in air before choking out three words that would break us both. *"Feed from me."*

A deep rumbling in my throat reverberated as I fed. Her body began to shudder from pleasure, and I picked up my pace, loving the way she came on my cock. Gold light flashed from her eyes, filling the car as I followed her into ecstasy with a roar.

She collapsed against my chest, gasping for breath, her hands gripping me like I might disappear. Stroking her hair in the silence, I listened to her heartbeat while it steadied. "I don't want to leave," she whispered.

"I'll stay here as long as you want." I wrapped my arms around her, holding her like she could be taken from me at any moment.

That was a possibility, now more than ever. She'd never admit it, but I feared this was her way of saying goodbye. Something tightened in my chest. Thoughts I'd pushed away began to resurface. Every time we were together, it felt like it could be our last. Maybe this time, it was.

16

NATHALIE

A DAY AND A HALF OF SEARCHING MEMORIES AND A DAY AND A half of trying to figure out how to find the shears using the Eye, and I had come up with nothing. As much as I didn't mind going at things alone, I knew when to call in the cavalry. Pulling this off was going to take a group effort, but Lucifer didn't know how to find the objects of fate any more than August did. It certainly didn't stop them from trying to get me some answers. If I didn't get some answers, I was going to fail everyone. The plan would be null and void if I didn't get my ducks in a row. And these ducks were acting more like rabid squirrels.

I needed a new perspective. I needed my best friend. Someone who understood what it meant to have the weight of the world resting on their shoulders.

It was decided.

Glancing at the clock, I knew she'd be awake. The twins were still on a bizarre sleep schedule. So, I freshened up and with keys in hand, I tiptoed to the door. I'd asked Lucifer to sleep in his room for the night. I just couldn't give him the attention I knew he needed. Just as I reached for the handle of the front door, I felt a familiar presence behind me. Lucifer stood, his arms crossed over his bare chest, his presence filling the room with a quiet intensity.

"Sneaking off to save the world?"

I huffed a laugh. "Going to see Piper, actually."

"At two in the morning?"

"She's awake," I said, shrugging. "Kids."

"That sounds horrendous." He wrinkled his nose.

Smacking him on the arm, I gave him a disapproving look. "Watch it. Those are my godchildren you're talking about."

"Forget I said anything." He held his hands up in surrender. "Want me to go with you?"

I shook my head. "No, I need to go on my own. Get Piper's input. Ronan's too. I'm not sure everyone is ready for a family gathering."

"By family, you mean my brother."

"Of course I am. I have enough on my mind as it is. I don't need to deal with the two of you right now. That'll come in due time." He raised a brow in surprise, and I put my hand on his shoulder, reaching up to kiss his cheek. "Don't burn the place down. And don't follow me."

The drive to Piper's house was a blur, the road passing beneath me without notice until I found myself standing outside her door. Piper opened up almost immediately, concern and exhaustion etching lines on her face, but the surprise of seeing me on her doorstep was evident.

"What's with the sunglasses? It's the middle of the night." She waved me in, and I stepped into the foyer.

"About that," I said, taking them off and turning to her. "We have some catching up to do."

Piper's mouth fell open but she didn't say anything, just watching me intently as a crease formed between her brows. Eventually, she nodded and cleared her throat.

"Ronan," she called, never taking her gaze off my face.

"Hmm?" His deep timbre rumbled from the other room.

"Put the kettle on for Nat, will you?" She paused. "And bring whiskey."

Several minutes later, I found myself sitting in Piper and Ronan's living room while they stared at me. The kids and Mist had recently gone to sleep, thanks to a concoction the Señora had put together to get the twins to sleep at the same time. It wasn't perfected yet, but the trials were getting closer.

"So," Piper began, her eyes peering over her cup at me as she took a small sip, "that is going to take some getting used to."

"That's what you focus on?"

"What? It looks . . . weird. I'm just saying," she mumbled, lifting a shoulder. "If I showed up on your doorstep with a golden metal eyeball, you can't say you wouldn't say the same."

"Yeah, I probably would. I plan on keeping it glamoured, so you won't have to get used to it too much. No one needs to know. I'd be killed in a heartbeat just so some idiot supernatural could steal it from me. I just figured the easiest way to get the conversation started was putting it out in the open." Letting the magic settle over my face, the glamour covered the orb, and Piper could stop staring at it. "Better?"

Ronan tilted his head. "Did my brother convince you to do this?"

I snorted. "Please. I make my own decisions. You know me well enough by now. He didn't know about it until the surgery was underway."

"Are you going to fill us in on why you did it, then?" Piper asked, setting her cup down on the table.

"Brace yourselves. It's a lot," I said, and began to fill them in on everything that had happened in the two and a half days. Carissa's death. Kat's family secret bomb. Morgan La Fay not being able to actually die and me being her ultimate vessel. My plan for how to trap her. All of it. Including my complete failure in locating the objects of fate.

"The *Morrigan* is in Sasha's body? Are you fucking serious? How is that bitch *not* dead?" Piper asked, a mild mix of panic and anger in her eyes. "We killed her. Or sort of killed her. Did we? If we didn't kill her, who was it?"

"We killed a vessel. Nothing more. Her soul jumped

to another one." I crossed my arms, wincing. "I just thought the coven had brought her back. I didn't have a clue she'd been alive-ish for centuries, bodysnatching."

"Fucking magic and glamours," she mumbled. "Looked just like her." She finally breathed out a long sigh, then nodded. "This a lot to take in."

I hated that she was worried. I could see it on her face. How could she not? She had her children to think about. This affected all of them too.

Pressing my lips together in a thin line, I gave her a look of apology and sympathy. "I'm sorry I didn't tell you sooner. There's just so much . . ."

"There's more you aren't saying, isn't there?"

I sighed. "Even with all of this, I'm also trying to think of a way to save Marcel, and I just . . . I don't know how. I check on him every day. He's weakening, and I can't do anything to stop it. I'm lost, Piper. I'm in over my head, and I genuinely don't know what to do anymore. Everything is a fucking ticking time bomb."

Piper wiped her palms on her pants, leaning forward. "You aren't kidding," she murmured, before shaking her head of whatever thoughts had crept into her mind. "So . . . what do we do? We're here to brainstorm, right?"

I gave her a small smile in thanks. "I'll take whatever advice you have. Give me any ideas."

It felt like hours had passed as we tossed suggestions back and forth, finding a hole in each and every one of them. Each idea we tossed around fell apart under the weight of practicality or unforeseen complications. It was frustrating, disheartening even, to come up against so many dead ends.

Three pots of tea had been consumed. Snack wrappers littered the coffee table. Piper paced the room, chewing her thumbnail as she thought in silence while I slumped on the couch, my neck bent back over a pillow while I stared at the ceiling.

"Maybe there's a way to go about it *without* the objects of fate?" Piper asked. "If you can't find them with the Eye, maybe it can do something else?"

"Not that I know of," I said, glancing at Ronan and he shook his head in agreement. "I can see the ties that bind all of us. Everything is covered in thin gold threads. I can touch them, but I can't do anything with them."

"Would she fall for a lure somehow? A way to coax her out of Sasha's body?" Ronan suggested.

I pulled my legs up on the couch, sitting crisscrossed. "Not likely. She's too cunning for that. She chose Sasha for the safety net. The Morrigan knows we won't just kill her out right."

"Even if we were willing to, how would we do that without putting anyone else at risk?" Piper sighed, running a hand through her hair, her voice tinged with weariness. "The moment she got a whiff of danger, she'd just jump into the body of someone else we care about. Possibly even one of the kids."

We were all in agreement as we sat in the quiet for several moments, the wheels turning in our brains. We needed a way to just get rid of her altogether. If there's a soul tie between two people, the only way to do that without getting rid of the tie, would be to get rid of the soul.

The Nats in the loci were just as silent until The Warden piped up. *"Maybe we don't need the shears?"*

"Explain," Ann said, pinching the bridge of her nose, not looking up from her file.

"If there's a soul tie, but we can't cut it, the only other option would be getting rid of the soul." The Warden tapped the table, getting everyone's attention. *"Don't you see? We have to get rid of the other soul."*

"Never gonna happen," Bad Nat chimed in, picking at her nails with a dagger.

"Wait," Ann mumbled, then pulled out a memory and slapped it on the table. I understood what they were saying.

"Ronan," I said, breaking the silence and looking at him as the tiniest spark of hope warmed my chest. "Can't you just consume Morgan Le Fay's soul?"

Piper looked at me triumphantly before looking back at Ronan. "Would that stop her?"

He hesitated, then gave us a single nod. "Yes, technically."

"Why technically? You're the Harvester," I said, waving my hand at him. "You eat souls."

"Happy to," he said on a sigh before adding, "Just one problem. I do that, and your friend's body dies. There's no coming back."

"Dammit," I whispered under my breath, deflating again.

"Told you," Bad Nat muttered, and I wanted to slap her.

Piper groaned. "Scratch that off the list."

Pressing my thumbs into my temples, I closed my eyes. "This list sucks."

"We really need those fucking shears," Piper said, dropping down on the coach next to me. "There's really just no other way."

"Mama?" Orson called out, coming down the stairs.

"I'll be back," she said, patting my leg as she got up and left the room.

Ronan looked at me with an intensity that told me whatever he was thinking was not something I wanted to hear. "Spit it out," I said, shifting my gaze to the hallway and then back to him. "She's out of earshot. Say what you need to say."

"I'd already considered that solution," he began, his voice firm and resolute.

"Why didn't you just say that earlier?"

He took a moment, his eyes narrowing just a fraction. "Because Piper doesn't need to hear the rest of it." Realization dawned on me, and I had no doubt it passed over my features. For a brief second, Ronan almost looked sympathetic when he saw that I understood. "If this comes down to protecting the kids, protecting Piper . . . I won't hesitate to take her soul. It doesn't matter whose body she is using as a vessel. Even if that vessel is you."

"Good," I whispered, giving him a resolute nod. "I expect nothing less."

"Say nothing to her," he said, his voice barely a whisper. "We both know she will do everything in her power to stop me. She'll believe there's another way."

"We both know there isn't."

No one needed to know. Not Piper, not August, and definitely not Lucifer.

This was my contingency.

A last resort to protect the people I loved the most, no matter the cost.

17

MARCEL

A COUGH RATTLED THROUGH MY LUNGS, AND I LURCHED OFF the bed, keeling over. As I straightened and laid back down, every breath felt like a struggle.

Living wasn't supposed to be this hard.

There were moments where I had dark thoughts that I was ready for all of this to be done. To finish this on my own terms, on my own time. But then, I pictured my sunbeam. She was determined. Nathalie always had a way of doing the impossible. I had underestimated her for so long. I could see that now. If I could live through this, I'd spend the rest of our lives making it up to her.

I tried to hold on to hope, but each passing hour became harder. Truthfully, I lived for the moments I could steal from her. Each text. Each phone call. It wasn't enough for her to check in on me once a day, it had now turned to every few hours.

I tried to lighten the mood with jokes about my condition, but most of them fell flat. She could tell I was trying to deflect, not that it wasn't painfully obvious anyway.

A sharp knock at the front door sounded. With great effort, I pushed myself up from the bed, ignoring the aches that coursed through my body.

The door swung open, and I couldn't help the way my heartrate picked up at the sight of Nathalie. Her brown hair was curling lightly around her face, hanging over her shoulders. Her brown eyes widened as she took me in, her plump lower lip being pulled between her teeth.

"Hey, you," she said with a small smile.

I watched her for a second, noting the way her eyes kept sliding past me, looking for something beyond me. Or someone. I swallowed my disappointment and petty jealousy so that I didn't lose a moment with her.

"Hey, yourself." I leaned against the door frame, feigning nonchalance, but really just needing the extra support. "August's not here. Business of some sort."

"Well, that's good for him. I actually came to see you." My heart skipped a beat, thrilled that the envy I'd felt was all for nothing. She'd come for me. When I didn't move or respond, she twisted her lips to the side. "You gonna invite me in, or . . .?"

"Right, sorry," I said, trying to be as relaxed as possible.

Her presence was like the universe handing me a small gift, and I wouldn't waste it for a second. Stepping aside to let her in, she moved past me and headed straight for my room. I shuffled slowly, trailing quietly behind her.

Nathalie plopped onto the edge of my bed, her eyes scanning the room briefly before settling back on me. "You can drop the glamour," she said, her voice forcefully casual. "I know it's draining your energy. You don't need to hide it in front of me."

I shrugged noncommittally, choosing to downplay the point behind her statement. I know she didn't like the glamour. She wanted to see what I looked like, wanted to watch my decline for herself, but keeping it up wasn't just about appearances and vanity. It was about preserving some sense of normalcy, of dignity, in the face of this fate I couldn't seem to escape.

Feeling her gaze weighing on me, I moved to take a seat on my bed, leaning back against the headboard. Nathalie moved to her feet, facing away from me as she moved to my dresser and began toying with the few trinkets on it. I watched her for several moments, at first content to let her come to me when she was ready.

"Are you doing okay?" I asked, starting to worry slightly. She was rarely this quiet.

She hesitated, her back still to me, her hand floating over a picture frame. "I've been better."

"Nathalie," I said in a flat voice, cocking an eyebrow.

"I can't figure it out." She sniffled and finally turned her watery brown eyes on me. "I don't know how to save you. I don't know how to save Sasha. I don't know how to do anything. I don't know what it's like to be this helpless and lost, and it's driving me crazy. I should have figured out something by now." She cleared her throat to hold herself back from crying.

"Come here," I urged softly, holding my arms out and gesturing to my lap to make it clearer what I wanted.

Nathalie hesitated; her concern etched across her face. I reassured her with a faint smile, "I'm not that weak. Come here, sunbeam."

Finally, she relented, stepping closer until I could reach out and pull her into my lap. She swung her leg over mine, coming to straddle me, face to face. She was stiff at first, trying to hold her weight off of me, but as my hand rubbed over her back, she slowly relaxed into my touch.

"I've always known that I had an early expiration date attached to me," I said, finally talking over the quiet. "Whether we find some miracle or not, I'm just grateful that you know the truth now. That you know all I ever wanted was to love you and protect you."

"It's not enough," she whispered, pulling back to peer at me with tears streaming down her face.

"It might have to be." It was the painful truth, and I hated to say it out loud. "Both of us know that if that happens, it wasn't for lack of trying. You put in everything you have. You're going to have accept that it was enough."

Her lips quirked in a small, sad smile. "Why is it that the dying are always comforting the ones who will survive?" she mumbled. "How backwards is that?"

I chuckled lightly, rubbing my thumb over her lower

lip. "I'll comfort you anytime if it means you'll sit on me like this."

Nathalie's small, sad smile widened a bit, but the tears in her eyes remained. Nathalie had always been like that. The type to take on the world's problems as her own, to believe that tragic moments of fate were somehow her responsibility. More than ever, I wanted to take it all away, to give her a moment of peace amidst the chaos.

She leaned forward, pressing her forehead against mine. "I wish we had more time." She sighed, her breath warm against my skin.

"We have this moment," I replied softly, brushing my lips lightly against hers. She froze for a second. The choice was hers. I wasn't going to push it on her and I wasn't going to make her feel like she had to.

Then her hands moved to cup my face as she pushed her lips against mine. The kiss was tentative at first, but Nathalie knew what she wanted, and I was happy to give it to her as she deepened the kiss. As our mouths moved together, the world outside of our small bubble just disappeared. There was no illness, no impending doom —just us and this precious, fleeting moment of intimacy. Nathalie's fingers traced the lines of my jaw, her touch sending shivers down my spine. My grip on her tighter as I held her closer.

"Marcel," she breathed against my lips, her voice breaking slightly. "I don't want to lose you."

"You won't," I promised, even though we both knew it was a promise I couldn't keep. Gods, did I want to.

Her kisses had become more urgent, more demanding. She pushed herself against me as if she were trying to imprint herself onto my skin. All hesitation in either of us had dissipated and given way to an almost rushed sense of passion.

She quickly pulled at her sweater, tugging it over her head, revealing a red, lacy bra with a front closure. I flipped us over, putting her body beneath mine. My lips skirted a path of nips and kisses across her smooth skin. I stopped my trail at the crest of her breast, placing one last nip before I unsnapped the clasp of her bra. The delicate material fell to the side. My hands were beasts of their own, cupping her breasts, each of my thumbs toying with the hardening nipples. I couldn't resist the temptation and leaned forward, latching my mouth onto one of the stiff peaks.

"Marcel," Nathalie groaned out as I rolled one of the little buds between my teeth before sucking away the sting.

Pulling away with a pop, my hands moved to her hips, dragging my hands slowly at the edge of her underwear, teasing.

Nathalie grabbed my wrist, pushing it further down. "Touch me," she said hoarsely.

Leaning back, I shimmied her leggings down, taking her underwear with them. I tossed them to the floor, not caring at all where they landed.

She knew what she wanted, spreading her legs to give me access. Lying beside her, I brushed my lips over hers while I teased her opening, coating my fingers in her wetness. Her breathing hitched every time she thought that would be the moment she got what she'd asked for, until finally I plunged two fingers inside her, and she gasped, her pussy clenching. I stroked her inner walls, lightly rubbing my thumb over her clit as I found the speed and angle I knew would make her come undone. Gods, I had missed this.

"Nathalie," I murmured, my voice rough with emotion as I watched her writhe against my hand. "You feel so fucking good."

Her lusty gaze met mine, and she bit her bottom lip, nodding her head. "I always loved what you could do with your hands."

With my fingers buried inside her, she fisted the sheets and moved her hips in a rhythm that felt like coming home. Watching her body respond to my touch felt as magical as any spell I'd ever cast.

"I want to look at me when you come," I whispered, planting kisses along her jaw before I pushed myself to sit on my knees. It gave me the perfect view. "Give me that, sunbeam. You know how pretty you look when you shatter."

Nat gave me a salacious crooked smile that made my cock twitch. I wanted to bury myself inside her for hours. But first, I wanted to watch her.

I flattened my palm on her lower abdomen as I curved my fingers upward, stroking her against the pressure I'd created. My thumb pressed into her clit and her legs began to twitch. Her mouth fell open, and her back began to arch, and still, she kept her eyes on me. Her pussy tightened around my fingers as the pleasure built. Her orgasm shook through her, a throaty groan escaping her as she trembled around my hand while I kept stroking inside her, drawing out the intensity and making her come again.

In that moment, a brief flash of gold appeared over one eye before a glamour flickered back into place. She threw her head back with a cry as the second orgasm tore through her.

Nathalie's body unwound, and she released her death grip on the sheets while little spasms fluttered around my fingers. I pulled my hand away while she caught her breath.

I leaned against the wall, trying to still my own breathing. It had taken more energy than I could have imagined. Sweat dripped down my temple.

"Marcel," she said quickly, sitting up next to me, checking me over. "Are you okay?"

I nodded. "Just a little winded."

She ran her hands through her hair. "We shouldn't have done that. I'm so sorry."

Turning to her, I met her gaze. Two brown eyes stared back, but I know what I saw. "I have no regrets, sunbeam."

"No, you spend so much energy keeping your glamour up—"

"You have a glamour too." I hadn't intended on blurting it out, but time was a luxury I didn't have anymore.

"I . . ." She stared at me, wide-eyed. "How did you know?"

Tilting my head back against the wall, I pulled my legs up and rested my elbows on my knees. "The second time you came. Your glamour broke."

"Fuck." She got off the bed, grabbing her clothes and putting them back on while I silently watched. She sat on the edge of mattress when she was done, keeping her back to me while she stared at the wall.

"Are you going to tell me what it was?"

Nathalie let out a deep sigh. "You're going to be pissed, and I don't want to fight with you about it, Marcel. Can we leave it at that?"

"I don't have it in me to fight with you either, Nat." It was the truth. I really didn't. My end was near, and I didn't want to spend it mad at each other. Not when we'd come this far. Not when she'd finally understood what happened. Last time she'd visited, she'd told me she didn't our last words being said out of anger. I agreed. "I'll drop my glamour if you drop yours."

She turned her head slightly, giving me a questioning look before she finally nodded.

I dropped mine, and I know how hard it must have been to keep herself together. I looked worse every day. Her lips parted slightly, and then she swallowed thickly. Letting out a shuddering breath, she closed her eyes. When she opened them up, it was my turn to stare in awe.

"Surprise," she mumbled.

"Indeed," I said, clearing my throat.

"You're awfully quiet."

"I . . . have a lot of questions."

"Ask away."

"Is that what I think it is?"

"If you're guessing the Eye of Parcae, you'd be correct."

I blew out a breath. "So it's not a myth, after all. How did you find it?"

"I didn't actually," she said, hoisting a leg onto the bed and turning her body to face me as we spoke. "Kat did. She gave it to me."

I huffed. "Of course she did. That's why you'd asked me what I knew about it."

"Guilty." Nathalie hesitated, her fingers toying with each other.

"Clearly you found someone who knows how to use it." *I hope.* Surely she wouldn't have done this without knowing for sure.

She nodded. "Señora Rosara."

A chuckle formed, and Nat looked at me curiously. "Honestly, I'm not surprised. If anyone would know about it, it'd be her."

"She's also the one who put it in me."

A small wave of anger rushed through me. That old witch put Nat in danger, but a whisper in the back of my mind was quick to remind me that I knew damn well Nat had made this decision all on her own. Instead of voicing any of it, I let it go. It was all I could do. What would be the purpose of saying it anyway?

"So? What's it do?"

She raised an eyebrow. "You're taking this awfully well."

"Nat, you have a golden eyeball right now. It's a little shocking, I'll admit. But you did it for a reason. No one makes you do anything you don't want to. Believe me, I've learned that."

She twisted her lips in a small smile. "Took you long enough."

"It's the one thing that just wouldn't sink in," I said, tapping my temple, and she let out a laugh.

"It's permanent, you know," she said softly, and I cringed. It's what I'd expected, but the confirmation stung. "I can see the threads of life with it."

"Jesus . . ." I whispered, genuinely shocked. "I just thought it was supposed to help you find the objects of fate."

"Sort of. It won't help me find a cure. It's supposed to allow me to wield the objects of fate, but I can't find them without a thread to follow. I don't know how to sort those out. The threads are like breathing entities. They pulse with life and power, and some . . ." She paused, her features softening for a moment before she lightly cleared her throat. "Some of them are brighter than others. Stronger." Nathalie winced, looking away from me. "I can see the bonds between people too. Even us. It's remarkable."

"And ours?" It was a fool's hope to ask.

"Fading," she said in a barely audible whisper. "I'm just at a loss."

I sighed. "I wish I could help you. I don't know any

more than what I've told you about it. It was always vague, at best. Sounds like Señora Rosara knew far more."

"Deep down I think the objects of fate will help me save you. I don't know how to explain it." Staring out the window, her shoulders slumped slightly. "How am I supposed to find three threads amongst the countless, Marcel? It's the universe's 'fuck-you-riddle'."

Tilting my head back to rest on the wall again, I closed my eyes. I was so tired, but my sunbeam needed me. "Might as well be searching in the dark," I muttered.

"What'd you say?" she asked, her voice lowered, and I shot my eyes open. She'd stopped pacing and had turned to me, her arms at her side. "Say that again."

"You might as well be searching in the dark?"

Nathalie went blank for a moment as she thought, and a panic started to fill me. Before I said anything more, her mouth fell open. "It's how I found my way in the darkness . . ."

"You found your way, what?" I asked, sitting up straighter and no longer leaning on the wall.

She began to pace again, flexing her hands. "It's something a . . . friend said. 'Eyes don't help you see what's already there.' You visualize what's real. Everything else, you imagine . . ." She trailed off, a crease forming between her brows before she muttered, "'My other senses became enhanced. It's how I found my way in the darkness.' That's it, Marcel!"

I stared at her blankly. "You're going to have to tell

me what that means. I don't know what's happening right now."

"Sit with me," she said in a rush, coming to the bed and sitting on the edge, patting beside her. I scooted toward her, completely confused. It was like she was having a conversation with someone else right now, and I was definitely not included. "Stay quiet. Not a sound."

Nathalie closed her eyes, and we waited in silence. The white noise of the fan hummed. I focused on her breathing as it became rhythmic and steadied. I had no idea how much time had passed. I watched in awe, recognizing that something was happening, some discovery was being made, and I wasn't about to interrupt her.

She licked her lips and murmured quietly, holding out her hands as though she were waiting for an offering. "The shears."

I practically choked on air when the space above her outstretched hands began to shimmer like someone was sprinkling gold glitter. An unremarkable pair of shears, plain bronze and antiquated, materialized in her hand.

Nathalie opened her eyes, a brilliant smile spreading across her face as she looked from her hand to me and back. "I think I've figured out how it works."

A cough wracked through me as I tried to smile and tell her how amazing she was. Instead, I tipped over, curling into a fetal position on the bed. Exhaustion overwhelmed me, and my body was screaming to rest. I had overdone it. But how could I not? My days were numbered, and I'd give anything to spend each hour with Nathalie.

"Marcel!" she yelled, jumping up from her spot and rubbing circles on my upper back.

August called from down the hall, surprising both of us. "Nat?"

"Slow breaths. Slow. It'll pass," she said, though I was sure she was trying to convince herself instead of me. August rushed into the room, making me feel worse than I already did. She looked at him, her glamoured eyes pleading. "Help me get him moved? He needs to rest."

The incubus scooped me into his arms and set me further up on the bed while Nathalie placed pillows under my head. A part of me died on the inside that he'd just picked me up. I wanted to push him off and tell him I could do it myself, but the truth was, I was too weak to even fight it.

When my coughing subsided, she pulled the covers over my chest. Brushing her hand over my forehead, she leaned down to place a gentle kiss on my lips.

"Don't go," I said, though it was barely a whisper.

"I have to," she replied softly, stroking my hair. "I will be back, Marcel. I promise. Hold on for me. I can fix this. I know I can. Hold on for me, okay?"

My eyelids fluttered closed as I tried to hang on to consciousness and her voice faded out.

I would hold on for her, as long as I could. Whatever darkness she'd spoken of earlier, she'd found her way out. She wouldn't stop trying to save me. A black, dreamless sleep had me in its grasp, but there was a bright light in the distance.

My sunbeam.

18

NATHALIE

Watching how quickly Marcel declined terrified me, but I had a direction now and that needed to be my focus. It was confusing to feel the tug between priorities, and the mixture of adrenaline and fear was rampant. The drive back to my apartment passed in what felt like seconds.

"Lucifer!" I called out as I opened the door.

The devil emerged from my library with a book in hand, his gaze appraising as he took in my excitement. "Well, well, well. I've never had a woman so thrilled to see me while wearing another man's scent. Did Marcel's attempts to please you fall short?"

I narrowed my eyes. Under normal circumstances, I'd tell him how talented Marcel was with his hands and egg on his alphahole nature, but this wasn't the time for games. "Can you stop with the pissing contest, please? I don't have it in me to deal with your jealousy right now."

He shrugged, but I could see him soften ever so slightly. "I can keep my thoughts to myself for a while."

"I figured it out," I said, getting right to the point and ignoring his half-assed promise. "Look."

Part of me was worried it wouldn't work a second time, but I knew that was nerves. I had found the thread. That was all I needed. Holding out my hands, palm up, I took a deep breath and exhaled slowly. The shears materialized in a shimmering of gold light.

"Impressive," he said softly, smiling in approval.

I preened, grinning as I continued to admire my discovery. It didn't take long before the joy I felt became a little less. "I need your help."

He glanced at his fingernails, ignoring my request. "Now you're letting me in?"

I sighed. "Are we really doing this?" Since when did the devil himself want to talk about his feelings?

Lucifer studied me for a moment, his expression unreadable. Then he grabbed my wrist, and he led us to the couch. I crossed one leg under me, angling my body so I could face him.

"If you want my help, you have to share with me what goes on in your mind," he finally said, his golden gaze cutting to the core of me.

"You want to know everything, that's fine. But you have to help me. At this point, I might as well put it on a billboard with how many people I've already told," I muttered with a long sigh.

"Who am I going to tell?" he countered with a chuckle. "I don't like anybody except you." His words caught me off guard. They caused a flicker of warmth to stir—which I promptly pushed away. Focus.

"Fair enough," I said, letting a tiny smile slip through. I spilled it all. Every last detail and discovery . . . with the exception of what Ronan and I discussed.

"I suspected it was Morgan Le Fay," he said, not showing any emotion alongside the admission. "Not-Sasha's interest in me has been unusually specific."

"You never said anything."

"Neither did you," he countered, raising a brow.

He wasn't wrong, but still, I rolled my eyes. "She 'suddenly' had a change of heart about August as well, you know? The Morrigan is pretty keen on me taking him for myself. Everything she does has a purpose. It's not just to throw me off you."

"What help do you want from me?"

"I need her out of Sasha's body, and I don't know how. I can't implement any part of the plan without that first piece."

Lucifer sighed in a way that was unsettling.

"What is it?"

"You won't like it."

"Since when has that ever stopped you?"

Golden eyes settled on me like a physical weight. "You won't be able to lure out The Morrigan. She's too cunning, and even if you did manage to—without a soul in Sasha's body to keep her alive . . . ."

"Señora kept her body alive before—"

"And she told you it was temporary. That if Sasha didn't return on Samhain, she wouldn't at all."

I shook my head. "No, I won't lose her in this. There has to be a way to do both."

"Do you want my help, or do you want me to placate you?"

Standing up, I began to pace. "Losing Sasha isn't an option, Lucifer. My plan will work. I just have to get her out—"

"You need to plan on how to cut the tie from *yourself*."

My jaw fell open. "You want me to only consider how to save myself? Are you serious right now?"

"What else would I be? She is going to do exactly as you said. The Morrigan will use Sasha to kill Kat, and when she's done, she's going to cut the strings on her puppet and go straight for you. You need to find out how to retreat into your memory loci, keeping safe long enough to cut the soul tie between the two of you."

"I can't believe you." Tears began to sting my eyes. I was so disappointed. I thought maybe he was a little better than the Lucifer of before, but here he was, pushing me to focus on self-preservation.

"He has a point," Ann said, whispering in my mind.

"Regrettably," The Warden agreed.

"I'm not like you, Lucifer. I care about others. I saved Piper, I saved you, and I'm going to save Sasha and Katherine. If you won't help me—"

"It's not a matter of caring, Nathalie, it's a matter of reality. I care deeply for Sasha and would never want to see her harmed. Her soul is in the veil. We can't change that. *You* can't change that." I started to shake my head, and he captured my chin between his finger and thumb. "But you can still save yourself."

"You'd have me abandon her. Abandon them both—"

"Katherine doesn't deserve this loyalty, but even if we put that aside—you don't know how to remove Morgan Le Fay from Sasha. She's hunting her. Eventually, one of them will mess up. Either Katherine kills Sasha's body and The Morrigan enters her, or she kills Katherine and abandons Sasha to jump into you."

"There has to be another way," I whispered. "Something we're not seeing. I just have to find it."

"Little witch," he began, stroking the side of my cheek with his knuckles. "I don't know how to lure the Morgan Le Fay out of Sasha, but after playing games with her for half a millennium, I can tell you that she won't be easily deceived."

"We've managed to keep her in the dark for days now. She doesn't know we know she's back."

"That you're aware of."

I paused, my eyes narrowing. "What reason would she have to pretend—"

"I don't know, Nathalie. What I do know is that she's over five hundred years old and consumed the life force of her children to keep her alive. She's certifiable, but not stupid. You're not the first Le Fay to try to find their way out of this, but I want you to be the last." Lucifer brushed his knuckles along my cheek gently. "You wanted my help. The advice I'm giving you is help, even if you're choosing not to listen. You don't have a backup plan. This is it."

A tiny bit of guilt fluttered through me, and I tried to school my features. If I told him, he would try to hide me away. He and August were no different in that. They would let the world burn so long as I lived. Ronan was the same with Piper.

The Nats in the loci were trying to talk, but I worried if I let them through, Lucifer would show up in my mind again. It wasn't his fault. At least I didn't think it was.

"I need to go," I said, removing myself from his embrace and walking back to the counter, grabbing my keys.

"The loci," he said softly, his gaze holding mine. When I didn't answer, he added, "I felt the pull."

I sighed, but finally nodded. "I just need to think."

"Ann knows I'm right," he said knowingly.

I grumbled incoherently, annoyed that he even knew their names and could argue with me using their feelings or logic.

"I'll give you your space," he said, lowering his voice to a sexy rumble. He leaned down to brush against me with a kiss, teasing as he nipped at my bottom lip. "Just come back to me when you're done."

"Thank you." I patted his chest with the palm of my hand. "I know you're only looking out for me."

"Always."

As I walked out the door, he whispered so quietly, I almost didn't hear him.

"Careful, little witch."

~

I didn't even bother taking the elevator. I sat at the bottom of the stairs in my building leaning up against the wall. It seemed like the safest and most private place for the time being.

The loci was surprisingly somber.

"I don't understand how you could even consider this a good plan," I began, taking a seat at the table.

"You know damn well why," Bad Nat said, crossing her legs and not propping them on the table for once.

"While I don't share her exact sentiments, she's not wrong," The Warden said, side-eying her bad counterpart.

Ann pushed her glasses up her nose. "This could be the contingency plan. Ronan's could be the last resort."

"But we would be letting Sasha and Kat die," Peace said softly.

"No," Caretaker said. "We're not letting them die. This is just a worst-case scenario."

Bad Nat scoffed. "Is it? Sugarcoat it all you want. She knows what it means."

"That's not how Lucifer presented it," Peace countered.

"But that's how we can consider it," Ann added. "While we don't have to take his suggestion exactly as it is, we have to consider the possibility. If we are unable to take Morgan La Fay out of Sasha, she will Kat. We know her next moves in that sense. Surely there has to be a way to protect ourselves here in the loci."

"Well, if there's a soul tie between you and Morgan La Fay, then she would be able to access the loci once the bitch body snatches us," Bad Nat said. "She may not even need to take you over to get in here."

Peace whimpered and Caretaker rubbed circles on her back to soothe her.

"Shit," I whispered, thinking through the scenarios. "Is that even possible?"

Ann shrugged. "I don't know, but Lucifer is your familiar and there's a bond allowing him to come into the Loki. Logically, there's a possibility she could, right? Have you taken a look at that particular thread?"

I shook my head. "No, not close up. I just know that there's a bond between us." One more thing on the never-ending to-do list. I looked at the two calmer versions of myself. "I expected The Warden and Ann to be on the same page here. Tell me what your thoughts are."

"I think it's the middle ground," Caretaker said after a moment. "Obviously the goal here is to save everyone, but you have to admit it. We may not be able to. And the only contingency you do have is sacrificing yourself. This is the in-between. It's a way to save the ones you love, and also a way for you to survive. If it doesn't work, we still have our final backup plan. We know Ronan will end us. There is no question."

"Peace?"

She sniffled. "I don't like any of this. I just want everyone to be okay."

Bad Nat huffed loudly and rolled her eyes while The Warden shot her a dirty look.

I chewed on my lip, rolling the idea around. "Let's say

Bad Nat is right and she ends up here in the loci. What would we even do in here? Am I supposed to hit her with a library book? This is a part of my subconscious mind. It's not like Bad Nat can stab her." I could feel myself getting more frustrated. It felt like each step I took toward a solution, a new problem would take us five steps back.

The door in the attic rattled harder than it had before. Papers on the table vibrated.

Bad Nat grinned, looking at the ceiling above us. "Let her take a swing."

"Be useful for once," Ann snapped.

I exhaled, taking the time to process what I wanted to say. "Look, I understand that Lucifer has a point, as much as I hate it. But this can't be the contingency. If she gets here, we can't risk her accessing my magic. Ronan has to do what he has to do. There won't be any time."

The Nats looked displeased with my decision. Ann pursed her lips, the corners of her mouth crinkling. "And what do you want us to do in the meantime?"

"We have to make this plan work first so I don't end up dead." I ran my fingers through my hair. "Ann, search the library for every memory we have on looms, spindles, and shears. Even if they aren't the objects of fate. Maybe something will spark an idea, or maybe something was said in code. Warden, Caretaker, everything on transfiguration. Every detail. Peace—"

"Nathalie?" A voice caught me off guard, pulling me from the loci and into the real world where I sat on the concrete stairs.

Not-Sasha stood at the door to the stairwell, her head cocked to the side.

"Hey, Sasha," I said, trying to disguise the suspicion in my voice. "What are you doing here?" She was supposed to be with Sienna, but her twin was nowhere in sight.

"I was actually just looking for you," she responded with a smile that didn't reach her eyes. "Can we grab coffee together? I feel like we haven't had a chance to really talk since I came back."

"Oh, right now?" I asked, standing up and smoothing my palms over my skirt. "I was just getting ready to head out. A lot on the agenda. You know how it goes. The city can't run itself."

"Oh, come on," she insisted, using a coaxing tone. "It'll just be a quick coffee date. I promise I won't keep you too long."

I was reluctant to agree, but she was without her sister, and I needed to keep an eye on her until I figured out why.

"Okay, yeah. Let's go. I know a great place." The truth was, Real-Sasha knew the great place. It was a small shop owned by a succubus that Sasha had introduced me to.

Internally, the Nats were buzzing with concern. Why was she so insistent on spending time with me? What did she hope to gain? Where the hell was Sienna? Was Kat still alive? All valid questions.

Not-Sasha's presence was like an itch I couldn't scratch. Every word, every gesture felt calculated. Just a performance for my benefit. I wondered what The Morrigan wanted. The air between us was thick with unspoken tension, a dangerous game of pretending everything was normal when it was anything but.

As we walked, Not-Sasha glanced at me, her eyes glinting with something I couldn't quite place. "Have you seen your sister lately?" she asked casually.

"Which one?" I asked. I wasn't sure if she knew that I was aware Carissa died. I'd rather give nothing away if I could help it.

"Katherine?"

I scoffed, answering in a way that should be expected. "Thankfully, no. Not that I prefer Carissa's bitchy attitude over Kat's. The longer I go without talking to either of them, the happier I am." Not-Sasha made a sound of sympathy, her eyes scanning my face as if searching for something.

"It's a shame, really. Family bonds are so important."

I resisted the urge to snort at the irony of that statement coming from Morgan LaFey of all people. I forced a smile, feeling the weight of the charade bearing down on me. "Speaking of sisters, where's Sienna?"

"Here and there," she answered vaguely. "She's been hovering since I came back. Trying to make sure I'm okay, but I'm ready to do my own thing again. You know how I am."

"Ready for anything," I said, keeping the tone of the conversation light.

She fell silent, seemingly lost in thought for a

moment before shifting the conversation. "And how are you and August?"

I felt myself stiffen, but I released the tension quickly. "Oh, you know that's a weird topic to discuss with you. I'd rather do it another time. After all you've been through . . ."

"What better time than the present?" She shrugged. "I'm over him. The veil made me see things more clearly. Truly. You should take him for yourself."

"I . . . will think about it." I wasn't sure what else to say, but she had an agenda and wouldn't drop it.

She playfully elbowed me. "Enjoy all the perks of an aurae bond, Nat. How lucky are you? I mean, he can give you so much more than Lucifer ever could."

My heart skipped a beat at the mention of Lucifer. What was her point? "How so?"

Not-Sasha chuckled. "Please. He's the devil. He'll never change. He's better suited to finding someone that can feed that desire. It's his magic, after all. The witches he's had in the past? He just uses them up until he's bored. I'd hate to see him do the same to you."

I couldn't help myself from feeling territorial, but I shoved it down as deep as I could. This was not my friend speaking. "Hadn't thought of it that way."

The coffee shop came into view as we rounded a corner. It stood out vividly against the otherwise muted tones of the street. Its exterior was a burst of cheerful color, with bright teal walls adorned with whimsical, hand-painted flowers and vines that seemed to dance up toward the roof. *Perk & Petal* was emblazoned in bold, golden letters on a rustic wooden sign that hung above the entrance. A few small tables and chairs were arranged outside on the sidewalk, each set adorned with a tiny vase holding fresh flowers, adding a personal touch to the scene. The windows were large and inviting, allowing passersby to glimpse the cozy interior filled with soft lighting and comfortable seating. The door was painted a sunny yellow, standing open to welcome patrons with the rich aroma of freshly brewed coffee and baked goods. It was a bright spot in the city, really focusing on bringing back some beauty and charm into New Chicago.

It only took a minute before I was holding the door open for Sasha, allowing her to enter the coffee shop ahead of me. The familiar jingle of the bell greeted us as we stepped inside. It was packed, and I cursed internally. The girl at the counter, a young werewolf with blue streaks in her hair and a septum piercing beamed at me.

"Hey, Nat."

"Hey, Melinda," I greeted with a forced smile. Melinda looked at Sasha expectantly, but of course, the imposter had no knowledge of their previous inter-actions.

Not-Sasha noticed the lull in conversation and proceeded to start asking about the menu without missing a beat. While she focused on that, I swiftly texted Piper and Ronan: ***Sasha with me. At P&P.*** I tucked my phone into my pocket just as she finished ordering and turned around, both of them looking at me.

"I'll have a cinnamon dolce latte, please," I

requested, catching a flicker of surprise on the barista's face. It was fleeting, quickly replaced by a practiced smile.

"Sure thing," she replied smoothly, punching in my order. "Want me to put it on your tab?"

"That'd be great." I gave her a subtle nod.

Sasha had already moved to wait for our drinks, her attention momentarily captured by something on her phone. There were a good number of people in the seats, but I watched surreptitiously as a barista began moving from table to table. People were calmly standing and gathering their things to leave, keeping cheery tones as they waved their goodbyes.

That was good.

I turned away, not wanting to bring attention to it. Sasha continued tapping at her phone and not for the first time, I wondered what she was doing and who she could have been talking to.

When the drinks were ready, I grabbed the coffees, turning to Not-Sasha with forced warmth.

"Here we go," I said, handing her drink over. "So, what did you want to catch up on?" We grabbed a table, our choices freeing up more and more as the shop was practically empty by now.

"You know. Life. What happened while I was gone. What you're working on now."

I shifted in my seat, a sinking feeling settling in my stomach. Whatever she was fishing for, I didn't know yet. I had to keep my answers as vague as possible.

"While you were gone, we just kept looking for you.

That was our focus. Of course, Sienna was distraught, so we had to make sure she was okay."

She nodded along, but any real warmth was lacking. She didn't care how Sienna reacted. "Well, I'm back now. So everything is fine. We can just get back to work."

I took a sip of my latte and tried not to cringe. It was so damn sweet. "Have you seen the Señora so she can check you over?" I knew she hadn't. Morgan Le Fay would want to stay as far as possible from a witch with that much power. She had been careful to avoid her at all costs. "I know she said she'd call you."

"No need." She waved me off, changing the subject and not even bothering to transition.

My phone rang in my pocket. I pulled it out and set it to vibrate it without looking at the caller ID. Vibrations, back-to-back, continued moving the table.

"Not going to check that?" Not-Sasha finally asked, her tone light.

"Oh, the city always needs something. The calls can wait." I forced a smile, attempting to dismiss the significance of my ignored phone. "I'm with you right now," I replied casually, hoping to deflect her attention.

"With how much you've been avoiding me, I'm surprised to hear you say so. Almost seems insincere," she deadpanned and the hairs on my arm stood on end.

"I've been so busy," I began, but she didn't let me finish.

"So busy you couldn't be with a friend you dumped in the void? You and Marcel fucked up and left me to die in there. It's the least you could do." I felt the sting from her lashing, but that was because I felt guilty over Real-Sasha still being stuck there. This was an imposter trying to hurt me, and I couldn't let it work.

I pressed my lips together. "You're right, Sasha. I can do better."

She traced a claw along the rim of her cup, a smirk curling up one side. "Yes, you most certainly can."

"So, what's your plan?" I said, ignoring her slight.

Not-Sasha hummed, taking a sip of her coffee. "Regarding?"

"Well, now that you're back. I know you don't want to talk about it, but I'm sure the veil has changed you in many ways." I sniffled, taking a pretend sip of my drink. Of course I knew she would never come out and admit anything, but I hoped for a nugget of information that would let me know where her thoughts were. "That's a lot to go through, I mean. Were you wanting to resume your work with Piper, or were you thinking of another direction?"

"Oh, Nat, I'm done with New Chicago," she said, a smirk pulling at her lips. "But I think you knew that already."

I schooled my features, trying to figure out her angle. "Oh, I didn't realize you wanted more than what our city has to offer."

"I just want what every woman wants." Her eyes darkened, and the intensity of it made my skin crawl.

I swallowed thickly, feeling a new buzz in the air that hadn't been there before. "And that is?"

"Power."

My breath caught in my throat as she spoke, her voice now laced with an unsettling familiarity as she dropped the façade.

"I'd like to say it's nice to see you, Morgan, but we both know that's a lie," I said smoothly. All pre-tenses were gone. The jig was up. I sighed, almost as relieved as I was terrified. I leaned back in my chair, trying to come up with an escape plan. Some way to fight her if she tried to take me over.

"You're good, Nathalie," Not-Sasha said, her voice low and taunting. "Better than the sister, but you made a crucial mistake today."

"What gave me away?" I asked, raising a brow.

"That ridiculous drink you ordered," she whispered, her tone dripping with malicious humor. "You despise sweet. Did you really think I wouldn't notice the sudden exodus in the last fifteen minutes? Or that the child at the counter has told the last three people their coffee machine is broken?"

I shrugged. "Best I could do was hope."

She leaned forward, her gaze piercing. "Out of all of them, you were the best liar. Always have been. Well, apart from Lucifer, perhaps."

"How long have you known?" I asked. My tone was relatively calm, but my brain was scrambling. What would her next move be?

The Morrigan's laughter echoed in the quiet. "Since the moment Sienna returned from her 'business' talk with you. She's not as good an actress as she thinks."

"So, why wait until now?" I remained steady despite

the turmoil rolling inside me. I needed to keep her talking, grateful that the shop was finally clear. Even the baristas had moved to the back rooms.

"I was biding my time," she said simply.

"For what?" Gods, I hoped my sister was still alive.

"*You*," she replied with a vicious grin. In a flash, she transformed into a sleek, black bird, spreading her wings and darting out of the open door in a flurry of feathers. I watched in stunned silence as she vanished, leaving me shaken and alone.

I reached for my phone, my fingers trembling as I went to unlock it. I had every intention of informing Piper and the others. But as I scrolled through the notifications, my heart pounded in my ears and emotion clogged my throat. August's name stood out among the missed calls and urgent messages and deep down, I knew why.

He picked up on the first ring, his voice tense and strained.

"Marcel's dying."

19

NATHALIE

The bell above the door slammed around as I burst into Señora's shop, fear and urgency pushing me forward. Inside, the room was thick with tension, the scent of herbs and the faint hum of magic weaving through the air. As I came to a halt, I took in the scene before me. August was already there, cradling a limp and emaciated Marcel in his arms, his own face etched with worry. Lucifer stood nearby, his expression grave as he watched me enter.

"August," I breathed out, rushing to his side and grabbing Marcel's limp hand. The coolness of his skin sent a shiver down my spine, amplifying the fear gripping my heart. "What happened?"

"I don't know," August replied, his voice steady but tinged with concern. His usually calm demeanor was replaced with an edge of panic, something I rarely saw in him. "Estrid started pawing at his door and crying

200

loudly. She's never done that if it wasn't for food. I found him on the floor."

"How long?" I asked, brushing a lock of hair away from Marcel's damp forehead.

"I called you and the Señora as soon as I found him. Before that, I don't know."

The sight of Marcel, so lifeless, pale and hanging from his arms, was almost more than I could bear. My mind raced, searching for answers, or for anything that could explain why this was happening, besides what I already knew.

Marcel's time was up.

He paused, his gaze flickering to Marcel's. The dark lines of magic that usually sat beneath Marcel's skin were now pulsing and vibrant, dancing in victory as if it won the battle and would soon consume its host. Cracks formed as if the magic were threatening to burst out of his body at any moment.

"I'm going to get Señora Rosara," Lucifer announced, breaking the tense silence. He gave me a meaningful look before leaving the room. His usually confident demeanor was overshadowed by concern.

"Let's get him to the side room. That's where she'll want him," I said, motioning toward the back of the shop.

August followed me as I led him past Señora's curious cats and into the small room that had been my own sanctuary during my eye surgery. The room was dimly lit, the air thick with the scent of lavender and sage, a stark contrast to the sterile environment I'd been in not long ago. August gently laid Marcel's unconscious body on the long table, then stepped back to stand beside me.

August placed a comforting hand on my shoulder, squeezing gently. His touch was warm, grounding me in the moment. "For what it's worth, I'm sorry I couldn't do more, Nathalie."

Pressing my lips together, I nodded and swallowed the lump forming in my throat. This was it. I was no closer to a cure than I had been when I started.

I said none of that, keeping my eyes on Marcel, blinking back tears. It wasn't long before Señora swept into the room, Lucifer hot on her heels. She barely acknowledged us, her gaze fixed on Marcel. She retrieved herbs and magical instruments from the shelves around her, creating a small circle of items around his body. We all stood back, giving her the space she needed to work. Señora tsked softly as she assessed Marcel's condition, her movements precise.

The threat of losing him became more real than it ever had been. August kept his hand on my lower back, swirling his thumb and grounding me as best he could. Lucifer stood next to me; his arms crossed as he watched for my reactions. I stepped away from them both, knowing that if Marcel was ever going to have a chance, I needed to come up with some last-ditch effort. No matter how wild or unlikely, I just needed something.

Gods. Everything was happening all at once. The Morrigan was out there somewhere, plotting her next move. She wasn't even hiding it anymore. I didn't have the chance to tell anyone what had just happened. I couldn't. I had more questions than answers, all while Marcel's chances at surviving were plummeting by the second. Somehow, with all of that, he was all I could focus on.

His breaths were shallow and raspy. Running a shaky hand through my hair, anxiety tightened its grip around my heart as I turned to face Señora. My heart dropped as she looked up at me with a pitying gaze and she shook her head slightly.

"No, not yet," I whispered, cutting her off before she could say anything, shaking my head in defiance. "Keep him alive. Do whatever you have to do."

Señora's expression softened just a touch, and her voice carried the weight of the truth we all knew. "Nathalie, there is nothing more I can do. His time draws near."

"I know there is something you can do to fix him, Señora. I don't care what it costs."

Her eyes narrowed slightly. "You will."

The harrowing way she spoke sent a shiver up my spine. "Tell me."

"He will not be himself when I am done. The man you love will not be saved."

Whatever level of dark and seedy magic she was referring to remained unnamed, but the insinuation was enough for me to understand. I nodded, and she pressed her lips together, allowing me to accept the gravity of the situation in silence.

The whispers of my loci pulled me in, where I found

every version of myself scrambling. Peace was crying with hyperventilating hiccups, and even then, she was pushing herself through every plant book we had, furiously wiping the tears away with her arm. Caretaker was by her side, sifting through books of spells we had watched or had read about over my lifetime.

Bad Nat threw another book across the room, kicking the table as she did. "This is pointless. He's on death's doorstep and we have no way to slow it down, much less stop it."

"Keep looking," Ann muttered, pushing her glasses up her nose while she scanned a shelf in the library.

"For what?" The Warden asked, tossing her hands up. "I hate to agree with her, but Bad Nat is right. It's not as if we haven't been looking. The sudden pressure to find something isn't going to make it miraculously appear."

Peace sniffled. "There isn't a plant or flower on this realm that can save him." She pushed her book away, grabbing another one. "I wish we could just turn him *into* a flower," she whispered.

Bad Nat scoffed, rolling her eyes. "You and your stupid movies. Even the other two fairies thought that was dumb."

The Warden looked up. "Which movie was that?"

"Sleeping Beauty. Animated one," Ann muttered, blowing a lock of hair away from her face while she read.

"Wait," Caretaker said, looking at me. "Can we do that? Can we turn him into something?"

I scrubbed my hands down my face and shook my

head. "The death magic that's eating him now will just eat the new form he'd take. It's not killing his soul. It's the vessel, the part that's living . . ."

As I trailed off, thinking of how crass I sounded, Bat Nat's assessment sounded significantly worse. "Well, he's mortal, just like us, and there's nothing we can do to change that. He's going to die someday. Might as well let it happen now."

Caretaker threw a pencil at her. "Could you, I don't know, *not* be yourself right now?"

Bad Nat took a step forward, fists balled up. The Warden stepped between them before they took it any further, and she began shouting over them to calm them down. "Stop it! What's gotten into you?"

"She started it," Caretaker said, jabbing a finger in Bad Nat's direction.

"I didn't start shit. You're just too caught up in emotions to see the fucking truth. This is reality, you twat. Welcome." The same pencil that had been thrown at her went flying back toward Caretaker.

The Warden swatted it out of the air, midflight. "What the hell, you two? You're acting like children!"

Ann snorted, turning away disapprovingly before tossing another book aside. "Hardly. Honor and Orson are children. Don't insult them by putting them in the same category."

This was a disaster. Not only was I losing Marcel, but the pieces that lived within me were falling apart. Which meant, in fact, *I* was falling apart. I sighed.

"Wait!" Peace shushed everyone, waving her hands

wildly and standing up. The loci paused the bickering long enough to look at the frantic version of myself, her eyes swollen and her nose rubbed raw. "The children!"

"Come again?" Ann turned, giving Peace her attention, but she only looked directly at me.

"You wanted to change him into an immortal—"

"We can't," Ann said, dismissing her. "He's too weak."

Peace ignored her completely, walking toward me and grabbing a picture of Honor and Orson that was kept on a small table by the couch. She held it out to me. "*Change his reality,* Prime." Her eyes widened as she stared at me, dipping her chin slightly. My lips parted as I inhaled sharply. All at once, the rest of the loci caught on.

Within seconds, I'd jolted myself back into the reality of Señora's shop. August and Señora looked at me quizzically, but Lucifer only smirked. Part of me wondered if he'd been there and I was so frantic that I hadn't noticed. It didn't matter.

"I'm going to change him into an immortal," I blurted out.

Señora's eyebrows pinched together, not understanding. "I don't have that kind of power, Nathalie."

"You don't have that power," I began, pulling my phone out, "but I know someone who does."

20

NATHALIE

One of the many benefits of a best friend was they would show up for you, no questions asked. After what Piper and I had been through together, we were no different. If she called me and told me to bring a shovel, I'd ask when and where. So when I called to tell her Marcel was dying and that I needed her and the kids at Señora Rosara's shop, like a true best friend, she said they were on their way.

Within minutes, Piper and Ronan arrived, each holding the hand of one of their twins as they walked through the light realm and appeared inside the store. Honor and Orson smiled as they saw me.

"Auntie Nat!" they said in unison as I scooped them into a hug.

"Hey, guys," I said softly, glancing up at their parents. No doubt they could see the urgency in my eyes. I gestured to August standing beside me. "This is my friend, August. He's safe. Can you hang out with him for a minute while I talk to Mom and Dad about something?"

August snapped his head in my direction, giving me a quick look of uncertainty.

"It's fine," I whispered. "Just show them the gemstones on the shelves over there. Honor likes geodes. They can pet the cats. But not the tuxedo cat, and not the orange tabby. They're both pissy."

Piper inclined her chin when they looked to her for confirmation, and August reached his hands out for each of them to take one. I could feel Ronan tense at the sight of another man walking away with his kids, but August was the safer choice. Lucifer had stayed in the back room with Marcel, though I knew he was irritated by it. I would have to tell him at some point that I appreciated the fact he didn't fight me on it. We both knew that if he were present, it would make this harder for Piper and Ronan. My eyes strayed to the back room, my heart clenching at the thought of Marcel being so frail and vulnerable.

"Where's Hallie?" I asked.

"With Morfayus and Ailaine," Piper answered, watching her kids walk away. "If you need her too, Ronan can go get her."

I shook my head, but before I could speak, Ronan glanced at the back room, no doubt sensing his brother's presence. "I'm not leaving."

Piper elbowed him in the stomach. "Nat wouldn't put the kids in harm's way."

"You said Marcel is dying," Ronan began, crossing his arms. "Why are we here?"

Piper glared at him. "A little tact, maybe?"

I waved it off, placing a hand on Piper's arm. "No, he's right. There's no time to sugarcoat any of this."

She pressed her lips together. "Fair enough. What can we do?"

I looked between Piper and Ronan, knowing what I was about to ask would worry them both. I knew Ronan wouldn't like it. I knew Piper would be hesitant. But it was all I had.

"The death magic in Marcel can't be slowed down anymore. He's about to die," I said, pausing as emotion began to clog my throat. I cleared it out, trying to keep my composure. If I didn't remain calm, this wouldn't work. "I need to change him into an immortal."

Piper's brows furrowed. "I don't understand. We talked about this already. You'd said his body can't handle it."

"It can't. I need Honor's magic to change his reality," I said quickly, holding my breath and waiting for Ronan to shut me down.

I volleyed between Piper and Ronan as they exchanged a heavy look. I could practically see the silent, mental conversation happening between them. Their hesitation was palpable, the heaviness of the decision pressing down on all of us.

"That's . . . risky," Piper said softly. The concern in her voice was evident, and it mirrored the fear gnawing at me. "Honor's magic isn't stable, Nat. We can't ask her to use it. Hell, we've done everything possible so she *won't* use it. She can't control it."

"But I can," I said, placing a hand on my chest. "I can channel and control her magic." Their silence indicated more mental conversation, so I pressed on. "She needs to be okay with me doing this and give me consent, of course, but there's no risk to Honor. She'll be perfectly safe, and Orson's presence brings her comfort. I knew if she said yes, she'd want him here."

Ronan spoke up, his voice low and stern. "There's no question that she'd say yes, but we're not worried about Honor's safety. We're worried about yours."

I raised my brows, almost chuckling internally. Considering the deal Ronan and I had, his concern for my well-being tickled me a bit.

"I can handle it. You both know what I'm capable of."

"Nat," Piper began, blowing out a breath as she considered her words. "Honor's power is immense. She literally holds part of the source of magic itself. Not only is she a demon, but she's damn near a god. The strain of channeling that will overload you. It would overload anyone. It's not that we don't trust you to not hurt Honor. It's that we don't trust her magic not to kill you. Even if she's not the one using it, it doesn't change its strength. You can channel her magic, fine. But who will protect you when it becomes too much?" Her voice was gentle but serious.

"I . . . then . . . I don't know." With a stuttering and uneven exhale, a tight ball of anxiety twisted in my gut. Hope drained out of me, and my fingertips felt numb as a result. The truth was I didn't know what to do. I knew for certain I had the ability to *channel* her magic, but if I didn't have the strength to ground me through it, none of this mattered. I'd just end up dead and that helped no one. And gods forbid something did happen to Honor if I wasn't able to ground myself.

"I'm so sorry," Piper said, wrapping her arms around me. "If there was a way to stabilize you . . . It's just—"

"Perhaps I can offer my assistance," Lucifer said, his voice steady and confident. Piper tensed around me, and I glanced at Ronan as she did the same. The devil strolled out from between shelving units in the shop, his hands in his pockets.

"No," Ronan said gruffly, his jaw clenching.

Lucifer glanced at his brother, but ignored him, choosing to address me and, to an extent, Piper. "I'm your familiar, Nathalie. I can act as your anchor as you channel Honor's power."

Piper raised a brow, assessing him. "Can you?"

He lifted his shoulder in a slight shrug. "As the power channels through her, who better to take the brunt of it than an undead demon? It can't hurt me."

That little glimmer of hope reappeared, and I played out the scenarios in my head. Ann scrambled in my mind, doing the mental math, and calculating how to perform the spell in this way. While Piper and Ronan were no doubt having their own mental debate, I was figuring out the probability of success.

"It will work," I whispered, nodding my head as Ann

and I had come to the final conclusion. "He's right. He has the strength to anchor me."

Piper and Ronan exchanged another glance, silently weighing the proposal. Ronan's nostrils flared at the idea his brother would be involved.

"You may be overestimating yourself, Nathalie," Señora Rosara said, coming into view. My eyes shot toward the back room. She'd left him. He was alone. Not that he was conscious, but the thought still terrified me. My heart skipped a beat, and she rested her hand on my arm. "Nevertheless, his breathing has slowed, and his heartrate has begun to drop. You are out of time, child. The veil calls to him."

"Lucifer will have no contact with Honor," I said quickly, looking directly at Ronan. "The spell requires a three-looped salt sigil; one loop for each of us. Marcel in the middle. She wouldn't even be near him. He can't touch her magic. It'll flow through us like a circuit breaker. Nothing more." When I glanced at Lucifer, he held his hands up and raised his brows. "This is the only shot I have to save Marcel, you guys. I've got nothing else. Whatever shit is between brothers, this has nothing to do with it. Lucifer is my familiar. He knows how I feel about Piper. How I feel about the kids. He would never harm someone I love."

A parent was protective, no matter if they were human or immortal. Even demons that were almost untouchable. They looked at each other, and Ronan's shoulders lost some of their tension.

"Okay," she said, dipping her chin. I could still sense

their discomfort, but I also knew Piper and Ronan would never agree if they weren't actually okay with it.

I threw my arms around her. "Thank you," I breathed.

"If you plan on doing this, I would save the hugs for later," Lucifer said, putting a hand on my shoulder and tilting his head toward Señora.

She squeezed my hand, turning and walking toward the back room, her skirts shuffling.

I shook my hands out, wishing I could make the anxiety leave my body. "Ronan, will you bring Marcel into my living room?"

He nodded, following the Señora.

Without another word, Piper turned to get the twins. We didn't need to speak. She knew where we were going, and she knew how urgent this was.

I turned to look at Lucifer. "Bring August."

After running up the stairs to my apartment, I left the door open as I quickly moved things out of the way, not giving a care about where I shoved things. August and Lucifer came in and didn't question anything. They both jumped to action and moved what furniture was left while I grabbed my supplies. The middle of the living room floor was wide open, with the couch and chairs haphazardly shoved against the walls and windows. We'd done some version of this routine quite a few times now.

I hoped this would be the last.

Ronan appeared, cradling Marcel's frail body, and Piper and the kids were right behind him.

"She's ready," Piper said, giving me the go-ahead as Honor gently waved at me. I wanted to save Marcel more than anything, but if Honor had said no, I never would have forced her.

I gave them a tight-lipped acknowledgment as I kept moving. With a deliberate process, I let salt flow from its box, drawing the sigil with three loops, all connecting at a common point. Each line was precise, each curve intentional. This symbol would serve as the foundation of our ritual and allow for a continual flow of magic between all of us.

Lucifer handed me my athame, and I carefully cleansed it, making sure it was purified for the new spell work. He snapped his fingers, and each candle flickered at once, the tiny flames dancing and creating shadows in the room. The blade gleamed under the dim light, and the weight of the athame in my hand was both comforting and daunting.

Ronan laid Marcel in the center of the sigil, and I pushed emotion aside. There was no room for that right now. His breathing was even more shallow than I'd expected. As if the pulsing death magic ravaging his veins wasn't enough of a reminder of how close he was to dying, each raspy rise and fall of his chest certainly did the trick.

"Okay," I began, my voice clear and firm as I turned to Honor, giving her a reassuring smile. "All you need to do is stay in your loop, okay, honey? I'll do the rest."

Honor nodded happily. "Yes, Auntie Nat. Mama told me."

I thanked her, giving her shoulder a gentle squeeze, and then looked to Orson. "Thank you for being here too, kiddo."

He smiled, looking at his twin as they made eye contact and shared some secret moment between them.

Piper led her to sit in the top loop. Honor watched us with curiosity as Lucifer and I positioned ourselves in the two loops at the bottom, side by side. The air was thick with anticipation, every moment stretching out painfully.

With a deep breath, I closed my eyes and refocused my thoughts and my energy, willing the object of fate to appear.

The spindle.

The loom.

The shears.

Ancient and powerful; the coveted tools of destiny.

I vividly pictured them as they hovered in my mind. They were mine to control. I reminded myself of my strength. What I had done to get here. That these objects belonged to me.

Honor let out a tiny gasp, and Orson whispered, "Mama, did you see that?" Piper lightly shushed him.

When I opened my eyes, the objects sat in front of me, gleaming in the candlelight. Señora Rosara and August stood near the door, a stoic expression on her features and a smirk of pride on his face. Orson stood between Piper and Ronan as they watched the circle.

My gaze found Lucifer's and he dipped his chin,

silently encouraging me. Steeling myself, I looked at the others and gave a determined nod.

The Nats of the loci sat at the table, waiting with bated breath. Everyone was holding hands, except Bad Nat. She paced and flicked at her thumbnails anxiously instead.

"Don't fuck this up," she whispered in the recesses of my mind as I put up walls to shutter the outside world.

It was time.

21

NATHALIE

As I began to chant, I took my athame and made a clean cut across my palm, wincing as the pain bit into my skin. Blood welled along the line left by the blade. The coppery scent filled the air, mingling with the salt and incense smoke that swirled around us. Carefully I dragged the blade along the lines of my palm, ending with a rune carved into my skin.

My teeth dug into my bottom lip as I cut. The lines had to be precise, and I had to dissociate myself from the pain. Taking a steadying inhale, I turned to Lucifer, who held out his hand without hesitation. I carved a matching rune into his palm, the lines painting a red design across his broad hand.

Setting the athame down next to me, I held out my bleeding hand and Lucifer placed his in mine. They clasped together, mingling our blood. I pulled our connected hands forward, allowing the flow of blood to drip over the salt outlines of the sigil.

I was still chanting, my words almost hymnal as I recited them meticulously, putting every fiber of my being into the spell.

It had to fucking work.

It took a moment, long enough for panic to flare, but the salt began to sizzle as our blood activated the intricate loops of the sigil. A soft hum filled the room; a low vibration that resonated in my bones. A glow climbed along the curves of the sigil as the entire emblem came to life, the light pulsating in rhythm with our heartbeats. My chanting never ceased as I called forth the power we needed, the ancient words rolling off my tongue, each syllable infused with intent and desperation.

As the glow from the sigil finally reached the portion that Honor occupied, I felt the first rush of her magic. It was an overwhelming surge that burned through my veins. A sob threatened to pass my lips, but I held it back. I couldn't risk breaking my concentration. I couldn't risk Piper stopping this, thinking I couldn't handle it. Still, it was too much, too fast. The raw, unbridled power of the Source threatened to consume me.

Piper and Ronan had been right.

Honor remained still, unaffected by the channeling. She tilted her head slightly, watching me, her curious expression giving me a sense of peace that she was completely okay. The pain was mine. Not hers.

Lucifer tightened his grip on my hand, his presence a steady anchor in the maelstrom of energy. I connected my eyes with his and saw the concern, but also the confidence. He knew it hurt, but he trusted me at that moment. He knew I could handle it and that gave me the push I needed.

I closed my eyes, concentrating on changing the way the magic flooded through the channels. Slowly, the burning sensation began to lessen as I reversed the flow, using Lucifer as the first conduit before it reached me. It had become tempered and manageable. I glanced over to see Lucifer's jaw clenched, his gaze trained on me only, his eyes glowing with a bright, fierce light.

The channel was complete, and the lines of salt glowed with energy. Ceasing the chant, I released him, turning my hands palm up and holding them out as I continued.

Marcel coughed weakly, a dribble of blood trickling down the corner of his mouth and down his neck. My stomach clenched, and sigil pulsed as my attention on the spell waned. Lucifer reached over to squeeze my hand, and I nodded, speaking the spell through the lump in my throat.

I concentrated on the objects of fate before me, and then I called further to the power of the Eye, allowing myself to refocus on the threads in the room. I only needed to see what was attached to me.

There were several threads linked to my existence, but three were strong, bright and connected straight through my heart. Two of them shone brighter than the other, one a little duller, as if the connection was incomplete. I sifted through them, passing by the one that I knew had been connected to me the longest.

It wasn't hard to find Marcel's, weak and frayed. The

irony of its dimness standing out against the bright gold of everyone else in the room was not lost on me. I reached out and gently plucked the thin thread between my thumb and forefinger. I wrapped his thread twice around the spindle before setting it down.

Grabbing Marcel's thread hanging from the spindle, I picked up the loom with shaking hands and then placed it in my lap. Sourcing my own thread, I pulled on it, feeling the tug in the pits of my soul when I draped it over the loom.

Using the spindle to guide Marcel's thread and the loom to twine him with mine, I began to work. I bound us together. With each weave of the loom, Marcel's thread changed. First it became a thicker strand. Then it became brighter and stronger, feeding from my own.

I looked at Marcel, and the death magic in his veins dimmed beneath his skin. His sickly color began to improve. Sweat dripped down my forehead, and a small smile formed on my lips.

It was a fleeting victory.

The strand frayed again, turning from a light gold to a muddy shade of purple, traveling the length of the thread connecting straight to my heart. His body jerked twice in a harsh, forceful motion. The hopeful change in his pallor disappeared as quickly as it had come.

"No!" I barely recognized my own voice.

Panic flooded my senses.

Pain coursed through me.

I ceased weaving through the loom any further as I coughed, and the same trickle of blood I'd seen in him came sputtering out of my mouth, spraying on the floor in front of me.

"Nathalie!" August shouted, stepping forward, but Señora Rosara placed her arm in front of him. Ronan held Piper back as she lunged toward me.

I shook my head violently, holding my hand up. Honor remained the same, watching me closely.

"Are you okay?" I asked her, and she nodded, completely unaffected.

"Natalie, you cannot hold the tie," Señora said, her voice rising.

"I can! I just need to fix the thread!"

"Listen to me now! He needs an immortal tie. The death magic is transferring through the thread. If you bind him to you, it will kill you both!"

"No," I whimpered, swallowing thickly. "I can . . ."

"You cannot hold him to this plane!" she shouted, stepping forward but stopping before she crossed the sigil.

"I can change myself to an immortal," I countered, thinking quickly. "I'll change my reality first—"

"You can't," she argued, frustration radiating in her tone. "What you are doing is not that spell."

"I have to try—"

"Tie him to me." All eyes in the room turned to Lucifer. His jaw was still clenched tight as Honor's power circled through us. He dipped his chin once.

Pain wracked my body, and I nearly doubled over as the death magic attacked my insides. Tears stung my eyes, and I choked out a sob. Exhaustion washed over me, threatening to consume all my energy. Marcel's color had paled. His cheeks were gaunt. Tiny purple lines appeared beneath my skin.

"Move the godsdamned thread now!" August ground out, his fists clenching. "I'm not losing you!"

My hands trembled as I found Lucifer's thread, gold and vibrant and strong.

I tried to move quickly, but I couldn't. Tremors rippled through me. Keeping steady was imperative while also seemingly impossible.

I wove Lucifer's thread through the spindle, pulling mine away from Marcel's so I could unravel what I had started to connect.

The moment I did, Marcel's body convulsed. The muddy purple in the thread wound its way out of me, traveling down the length of the thread . . . and thereby taking away the life source that had been keeping him alive.

I watched in slow-motion as that death magic drove down the thread, pieces fraying behind it, heading straight for him. That's when I knew in my heart he was going to die. He'd been on the cusp when we started the spell, and the threads had pulled from me to give him life. Without it, the magic was able to fully devour him.

A scream filled the air, and I realized it was mine as I reached my hand toward him as if it would do something to stop the inevitable. As if I had some magic that could save him. Some magic that could stop—

An errant wind rushed through the room until all I

heard was the sound of my own sobs. The magic in the thread had paused, millimeters from his heart.

Everyone in the room stood still, frozen.

Orson was behind his sister, his hand on her shoulder, with her hand resting on top of his. He held his arm out, as if he was manipulating a spell.

He'd stopped time.

"Orson," I breathed.

His gaze drifted down to Marcel.

The sound of a weakened heart thumped pitifully, once.

Twice.

Long pauses between each beat, but Marcel was still alive. Barely.

Tears streamed down my face.

"Now, Auntie Nat," he whispered, and Honor gave me a smile of encouragement.

Grabbing Lucifer's thread, I wound it with Marcel's, moving swiftly as I wove them together in the loom, over and over, repeating the spell as I did.

The loom seemed to hum with energy, each pass of the threads through the warp and weft creating a resonance that vibrated through the strands. The threads became hard to distinguish from each other.

With each second that passed, the thread grew stronger. I whispered my incantations under my breath. The loom glowed with a soft, ethereal light, each weave making it pulse brighter.

I may not have bound him to me, but I felt the

connection we had strengthen as his proximity to immortality neared.

I put the loom down and picked up the shears. One wrong move, and everything could unravel. The shears felt heavy in my hand. Pulling the thread taut, I carefully snipped Marcel's connection to the mortal realm, leaving him bound to Lucifer.

The new thread flared brightly. As the severed ends of the threads wove themselves into a new pattern, I felt a surge of energy pass through me. I may not have been holding him to this realm, but he had always been tied to me.

The sigil on the floor pulsed with Honor's power, the magic within it reacting to the completion of the ritual, sealing the new reality I'd just created. Marcel's thread, now intertwined with my familiar's, glowed with a renewed vibrancy, the life force within it strong and steady.

Immortal.

The glow slowly dimmed until second by second, everything around us returned to normal. When the final bits of light faded from Marcel's face, his features were radiant and free of the magic that had been marring his body. His breathing was steady, his heartbeat strong.

"It's done," I said, my voice cracking.

Orson released his hold on time, and the room exploded into life, everyone talking and reacting all at once.

"Orson!" Piper scolded, shock and fear on her face.

"I had to, Mama. I had to help Auntie Nat," he said softly, not apologizing.

Honor stood up, hugging her brother.

Lucifer twisted his face, wrinkling his nose. "Nope, didn't like that one bit."

"What just happened?" August asked, patting down his body.

"The boy can control time," Señora whispered.

"That's...unnerving," he muttered in return, taking in the chaotic room.

I looked up at the others. "I did it."

That was when they all stopped and realized Marcel looked healthy again.

"Holy shit," Piper breathed. She walked forward, extending her hand to help pull me up. "He's tied to Lucifer now?"

I nodded, giving him a small smile. Holding my arms open, I gestured to the twins, and they came to me, allowing me to embrace them in a tight hug. "Thank you both," I said softly, resting my cheek on Orson's head. "I couldn't have done this without you."

"He did it too," Orson said, and I followed his line of sight. Lucifer had stood up and was running his fingers through his messy hair.

"He sure did," I said in agreement. After I kissed their heads, I let them go, walking over to Lucifer while the twins went to their parents.

"I suppose I owe you a pretty big thank you," I said, brushing some of the salt off his shirt.

"I can think of a few ways you could show your appreciation," he whispered, winking at me.

My heart sank. "Is that why you did it?"

"Of course not."

"Then why did you?" I asked. "You don't even like him."

He shrugged. "He matters to you."

"And?"

He leveled me with a stare that threatened to send shivers down my spine. "Little witch. You said so yourself: I would never harm someone you love. Watching you lose someone you love—and being able to prevent it—falls into that category. Even if it's someone like Baggage. If I'd have let him die, a part of you would have died with him, and that I can't allow."

Nickname aside, my chest filled with warmth, and I wrapped my arms around his waist, pulling him close to me. "Thank you," I whispered.

Stepping back, I wiped the tears from my face. Ronan and Piper had watched our exchange with what could best be described as curiosity. An unreadable crease had formed between Ronan's brows as he let out a deep huff.

August had picked up Marcel, cradling him while Señora Rosara was speaking softly and rubbing a salve on his head.

"Your bedroom?" August assumed, tilting his head toward the open door.

"Yes, I need to keep an eye on him. I don't know why he's not awake yet."

Señora closed her eyes, placing her hand on his forehead for a moment. "His body needs rest. Even immortals sleep after battle." She shooed August toward the room and Lucifer followed, pulling down the blankets so August could lay Marcel down on the bed.

"Is the death magic gone?" I was fairly sure I knew the answer, but I wanted confirmation.

"No." She pursed her lips and gave a subtle shake. "That magic is irreversible and will forever be in his body. His immortality will save him. It can't harm him anymore."

I'd suspected as much. A part of me hoped changing his reality would cancel out the death magic that plagued him, but I'd doubted that could happen. In the end, it didn't matter.

Piper scrubbed her hands down her face, glancing at the twins. "I think I've had enough excitement for one day. I hope your next call is because you're bringing milkshakes over."

"Or because she's bringing me blueberry muffins," Honor said, smiling big. "Those are my favorite."

I chuckled. "A milkshake sounds amazing, but what I could really use is a cup of tea. I don't even know the last time I had a cup."

"I thought you were at Perk & Petal earlier?" Piper asked, pulling out her phone. "You sent a text. . ."

The day's events came rushing back to me, and I felt a pit grow in my stomach. The urgency of saving Marcel had consumed every part of me once I'd heard, but now . . .

My lips parted and my breath stuttered.

"What's that look for?" Piper said, her tone flattening, knowing damn well I didn't have good news.

"The Morrigan isn't pretending to be Sasha anymore. She knows that we know." I told them everything that happened. Every word that had been exchanged. Lucifer and August had come out of the bedroom, arms crossed and posture stiff.

Piper groaned, and Señora Rosara stepped forward, grave concern etched in the lines around her eyes. "Is Katherine still alive?"

I shrugged, rubbing my arms as a chill crept over me. "I think so. Otherwise she would have tried to take me, right?"

"I can't presume to think the way she does," Señora answered, glancing at August and Lucifer. "Nathalie will need your help before this is all over."

What felt like guilt began to crawl over my skin while I attempted to avoid contact with everyone in the room. I could feel Lucifer's gaze practically burning a hole in me. As much as he knew, there was still one detail none of them were privy to, except Ronan.

"Where's Sienna?" Piper asked in a panic, looking at her mate with wide eyes.

I felt horrible that I hadn't questioned it yet. "Check my phone," I said, pointing at it on the counter where I'd dumped my things earlier. "Not-Sasha would have told me if she'd killed her, just to watch me suffer."

Piper quickly grabbed it, scrolling and sighing in relief. "She's okay," she breathed. "You have a ton of missed messages and calls from her after she couldn't find Sasha."

"Get her to safety. The Morrigan kills when she feels like it, with or without reason. She's playing a game with Nathalie now, and everyone will be a target," Señora said, before turning to Piper and Ronan. "It's time to take the children somewhere they can't be found."

Piper walked to the kids, taking their hands, and preparing to leave through the light realm. "Ronan, get Sienna and bring her. She needs to be with Hallie. I'll meet you at home."

Glancing at Ronan, I inclined my chin slightly, holding his gaze while he spoke in my head.

Get to her first, Nathalie. Don't make me kill you.

Just as Piper had, he seemingly disappeared into thin air.

"Now what?" August asked, leaning against the door frame.

"All we can do is wait," I answered, knowing he would hate that response.

"Wait for her to come after you?" He scoffed.

"That's all we can do." Señora Rosara shuffled toward the door.

"You have to be joking," he said in return.

She turned to look at him. "Katherine is in hiding. Morgan Le Fay is playing with Nathalie now, trying to mess with her head, and we have no way to track her. Do you have a better suggestion?"

August looked at me, his features hardening. "Come to my place. It's safer."

I smiled, walking toward him and cupping his face in my hand. "It's not." I stood on my tiptoes, pressing a gentle kiss to his lips. "She'll find me wherever I go. I can't hide from her. Right now, Marcel needs rest, and I'm going to watch over him."

"Then I'll stay here." He leaned down, pressing his forehead to mine.

"Go feed Estrid. I know she's clawing your favorite chair right now for missing lunch." I smiled, but I knew it didn't reach my eyes. "I'll be okay. I need some time with him . . . you understand . . . he's going to wake up and have a lot of questions. I just . . . need to be alone with him for a while. Maybe Lucifer can come with you?"

"Wait, what?" Lucifer said, tensing immediately.

They spent a moment staring at each other. Sizing up the other. I could feel the testosterone radiating between them.

August contemplated what I'd suggested in silence before he lowered his eyes, exhaling in resignation. "Of course he can. If that's what you need, then it's done."

He held my chin between his forefinger and thumb, tilting me up to envelope me in a kiss that sent electricity all the way to my toes.

My heart clenched tightly, not wanting him to go, but needing him to all the same. I prayed to whatever gods that existed that I would see him again.

He tilted his head toward the door, addressing Lucifer. "I'll give you a minute and wait downstairs."

After he and Señora left, I stood for a while, staring at

the spot where he'd just been standing. Lucifer came behind me and wrapped his arms around my waist, burying his face in my hair. I turned, and he watched me closely, suspicion in his eyes.

"Sending me off with the incubus? I know he babysat Marcel, but I can assure you, I don't need to be watched over."

"I need the two of you to get along. Get to know him."

He huffed through his nose mockingly. "I'd rather not."

I sighed, twisting my lips to the side as I frowned. "For me, Luci. Do it for me."

"You drive a hard bargain, little witch." Lucifer rubbed small, gently circles into my lower back as he held me.

I chuckled half-heartedly. "I didn't say anything about a bargain."

"Everything is a bargain," he said, lowering his voice to the edge of seduction but stopping short. Almost as if he were teasing.

"Cute," I said flatly. "But no bargain. Just . . . me asking you for some time with him." I glanced away briefly, my eyes catching the sigil left in the middle of the room. I'd clean that up later. As much as I liked a clean home, it wasn't at the top of my priority list.

"You seem intent on sending August and me away. Anything else happen?" he asked, examining every inch of my features as I formed my response.

"Isn't Morgan Le Fay's coming out enough? I don't need anything else to happen for at least twenty-four hours." I tried to stifle a yawn but failed. I could feel my eyes glazing over. "It's not sending you away either. Stay in the guest room if you insist. I don't have the energy to make you go."

He hummed, kissing my forehead. "I can't stay away long, but I'll go with him for a while."

"Can't stay away, or won't?" I asked, raising a single brow.

"Same difference."

I couldn't help but smile. Of course he didn't want to be there. Marcel was in my bed, and that was where he always wanted to be. "Thank you," I said, patting his chest and stepping away from his embrace. "That means a lot to me, you learning to give me space when I ask for it."

As I walked away toward my bedroom, a sense of dread formed in my gut. Marcel was recovering and that was the best news of the day. It didn't stop the weight of the world from sitting on my shoulders.

I feared what would come next.

I feared I didn't have twenty-four hours.

I feared that no matter what I did, I would fail.

My breath stuttered slightly, and I shook it off. As I closed the door, I looked up, Lucifer and I locked eyes, and he held my gaze until the door clicked shut.

He whispered so quietly, I barely heard him. "I'd hate to think there's something you aren't telling me, little witch."

Guilt was Piper's shtick, but I was apparently not immune. Mine was just a different kind. The more you kept secrets from the people you loved, the more that guilt began to fester and build, slowly devouring you.

I was being served up on a silver platter, and it was my own doing.

22

NATHALIE

Surreal dreams with faceless enemies filled my sleep. I tossed and turned, never feeling that I truly rested. Death. Destruction. The Morrigan hurting those I loved. It was too much. With a sharp inhale, my eyes flew open.

"Hey, you," Marcel whispered, and my stomach fluttered hearing his voice so strong and healthy. He was pressed against me, propped up on his elbow, his cheek cradled in his hand.

"Hey," I whispered, turning to my side. "When did you wake up?"

"About an hour ago."

"Why didn't you wake me up?"

"I wanted to watch you sleep."

"How do you feel?" I asked, brushing a tendril of hair away from his face.

"Alive." He smiled. "What happened?"

I sat up, letting the sheets pool around my waist as I scrubbed my hands down my face. "August found you on the floor. I guess Estrid was getting shouty at your door, and she doesn't usually do that. Tipped him off something was wrong."

He laid back, crossing his hands under his head. "So I have a cat to thank for saving my life. That's interesting."

I huffed a small laugh. "You have a lot of people to thank, actually. Estrid tipped off August, he brought you to Señora Rosara's and then called me . . ."

He glanced at me, waiting for me to finish. I hadn't thought about how to tell him everything. He shouldn't care. He was alive, and that was the outcome we wanted. Still, everything I did, I did without his consent.

"That sounds like two people," he said, breaking the silence. "Well, one person and his cat—and honestly, Estrid is significantly better company."

I picked at my nails. "You're immortal now," I blurted out, ripping off the band-aid instead of finding a smoother way to go about it.

He sat up. "Come again?"

"I, uh, I used someone else's power to change . . . you."

"Change me?" He blinked, trying to process what I had said. He ran his tongue over his teeth, looking for fangs. "What the hell am I?"

"You're still the same, actually," I began, taking a deep breath before dropping the big reveal. "I had to bond you to an immortal to keep you on this plane. You're the first of your kind, actually. An immortal warlock."

"Gods, I'm not bonded to August, am I?" A crease

formed between his brows as he scrunched his face at the possibility.

"No—"

"Thank fuck. That would be the worst."

My lips parted as I tried to speak, but I closed them and cringed. "Um . . ."

"Nathalie, who am I bonded to?

"Lucifer."

His mouth fell open. "What? The devil? I'm bonded to the fucking devil? Why him, of all people?"

"Look, the moment was a little tense, okay? You were trying to die, I couldn't tie you to me, and he offered. I didn't think too much about whether or not you'd like it, but I figured you would like *not dying*, so I used the objects of fate to detach you from mortality and bound you to him." I crossed my arms, holding my chin out.

He pinched the bridge of his nose as though he were fighting off a headache. "I think I'd prefer August. Or the cat."

"Well, you were on the cusp on death, so I didn't have time to ask your thoughts on the matter, and either way, Estrid wasn't available, I'm afraid," I said defensively. "And you're welcome, by the way, since you have yet to say thank you, you asshole."

"I . . ." He sighed and his face fell as he realized how he was acting. "You're right. It's just a lot to take in at the moment. The last thing I remember was feeling cold. I got up to get a blanket, and then I must have passed out. I woke up feeling healthy, and not knowing what happened. I'm alive because of you—and others—so for that, thank you."

I softened, knowing my defensiveness wasn't warranted. It was a lot to process. I knew it would be. Finding out you're alive and immortal is one thing. It's another thing entirely to learn you're bound to the devil for eternity.

"The death magic is still in you, though. We still haven't found a way to stop it. The only difference is your body will be able to fight against it since you can't die now. I think you'll experience some symptoms still, like needing more rest, but I don't know. This is all so new, so no one knows. It makes sense in my head. Piper is an immortal badass, but twins on an opposite sleep schedule still exhausts her. I would think it works the same here. The body can still get tired."

"What about you?" he asked, running his fingers through my hair.

I tilted my head, confused. "What about me?"

"You aren't . . . immortal, sunbeam." He grazed his thumb across my cheek tenderly. "I'm not living in this world without you in it."

Emotions clogged my throat. "Well, I wasn't going to live in a world without you, so I understand."

"I'm here now," I whispered. "And I'm not letting you go." I leaned into him, our foreheads connected, our breaths mingling as we both tried to work through the emotions lingering in the air. He lifted my head by my chin and brushed his lips against mine.

The kiss was gentle as we explored each other,

savoring and soaking it all in. Marcel cupped the back of my head, and I couldn't help but notice how much more strength there was to his hold. Compared to the last time I'd kissed him, his hands were steady, his body warm and inviting.

"I never stopped loving you, sunbeam," he murmured, his mouth so close to mine. "It's always been you."

I pulled away slightly, my eyes skimming over him, truly taking him in. He looked how he was supposed to. His skin had a healthy glow, and his body was filled out rather than the gaunt frame he'd been struggling to hide. He looked even better than the glamour he once wore and not an ounce of magic cracked through the surface. "I know," I breathed, nodding my head in short, tight bobs. "I thought I'd lost you. You almost broke your promise to me, Marcel. You almost left."

"I held on with everything I had." He pressed his lips to mine again, but the kiss quickly deepened, the desperation and relief we both felt fueling the sudden intensity.

He responded to my heat immediately, his fingers threading through my hair and gripping just tight enough to send a thrill through my body. His free hand moved down, grabbing at my waist and pulling me closer. Never pulling my lips from his, I rose onto my knees, swinging a leg over him until I straddled his lap, my hands tangling in his hair as the kiss grew more passionate. His heart beat against my chest, a steady reminder that he was alive and here with me.

"Gods, I want you," he murmured against my lips, his voice filled with a mix of need and love.

"Then take me," I whispered back, my hands slipping under his shirt, feeling the warmth of his skin beneath my fingertips.

He didn't make me beg as his big hands slid under my shirt, his touch sending shivers down my spine. He lifted the fabric, and we broke the kiss only long enough for him to pull it over my head, discarding it to the floor. When he saw I'd been in nothing but a t-shirt and underwear, he gave me a smirk of approval, admiring my body. I ripped his shirt as I pulled it off, needing to feel the skin-to-skin contact. Needing the warmth of him to seep into my very bones.

Marcel's lips moved from my mouth, trailing along my jaw and down my neck, leaving a path of fire in their wake. He latched immediately onto my pebbled nipples, and I gasped, arching into him. He sucked and nipped, the warm wetness of his mouth teasing my sensitive skin.

I moaned, and my hands started moving with urgency, fumbling at his pants. I needed him, all of him, *right now*. My movements were far from smooth, leaning heavily into desperation, but I didn't care. Marcel didn't even seem to notice, his mouth still on my breasts, his tongue teasing me.

Raising myself off him, I shimmied his pants down. His cock was freed, hard and jutting towards his chiseled abdomen. I leaned back, forcing Marcel to break contact with me, as I fisted him, stroking him as my thumb rubbed his own arousal over the length of him. Locking my eyes with his, he reached between my legs, ripping the fabric of my delicate underwear to shreds, exposing me fully. I positioned myself over him, and his hands went back to my waist, guiding me down, a groan escaping his lips as I slid down him, inch by inch. I moaned, deep and guttural as I stretched around him.

"Fuck," he breathed, his voice rough with emotion. "You feel so damn good."

The connection was electric and the moment my body began to grind against him, I felt tension coiling in my core. Marcel gripped my hips, his brown eyes locked onto mine, filled with something headier than desire and softer than adoration.

My head tilted back as he began moving, his hips matching my rhythm, thrust for thrust. A hand strayed up my body, tweaking a nipple on its way and coming to clench around my throat. A twitch fluttered through my pussy, coating him in more wetness, and he grinned.

"You still like that," he growled, digging his fingers into my hips as I clenched around him. He used his hold to pull me forward just a bit, but the change of angle almost did me in as the tip of him hit over and over and over in just the right spot inside of me.

"I love what you can do to me," I whispered, my own voice barely more than a breath as my body moved over top of his. My fingernails dug into the skin of his chest.

"You've always been mine," he said between breaths. He talked through every thrust of his hips, telling me how pretty I looked around him, how much he missed being able to take me the way he liked, how good I felt. His words ignited my insides and my movements became faster, his jerkier, and both of us more frantic as every pump drove us higher and higher. I felt the edge approaching, my body dangling over the precipice of pleasure as a whirlwind of sensations built within me. Marcel's hands guided me, his touch grounding me even as I felt myself slipping over the edge.

My eyes started to close as my head fell back, but he wouldn't let me get away that easily.

"Eyes on me, sunbeam," he forced out through gritted teeth. "I want to look at you while you come on my cock."

My eyes snapped open, locking on his as his free hand moved between us to find my clit. The instant electricity I felt with a few quick circles was bliss. It only took moments of the combination before I let out a scream, pleasure pulsing through me while I came.

With a feral grin, his upward thrusts became punishing, bringing me close to the edge once more.

"Are you going to come again, sunbeam?" he asked, angling his hips and hitting me deeper inside. I gasped, trying to swallow, feeling my throat bob against the pressure of his hand.

"Yes," I breathed, trying to get the friction against my clit.

"Tell me to make you come," he said, his voice becoming shaky. He was close. I was close.

"Fuck me harder, Marcel," I ground out. "Make . . . me . . . come."

He growled, slamming into me faster. Harder. Deeper. As my brows pinched together and my lips parted, he squeezed around my neck, cutting off my air.

The tension built.

Seconds passed.

The lack of air was sending me into a spiral of ecstasy.

Each sensation inside me intensified.

Every electric touch sent jolts through my body.

I fluttered around him, my inner walls clenching him tight as my orgasm spasmed uncontrollably. My eyes rolled as I came so hard I almost passed out. When he released my throat, stars exploded with the onset of air. A tidal wave rushed through, coating him beneath me as I cried out. He let out a low, deep groan when he pulled my hips down hard and thrusted up, bottoming out and emptying inside of me.

Aftershocks rolled through me, and I fell forward, exhausted, and intensely happy. My head nestled into the crook of his neck. His heartbeat was fast and strong. Healthy.

"I've waited so long," Marcel said softly, splaying a hand on my back and caressing the skin. I hummed, not having the energy to form words. "All I ever wanted was a future with you."

"I'm here now," I whispered, mirroring the sentiment he'd shared with me earlier.

The beauty of the moment stalled, but I didn't want to let him know. There wasn't time for me to think about the future. I didn't know if I was going to survive another day.

Living in the moment was all I had, and I wanted to give myself to him without that hanging in the balance. We'd finally stopped the sand in his hourglass, but a new hourglass had been turned, and this one affected everyone I loved. I would do anything to protect them.

Only I could shatter the glass before time ran out.

I just didn't know how.

23

NATHALIE

Fucking dreams.

You'd think after mind-blowing orgasms, you'd sleep soundly. Apparently not.

Too many times I'd startled myself awake, my hand clutching my chest and feeling my pounding heart while my breath came in ragged gasps and sweat coated my body.

Each time, Marcel woke with a jolt, pulling me back into his arms and lulling me back to sleep with his warm embrace.

Visions of raging fire and fields of glass. Wolves and ravens attempting to shred each other to pieces as they fought. Everyone I loved standing on the other side of a dark, bottomless canyon while I helplessly watched The Morrigan destroy them.

"Marcel?" I whispered softly, checking to see if he'd stir. The gentle rhythm of his breathing was my only answer.

Good. I felt bad enough waking him up so much. He'd always been a deep sleeper, but someone thrashing next to you was hard to ignore.

A glance at the clock told me it was nearly three in the morning. If my anxiety refused to let me sleep, so be it. I slipped out of bed, deciding that tea and a comfy blanket in my reading chair might be what I needed. Grabbing sweatpants and an oversized sweater, I pulled them on quickly and left, shutting the door softly behind me. The floorboards creaked under my feet as I made my way to the kitchen.

The familiar routine of making tea helped to steady my racing thoughts. As the kettle heated up, I leaned against the counter, staring out the window into the dimly lit, sleeping city.

My sister was still out there somewhere. So was Morgan Le Fay. Katherine was biding her time, staying hidden. She was good at it, thankfully. My hope was that bought me a few more days. For someone who had been in control for so long, it was terrifying to know how much of this wasn't in my hands, but I wouldn't let fear paralyze me. The fact I wasn't in control pissed me off as well. This was my city. My family. If I was going to let an emotion drive me, I'd choose the latter.

The kettle whistled, pulling me from my thoughts. I poured the hot water over the tea leaves, watching as the steam curled into the air. The scent of jasmine filled the kitchen, soothing and familiar. I wrapped my hands around the mug, letting the heat seep into my skin.

Tea in hand, I walked around the sigil and headed to

my den. The French doors creaked lightly as they swung open. The smell of books mingled with the scent of jasmine, and I felt at ease.

"Maybe I can sleep sitting up," I said aloud to no one but myself. Even if it were a small cat nap, if it was dreamless, I'd take it.

I audibly sighed in relief as the comfort of the chair held me. *Mindset,* I told myself. *You can sleep. Safely. You can rest."*

My body relaxed. The tea had worked its magic, and I was in my favorite spot. As I began to drift . . .

Tap, tap.

I cracked an eye open, looking around to see if Marcel had come in, but no one was there. I paused, straining to hear it again, but no other sound came.

The moment I closed my eyes, it happened again.

Tap! Tap! Tap!

"What in the Edgar Allen Poe nightmare is this?" I grumbled, standing up and walking into the living room.

Tap! Tap!

It was coming from the window. I caught a glimpse of what was making that sound and at first my heart jumped in my throat.

"A fucking raven? Are you kidding me? This really is some Poe shit," I whispered, taking a closer look as I took slow, hesitant steps toward it.

It continued to hover in the same spot, flapping its wings. The bird cocked its head, watching me with intelligent eyes before it lifted its body slightly, showing me its legs. A small, rolled piece of paper tied to it.

I blew out a breath, steeling myself before I opened the window, and it landed on the ledge. Holding its leg out for me, I reached toward it slowly so I could untie the parchment.

I couldn't help but feel a shiver run down my spine as I touched the cool, smooth feathers. "You really are something," I whispered to it, wondering if it understood me. Part of me waited for it to say "Nevermore" in response. I might have fainted if it had.

Instead, after I'd relieved of its message, the raven gave a soft caw and flew off into the night. I watched it for a long moment before turning my eyes back to the small slip of paper, unrolling it to reveal a short script.

Rooftop.

~K

I immediately recognized the scrawled handwriting and breathed a sigh of relief. Katherine was here. She was still okay.

I almost yelled for Marcel but stopped myself. They were still technically married, and that was weird, wasn't it? I needed to see her alone, and not invite whatever tense reunion that would occur if I brought him with me.

I left the note on the kitchen counter and grabbed some boots and a jacket by the door. The night air would be chilly enough simply for this time of year. Add the New Chicago wind while standing on a rooftop? No thanks.

Leaving the apartment was easier when your houseguest didn't have supernatural hearing. Marcel might have been immortal now, but he was still a warlock. Lucifer would have already been glued to my side, refusing to leave. I made my way up the stairs to the rooftop, my mind racing with what new my sister had. We had a lot to talk about, and knowing Katherine, she was going to be vague and disappear as quickly as she'd arrived.

When I finally pushed on the thick metal door leading to the building's roof, it screeched as it opened, and the cool night air hit me, bringing with it the faint sounds of the city around us.

As I rounded a corner, Katherine came into view, standing near the edge, her silhouette framed against the night sky, dramatic as always.

"Fancy way to get my attention," I called out, my voice echoing slightly in the night air. "I—"

My words broke off and I froze as she turned to me.

Katherine wasn't alone. She was gripping Sasha's lifeless body by her hair. In her other hand, a blade, gleaming in the moonlight.

My heart pounded in my ears. A grin stretched across Katherine's face, vicious and unsettling. It was like looking at my own reflection twisted into something sinister. I didn't get closer, knowing it was safer to keep a good distance between us. Panicking would get me nowhere, but fucking hell did I want to panic.

"Hello, Nathalie." She cocked her head, looking behind me and then giving a tut of disappointment. "Didn't bring Marcel, I see? That's a shame."

My heart skipped a beat. She had known we saved

him. She knew I was with him, and that meant she knew no one else was here.

The Nats of the loci were still, but fear and anger radiated from them in waves.

"It didn't take you long," I said, attempting to keep my voice calm. "I saw you, what, fifteen hours ago? How long before you found my sister?"

The Morrigan chuckled, smirking at me while she did. "Katherine isn't as smart as she thinks she is. She's been shadowing you once a day. Probably to check in on her dear sister. Isn't that sweet? All I had to do was wait."

"Couldn't have waited a little longer?" I asked, my voice dripping with sarcasm. "I was trying to sleep."

"What's the saying? There's no rest for the wicked?"

I scoffed. "Lame. Getting slower in your old age, Morgan. You can do better than that."

"*Why are you taunting her?*" Peace whispered from the loci, her body shaking.

"*It keeps her talking,*" The Warden said, shushing everyone by gesturing her hands.

The Morrigan sneered. If there was one thing I knew about her, it was that she was as vain as she was power-hungry. "My, my. Filled with unearned confidence, aren't you, Nathalie?"

I shrugged, but the entire time I feigned noncha-lance, my mind raced. "Oh, no. I think I've earned my confidence," I said, placing my hand behind my back.

The Morrigan laughed, the sound eerie and wrong coming from my sister's mouth. "Do you think Marcel will know it's not you?"

My attempts to focus halted the moment she said his name. I tried to school my features, but I knew she'd seen me slip.

"Or Lucifer, even," she said with a salacious smile. "Oh, that will be a fun victory."

"I doubt it," I said, clenching my teeth.

"That's your flaw, Nathalie," she began, giving me a look of pity. "You doubt too much. You never *see* the possibilities for what they are. Did you doubt it would ever come to this? I bet you did."

In the time it took me to understand what was happening, she swiftly dragged the knife across Sasha's throat. A curtain of crimson poured out, and Sasha's blank green eyes rolled into the back of her head. The Morrigan shoved the lifeless body forward, letting it fall with an unceremonious thud. A scream tore from my lips as Sasha's head smacked against the concrete with a sickening crack. Her soul was lost, forever disconnected from her body. My breaths came in ragged gasps as my brain spiraled. My memory loci was a mess of chaos.

"What's the plan here, Morgan?" I asked, my voice trembling with barely contained fury. "Take over my body and rule the world? You've been making babies and killing your own family for centuries now, and you're still at it. Really playing the long game here, huh?"

The Morrigan scoffed. "Witchcraft and magic are about power, Nathalie. We're better than every super-natural out there, yet the gods didn't give us immortality. Fuck the gods. I found my own. I can control life and death. I can create my immortality."

"Guess that's the constant wrench in your plan, isn't it? Witches have an expiration date. Must be exhausting jumping from body to body."

It was incredibly hard to use the Eye to search through threads while seemingly keeping my focus on the enemy in front of me. One wrong move and she would suspect something else was happening. Thousands of threads. Millions. I just had to find one.

The Morrigan tilted Katherine's head, a mockingly thoughtful expression on her face. "Just as I said. You just don't see the possibilities." She smiled, baring her teeth. "When I take over your body, I'm going to fuck that delicious incubus of yours. Complete that aurae bond you've been denying yourself, annoyingly I might add."

My stomach roiled. There it was. Her key to immortality. My body. My chaos magic. My aurae bond with August.

A humorless laugh bubbled up. "He'd never fuck you, Morgan. He'd know it wasn't me. Surely you aren't that stupid."

She glared at me, something sparking in her eyes. "He doesn't have to be willing, Nathalie. Surely you aren't that stupidly innocent. He can barely hold the aurae bond back. His desire to feed will override everything. He's putty in my hands. Or your hands, really."

Bile rose. Anger flared. The Nats of the loci tried to calm me down, reminding me to focus. I had to get her to stop talking about him. It made me vulnerable. "Honestly, I have to admit, I thought you were going to have

Sasha kill Kat so you could just skip over her entirely and come to me."

She walked around, light on her feet, not a care in the world. She didn't suspect danger. She thought she was in control. "Again, without seeing the possibilities, Nathalie. It's a wonder you're a Le Fay. Of course I could do that. But where's the fun? This way, you get to watch poor Sasha here die." She kicked my friend's lifeless body with her boot and Sasha's head lolled to the side. A flood of anger washed through me. The Morrigan knew her taunting had worked. She met my eyes, relishing her small victory. "She saw me in the veil, you know. Remember when I came out and told you something was hunting in there? It was me, naturally, but she knew. Oh, and she was so close to your lure. So close to getting back to her body." She looked down at Sasha and pouted, flicking her boot against Sasha's feline ears. "Alas. I got there first. A for effort, though, eh, kitty cat?"

"Fair enough," I said, playing along and trying to swallow the emotions. "You fooled me. Still. We both know you aren't going to kill Kat," I said, tilting my head and raising a brow. "You can't."

She shrugged, flicking the blade to the side and spattering droplets of blood on the floor. "I don't need to. Your friends will do that for me."

I barked a laugh. "Okay, you're crazy, we can both agree on that, but this one takes the cake."

"You don't have the power to fight me." Anger flashed in her eyes. "All it's gonna take is one of your friends, one of your *lovers* to see Kat hurting you.

Standing over your unconscious body. They won't think twice to save their precious Nat." She chuckled, skipping around Sasha's body while I kept myself angled away from her. "You don't think that my power, my magic, is stronger than yours? Please. I've spent lifetimes perfecting chaos magic. You're just a baby. You have no idea how much power you hold, or how to use it. And you never will."

"My friends aren't going to kill my sister."

The thread came into view. An eerie, sickly-looking strand warped, but strong. It pulsed with a sinister energy, intwining itself between Kat and The Morrigan.

She gave me a sardonic smile. "Why not? If you thought I would take Sasha's body to kill Kat and then take you, I'm guessing you shared that same little tidbit with all of your friends. They'll kill her without a second thought. And you know why? Because she's always been a villain. No one trusted her. But they'll trust their eyes the moment they see you in harm's way."

My lips parted as my breath stuttered. She was absolutely right that would happen.

"Focus! The shears! Get the fucking shears!" Bad Nat shouted.

The Morrigan carried on, unaware. "And better yet. You didn't tell anyone you were coming to see me. Did you? I'm willing to bet you didn't share that note with anyone. No one knows you're here with her. Tsk-tsk. Always trying to jump in and save the world on your own."

I glared at her, trying to clear my mind and focus on one thing.

The shears.

It was becoming seamless. Finding the right threads was harder than calling the objects into my possession. Heavy, cold scissors materialized into my hand.

"Cut it," The Warden yelled from the loci.

"Her thread could tie to yours quickly afterward. Cut it as soon as it starts to weave around yours," Ann said firmly.

Then what?

"Fight like hell," Bad Nat said through gritted teeth.

"You have a flaw too, you know. Quite similar to mine."

Morgan raised eyebrow in genuine surprise while she giggled, almost childlike. "And what's that?"

"You don't see all the possibilities either."

I pulled the shears from behind my back. Holding them in my right hand as my left hand reached forward and grabbed a thread that now stood out against all others. Pulling the thread that bound her to Katherine, I slid it between the shears, swiftly closing them tight.

The Morrigan's eyes widened as an explosion of gold flashed, blinding me for a moment. As the two strands unraveled. I tried to grasp the strand connected to Morgan Le Fay, but it snaked and slithered, sliding off of Kat's in a flurry. I couldn't grasp it between my fingers.

For a moment, Morgan Le Fay stood still, frozen as her line disconnected from Kat. Where her psyche went, I didn't know. When Kat's eyes rolled into the back of her head, her body dropped to the floor.

It happened. Everything, everywhere, at all once. The Morrigan's loose thread whipped around until a new thread emerged, and it pulsed, spiraling around a new strand.

Mine.

A shock reverberated through my body.

"Get rid of the shears!" Ann shouted, and I had enough wherewithal to will them away. They disappeared as quickly as they'd come.

The soul tie choked my thread, suffocating it and my sense of self along with it. A cold current rushed through my veins.

"Gods," Bad Nat breathed, and for the first time, I heard fear in her voice.

"It's happening," The Warden said.

"What do we do?" Peace asked, her voice shaky.

"Hide," Caretaker and I said at the same time.

I managed to call out to one person before darkness enveloped me. I knew he'd hear it.

"Ronan . . ."

<h1 style="text-align:center">24</h1>

LUCIFER

Never did I think I'd find myself drinking with another man that shared my little witch's heart. We'd sat in silence, staring at each other.

"Well, I don't like this much."

August barked out a laugh and held out a glass. "Nat will be pleased we can agree on something."

"We agree that Marcel is baggage," I said, sipping the liquor slowly.

August nodded. "Not untrue," he began, "but I'm fairly certain that's not something we should share with her. Also? Doesn't matter. Nat loves him." He side-eyed his cat, who had curled herself up in a chair. "So does Estrid, who is generally a good judge of character, but we'll see if she's lost her touch."

"At least you aren't bonded to him," I muttered.

"That was all you, my friend." He raised his brows, gesturing his hand in my direction. "And not a bad move in Nat's eyes. All the same. You saved him, and you weren't wrong about a piece of her dying with him."

"I'm aware I was right."

"That's not how I phrased it. I said you weren't wrong," he said in a flat tone.

"You don't like me," I stated plainly, taking a long sip and feeling the delicious burn. Not that whiskey would do much for me, but it gave me something to do instead of thinking about my little witch in bed with Marcel.

"What tipped you off?" he asked sarcastically. When I didn't answer, he sighed. "What's to like, Lucifer? You ruined this city. I know who you are and what you've done. I know how you are." He quieted a moment, contemplating if he was going to speak again when he opened his mouth and then shut it again. After some thought, he finally added, "I also know you're Nat's familiar. I also know that you saved someone she loved, and oddly enough, not for your gain—which might be the first time you considered someone outside of yourself. I'm not sure if you're clued in to how relationships work, but we call that 'growth.' Look it up sometime."

"How old are you?" I asked, flicking off a piece of imaginary lint from my trousers.

"Are you attempting to play the elder card here?"

I hummed noncommittally. "I'm nine thousand years old, August. I'm guessing you aren't quite up there yet." He shook his head while watching me with slightly narrowed eyes. "Mmm. It's a long time. I've been a possessive demon the entire time. I don't have to like you to make this work. It might take a while for me to get used to sharing what's mine."

"Ours."

"If she accepts your aurae bond," I said, smirking. August twisted his lips.

"You know, you and Marcel both have something in common too." He waited a beat as I looked at him in question. "You're both assholes who think they know what Nat wants."

"I suppose only you know what she wants, incubus?"

He shrugged. "I do because I ask her. That's called 'communication.' You can look that one up too."

While he was insulting me, he was also correct. I would never admit such a thing to the likes of him, but his connection with Nathalie was strong, and it was likely due to his ... *communication*. She may not have realized it yet, but she was going to accept the aurae bond. I saw the look in her eyes when she was with him. What he made her feel. I saw how she lost herself in him when they fucked. Each and every time they were near each other, there was an electric current in the air.

And I hated the bastard for it.

"So where does that leave us?" I asked, cocking my head and raising my brows. I gestured and him and then myself. "You hate me for what I was, I hate you because you take Nathalie away from me, and I don't like sharing."

August leaned back, crossing his leg and rested his ankle at his knee. "For some reason completely unknown to me, Nat loves you. You are also what she wants. She sees something in you that I don't. Not yet, anyway." He inhaled, long and deep before exhaling. "Ultimately, that's good enough for me."

I stared in shock, blinking a few times to process what he'd said. "Are you proposing a truce?"

"Sure," he said, crossing his arms and lifting a shoulder. "Jealousy will run rampant, but life will be easier if the four of us get along. And if that makes her happy . . . The kid has a lot of work to do, so the best I can do is tolerate his presence. I've had some practice since he moved in." He looked down the hall, a frown forming between his brows. "Which reminds me . . . now that he's alive and well, he needs to move the hell out."

I laughed, then quickly realized that meant Baggage would be moving in with me. When August saw my face, he grinned. "Hmm. Maybe we should find him somewhere else to live. Away from me. And you, of course."

"I'm happy to pay for the apartment.," August said.

I nodded. "I'm more than content to find one for him, with Nathalie being so busy."

"*Far* away from her apartment, naturally."

"Naturally." I waved my hand in agreement.

A brief moment passed between after we spoke back and forth. A shared understanding.

"Why, Lucifer," August said smoothly, with a hint of humor in his voice. "Did we just become friends?"

My laugh was cut off when a sudden, overwhelming wave of fear crashed through me. I clutched my chest as it threatened to take the air from my lungs. The intensity bowed my body back first, then I doubled over. In the next instant, there was nothing—no fear, no emotions at all. Just a terrifying void.

August flew off the couch, his glass falling to the floor and spilling the amber liquid. "What's wrong with her?"

I met his eyes, wild with anxiety and dread, likely mirroring my own. I didn't waste time explaining. Lunging forward, I grabbed August by the arm and pulled him with me through the veil. The transition was seamless, a blur of light and energy, and we appeared in Nathalie's living room. August stumbled forward, before righting himself.

"Jesus-fuck, I feel like I just died," he coughed out.

"Nathalie!" I shouted. August reoriented swiftly, calling for her just after I did.

Panic fueled my movements as I ran towards her bedroom door, my mind racing with possibilities. August ran down the hall to search the other rooms. Bursting into the bedroom, the door smacked against the wall and bounced back violently. Marcel was pulling on pants while he looked around, confused.

"Where is she?" I demanded, my voice tinged with fear. "Where's Nathalie?"

"I don't know! She was right here—" he cut off as he looked at the empty space next to him, then seeing the bathroom light off with the door open. "Fuck! We went to sleep, and she was in bed with me. I never felt her leave."

"I felt her emotions," I explained quickly, turning around to exit the room and find something that could tell me where she went. "She was terrified, and then there was nothing. Fucking nothing! We need to find her *now*."

"Her car keys are still here," August growled, taking them off the hook and throwing them against the wall.

"So is her phone," Marcel said, holding it as he came out the bedroom. His eyes darkened. "I can scry for her with my magic. I just need her hair."

He immediately headed for the bathroom, but I paid him and August no attention as my eyes focused on the deadbolt on the front door. Unlocked. The bomb Piper had placed was deactivated. She was here. In the building.

Scanning the room, I saw a furled piece of paper that looked out of place. Parchment. I picked it up, taking in the message.

Rooftop.

~K

Without a word to the other two, I tossed the note back on the counter and pulled myself through the veil.

The scene that greeted me stole my breath away.

Sasha's lifeless body lay on the ground, a massive pool of blood spreading around her. A clean line across her throat.

Katherine was cradling an unconscious Nathalie, her face a mask of worry and guilt. Rage flared up inside me, burning and uncontrollable. I disappeared and reappeared several feet ahead, grabbing the twin by the throat and lifting her off the ground. Her panic flared as she gurgled, trying to breathe. I brought her close to me, knowing an inferno blazed in my eyes as fury coursed through me.

"What did you do?" I snarled, my voice echoing across the rooftop. Kat's eyes widened in terror as she clawed at my hands, gasping for breath.

"It was The Morrigan!" she choked out. "Not me!"

"I saw the fucking note. You signed it." She slapped at my hands as her face turned red, her legs kicking wildly as I squeezed harder.

"I swear." Her words were strained and cut off with a strangled wheeze.

I let her drop to the ground, and she rolled to the side, forcefully inhaling and coughing, trying with desperation to fill her lungs with precious oxygen. I knelt beside her, glancing at Nathalie for a moment—laying prone, pale and fragile. My heart clenched painfully at the sight. I turned my gaze back to her twin, demanding answers.

"You have ten seconds to tell me what happened before I kill you—"

A metal door slammed against the wall and two sets of heavy footsteps sounded. Marcel and August finally made it onto the roof, their expressions a mix of the same horror and anger I felt.

"Kat, what the fuck?" Marcel bellowed as he came to kneel next to me, his hand immediately stroking Nathalie's hair out of her face and feeling for a pulse. "What the fuck did you do?"

"For gods' sakes, I didn't do anything," Katherine

said through a cough, her face contorting. "The Morrigan took over my body."

"Explain. Now," I growled through clenched teeth.

Katherine struggled to catch her breath, bent over at the waist, her hands on her knees, before she started speaking. "I was in my hideout, a small apartment no one was supposed to know about. Someone knocked at the door, and when I opened it, Sasha was there. She grabbed my face, and everything went black. When I came to, I was conscious but trapped inside myself, like I was in the backseat of my own body."

"How did you end up here?" August asked, standing over Kat and shaking with unbridled rage.

"The Morrigan set the trap for Nathalie, but I couldn't do anything to stop her, okay? Backseat. I literally watched it all happen, and there was nothing I could fucking do, you get it?"

I pointed to Sasha. "And this?"

Kat narrowed her eyes at me, even as they filled with tears, she glared at me just as angrily as I glared at her. "I didn't do anything, you delusional asshole! I wouldn't hurt my sister, and I have no reason to kill Sasha." She rubbed her throat, turning her head to stretch. Bruises were beginning to take shape on her delicate skin. "The Morrigan taunted Nathalie. Sliced her open knowing there was nothing Nat could do, then told her how she was going to fuck you for the immortal aurae bond," she said, pointing at August. She looked at me. "Said fucking you was going to be a victory." She waved her hand haphazardly. "Said you'd be the ones to kill me, thinking

I'd hurt my sister"—she gave us a dirty look—"seems like she was on the money with that part of her plan."

"How are you here now?" Marcel asked, extending a hand to Kat and pulling her up. I refrained from slapping him away until I had all my answers.

She shook her head. "I don't know. Nathalie did something I couldn't understand. Shears appeared out of thin air, and she cut the air. Nothing was there. Then she just collapsed as I felt The Morrigan leave my body."

August and I looked at each other, both understanding exactly what that meant. "She cut The Morrigan's thread to Kat," August said quietly.

"And it tied to hers," I finished.

"Fuck!" Marcel yelled, running his hand through his hair as he started pacing.

Katherine's brows shot up in surprise. "She found the objects of fate?"

"Wait," August said, holding his hand up for us to stop talking. "The Morrigan needs Kat to die before she can fully take over Natalie, right? We just need to keep Kat alive."

"Easier said than done," Marcel grumbled.

"You have no idea how many people want me dead," Kat said in agreement. "And even then, I'm still mortal."

Completely ignoring the other three, I gently lifted Nathalie's head onto my lap, my hands gripping either side of her head as I tried to concentrate. I'd never forced my way into her memory loci on purpose, but this was the perfect time to try.

I'd told her to escape into her loci. To find safety

there if this happened. I also warned her that The Morrigan could find her way there as well. For once, I hoped I was wrong. The space around me grew silent and I could feel the others watching me, their curiosity and concern palpable.

"What are you doing?" Marcel asked, his voice tight with anxiety.

"I'm trying to reach her mind," I replied, my eyes closed in concentration.

"You can do that?" August asked incredulously.

"It's weird. The familiar bond. I can connect with her mind." I measured my next words, balancing guarding Nathalie's privacy while still giving necessary information. "She organizes her thoughts in one space, with all her memories filed away. That has to be where she went. I'm going to try to push into her mind and see if I can find Nathalie and help her. Now shut up so I can focus."

I closed my eyes tighter and took a deep breath, pushing myself into the mental connection we shared. At first, nothing happened, and I started to fear that I couldn't find her loci on purpose. That I could only get there when it was pulling her, thereby calling out to me as well. But then, the familiar sensation of slipping into Nathalie's loci washed over me, and I felt myself slide into her mind.

But everything was wrong.

I stood outside of the house she'd built, where all her inner-Nats lived.

A scream rent the air, coming from inside, and I thundered up the porch steps. When I grabbed the doorknob, it jiggled but wouldn't turn. The metal began to burn, searing into my palm and burning my skin. I yanked it back and then banged on the door, throwing myself against it, but it wouldn't budge. It didn't crack. Nothing. The powers of an immortal demon couldn't even break it down. I couldn't make a dent.

"Nathalie!" I shouted, desperation seeping into my voice. I could hear voices and more screaming on the other side. I called her name, over and over while I kept trying to bust into the house. I called the other Nats, yelling for Peace or Ann—any of them—but there was no response.

A nauseating resignation took hold of me. There was nothing I could do. I pulled out of her mind, snapping back to reality and facing the others.

Three sets of expectant eyes held my gaze, waiting with bated breath.

"I can't reach her," I said, my voice hollow.

A familiar presence appeared, and the hair on the back of my neck stood on end.

"Ronan," I said flatly. "What are you doing here?"

His features held a darkness there that answered my question when he looked at Nat's prone body. Scanning each of us, he landed on Kat, and he narrowed his eyes. "You're alive."

Kat stood up, blocking her sister's body. As if she could protect her from The Harvester. "I am."

Ronan's gaze shifted between them, then to me. "You know why I'm here."

I sighed, feeling my insides clench. "She made a deal with you, didn't she?"

He nodded, the muscle in his jaw clenched.

"No." Marcel stepped forward, and August grabbed him by the collar, pulling him back.

"While I don't share his idiotic approach," I said, kneeling down by Nat, stroking her hair, "he's right. No."

"The Morrigan is in here, is she not?" he asked.

"She is, but Kat is alive. I'm assuming the deal you made included Katherine's death first?"

"It did."

"Then wait."

His brows lowered. "Until when?"

August stepped around Marcel, also blocking him from Nathalie. "We'll know if it's her when she wakes up. Lucifer is her familiar. He'll know. The aurae bond is almost solidified between us. There's a strong semblance of a bond connected between us already. I'll know."

"And you know what I have to do if it's not her." Ronan looked down at Nat, then back to me. "And anyone that tries to stop me."

"Where's Piper?" I asked.

"Don't make me kill you now," he growled.

August stepped between us slowly, turning to face Ronan. "Why did she make a deal with you?" My brother glared at August. "She came to you about this. And if you're here, she called out to you somehow when The Morrigan took her. So tell me what she said."

"I don't owe you any answers," he said.

"No, but you will have to answer to me," Piper said,

appearing behind him. A part of me smirked, but I schooled my features. Piper was pissed, and I was not stepping into that marital trap.

Ronan's eyes closed in frustration as his mate came around, kneeling beside her best friend. "Spit it out, Ronan. Tell me why you're here. Tell me why I didn't know about it."

He sighed, crossing his arms. "We agreed that if The Morrigan took her, I'd end it. She didn't want you to know because you'd try to stop it."

"You would kill my best friend to save me and the kids," Piper surmised. Her tone was resigned, but there was a pain behind it she couldn't hide.

"That's why I would do it, yes. Without question."

"And what was Nathalie's reason?" August prompted.

Ronan looked at each of us there—Piper, August, Marcel, Katherine, and me—"To save everyone she loves."

A piece of my heart began to fracture. I didn't know something could hurt like this. Nathalie kept this from me. Always trying to fight battles on her own. Always one foot in the door and one foot out. If she made it through this, we'd have to work on that communication thing August was going on about.

"I won't let you take her soul," I said, looking at my brother and knowing full well how this would all end if I got in his way.

"You know what will happen if you try to stop me."

I inclined my chin. "I do."

He shrugged. "So be it."

The physical pain I'd endured, the sacrificial exsanguination, losing my atma—none of it compared to the mere thought of her not existing in this world.

I'd like to think it wasn't a bad way to go, but I wasn't sure. I'd never had a harvester consume my soul.

If Nathalie didn't find a way to kill The Morrigan, I guessed I would find out soon enough.

25

NATHALIE

I LANDED FLAT ON MY BACK, THE FLOOR OF THE MEMORY LOCI rushing up to greet me. My head cracked against the hard surface. I blinked away at the spots in my vision, gingerly touching the back of my head.

The spot hurt.

I couldn't recall the last time anything hurt in the loci.

Ever.

Yet the back of my skull ached as if it had been bruised.

This wasn't good.

Above me, the Nats peered down. Well, two of them did; The Warden and Ann. A boot nudged my arm, drawing my attention to the side where Bad Nat sprawled. She sat with one leg bent at the knee and the other stretched out, nudging me. I blinked a couple times, taking it all in.

"What in the—"

A single finger pushed against my lips. The Warden.

"Nathalie, oh Nathalie," The Morrigan said my name in a sing-song voice. A crazed sort of mania bled into the syllables, carrying from somewhere else in the loci. We were in the library with the chairs wedged beneath the doors to barre her from entry. Peace and Caretaker were nowhere to be found. "Where are we, *little witch*?" She used Lucifer's nickname in the most mocking of tones, making sharp indignation fire through me. "Did you build a place in your mind? How quaint."

I breathed in through my nose, my nostrils flaring.

"Lucifer and Bad Nat were right," Ann whispered. "When we cut the line to Kat . . ."

"We opened the door for her to come here," I finished in an equally hushed tone.

"This is good," The Warden continued quietly.

"In what world is this a *good* thing?" Bad Nat stage whispered.

"Because if she's here, she's not *in* us. She can't control our body from the loci."

"Um, newsflash, neither can we."

A floorboard creaked outside the library doors. *Shit.*

"There you are," The Morrigan practically purred from the other side of the door.

"Time to move," The Warden said. She grabbed my upper arm, and we disappeared right as the wood splintered. We were only in the same place for a fraction of a second, but it was long enough for me to see. Morgan Le Fay was in her true form.

Old, weathered skin stretched taut across the bone

and was nearly as white. Her hair appeared greasy at the scalp where it was falling out in clumps. The long silver strands hung limp at her waist. She wore some sort of ancient garment steeped in black magic. A dress that was the dark reddish brown of dried blood, as though it held her body together.

Despite her haggard appearance, the light brown eyes that matched mine were alight with a madness I couldn't even fathom.

We reappeared in the greenhouse. I sat up, brushing the wooden shards from my chest. Peace and Caretaker sat in front of the door, bracing it with their bodies. From deeper in the house, the crack of wood splitting echoed.

"Well fuck. That answers that question." Bad Nat sighed.

"What question?"

"Whether the old hag has her magic."

"That *hag* just destroyed the library without a second thought," I said. "And you're bleeding." It was slight, but a red slash stretched from the arch of her eyebrow to her hairline. A thin trickle of blood ran from it.

"It's nothing."

"It's everything," Ann snapped back. "We're invincible here. The loci is made for us. Shaped *by* us. It's a physical manifestation of our psyche. It can't be hurt, and neither can we. You aren't supposed to *bleed*. The Morrigan's soul entering must have changed that."

We all stared at one another, the quiet truth hanging over us.

Morgan Le Fay's voice rose from within the house

once more, breaking the silence. "Oh *little witch*, you can't hide forever."

A chill ran through me, starting at the base of my spine and working its way up. The hairs on the back of my neck rose. She was right, of course. Hiding would only work for so long. If the sound of things exploding was anything to go by, she'd level the house before long and there would be nowhere left to run or hide.

"She's not wrong," I said quietly. "We have to face her."

Peace made a face. "Are we strong enough?"

"It's six against one," The Warden pointed out.

"Be better if it was eight."

My neck cracked from how hard my head whipped around to stare at Bad Nat.

"Rage is unpredictable," I started.

Bad Nat shook her head, an almost pitying look in her eye. "Rage is one of us. So is Little. If this place dies, we all die with it."

I inhaled sharply. "What if she just makes it worse?"

Bad Nat threw her arms wide, motioning to the greenhouse around us. "I hate the be the bearer of bad news, but how much fucking worse can it get?"

"She's got a point," Ann said quietly.

"What?"

Ann pinched the bridge of her nose. "Don't make me say it twice."

I turned to The Warden. "What do you think?"

"She never should have been locked up to begin with," my strength answered.

I flinched at the accusation. "We were in agreement—"

"You would have done it regardless of what we said. You weren't ready to hear the truth." She added, blunt but not cutting. There was a gentle edge to her voice as she said it. Sympathy. Pity.

I turned to Caretaker and Peace last. "Is that true?"

Caretaker tilted her head, eyes softening as she said, "You were in a bad place."

"That's not what I asked."

She took a deep breath. "My purpose is to take care of us. All of us. Rage and Little are part of that." She stared at me, unseeing for a moment as pain flashed through her features. It would have been undetectable to anyone else, but this was me. I saw it in the tightening of her jaw, the purse of her lips, and the tiny hunch between her brows. "I had to neglect them for the betterment of the whole."

Speechless. I looked at Peace.

If there was anyone that was against Rage, it was always her. They were the antithesis of each other.

Peace sighed. "I agreed with you. I thought it's what we needed to move on . . ."

"But?" I ground out.

She smiled sadly. "You can't have peace without war. Rage is war, but she's also *needed*." My kinder, softer self scootched across the floor to take my hands. "We're two sides of the same coin. You can't have me without her."

"It's time," Bad Nat said. "Put on your big girl panties and woman the fuck up. Open the door, Prime."

I swallowed hard, my throat dry as a desert. "What if she tells me to go fuck myself?"

"What if she doesn't?" Peace countered.

"Oh, she totally will," Bad Nat chuckled.

"I—" The words halted on my lips. Excuses. It was all excuses, and we didn't have any more time for them.

I had to make a choice.

Admit my mistake. Ask Rage to rejoin us. To fight with us.

Or die.

The six of us could fight Morgan Le Fay, but I had this feeling, this premonition, that we wouldn't win. Not as six. Even with Rage, nothing was guaranteed.

But it was something.

More than the hopeless crushing feeling in my chest that we would fail. That I would never make it back to August, Marcel, or Lucifer. That all of the suffering we'd been through was for nothing.

I couldn't accept that.

No one liked to be told they were wrong. Fewer would admit it. I promised myself then and there that if we came out of this on the other end, I wouldn't stop there. I would learn from it.

And I would stop shutting them out and keeping secrets from them.

"I grow tired of the hide and seek, Nathalie," The Morrigan's haunting voice trilled. Another explosion sounded from in the house that I knew to be the dining room.

"I need to talk to Rage," I said. "Can you buy me time?"

Bad Nat summoned a baseball bat out of thin air. She twirled it in a circle with her wrist and slapped the blunt end against her palm. I arched an eyebrow. "What are you going to do with that?"

Bad Nat rolled her eyes. "What do you think? Swing it at her. Duh. If we can bleed, so can she."

Beside her, The Warden summoned a short sword. Something I saw years ago when I went through a phase where I was obsessed with human weapons. I learned everything I could about them and how to wield them.

In the real world, I probably wouldn't stand a chance at being successful with these weapons. But here, in my domain?

I was going to fucking slay.

Me and my others.

As if on cue, Ann called up a utility belt filled with different colored vials. I'd bet the whole loci that those chemicals, when combined, exploded. It was a fitting weapon for my least emotional self.

"Alrighty then, you guys ready to do this?"

Ann, The Warden, and Bad Nat shared a look then nodded once. They disappeared a second later, leaving me with Caretaker and Peace.

"Where do you need us?" Caretaker asked hesitantly.

"Not with me." I shook my head. "Join the others. I need to take of this myself."

Peace gave me a slight encouraging smile and Caretaker's eyes softened. "Speak from the heart," the latter said.

I nodded once and they disappeared too.

Taking a deep breath, I closed my eyes and moved silently from the greenhouse and appeared at the door outside the attic. All was quiet, apart from the distant sounds of battle.

My throat constricted. A knot tightened in my stomach as I slowly unlocked the door—mentally breaking the chains. They hit the wooden floor with a thud. The door swung open on creaking hinges.

Everything was as I remembered.

Blood-stained floors.

A dozen candles, all burned to the base and smoking.

Thousands of glass shards floating in a circle.

In the center of it all was Little. A small, brown-eyed girl with tear-stained cheeks. She huddled in on herself, knees pulled to her chest. Her arms wrapped around them tightly.

My heart stuttered.

Then *she* appeared.

Rage.

Her hair floated like the glass, eyes glowing a burnished gold color. Her clothes were ripped, her fingers stained red. She looked more than a little feral.

I opened my mouth to speak but the words wouldn't come.

How did I apologize to myself for all the time spent with my head in the sand? How could I find the right way to own the injustice committed?

Everything felt so hollow when faced with the reality of what I'd done.

"What? No words?" Rage said, voice dripping with poison. "You're here to apologize and ask for my help, are you not?"

"I—yes, but how do you—"

She huffed a bitter laugh. "The memory loci is under attack. I don't have to be Ann to know that you'd come for me when it suits you."

"Rage, I'm sorry—" I stumbled over my apology. Her upper lip pealed back in disgust.

"Save it. It's not like you mean it anyway."

"That's the thing. I do mean it. The others—they were right. I was wrong to lock you away. What happened . . . it wasn't your fault, even though I blamed you for it. I . . . I don't have the words to express how sorry I am for locking you both away, because the words don't exist. Nothing I say will compare to actions, and for nearly a decade mine have been atrocious." I sucked in a tight breath, trying to get my lungs to expand despite the uncomfortable tightness in my chest.

"You're right," Rage said, that all too familiar fire burning in her golden gaze. "But I meant what I said. I don't *need* your apology. Not now. Not ever."

"But I—" My lips parted in shock.

Rage extended a hand. The glass parted. Little got to her feet and slowly padded forward. Small fingers closed around the offered hand like it was a lifeline.

"How do I make this right?"

Rage stared straight ahead, not looking at me.

Beyond us, explosions went off. Wood splintered. Furniture was thrown from one end of the room to the other. We heard it all. And yet there was only silence in that moment.

I didn't think she was going to answer, but she did. "I don't know that you can ever make it right, but I can promise you this—when it's done, if we live, you will *never* lock me away again, or *I* will tear this loci apart myself."

I swallowed hard. It burned, her ire, but I'd earned it. And if we survived, I'd find a way to live with it too. "You have my word. I won't lock you up again. Either of you."

Rage's gaze slid to me, measuring what my word was worth. She must have found it worth something because she nodded once and strode past me, taking Little with her.

Before she could make it to the door, the floor began to shake. A shudder went through the house, and then the ground gave way. We fell through the air, no more than a second before landing on broken wood and shattered glass.

I tried to sit up, but the glass was embedded in my hands. Every twitch of muscle, pushing it deeper beneath my skin. The breath hissed from between my teeth. An eerie laugh surrounded me.

"What have we here?" Morgan Le Fay mocked as she walked around us in a circle. Her bare feet stepped on broken glass, but she didn't seem to notice. I wasn't sure if she was immune to the pain or if her tolerance was just that high, but either way, she left bloody footprints in her wake. "Is that a little girl? You really did create multiple versions of yourself in this place. It's almost impressive what you've done here. I've been in many minds over the years, and none held up against me."

She stopped before me. I spat; blood mixed with broken tooth landed in a wet glob on her left foot, and The Morrigan sneered. Lifting a bloody foot, I closed my eyes in preparation for the blow—but it didn't come. Not immediately.

"Oh no you don't." Bad Nat appeared beside her, baseball bat swinging before she was even full material-ized. Morgan Le Fay caught the blunt end in one hand and squeezed. The wood cracked under her grip. She switched direction and planted that foot in Bad Nat's stomach, sending her flying across the house.

I winced.

From behind her, The Warden appeared. Blood already splattered her clothes. She was sporting a split lip and a black eye, but determination still glinted in her gaze. She stabbed at the spot where The Morrigan was, but the evil of old parried, sending another swift kick into The Warden's ribs.

A crack echoed through the room as she soared a few feet and crashed into Ann. They both went down in a tumble. The potion Anne was mixing spilled. Green liquid rolled across the floor in a glass vial that stopped just short of Morgan Le Fay's feet. With a flick of the witch's wrist, the vial shot back, flying across the room toward them . . . and detonated.

The explosion that rocked the house shook me to my core.

Ann . . .

Warden . . .

My eyes watered. I felt their passing. Their pain. The way the flesh melted off their bones, the only consolation was that it was fast. Blindingly so. They had no time to scream.

But I did.

A sound I'd never made before crawled up my throat. Somewhere between a growl and battle cry. I launched myself at The Morrigan. Golden magic pouring from my skin, filling the room.

My analytical self was gone. My strength was gone.

Caretaker joined me, brandishing a cast iron pan in one hand and rolling pin in the other. My magic clashed with Morgan Le Fay's as Caretaker went at her. The bitch danced on her bloody feet evading us both.

Then the worst happened.

The Morrigan sent a shot of black magic at Caretaker and struck true. Her head fell from her neck, a scorched hole appearing where it once was. Her body stood there, suspended, not quite realizing she was dead. And then it fell.

Caretaker hit the ground with a thud.

Gone.

Just like Ann. Just like The Warden.

An earsplitting scream stopped us both in its tracks.

Across the room, Peace stood with her fingers tense

in a clawed motion. Nothing moved. No one reacted. It was like time sat still for a single second.

And then there were plants everywhere.

They burst from the hallway that led to her greenhouse. They climbed through the broken windows. They split the ground beneath us, slithering and snaking around corners and objects.

Green thorned vines appeared with a vengeance, Peace's vengeance.

One caught the ancient witch by her ankle. Another her bicep. Quickly, they attacked her limbs, wrapping around everybody part, including her neck.

Then they squeezed.

And squeezed.

And—

Exploded.

The vines disintegrated in the face of her black magic and the force of it cut through my own. It hit me square in the chest like a stab wound. I clutched at my heart, feeling it tighten. My head became warm. Nausea churned in my stomach.

Oh my gods. Was I having a heart attack? Sweat slicked my skin, mixing with the dirt and debris. I dropped to my knees, blinded by the pain.

But I felt it. The second Peace left us.

The moment The Morrigan killed her.

I don't know how, but the pain that went through me at her loss . . . it was visceral. Somehow deeper than the others. It's like each piece she took from me left my heart hollow and my mind splintered like the wood beneath my knees.

She was chipping away at my defenses. Taking us down one by one.

Pretty soon there would be nothing left.

Just shattered glass and an empty house of horrors.

My body seized. I fell sideways. My head cracked against the floor.

Stars danced in my vision.

Then it cleared and there she was, wiping her dirty foot across my cheek.

"Admit it, little witch. Try as you might, I will always win. It would be better if you surrendered. I could make it painless. The rest of you don't have to suffer if you choose wisely."

"Never," I spat as best as I could between gritted teeth. Morgan Le Fay tutted like I was an errant child doing something naughty.

"Very well. Just remember, I gave you a choice. That's more than either of your sister's had."

She lifted her hand, and I instinctively knew it was the end. She'd obliterate me. She would have full control of my body, and my magic. It was over.

A tear slipped down my cheek as I waited.

I silently said my goodbyes to the men I loved.

To Piper and the kids.

Ronan would save them. I took solace in that.

He would come through.

Then, so softly I almost missed it, a low chuckle sounded behind me.

My heart felt as though it had jumped into my throat.

The Morrigan cocked her head. "Why are you laughing?"

"Because," Rage murmured, *"it's my turn."*

Glass lifted from the ground. A cold wind swept through the house. There was no sky above us. No demons or gods that could hear us. Yet, I felt a darkness within her—within me—that I'd never touched before.

They say you should never take blood from more than one demon. That the results could be catastrophic. Morgan Le Fay had defied that. But she wasn't the only one.

Ronan. Piper. Lucifer.

I may have been born a witch with weak chaos magic.

But I was not weak.

Not anymore.

I just needed to hit rock bottom to see it. See *her*.

Rage in her truest form.

Raw. Unrestrained. Immeasurable.

Her hair lifted on end, the strands whipping around in that magical wind. Her eyes glowed with the fire of a thousand suns. Gold filled my vision, coloring every fiber, every inch, every particle.

Amid the chaos, one thing remained untouched.

Little.

She stood strong, gripping my other's hand, grounding her when no other could.

I thought I'd unleashed myself before, but the truth

was I'd buried my power in chains. I punished it for being tied to my emotions. Because Rage was so much more than her name. She was power. She was passion.

And right now, she was finally free.

Gold settled over Morgan Le Fay's skin. It buried deep into the rot of her black magic. She didn't have time to scream. There were no last words.

The golden shards spun faster and faster. Their wicked edges slicing her skin open, making way for more gold magic.

More chaos.

More . . . *me.*

She tried to fight. Her dark magic attempted to lash out, but like with Carissa, the second it encountered mine, it became *mine.* I took control of her body, her blood, her magic, her very being.

I absorbed it. Absorbed her into myself.

I took every blackened spec and made it gold.

I tore apart her form to feed my own.

Until Morgan Le Fay was no more.

Fingers wrapped around my own. I looked up to see Little's hand clasped with mine, linking me to Rage.

"It is done," my seven-year-old self said.

My chest caved in. Tears I couldn't stop poured from me. We might have survived but my others . . .

I sobbed. "Peace. Caretaker. Ann. The Warden. I—I can't do it without them."

"Then we won't," Little said.

I blinked away my watery vision, letting it sharpen

enough so I could focus on her face. "But they're . . ." I couldn't say it. I wouldn't.

"Pieces of you," Bad Nat interjected hoarsely, stumbling forward from the wreckage she'd been trapped in. One hand fisted in her band shirt, where her ribs were broken and were now healing. "We all are. With The Morrigan vanquished, they will come back."

"But when?" I asked.

Bad Nat lifted a shoulder. "I don't know, but that bitch Ann would never stay down for long. Even if you're shattered right now, you're still you. The others will return in time."

"How do you know?"

Bad Nat grinned. "I've been telling you this all along. I'm the truth. The bitter, usually sucky truth that exists when you strip everything else away."

"I . . . how do I just leave? How do I move on? The loci is a mess, and we've lost half of us. What do I even—"

Little squeezed my hand.

Bad Nat patted my shoulder awkwardly. "I'm not good with the touchy, feely shit. Go back to your mates and heal. That's what you do. Leave the loci to us."

"I don't know if I can . . ."

"Don't make me yeet you," Bad Nat deadpanned.

"What the fuck is a yeet?" Rage asked, scrunching her brow.

"It sounds like a vegetable," Little whispered.

Bad Nat winked at them. "I'll catch you up."

I sighed softly, looking between the three familiar

faces. They were the pieces of me that were still intact. My young self. My passion and power. My truth.

I was missing my strength, my peace, my love for others, and my brilliant mind.

But they would be back. They had to.

Eventually.

26

NATHALIE

My eyes fluttered open, and the first thing I saw was a trio of concerned faces peering down at me. I grinned up at Marcel, Lucifer, and August, the familiar warmth swirling in my stomach as they looked back at me with hard expressions. I tried to sit up, eager to shake off the remnants of sleep and disorientation, but Lucifer's hand pressed firmly against my chest, gently but unmistakably forcing me back to the bed.

Marcel stuck out his hand and snapped and a black flame flickered to life, licking ominously over his skin, casting eerie shadows on his face. He gazed down at me with unmistakable distrust and hesitancy, and it didn't take a genius to realize that black flame was definitely a silent threat.

August was the one who spoke up, his voice carrying an edge of caution. "Prove you're Nathalie."

I felt the bond between us. Why didn't they?

"Now," he commanded.

"Juniper," I said, the codeword slipping off my tongue as I looked at Lucifer with a soft smile.

"Wouldn't The Morrigan know that information if she took over Nathalie?" Marcel asked, keeping his harsh gaze on me.

"Probably," I answered, groaning as I felt my muscles ache. "But I'm not her."

August narrowed his eyes, glancing at Lucifer. They both nodded to each other slightly.

"*NATHALIE!*" A voice roared in my head, and I was startled, my eyes going wide.

"What! Jesus! I'm right here!" I cried out, clasping my chest and sitting up in a flash.

"It's her," Ronan said, tapping his temple as he stood by the door.

My heart was racing. "Asshole."

Lucifer's stern expression softened into one of profound relief. He enveloped me in a tight hug, his arms strong and reassuring around me.

"Little witch, you made me question if my immortal life can withstand this much stress," he murmured, his voice vibrating against my ear.

I laughed softly, my arms wrapping around him. Peering over his shoulder, I took in the familiar sight of my bedroom, and I wondered vaguely what happened while I was out. Finding the clock on the nightstand, I read the time.

"It's four p.m.? How long was I out?"

August answered immediately. "Nearly nine hours and twelve minutes."

As Lucifer pulled away, he captured my lips in a desperate kiss that said everything he couldn't. Then he released me into August's waiting arms. From him, I was greeted with a warm embrace and a gentle, teasing kiss. August's touch was tender, but there was an undeniable intensity to it. His usual composure was rocked by a genuine relief that was almost palpable.

When I was released, I was immediately gathered in Marcel's arms. Marcel, whose embrace was a mix of firm reassurance and quiet strength, kissed me deeply and slowly. By the time he let me go, the combination of their affections left me breathless and tingling. I had always had a problem with craving sex when even remotely stressed, and the stress that I just experienced was definitely influencing me. Still, I pushed it aside.

"I feel the bonds between us. I can see the threads. Why didn't you feel it when I woke up?"

"You tell us," Lucifer said. "We feel it, but something happened while you were out. It's like we felt a fracture."

August nodded in agreement. "It's still there, but when we felt whatever that was, we didn't know if The Morrigan had somehow taken control of the bonds as well."

I had a feeling I knew when that happened. As pieces of me were lost, the bond would have been shaken. I was so close to losing every part of myself. My guess was that nothing would have been left to be bonded to.

"You know what happened, don't you?" Marcel asked.

"I have an idea."

"Fill everyone in," August said, stepping back and giving me more room.

"Everyone?" I asked, raising a brow.

"Your life was hanging in the balance, and my asshole brother was prepared to harvest your soul if The Morrigan took over," Lucifer began, though I didn't miss the look of annoyance that he knew I'd kept a secret from him. "That affects everyone, little witch. So everyone is here."

"Well," I breathed out, "might as well get it over with."

At that moment, I wished more than anything we had space and time. The three walls of warmth surrounding me were beyond enticing and if there weren't supernaturals with superhuman hearing outside I might have considered delaying the storytelling a little bit. But it wasn't meant to be.

Not right now, at least.

I pushed myself up from the bed, swinging my legs over the edge to stand up. The three of them hovered around me like protective shadows. Their concern was palpable, but I waved them out of the way.

"I'm fine, really," I said with a steady voice. "Everything I faced was mental. Physically, I'm okay."

It was true. When I looked down, I wasn't wearing the sweatpants and oversized sweater I'd worn before and during the battle in my memory loci. I'd been stripped back down to my tank top and shorts, which meant I could see that all of the tiny cuts I'd had from the mental storm were nowhere to be found.

"Come on," I called over my shoulder, striding past them and to the door. Ronan gave me a slight nod, moving his large frame out of the way. As I entered the living room, I was immediately met with the gaze of four pairs of eyes each holding suspicion, relief, and some weird mix of the two.

I saw the relief settle over Kat's face right before Piper stormed forward and pulled me into a punishing hug.

"Next time a random bird gives you a note, don't follow it. And don't make deals with my mate to kill you, dammit," she muttered as she squeezed me tight before stepping away.

Sienna followed close behind, tears streaming down her face as she joined the hug. The sight of her tears made my heart ache deeply. I'd succeeded in many ways in the last forty-eight hours, yet it felt like the ways I'd failed were some of the worst I'd experienced.

Her voice trembled as she pulled out of the hug, and said "I couldn't afford to lose another person today." The words hung heavy in the air.

"I'm so sorry, Sienna," I said, my voice breaking just the same as hers. "I couldn't save Sasha. I wish I could have done more."

Sienna's tears continued to flow, but she managed a small, sad smile. "I'm not sure where I go from here," she admitted quietly. "But I know you did everything you could and at least I know Sasha has the chance to wander to peace now that her soul isn't tied by her living body." There was a sense of resignation in her words, a bittersweet acceptance of her loss.

Before I could say more, Kat stepped forward and Sienna moved to stand back by Anders. There was a moment of silence between my sister and me then, with a decisive movement, she pulled me into a firm hug.

"I'm glad you're not body-snatched," Kat said, her voice a mix of relief and stern affection.

When Kat finally pulled away from the hug, Ronan was, of course, the one to end the sappy greetings.

"So, what happened?" he asked, his voice carrying the weight of everyone's unspoken questions.

I gave them a streamlined version of the battle, carefully omitting the more personal details about the versions of myself that had died. It wasn't about keeping secrets right now. It was about the fact it was too painful to talk about. And instead, I focused on the key points— the confrontation, the chaos, and ultimately, how I had managed to kill The Morrigan.

The room was quiet as I spoke, the tension palpable as everyone listened intently. When I finished, a silence hung in the air before Anders broke it. "You killed her . . . in your mind?"

"My magic is chaos. It doesn't work like a normal witch. It rises in defense of me, and it takes control of whatever magic it's facing. All that was alive of The Morrigan was her soul. The soul is magic. I took her magic, which took her soul."

"You're sure . . ." Piper hesitated as she trailed off.

"Positive," I confirmed. "Ronan and Lucifer can confirm. Her magic and mine aren't the same color. The foundation of magic can't be manipulated. If she wasn't dead, mine wouldn't be gold." I summoned a wisp that played between my fingers for a suspended moment. Liquid gold that moved like molten metal but never burned and never settled. It was a wild thing, chaos magic.

"It wouldn't smell the same either," August added, inhaling deeply. "Morgan Le Fay left behind traces of her magic, and every time, it smelled like decay. And you smell like . . . sunshine. Life."

My cheeks warmed. For the first time in what felt like an eternity, the overwhelming weight of impending doom had lifted, leaving a fragile but precious peace in its wake—a peace I knew existed but a peace I couldn't wholly feel. I could see the exhaustion etched into everyone's features. We'd all been facing off one evil after the other for months. I could only hope that this was the beginning of rest.

"I'm glad you're okay, Nat." Sienna's voice broke through the quiet. "I really am. But I can't do this right now. I need to be alone with Sasha . . .her body . . . I—" She broke off in a quiet sob. "I just need to be alone."

I pressed my lips together, fighting back tears. "I'm sorry, Sienna. If I could change it, I would."

She sniffled and started for the guest room where I'd assumed they'd placed Sasha's body. An ache started in my chest and spread to my head as I considered the thought of Sienna going through life without her sister. Not just separated by distance, but by the veil.

"Actually, you can," Kat began, stopping Sienna in her tracks. "I want you to consider a resurrection."

Her words hung in the air for a long beat before Marcel spoke slowly, his brows furrowed in concern. "We'd need to kill someone for a resurrection."

"No," I said incredulously, responding to my sister. "I'm not choosing some poor innocent to die. None of us are."

"I know," Kat said solemnly. Her gaze remained steady, unwavering. Horror settled in my stomach, spreading like a sickness through my body. Marcel's face contorted into shock as he seemed to realize what she was saying.

"You're not saying . . .?" Marcel asked in awe.

"I'm volunteering."

"Kat," I began, my voice shaking despite my best efforts to remain composed, "we wouldn't be able to bring you back. We'd be exchanging one soul for another. You'd be dead."

Katherine met my gaze with a serene smile.

"I'm aware," she said softly.

No one spoke. Kat moved toward Marcel, grasping his hand in hers. "How could you—" Marcel whispered harshly. Betrayal shone in his dark brown eyes as he stared at her.

"Shh," she quieted him, throwing one arm around his shoulders to pull him in for a tight hug. "This is what I've always wanted. You know that better than anyone." She reached up with a small smile and affectionately cupped his face. "The veil is where Prudence is. For years we tried to find a way to bring her back. There isn't one. A soul sacrificed for resurrection can't come back. But . . . I can follow her." Kat swallowed hard.

"Do you understand what you're asking for?" I said with disbelief. "You want us to kill you—"

"I want to be with Prudence." She shrugged. "Life or death. I just want her. If we can't have life together, then death it is."

"I know we did the rituals so you could visit her, but I didn't think you'd go this far. . ." Marcel choked out, hands hanging limp at his side as he refused to hug her back. She let go and stepped back.

"The only thing that stopped me was being connected to Nat." She looked at me now.

"You what?" So much was happening all at once, and the shock rode through me in waves. My sister was saying that she'd thought about me—still protected me—all these years. I had no idea. Emotion clogged my throat, and I tried desperately to swallow around it, but it wouldn't go away.

"I know we weren't as close as we once were, but I couldn't leave you to deal with a severed psychic bond. Not when you struggled so much with your sanity as it was. . ." Several pairs of eyes focus on me, but no one questioned it. "You have mates now. An aurae bond, a familiar, and Marcel. They'll keep you balanced." She gestured toward my men. "I know you'll be fine."

"Kat . . ." My voice was strained as I trailed off.

"I *want* this—*have* wanted this, and now my death can actually mean something. Don't you want Sasha back? You've been scouring the city for a way to bring her back. With Morgan gone, you finally can. Let me have this." She glanced between me and Marcel. "Please."

The room was filled with a tense silence as Katherine's words sunk in. My heart ached with profound sadness. I couldn't bring myself to agree with her. I knew deep down that I had no right to refuse her wish, even if the thought of going through with it was more painful than I'd have expected. Carissa's death didn't faze me much, but Kat's... no one understood what it was like to lose a twin.

Except, perhaps, Sienna.

And Kat was offering a way to bring her back.

Could I really deny Sienna that? Deny Sasha a second chance?

Could I stand in the way of Kat's happiness and live with myself?

I technically already had. I just never knew it.

I couldn't do it again.

I expected Marcel to object, to find a reason to stop this from happening, but after a pregnant pause, he looked at me.

"Nathalie?"

I swallowed hard around the knot in my throat. I was going to be sick, but I still pushed the words past my lips. "What right do we have to stop her?" I sounded hopeless. It's how I felt. "I don't like it. I selfishly want to say no . . ."

"But," Kat prompted, her voice gentle despite the years of animosity.

"You love her. You've loved her for years. You won't

accept no because I know you. You're like me. I already . . . I was faced with it once. I made my decision because I wouldn't accept the alternative." I took a deep breath, feeling it stutter slightly. "I know if one of my mates were dead, I'd fight magic itself to bring them back or . . ."

"You'd join them," she said, and I nodded. "And Marcel, what would you do if it was Nat?" Kat asked. "If it had been her that died instead and you who'd been visiting her in the veil. Would you give up your chance to be together, or would you take it?"

Marcel shook his head, brushing his hair back from his eyes. "You're right. Fuck, do I hate you right now, but you're right." She took another step toward him, pain reflecting in her eyes. Pain for him. His sadness. "We'll do it tonight at the Wicked Haunt."

The words hit me like a physical blow, but I didn't dispute them.

One way or another, Kat would find her way back to Prudence.

At least this way, we'd get Sasha back in return.

Sienna, who had been standing quietly at the edge of the room, suddenly rushed forward and enveloped Kat in a heartfelt embrace. The gesture was strained but sincere, and Kat awkwardly patted her back. Sienna's tears soaked into Kat's shirt as she choked out her gratitude.

"Thank you. I know you're not doing this for me or for Sasha, but thank you." She pulled away and stepped back again.

"I want to be there this time," Piper said. She stared at me, and I heard the silent *for you* added on.

Anders nodded in agreement, "We should all be there."

"We'll hold a vigil," Marcel said his voice steady but hollow. "Be there at 11:30 and not a minute later. I don't want to risk anything going wrong because of the time."

Time.

Everything came down to time.

It didn't matter what I did. No matter how many times I'd run down the clock to protect someone or helped to save the fucking world with a minute to spare, time had a way of reminding me that I controlled so very little.

Immortality wouldn't even change that.

Somehow, some way, time would always win because there was simply never enough of it.

27

NATHALIE

"Are you all right, little witch?"

"Huh? What?" I swallowed, throat dry. "I–I'm fine." My voice shook. Why was it shaking?

Lucifer narrowed his eyes. "You skipped over details in recounting what happened. You just sort of disappeared."

My temperature was rising. I felt like I was being edged with physical affection. *Affection*. What the hell was that?

A brush of a hand here. A massage there. The guys were comforting me as I talked. It wasn't sexual in nature. I didn't know what was wrong with me, but it was only getting worse as the time went on now that we were alone. I jumped, startled when long fingers touched my thigh on my outstretched leg.

My eyes locked onto Lucifer's pale fingers as his thumb rubbed circles just above my knee. *You've got to be kidding me.* I trailed my gaze up and Lucifer was staring at me, his eyes concerned.

"Do you want to talk about whatever has you rattled?"

My lips parted. What? "How do you—"

"Because we *know* you," Marcel interjected. "You're a good liar, sunbeam, but something has you shaken."

That was putting it mildly.

Whatever was happening with my body was weird, but the thought of my dead others cooled the heat that was burning inside me. "I . . . lost some of my selves. In the fight."

Lucifer's expression shuddered. August's hands tightened around my waist. Marcel's gaze sharpened. "Your selves?"

I explained how my mind worked. That it wasn't just the memory loci, but that there were versions of me. My personality. When I came to talking about each of them though, I choked. I just—couldn't.

"I feel broken," I whispered.

August shifted, handing me over to Marcel who sat beside us at the head of the bed. "You're not broken," August reassured me, running his fingertips down my temple and across my cheek. "You're a survivor."

"They'll be back," Lucifer added. "I'm with Bad Nat on that."

"I hope so." I tilted my head back to rest against Marcel's chest. The familiar comfort only lasted a moment before I found myself hyper-fixated on where we touched.

What the hell was wrong with me?

Why was I thinking about sex of all things right now?

"I want you to know that I have never felt more fear than when I found you on that roof and you wouldn't wake up," Lucifer said quietly. His admission didn't surprise me but admitting it in front of Marcel and August did.

My heart ached at the slight crack in his voice, but with every sweep of his thumb over my exposed skin, my body thrummed with adrenaline. "I'm sorry I scared you."

"I tried to get to you," he added, his eyes boring into my meaningfully, "but I couldn't get inside of your mind."

"I won't be diving headfirst into situations alone again," I said, breath hitching.

He squeezed my thigh, and the pressure resounded in my core. "Good, but you'll have to forgive me if I'm not sure I'm going to let you out of my sight for the foreseeable future."

"Agreed," Marcel cut in and, *for the love of the gods*, he put his hand on my other thigh and started massaging gently. "Don't scare us like that again, sunbeam."

Just barely resisting squirming, I cleared my throat and choked out, "I won't, I promise."

Silence filled in the cracks of our conversation, and my eyes finally took in August fully, realizing he was uncharacteristically silent. Had been for a while now. His eyes were trained on my comforter, lying on his side with his head propped in his hand. Despite the lounge position, his body was tense, his jaw tight.

I cocked my head slightly and watched him for a moment before calling his name, "August?"

He hesitated for a second and then his eyes met mine. "Yes, sunling?"

"Are you okay? What's wrong?" His expression contorted, flickering with a mix of unease.

"Nothing, I'm okay." I frowned at him, continuing to stare as if to say *yeah right, spit it out.* With a deep exhale through his nose, he pulled his eyes to the ceiling and said, "I think the fervor is starting."

The hands on my thighs stilled.

Of course. For a second, I felt intense relief. I couldn't understand what was happening. I thought I was now one of the people who got turned on by my grief. It had never happened before. Sex to relieve my stress? All day, yes please. Sex to relieve my sadness? It just wasn't me. But this made sense. I was just going into heat for my soulmate. Or something like that.

"That explains a lot," I admitted softly, and his eyes found mine again, pupils blown wide. "Weird timing, huh?"

"I think it's because you fulfilled your soul bonds when you cut ties with Morgan Le Fay," he replied in a strained whisper. "Terrible timing. It's okay, Nat. It can wait. I can control myself."

Heat crawled over my skin again, an ache pulsing in between my legs. *Gods.* I chewed my lip watching him thoughtfully before I glanced to each side. Lucifer and

Marcel watched us with rapt attention and either I was imagining things or there was a dark sort of hunger in both of their eyes. I had a feeling they could all smell my arousal. It was getting worse and there was nothing I could do to stop it.

I gently cleared my throat. "What if . . . what if I can't?"

The words hung in the air for a heartbeat before August groaned. "Don't say that. You're fucking with my restraint." His gaze flicked between the other two. "And we have an audience."

Lucifer held up a hand in mock surrender before giving a wicked grin. "Don't stop on my account. I've watched you two before—when I was a ghost, of course. But this wouldn't be the first group encounter if it swings that way. I am all for giving Nathalie what she needs."

August and Lucifer stared at each other until Marcel broke the tension. "It would be my first . . . but I could use a distraction."

All three heads turned to him, each of us shocked. Despite the dislike of sharing from all three men, it was not a secret that it was the hardest for Marcel. He met each of our gazes easily and shrugged in response leaning against the headboard and raking his eyes slowly over my body. It didn't pass his inspection that I wasn't wearing a bra as he lingered on my chest.

Wait until he found out I didn't have on underwear either.

My blood heated under his gaze and when Lucifer started caressing my thigh again, his hand inching up this time, I couldn't stop myself from squirming in my spot. The next several seconds were a showdown, a sexually charged game of chicken as we all waited for someone to tip the scale.

Shocking everyone, it was Marcel that went for it.

Shifting in his spot, he leaned toward me as he ran his fingers through my hair, his hands stopping at the base of my neck and gripping the strands. He tipped my head back. His eyes swept over my face.

Then, slowly, one hand released my hair and began drifting down my body. He skimmed the outer curve of my breast, over the plains of my stomach and to the waistband of my sweats. His fingers toyed with the edge while he cocked an eyebrow, asking for permission.

I arched upward, capturing his lips in a passionate kiss. I couldn't help the moan that slipped out when he forced his tongue into my mouth.

Marcel's touch was feather light as he pushed beneath the band of my pants and his fingers found my weeping core. I almost flew out of my skin, my hips jerked so hard.

"You're wet for us, sunbeam."

I heard the low growl from the end of the bed, and I knew in that moment August's control broke.

The bed shifted around me before hands settled at my hips gripping the waistline of my pants and tugging. In shifting to let August slide my sweats off, my connection with Marcel severed and I whimpered, reaching a hand behind me to wrap around the nape of his neck.

Marcel wasn't having it. He lifted both of my arms in

the air and Lucifer easily pulled my shirt over my head, leaving me completely naked to them.

"Fucking love your tits," he groaned against my neck. Both his hands came up to cup my breasts, playing with the neglected buds. He pinched and tweaked them, and his every touch was driving me crazy, sending jolts of pleasure through my body. I arched into his touch, a breathy sound escaping my lips.

My legs fell open just slightly as my head lolled to the side. August and Lucifer both took their opportunities. August grasped my hips before throwing a leg over his broad shoulder. A second later his tongue parted me as he licked up my slit and ended with his tongue flat against my clit.

I exploded with pleasure, a loud moan echoing in my ears before it was swallowed in Lucifer's brutal kiss.

I knew at this rate I would be covered in marks from all of them by the time this was over, but gods I didn't care. I craved it. My body was on fire and their touch was the only thing that was quenching the inferno raging through every inch of me.

I was still rippling with pleasure when August sucked hard on my clit. A cry tore through me as my hand buried itself in August's curly hair. I pulled, probably harder than I meant, as he began to roll his tongue over my center, slow and sensual.

"You're so pretty like this, little witch," Lucifer murmured against my lips. "So gorgeous and hungry for us." August took that moment to thrust a finger into me and I bowed against Marcel's chest, a guttural sound ripping from my throat.

Lucifer's hand grabbed my jaw and wrenched my mouth to his, the kiss demanding and heated. I felt Marcel move his hands from my breasts and I missed his warmth immediately, but then two large palms rested against my thighs, before wrenching them apart.

"Oh gods," I groaned softly, hardly able to believe that we were doing this, let alone that Marcel would hold me open for another man to eat me out. It was filthy in the best possible way.

"I'm the only god here," Lucifer chuckled. August rumbled in protest, and I felt it where his mouth was on me. My eyes were locked with Lucifer's as he brushed his thumb over my bottom lip. And then he dipped down and captured my lips in a slow kiss that teased every bit of restraint out of me.

August's fingers picked up speed inside of me and my breaths started to come in pants against Lucifer's lips. He bit my bottom lip as Marcel leaned forward and whispered in my other ear, "You're so close, sunbeam. I want to see that gorgeous face you make when you come."

August lapped at me and Lucifer eased back, guiding my head to look. "Watch him taste you."

Watching August between my legs with so many hands and mouths on me, had me on the brink. When cool slender fingers gave both of my nipples a hard pinch, that was it for me. My entire body jerked as a scream I hardly recognized as mine pierced the air. August didn't stop, riding my climax out with me until my body became languid, twitching slightly. He pulled away, biting my inner thigh. I peered at him through hooded lids, taking in the sight of his mouth glistening, and the dark look on his face while his hair—out of its usual ponytail—hung around his eyes.

My fingers gripped him hard as I tugged up. He complied with my silent request rising over my body until his lips met mine and I tasted myself on him. My hands roamed over his chest, and I growled half-heartedly in disappointment at the lack of exposed skin.

Pulling away, I rasped out, "I'm the only one naked. You need to fix that. All of you."

He chuckled darkly. "Anything for you, sunling, especially after the way you came on my tongue." He pushed away from me, sliding off the bed. I didn't get to watch him because Lucifer grabbed my jaw and twisted my face back to his. Unlike the others, he could blink in and out of the veil to rid himself of clothes.

"Anything you don't want to do?" I knew exactly what he meant, and I felt my body clench, already excited and ready again. The ache inside of me needed to be filled or I was going to lose my mind.

"No," I whispered back. "There's lube in my closet."

"Thank you for the offer, little witch." His lips pulled to the side in a satisfied smirk as he grabbed me by the hips and guided me off of Marcel. Then he turned me around so I was on all fours facing the headboard. "But what good would I be if I couldn't do this?"

I gasped when I felt a wetness suddenly gather at my

core. With little more than a touch, he'd made me slippery for him.

I felt the bed shift behind me before his fingers stretched me in a way that made my next words come out as something more like a groan than a coherent sentence. "That is a wild use of magic."

My words failed me after that as a second finger joined the first and each thrust had me rocking back to meet it. The stretch was delicious, but it wasn't enough. The fervor coursed through me, and it demanded one thing and one thing only.

"If one of you doesn't let me take your cock soon, I'll lose my mind," I ground out as I pushed back against Lucifer's fingers with more force.

Three throaty chuckles sounded from every angle.

"So impatient," Lucifer said, stilling his fingers and making me bite back a growl.

"She always is when it comes to her pleasure," Marcel added. I realized that he was at my side right as I caught sight of the swing of his hand just before his palm cracked against my ass. I'd be embarrassed of the sound I made if I were in my right mind.

"I love seeing our witch so cock hungry." Lucifer leaned forward, his front touching my back as he rubbed a thumb over my hanging nipple. "Patience. Good things come to those who wait."

I glared at him and barely resisted telling him to shove his patience. Tired of the teasing, I decided to take matters into my own hands—literally. I pushed onto my knees, ignoring the eyes on me. I knew who was most likely to crack first at this moment and so I wiggled myself around until I faced August. He was on the side of the bed, one knee braced on it, his cock in his hand. With a promising smile, I reached forward and wrapped my hand around his. I got through two pumps before his hand fell away and he let me take over.

I pumped August slowly, my eyes fixed on his face as I watched his expression. If he was feeling a fraction of the hunger the fervor was causing me, I knew this was bliss. So when I pulled away and his eyes narrowed in a challenge, I just grinned.

"Now who's hungry?"

He arched an eyebrow. "I think it's my turn," he said. Lucifer shifted back further on the bed just as August reached forward, grabbing me by the waist. With one smooth motion, he twisted us until he landed on the bed, and I straddled him, chest to chest. His hands gripped my hips, pulling them forward and backward, grinding me against his hard length. I choked out a moan.

August smirked as I moved against him, trying to find friction.

"Good, now scoot down to the edge," Lucifer instructed, and with August's fingers digging into my hips, the two of us slid down the bed toward Marcel, who'd stepped back as we got to the foot of the bed. August's legs were over the edge, his soles touching the ground. Without warning, he flopped back, pulling me forward until my chest was flush with his and I loomed above him, the back of me open to their eyes.

His eyes skimmed mine for a second as I felt other

hands kneading my ass. "You sure you're ready to be with us? All of us? For eternity?"

Eternity wasn't something I'd thought about much. Death had been looming a little too close as of late. But I knew that completing the bond with him today meant forever. It meant forever with him and with the other two just as intricately tied to me, it meant forever with *them.*

"Never been more sure," I murmured back, brushing my lips over his as I reached a hand between us and lined him up with my entrance. As I sank down on him, I felt it and saw it. The gold thread between us tightened, thrumming with energy as the aurae bond locked between us.

I moved against him and his eyes closed with ecstasy. It still wasn't done for me, though. I looked behind me and Marcel took me in before he stepped toward the bed. I nodded at him groaning as August's cock slid in and out of me. I felt a tip prod at my other exposed entrance and a flood of liquid that I knew was Lucifer making sure the stretch would be smooth and comfortable. As Marcel slid home, he growled deep and low, his fingers digging into my ass cheeks as he found the rhythm with my movements over August.

"Fuck, sunbeam," he groaned out as he pushed in and out of me. "So fucking tight for me."

I looked to the side of me and reached out my hand for Lucifer, needing his presence to feel like this was complete. He grasped my hand, and I pulled at him until he dug his knees into the bed and knelt beside me. His cock jutted out, proud in the space between us. I turned my head fully and let my tongue slide over his tip. His groans joined the sounds that came from all of us, tangling in the air until it was hard to tell which sound came from who. August and Marcel controlled my movements at my hips, but I found my own rhythm for Lucifer as I dropped my jaw and took him fully in my mouth.

And I felt complete.

"So, fucking perfect, sunling," August rasped out as he met every thrust from Marcel with a plow of his own. "Clenching around me. I'm going to fuck this pussy forever."

My sounds vibrated around Lucifer's length, and he let out a snarl, threading his hands in my hair, taking over as he thrust into my mouth.

All I could do was brace my hands on August's chest and moan around Lucifer's cock as I was pounded into from every angle, my body desperately riding the high climbing in me. I was so full it was almost overwhelming, but I couldn't imagine anything sweeter in that moment.

Call it the fervor, or maybe it was the fall out of everything that had happened, but I'd never felt anything so intense. I was climbing again, and fast, with every pull of Lucifer's hand in my hair, and every scrape of August's cock against my inner walls, and every pump Marcel thrust into my ass. The reverie climbed until all of us were racing toward the edge of a cliff.

"Come for us." August slid a hand between us and started making soft circles around my clit. It took exactly four turns before I detonated like a bomb, clenching hard as my body jerked and gushed for the men who had taken my heart in their shared hands.

I felt August give a few more erratic thrusts before he pulsed in me, his head pressing back into the bed as he came. Marcel's fingers dug into my hips and his movements picked up as he followed us both over the edge. My mouth grew slack around Lucifer as he grabbed both sides of my face and began to fuck my mouth.

"Come on, little witch," Lucifer grunted, his movements picking up, "I need to see you swallow me." That was my warning before his essence flooded my mouth and I gulped around him.

When he pulled out of my mouth my whole body sagged. Six hands helped me roll over until my back hit the bed. My eyelids were heavy, and I fought to open them, but couldn't quite manage. Movements happened all around me as I was petted and stroked. A second later, a warm, wet cloth stroked between my thighs, cleaning me up.

Finally managing to fight the daze, I cracked an eye open and met three sets of eyes. With a satisfied smile, I extended an invitation I never thought would happen between the four of us.

"Sleep with me?"

28

NATHALIE

MARCEL DROVE MY CAR WITH A STEADY HAND, HIS FACE ETCHED with concentration as he navigated the winding road leading to Wicked Haunt. We could have probably gone the faster way, traveled with Piper and Ronan through the light realm, or with August and Lucifer through the veil, or Marcel could have just popped us in the cemetery. But I'd asked for this drive. I needed the chance to sit and watch the scenery pass me by before I had to face the shitshow that was to come.

I couldn't believe I was on my way to attend my sister's assisted suicide, and there was absolutely nothing I could do about it. Maybe it was the release of Rage and Little that had me feeling the way I did. Maybe it was the fact that a secret part of me had hoped that now that our family was out of the way, Kat and I could have reformed what we'd lost. I mean, if Piper and Bree could scrape back together a semblance of a relationship, then so could the two of us, right?

Except I would never, ever get to find out.

The loss of my sister was as hard to deal with as the loss of my opportunity to know her again. Our time was up. Fuck, I hated feeling helpless and it was a feeling that I was reluctantly becoming used to.

All too soon, Marcel pulled down a gravel road and the large church loomed in front of us. He kept driving until the attached graveyard came into view. My heart rate kicked up and my palms became slick. I tried to surreptitiously wipe them against my jeans.

When Marcel finally parked, my eyes jumped immediately to the clock. 11:23. It felt like I could hear the ticking of an invisible clock in my ears. He turned off the engine and an oppressive silence settled over us. I fiddled with my fingers, picking at the skin around the cuticle. He reached over and grabbed my hands in his, stilling the nervous fidgeting.

I looked at him and saw the same grief I felt reflected in his eyes.

"I know this is hard for you," he said softly. "It's hard for me too, but you know that this is her choice. Kat deserves the chance to follow her own path, whether we agree or not."

"I know. I just don't know how to accept that." I swallowed hard, tears threatening to spill. "I used to think I'd feel nothing if she died, after everything that's happened, and that is the furthest thing from what I feel."

"She's your twin. I would be shocked if you felt nothing about this."

"I'm going to miss her," I said with a sullen chuckle. "I've spent years avoiding her and now I'm going to miss her."

A tear escaped and traced a path down my cheek. Marcel reached over and gently wiped it away with his thumb before pulling me into a tender kiss. The kiss was gentle and full of shared sorrow, his warmth enveloping me.

"I'll miss her too," he murmured against my lips.

We rested our foreheads together, our breaths mingling in the quiet of the car. I worked to match my breathing to his, letting his steady rhythm bring my panic down. Slowly, I regained composure, the tears drying in my eyes.

After a few moments, I pulled back slightly, taking one last deep breath. "Thank you," I said, managing a faint smile.

"Anytime, sunbeam," he replied softly, giving my hand a reassuring squeeze. Not letting myself think about it anymore, I pushed open the car door and climbed out closing it behind me. I walked a few steps forward, stopping to wait at the front of the car as Marcel went into the back seat and grabbed the duffel bag filled with supplies. Slinging it over his shoulder, he stepped up beside me and linked his fingers with mine. Together, we walked toward the graveyard, the chill of the New Chicago night biting through my clothes.

As we approached, I could see Lucifer and August standing by the wrought-iron entrance. The moment we reached them, they fell into step with us. Lucifer on Marcel's other side, August on mine. The graveyard was hushed, the only sounds were the faint rustling of leaves and the murmured conversations of everyone else. Everybody stood around expectantly, including Kat, who had disappeared from my apartment with the excuse of "getting her affairs in order."

Piper and Ronan stood side by side with matching faces of consternation. Anders was cradling Sasha's lifeless body with a tender reverence while Sienna stood by him, holding on to one of Sasha's dangling hands.

"I will do the setup with Lucifer and August," Marcel said just before we reached everyone else. "Go talk to her." With those words, I received three forehead kisses before I was left to walk to my sister alone.

Katherine stood off to the side, a picture of calm while all I felt was turmoil. I walked over to her, my steps slow and deliberate. She looked up when I came to stand by her but said nothing. For several moments, we stood in silence watching as Marcel instructed Anders to lay Sasha down and worked with Lucifer and August to create an extra-large salt circle.

Finally, Katherine broke the tension. "I don't blame you, you know," she said, her voice steady but tinged with a sadness that mirrored my own.

I turned to face her, definitely lost. "For what?"

"For Prudence," she continued. "I believe you. I always have. Pru always had a cruel streak and was too jealous and impulsive for her own good."

I snorted softly. "That's putting it mildly."

A reluctant smile touched Katherine's lips. She nodded toward Lucifer, August, and Marcel. "Well, we can't help who we fall in love with, can we?"

"No, I suppose we can't." I glanced over at my guys, a warm feeling spreading through me despite the heaviness of the moment. I fidgeted with my thumbnail, looking down at it while I tried to find the courage to say more. "If you didn't blame me, why . . .? Everything that happened between us started there."

"Grief. Anger. Jealousy that you got away," she said simply. "It was a bottomless pit of unimaginable sorrow, yearning for one more chance to be with the one you love, only to be met with denial and loneliness. I had no way to process it. Our family certainly didn't help it." She huffed, shaking her head. "I'm also as stubborn as you. We share that trait."

Silence fell between us again, and for a second, we watched Marcel cleanse the athame in ritual. I couldn't find the words to say it but knowing that she didn't blame me alleviated a guilt that was so heavy, I'd grown used to bending over to carry it. But I didn't let the silence sit between us for too long. This was my last chance, and I wanted to say everything I hadn't.

"I don't blame you either." She looked at me for an explanation, and I gave her the best one I could. "For everything that happened with Marcel, our family, The Morrigan—I realize now that there were a lot of things about our family that I got to evade when I left. You didn't. You were grieving and alone and left with *them.*

You didn't deserve to carry the weight of their sins any more than I did."

For a second she just blinked at me, her eyes misting over before she pulled herself back together. "Our family was so fucked up, but you were always the best of us, Nat. It only makes sense that you'll be the last Le Fay. You'll leave an entirely new legacy to our name. Something good."

I sniffled, trying to hold back the tears. "Tell Prudence I'm sorry, for what it's worth. I don't regret it, but it was unfortunate all the same . . . I don't imagine she cares, but—"

"She doesn't blame you either, you know."

"That's . . . surprising."

"Oh, she absolutely did at first." Kat chuckled and shook her head, a sad, tiny smile curling up one side. "She caused it. She knows that now. Death . . . death changes a person, oddly enough. I'll tell you the same thing I told her. If that day had been different, and it had been you dead and Marcel alive, I would have done the same thing. I would have taken the life of anyone in that room if it meant saving you. It wasn't personal."

Without thinking, I closed the distance between us and pulled her into a tight hug. Katherine embraced me just as fiercely, something she hadn't done since we were children, when she was my protector.

"I love you," I whispered, my voice cracking with emotion. "I hope that you find everything you're looking for in the veil."

Katherine's grip tightened around me. "I love you

too, Nat," she replied, her voice muffled against my shoulder. "I hope you get to live the life you've always deserved."

We held each other for a few more seconds before the moment was broken by Marcel's voice calling out from across the graveyard.

"It's time."

Katherine gave me one last, lingering pat on the back before stepping away from me and walking with sure steps toward the ritual circle.

"Only one person here knows what this looks like," Marcel began, flicking his eyes to mine briefly, addressing the others as they closed in around the outside of the salt barrier, "and even now it will look slightly different. We're trying to lure Sasha back, and she's been gone for some time. The salt gives us a stronger window, so don't fucking cross it. Sienna's blood is our lure. Nothing fancy. Just a cut on the hand."

Sienna nodded, squeezing her hands together.

"But . . . you're going to have to"—he paused, swallowing thickly.

"Say it, Marcel," I whispered.

Sighing, he closed his eyes. "You're going to see me kill Kat. If you can't handle it, turn around. Leave. Whatever you need to do."

"Then what?" Anders asked.

"Then I chant until dawn," he answered softly.

"All night?" Piper asked, and he pressed his lips together firmly, gently inclining his chin.

"And silence. Give him silence," I added. "It's a grueling thing to chant that long."

There was a general rumble of agreement. That meant we were once again, out of time. I finally dragged my feet forward, moving into the space Lucifer and August had left between them. Everyone spectating took a seat as Marcel held out his hand for Kat and she stepped over the salt.

Katherine assumed her position next to Sasha's lifeless body, laying down directly in front of me within arm's length. As she spread out, she arranged herself easily into the proper placement. Marcel set the cleansed athame on top of her stomach, keeping it off of the ground. Kat tilted her head towards the sky, staring up at the stars and full moon that illuminated everything.

Marcel gestured for Sienna, and approached him, holding out her arm.

"You ready?" he asked her quietly, and she closed her eyes, fisting her hand. He used a separate athame and sliced into her arm cleanly, an instant line of crimson appearing as her blood flowed into a stone mortar Marcel held up to collect it.

Her eyes welled with tears as she pulled her arm back, and Ronan bandaged her silently.

"Her hair," I said suddenly, thinking of other spells. Thinking of how long Sasha had been gone. If I was going to lose my sister tonight, Sasha better damn well return. Marcel looked at me in question. "Take a lock of Sienna's hair. Wrap it around Sasha's hand. It should strengthen the lure."

He didn't question how I knew it. He just trusted me, nodded in agreement, and did as I'd suggested. Sienna's blood was poured onto Sasha's arms, the bloody blade set across her thighs, and her twin's hair looped around her palm.

I looked away and my eyes connected with Piper's. Across the circle, she gave me a sad smile. I knew she could tell that this was hard. I didn't feel the need to try to explain myself to her; after all, she knew well the complexities of estranged sibling relationships.

The church bells began to clang the typical twelve peals as midnight arrived. Marcel knelt beside Katherine as the third toll rang, and he began to chant.

Without breaking rhythm, Marcel retrieved the athame from where it rested on Katherine's stomach. I knew what was to come and when I prepared myself for this, I told myself I would watch. I'd looked away during Sasha's ritual, but I wanted to be with Kat every step of hers. So, I kept my eyes trained on my twin's face, watching my other half contort with pain as Marcel slid the blade across one wrist and then the other.

With the blood of the sacrifice, the spell had begun.

The twelfth and final clang echoed deeply in my bones.

Lucifer reached and wrapped an arm around my waist. I leaned into his comfort, resting my head against his shoulder as I watched the steady rise and fall of Kat's chest. Fingers threaded in my hair, as August's nails began gently scratching my scalp. The chanting continued, Marcel's voice unwavering in its intensity, and I stayed enfolded in the comfort of two of the men who held my heart.

I couldn't help but think how dissimilar this ritual was compared to when we'd saved Marcel. And how different life was, and how different it would be going forward. Lucifer was alive again and bonded to me as a familiar. August was my Umbra. Marcel wasn't sick. So much had been gained, but the losses were numerous. If I'd let them, they'd consume me.

I watched Kat's chest expand less and less as her breathing slowed down. My eyes locked on my sister's body, finally letting myself fully take her in. She lay still, the flow of blood from her slit arteries slowed, and a massive pool of red framed her body, coating both Sasha and Marcel in the process. Her arms were outstretched as if in a final, silent plea to reach out beyond this plane and embrace the one waiting for her in the veil.

As my sister's chest gave one last shuttering exhale, I swallowed the sob that threatened to escape me. I stayed pressed against Lucifer's solid form the entire time, even as I swayed from exhaustion. The warmth of his body was a comforting anchor amidst the ritual's intensity. August held my hand, and I allowed myself to rely on their strength.

The moon traveled across the sky, time passing whether we liked it or not. Those hours dragged on; it would stay with me forever.

Life as it had been.

Life as it was.

Life as it could be.

The temperature changed slightly, and the scent of dew forming reached my nose.

The night was almost over.

I heard a breathy gasp, and my eyes locked on Sasha. I watched the line across her neck slowly knit itself closed, though I knew the scar would be there forever. Just as Kat had lived with the evidence of death, so would Sasha.

The gray pallor that had turned her light brown skin into a muddy taupe dissipated as brightness flushed over her. I waited, recalling what it was like to see my sister breathe again after chanting all night to resurrect her.

Then the moon crossed over the horizon, and dawn broke through, peeking out with a brilliant orange glow. Sasha's body shot upright with a loud inhale that cut through the silence we'd kept ourselves in for hours.

She gasped, clawing at her throat before she frantically patted her body as if shocked to be back in it. The entire group held their breath as we waited. She looked disoriented at first, her gaze sweeping around as if trying to grasp the reality of her return.

Then, her eyes locked onto her twin's, and a sob tore from Sasha's throat. "Sienna, oh my god." Without hesitation, she threw her arms around her sister's neck, and everyone seemed to collectively exhale.

My eyes strayed back to my sister's body.

Lifeless.

Cold.

Empty.

The juxtaposition of joy and sorrow in a resurrection is something that can never be described in words.

To resurrect the dead, you had to give the living.

All magic came with a price.

With shaky hands, I cupped her face, leaning down to kiss her forehead with tears streaming down my cheeks. "Bye, Kat. Find your peace."

29

AUGUST

Nathalie was finally asleep, her body curled up against Marcel's chest, the tension in her features slowly easing. It had been a long day for everybody, but especially those two. She'd been strong through the resurrection ritual and subsequent emotional appreciation from Sasha. They'd cleaned Kat and given her a proper witch burial. But when Nat finally climbed into bed, the dam broke and she cried herself to sleep.

Marcel held her close, his hand gently stroking her hair as if to soothe her even in her dreams. I watched her from the other side of the bed, listening to her steady breathing and wishing with everything in me I could take the pain for her.

Lucifer perched near the foot of the bed, his hand rubbing circles into her calf over the blanket. His gaze fixed on Nathalie with a similar mixture of concern and protectiveness that I know we all shared. He shifted slightly, his eyes meeting mine before he glanced over at Marcel.

"We need to talk," Lucifer whispered, careful not to disturb Nathalie. "Privately."

"This can't wait?" Marcel hissed back, his brown skin crinkling around the eyes as he glared at the demon.

"No. She doesn't need to be dealing with our bullshit while grieving her sister and the parts of herself she lost."

"Says the primary bullshitter," Marcel grumbled back. I didn't bother responding, simply sliding off the bed to my feet. I stilled at the door, waiting for them to both go ahead while I took one last lingering look at my aurae. She looked peaceful in her sleep, despite everything she'd been through.

My girl was a survivor. We had that in common.

The hallway was dimly lit, the shadows stretching long across the floor in the early morning night. I took the armchair, spreading my legs and crossing my arms over my chest as the other two filed in and found their own seats. Marcel took the other armchair by the window, his posture stiff, and a scowl etched on his face. "This had better be good. If she wakes up—"

"I'll hear her and be there before she realizes we're gone," Lucifer finished as he sprawled out on the couch.

Marcel grumbled under his breath, something about how he'd like that, wouldn't he?

"Now that Nathalie has completed the aurae bond with the incubus, she'll be immortal, which makes us all immortal." That was one way to start the conversation. I'd known in completing the bond with her that it was a package deal. Did I like it? Not particularly. Did I regret it? Fuck no. I wanted my sunling however I could have her. Whatever she gave me. Even if Tweedledee and Tweedledum came with it. "We need to figure out what our individual relationships with her will look like, as well as —much as this pains me to admit—the unit as a whole."

I watched Marcel's expression shift as the weight of Lucifer's words settled in. It came as no surprise to me. Lucifer and I had previously had some time to discuss Nathalie. I wouldn't call it bonding as much as it was an understanding. When it came to my relationship with Nat, my concerns were practically nonexistent. We were compatible in every way, from personality to whatever that elusive thing was that created a spark between two people. Now that we'd finally bonded and the issue of Sasha had resolved, I knew she was unequivocally mine.

The problem was, we weren't alone.

She was *theirs* too—which meant issues she had in her other relationships would inevitably bleed into our own.

We were now a unit, as Lucifer so delicately put it.

He continued, a wry smile playing on his lips, "There are logistics we need to sort out. For instance, as fun as the group sex was, I'd rather that didn't become a regular thing. I quite like having my own time with our little witch."

Marcel snorted. "That was a one-time thing for me. I have no desire to share her in that capacity again."

"I don't disagree," I acquiesced, before cocking an eyebrow, "but I think group sex will be the least of our problems in the future."

"And why is that?" Lucifer's eyes took on a more serious glint as he glanced toward me.

"We're in this for *her*. Each of us decided that we'd rather be with her than not, even if there is *baggage* so to speak." My gaze strayed toward Marcel and his lips thinned.

"Fuck you."

"I don't mean it personally." Mostly. "Each of us considers the other two baggage. We're the pieces of her that we accept because we have to for this to work. Hence, baggage."

"Uh huh," Marcel rolled his eyes. "Sure. That's what you meant."

"Either way, the point is, she's the reason. As long as we keep her needs at the forefront, I don't foresee there being many issues between us." I couldn't say *none* because let's face it, that was impossible.

"Much as it pains me to admit this, August and I agree on this. You get to get on board, Marcel." Lucifer sighed. "Which brings me to the next point of order. We need to nip this jealousy in the bud. The last thing she needs from us is fighting. If we make our issues her problem to sort out, I fear my little witch may, in time, come to regret binding herself to you both."

"Says the asshole who—"

"Ah-ah," Lucifer wagged his finger. "See? This is why we're out here and not in there."

Marcel got to his feet and started to walk by me but paused when I grabbed his upper arm. Firm, but not tight. Not threatening. "He's got a point," I said quietly. "Out of all of us, you're struggling the most because you had her first."

"I'm not—"

"Denying it won't help us," I said flatly, changing tactics. "Like it or not, we're in a relationship in some capacity. It's not just with her, but in a sense, with each other. If this is going to work we need to be transparent about our shortcomings and work through that shit. See a therapist if you need to, but don't let it sit and fester. She doesn't deserve that."

A slow clap came from the couch where Lucifer was bringing his hands together. "Well said."

It was my turn to roll my eyes. Marcel was her first love. I understood the original connection, even if it didn't make sense to me why he still mattered to her so much. But Lucifer? I had no idea what she saw in that hedonistic man child. Maybe one day I would. He had eternity to prove himself.

"Fine." Marcel's shoulders deflated as the tension eased out. "I have some issues I need to work through. I will. But none of us are thrilled about sharing in any capacity. I'm not alone in that." He backed up a few steps and collapsed in the chair he was sitting in only moments ago.

"You're not," I agreed. "But it's different for us. I knew the score from the beginning. Lucifer existed as a ghost for most of the last year. He watched her start to move on with me. We both knew that we wouldn't get her to ourselves and accepted it anyways. You weren't like that. You *had* her, until you lost her. This is a second chance for you."

"Do you have a point to make or . . ."

"See? This is why no one likes you," Lucifer said, gesturing to Marcel.

"Stop baiting him," I grumbled, then continued on. "You said you're up for this, that you're all in for her—but are you really? Can you stomach that she's not only yours but *ours* as well? Because if not—" Any lingering civility dropped from Marcel's gaze. He leaned forward, elbows on his knees with his fingers steepled. The scent of ink and parchment along with something else distinctly *other* permeated the air. His magic.

"Let me make myself clear," Marcel said, voice dropping to a lower tone. "I love her more than anything in this world, or the next. I'm willing to die for her. Putting aside my jealousy is the least of what I will do to make my sunbeam happy. So if you two neanderthals are part of the deal, so be it."

"Fair enough."

"Now that that's sorted," Lucifer started, then hummed. "The last thing I want to address is time."

"Nathalie said she'll choose how to spend her time," Marcel said, eyes narrowing. "Dictating what she does is only going to land us in the doghouse. By all means you're welcome to, but I won't be following."

"Right," Lucifer responded acidly. "But we have to agree there will be no monopolizing of her time. If she's ours then—well. I don't know where I was going with that, but there's no 'i' in team."

"There is a 'me'," I muttered to myself. Marcel cracked a smirk and Lucifer ignored it.

"Thought we were on the same side, incubus."

I sighed. "I think it's good to not knowingly monopolize her time, but something you both need to remember in all this is that she's a person. People can't equally split things all the time. She gets to choose. Sometimes she might need one of us more than the other, and we have to be okay with that."

"It's one thing if she wants it," Lucifer said, eyes narrowing on me. "It's another to knowingly sabotage another mate so you can have her all to yourself."

"No offense, but—" Marcel started.

"Offense taken."

"I haven't even said anything yet."

"Literally everything that comes after 'no offense' is offensive," Lucifer shot back dismissively. "Again, this is why no one likes you."

"Enough," I said to them both. Lucifer, it seems, had a decent point in calling this meeting if how they were acting was anything to go by. "I agree to not manipulate or monopolize our mate. Marcel?"

"I can do that; the real question is *can he*?" He thrust his chin in Lucifer's direction.

Irritation made Lucifer tighten his jaw. "Obviously. I'm the one that wanted the meeting. It's called *communication*. That's how relationships work. Look it up sometime."

I damn near choked. That fucker took my words and used them as his own.

"You didn't call this out of the good of your heart."

"How would you know? You're not privy to my feelings."

"That implies you have any outside causing anarchy."

Lucifer chuckled. "Oh I have them alright. Fortunately for you, I simply don't act on something if it's not in my best interest."

"Oh, for fuck's sake," I groaned, pinching the bridge of my nose. "Marcel, stop baiting him. Lucifer, quit with the threats. We know you aren't going to do anything."

"Do we?" Marcel huffed. "He's not above killing to get what he wants. He's proved that already."

Lucifer's response was as chilling as it was expected. A low, dark laugh escaped his throat, and he gave Marcel a smile that was anything but reassuring. "You don't need to worry about that," he said, his voice dropping to a menacing whisper. "Nathalie would be furious if I got rid of either of you. For what reason, I can't possibly fathom, but as long as she wants you, you're safe from me."

"Not to mention the tiny little detail that you're bound together," I added, mostly for Marcel's benefit. "Anything he does to you, he will suffer himself, so eliminating you won't benefit anyone but me."

"Don't count on it," Lucifer said.

"I wasn't." And much as that might be nice for me, I could only imagine the pain it would put Nathalie through. When she thought she had lost Marcel, something broke inside of her. I never wanted to see that again, even if it meant accepting the literal devil and her ex into both our lives.

"Was there anything else?" Marcel asked, impatient to return to Nathalie. I couldn't blame him; I was feeling the same way.

"No," Lucifer said, waving his hand as though he were dismissing a servant.

"Good. If you'll excuse me." Marcel got to his feet and padded across the living room floor. "I have a mate to take care of."

Lucifer rolled his eyes. "I take it you'll be joining them?" he asked me.

"You're not?"

He shook his head once. "Nathalie may be immortal now, but she's not unkillable."

I lifted a brow. "Your point being?"

"The Morrigan may be gone, but she's far from the only evil that lurked within this city. I can't lose my little witch again. I won't." His eyes glowed brighter in the low light of the room, radiating power from within.

"So you're going to what? Start hunting down anything that could possibly hurt her?"

Lucifer flashed me a smile. "That's precisely what I'm going to do."

"And if she wakes up and wonders why you're not there?" I asked quietly.

Lucifer grinned. "I'm sure you can find a way to distract her."

I sighed. "Why do I feel like this is going to end poorly?"

"Because it will, for those I hunt down."

I shook my head and got to my feet. "She's not going to like it when she finds out."

Lucifer let out a low chuckle. "On the contrary, I think she will. I'd be using my time cleaning up the city. She's been saying I need a hobby for a while now. I'd call it . . . growth." I gave him a deadpan look and he winked. "With you and Baggage here to watch over her, I finally feel comfortable enough leaving. Besides," he added on a darker note. "No matter how tame I may seem, it's best to not forget who I am. This will provide an outlet of sorts for my, ah, more demonic tendencies. One that Nathalie will be able to accept—which is really all that matters."

He had a point. A beast was a beast, even if you put a leash on it and called it a dog. Lucifer was the devil in his past life. He might have turned over a new leaf, but some things just couldn't be changed.

Perhaps he was right and Nat wouldn't mind so much.

So long as the people he went after actually deserved it.

"Well then, happy hunting, I suppose?"

"Take care of our woman," was his only response. Lucifer disappeared in a blink, leaving me to wonder whether that was a request or a warning. Not that it mattered.

As I turned around, Marcel stood at the doorway, arms crossed. "Thought he'd never leave."

Sighing, I stretched my neck side to side. I reminded myself he was young. He'd been a dying mortal for most of his existence. A lot of this was new to him. Still . . . I walked past him, patting him on the shoulder before heading into Nat's bedroom. "Get a therapist, kid. Forever is a long time to be a cunt."

30

NATHALIE

I made one last sweep of the house, checking that everything was in place. The interior designers I'd hired did an incredible job of taking my lists and vision and making them into reality. But still, I wanted everything to be perfect for the big reveal.

The last two weeks of my life had been a whirlwind, but in the turmoil of it all, I found myself more content than not. There were days that Kat's loss weighed heavier on me than others. There were days when the idea of being the last branch of my family legacy felt like a pressure on my chest.

Sasha had also been something that bothered me and seemed to have no real solution. I hadn't seen her since that night. I didn't want to push her. I understood that she needed time to adjust to being back in the land of the living. After everything she'd been through, how could I expect anything else?

I tried not to stress about it too much, telling myself

that Sasha just needed time. She'd find her footing again, and when she was ready, we'd figure things out. Until then, all I could do was give her the space she needed.

Aside from that, everything else in my life had found a strange sort of balance. Through it all, I kept finding moments of happiness. My house finally being finished was one of those—even with the last-minute changes I added in directly after the resurrection ceremony.

The keys to the place had been in my possession for a few days now, and I'd spent every spare moment putting in the final touches. Somehow, I managed to maintain the secret from the guys, despite the fact that all three of them tended to be at my apartment all the time.

That was partially why I chose today for the surprise. All three of them had things to handle, and my apartment was finally empty for the movers to clear out. They'd gotten the job done quickly and the unpacking done even faster.

It felt strange to know that the apartment that had been my home for so long was now an empty space, but it wouldn't stay that way for long. The Señora and I had talked and decided that it would become Mist's apartment. She'd be eighteen soon enough, but had lived through enough horrors to age her otherwise. Mist needed her own space sometimes, and so she'd have it. I planned to take her shopping next week with Piper and the girls to have her pick out furniture and decorations. Whatever she needed to make it feel safe.

And Piper's bomb would always be there too.

Not long ago I would have worried about her being

on her own, but she was far from alone. Mist was still training with the Señora every day to get ahold of her death magic, and when she wasn't doing that, she often spent time with Hallie at Sasha and Sienna's. This let her keep her regular schedule and a sense of normalcy, even though I wouldn't be around as much.

I glanced at my phone and cursed, then snapped my fingers a few times. Everything around me straightened. Books righted themselves on the shelves, clean dishes went back to their assigned cupboards, and the area rug that had become crooked righted itself. I smiled proudly. It wasn't fancy. It was far from what Marcel could do, but it was magic. *My magic.* And it was actually working for those simple spells that I could never perfect.

Since restoring my memory loci and bringing in Rage and Little, my magic had found its sense of harmony in the chaos. Having access to my emotions the way I did now was still new, but it was also liberating. I'd always been so guarded, so afraid of what might happen if I let myself feel too much. But now, those walls were coming down.

My loci wasn't back to normal, but just the other day, Ann seemed to fall out of the sky and land on a couch in the library. Bad Nat cackled at her expense while Little helped her up. It wasn't all my lost selves, but it showed that what Bad Nat said was true. With time, they would return. I just had to be patient.

Then there was Rage. She was quiet and reserved for the most part, but every day she seemed to change a little more. The baby fat that clung to her features shed away. She got an extra layer of hip and ass. She was filling out like all my other selves had, making their bodies identical to mine as I grew up. I couldn't help but wonder if she was finally getting the chance to grow up too now and find her own version of adulthood.

With everything ready, I took a deep breath, trying to steady my nerves as I made my way downstairs. I don't know why I was so nervous to show them. If they didn't like what I'd chosen for them, they could always change it. Still, I felt some kind of odd pressure about it.

Just as I reached the foyer, a wave of magic hit me, the familiar tingle spreading across my skin. Marcel appeared, his eyes immediately locking onto mine.

"Sunbeam," he murmured, a slow smile spreading across his lips as he crossed the distance between us in a few long strides. He pulled me into a deep kiss, one that made my toes curl and my heart race.

When he finally let me go, I was breathless, but before I could say anything, I felt another surge of magic. I turned just in time to see Lucifer and August appear out of thin air as if they'd always been there.

Lucifer was the first to reach me, his hands sliding around my waist as he pressed his lips to mine in a kiss that was all fire and heat. I barely had time to catch my breath before August was there, his kiss softer but no less intense. By the time they finally stepped back, I was dizzy with the sheer intensity of it all.

The biggest change in my life had been the solidifying of my relationships with each of them. It was still surreal to think that I had three men who cared about me, who were willing to share me in a way that I'd never thought possible. It was a strange dynamic, but it was ours, and it worked.

Marcel was the first to break the silence, whistling low as he looked around the grand foyer. "This place is amazing. They did such a good job with your house."

I couldn't help but smile. "I know, right? I actually wanted to give you guys a tour. Come on."

I led them through the first level, showing them the living room, the separate dining room, and the large kitchen. We stepped out onto the patio that connected to a back door in the kitchen. My backyard was something else I was proud of, with a pool sparkling in the late afternoon sun and a beautiful garden tracing the outline of the fence.

"I can think of several things that can be done in that pool," Lucifer commented, shooting me a heated smirk. "None of them involve a swimsuit."

I rolled my eyes but couldn't hide my grin. "Well, it's freezing in there right now, so no."

"I'm surprised it's not heated," Marcel said casually, and I smirked.

"An oversight. I can have it installed." As much as I wanted to linger there, I led them back inside and up the curved staircase, my heart pounding in my chest as we reached the second floor.

"There are six bedrooms in the house," I explained as we reached the first three rooms at one end of the hall-way. I opened the doors to show them the two guest rooms, each decorated in a neutral, calming palette, with a bathroom between them. Then I led them to my bedroom, pushing open the door to reveal the space I'd put the most work into.

"Thank the gods your bed is bigger," August commented, taking in the Alaskan king bed. "Marcel hogs space."

"It's called starfishing," Marcel retorted, shrugging unconcerned. I laughed at that because it was totally true. For three guys that didn't much care for sharing, they'd spent most nights in my bed. Not always in *that* way, but we always ended up asleep together. Well, August, Marcel, and I did. Lucifer couldn't sleep and the possibility of losing me plagued him. He'd taken to becoming some sort of vigilante enforcer at night, something I wasn't thrilled about but couldn't deny that he needed. I found it was best not to think about it too much.

It wasn't long before we were filing out of my room and heading past the stairs, down the other side of the hallway where three other rooms were. I led them down the other side of the hallway, stopping in front of the last three doors. Each one was painted a different color: a cool slate blue, a deep red, and simple black one with gold accents.

"This is the part of the tour that's a surprise," I said, my voice a little shaky as I started to ramble. "If you don't want it or don't like it, I won't be offended. And if you want to keep them but want to change anything, they're yours."

They exchanged confused looks, and Marcel came to the right conclusion first. "You're giving us rooms. . ."

I nodded, taking a deep breath before telling each of them which door to open. "August, you take the blue one. Lucifer, the black, and Marcel, the red."

The doors swung open, and I held my breath as they stepped into their rooms. Each one was decorated with them in mind, a space that I hoped would feel like home to them. I stood in the middle of the hallway, twiddling my thumbs awkwardly as I waited for their reactions. But as the silence stretched on, my nerves got the best of me, and I turned on my heel, heading downstairs to make myself some tea.

As I made my way to the kitchen, I chewed at my bottom lip. I'd put a lot of effort into each of their rooms and I hoped I captured what they would each want.

Marcel's room had been the easiest to design. I knew him well enough to understand that he would appreciate something functional yet personal. He had his own private library, and I'd lined the walls with floor to ceiling bookshelves, filling them with a mix of magic and non-magic literature. Some were volumes he already owned, but I'd also taken the liberty of adding a few rare tomes I knew he'd appreciate. The fourth wall framed a king-sized four-poster bed, the wood dark and rich, draped in deep red curtains. The bed itself was dressed in luxurious yet understated linens. I could almost picture him now, sprawled across the bed with a book in hand, the soft light from the bedside lamp casting a warm glow over him.

For August's room, I'd taken inspiration from his apartment in Paris. The room was filled with art showing abstracts and impressionist renditions of couples and bright sunsets. True love and new beginnings. It felt appropriate. The bed I'd chosen for him had a metal frame that mimicked the intricate ironwork you'd find on Parisian balconies. And of course, I had a miniature replica made for Estrid, placing it near the window so she could sunbathe. A hidden door had a room decorated right out of *Bliss*, where we'd met. A place for us to . . . indulge.

Lucifer's room had been the hardest to decorate. What do you get for a desire demon who'd had nine thousand years of wants fulfilled? The question had plagued me for days, and I'd gone back and forth on several ideas before finally deciding to keep it simple and sexy—just like him. I'd opted for a king-sized circular bed dressed in black silk sheets. The walls were painted an inky black, but instead of being oppressive, the color was offset by raised black accent molding that added texture and depth to the space. There was only one wall that deviated from the others—it was metallic gold, adorned with black cabinets and a custom tantra chair. The cabinets were already stocked to meet his sexual appetite . . . and mine. I added a few of my favorite romance novels on the nightstand. He still read them, even if it was behind the other guy's backs.

As the kettle whistled, pulling me out of my thoughts, I poured the hot water over the tea leaves and watched as the liquid darkened. I took a deep breath, the aroma of the tea calming my nerves. I wrapped my hands around the warm mug, letting the heat seep into my bones. And then I made my way into the living room just as I began to relax, I heard the sound of footsteps descending the stairs.

Steady and familiar.

I looked up as they entered the room, my heart skipping a beat when I saw the looks on their faces. August was the first to reach me, sitting down beside me with a big smile, while Marcel and Lucifer draped themselves over the edges of the loveseat, their gazes warm.

"So," I began, my voice betraying just a hint of nerves, "what do you think?"

They exchanged glances before August was the first to speak. "You've outdone yourself, sunling. The rooms are perfect." His eyes darkened a fraction as he added, "*All* of them."

Relief washed over me, and I couldn't help the small smile that tugged at my lips knowing he'd found the hidden door. "I was worried you might not like them..."

"Oh, I love mine." Lucifer chuckled, the sound low and rumbling, as he leaned forward and nipped my ear. "I see my room being incredibly useful." His smirk was downright sinful, and I felt a blush creep up my neck, heat pooling in my core at the thought of what he might be planning.

Before my mind could wander too far down that path, Marcel's fingers found their way into my hair, scratching my scalp in that soothing way he knew I loved. "Does this mean you want us all to stay here together?"

"Not if you don't want to. We can all live here, or you can live in other places. I'm all right either way. Regardless of if you decide to be here or somewhere else, each of you will always have a place in my home."

August was the first to respond, his voice soft but firm. "I stay wherever you are, Nat. Always."

Marcel nodded, though there was a slight hesitation. "I'm already used to having August as a housemate, so what's one more?"

Lucifer, never one to be outdone, added, "I wouldn't want to be anywhere else, but it better stop at the three of us." Marcel made a sound of agreement, and I couldn't help but laugh a little.

"I never meant to fall in love with one person, let alone three," I admitted, shaking my head in disbelief at my own life before teasing them. "Managing the three of you is a lot, especially with my work."

The guys quieted a moment, looking at each other as though they were having some sort of silent conversation.

"What is that look for?" I asked.

Lucifer's expression softened, his eyes dark with concern. "We've been talking . . ."

"About?"

"You, sunbeam. What else?"

"Elaborate."

August patted my thigh. "You have a tendency to . . . take on too much." As soon as I opened my mouth to argue, he said, "Let me finish. You take on the weight of the world. You look after everyone. You don't have to do that anymore. You have us."

"You have support," Marcel added, and my eyebrows shot up.

"He started seeing a therapist," Lucifer whispered. "He's full of new words, like 'trauma,' 'support,' and 'bandwidth.'"

August shot him a look, while Marcel's nostrils flared and he cleared his throat.

"Okay," I started slowly, thinking to think of how to manage everything they'd just said. "So, that's new information about Marcel. And explains where you go when you have 'things to do.' And I'm happy about it."

"But this is about you," Lucifer added. "The dreadful business with The Morrigan is resolved. You don't need to keep overworking yourself, little witch. You can scale back."

"I . . . I don't know how to not work."

"We're not saying don't work," August said quickly. "Gods, you'd be bored as hell. We're just saying you don't have to do it all anymore. Delegate. Outsource. Build an even bigger team and network. And lean on us when you need to."

I hesitated, the familiar tension of responsibility tightening in my chest. But when I looked at the three of them, I knew they were right.

"I'll try," I promised, my voice softer. "I've been thinking about taking on a second personal assistant to manage more of the businesses."

"That's a start," Lucifer said, then he shrugged. "I don't mind being in charge of the hiring process. I can run the background checks."

"You mean follow them around and decide if they end up crossed off that list you don't think we know about," August said with a chuckle.

"Same difference."

I groaned. "You keep an actual list?"

"I'm a busy man. It's hard work keeping the city clean."

"You're like a blonde Batman," Marcel said, smirking. "You even lower your voice like him. 'I'm Lucifer,'" he said, moving his arms around and lowering his voice mockingly.

August watched the interaction with disappointment. "Maybe group therapy is something we should look into . . ." he said quietly, watching the other two banter.

I barked a laugh, instantly feeling sorry for the poor soul that would take us on as clients. Even though they didn't sound like they were actually fighting, I knew if it went on too long, it might get tense. Clearing my throat loudly, they stopped the chattering and looked at me. "How about this," I began, looking at all of them one by one, "I will get a second assistant, full-time, and that person and I will begin the process of expanding my team, as you put it. And Lucifer, you can run the 'background check' but *cleanly*. I want to know the good, the bad, and the ugly about each candidate."

"I find that more than agreeable," August said, taking

my hand and kissing the top of it. The simple action sent delicious chills through my veins.

Marcel and Lucifer both nodded in agreement.

I patted their thighs and stood up. "Good. Now, if you don't have any objections," I said, pulling my shirt over my head as I walked out of the room. "I'm going to go for a swim . . ." I dropped the shirt on the floor and turned to leave.

"I thought you said it wasn't heated?" Marcel said, though he couldn't hide the hint of arousal in his voice.

A salacious smile curled up August's lips, and Lucifer's eyes glowed with desire.

I stopped, taking off my bra and letting it fall. Looking at them over my shoulder, I winked. "I lied."

31

NATHALIE

What did you wear to get lunch with the girl whose soulmate you stole?

I held up two hangers glaring at each dress as if they offended me personally. Clenching my jaw, I stormed out of my walk-in and presented both dresses to the mini audience in my room.

"Which one should I wear?" Three pairs of eyes found me.

The guys were scattered around my bedroom. Marcel had claimed the plush chair in the corner, his legs draped casually over the armrest, absorbed in a book. Lucifer was leaning against the wall, arms crossed over his broad chest. August was occupied by the window seat where he'd been sketching something.

"Blue always looks lovely on you," August volunteered first.

"Agreed."

Marcel pondered for a moment before nodding. "Blue."

I looked at the blue one critically before quickly changing. With the dress on and boots zipped over my calves, I made my way back into the main room heading for the floor-length mirror closest to the window seat. I fiddled with the hem of my dress and took a look in the mirror. I couldn't seem to stop adjusting it, smoothing it out, and checking my reflection. My nerves had been in overdrive since Sasha texted me yesterday asking to get lunch. She'd been absolutely radio silent for the last month and I'd started to wonder if maybe our relationship could never be rectified.

Family dinners had been temporarily stalled in the aftermath but were meant to start again soon. Things weren't as simple as they were before, for a number of reasons—chief of which being Sasha. I wasn't sure how she felt about me and August getting together while she'd been gone, but I couldn't imagine she was happy. In a lot of ways I'd been avoiding her as much as it felt like she was me. Sienna assured me it would be all right, but I wasn't so sure until Sasha texted me about grabbing lunch.

I turned side to side, just about to declare that I was changing again, when August stood up and moved toward me. He wrapped his arms around my waist from behind and rested his chin on top of my head. We both looked at our reflections in the mirror, his slate blue eyes meeting mine in the glass.

"You look beautiful, sunling," he said softly. "Stop stressing yourself."

I grimaced slightly, the tension in my shoulders not easing. "I can't help it," I admitted. "Sasha knows we're bonded but she's been silent for weeks. I have no idea what she's thinking or what to expect. What do I even say to her?"

"You tell the truth. You've found love and that's okay. She's still your friend and you want to be hers."

I scoffed and said, "Yeah that sounds perfect. 'Hey Sasha, sorry I bonded with your mate while you were trapped in the veil. Hope you're doing fine.'"

August's grip tightened reassuringly. "You're allowed to make decisions that bring you happiness. It's okay to prioritize your own needs sometimes. And you know as well as I do that she was never the one for me. Even without you in the picture, I wouldn't have accepted her. You're the only one I want, and you shouldn't feel shame for wanting me too."

Marcel, who had been absorbed in his book in the corner, looked up and gave me a gentle smile. "You're always the one to sacrifice. The martyr," he added. "After everything you've done for her and New Chicago, Sasha can get the fuck over it. It's not like you wanted to hurt her. In fact, you tried everything not to. Sometimes we find people and we can't help the way they make us feel." Therapy had certainly helped him so far, but I got the feeling he was talking about more than me and August by the twinkle in his dark eyes.

"Sasha loves you," Lucifer said, stepping forward.

"She might be hurting, but she won't hurt forever. It might seem like a long time to you, but both of you will see that in the grand scheme of things—finding a friendship like yours is rare. Even if it takes years, which I'm not saying it will, I know she'll come around."

I glanced between their reflections in the mirror and tried to let their words soothe the tension in me. With a deep breath, I gathered my thoughts and put my anxieties aside. I squeezed August's hand comfortingly before I stepped out of his embrace.

"All right, I'm ready."

Marcel closed his book. "Do you want me to teleport you, or would you rather drive?" he asked.

"I'll take you up on that," I said to Marcel after kissing Lucifer's cheek.

August pressed a gentle kiss to my forehead, wishing me luck. Then Marcel grabbed my hand and pulled me close. I felt the familiar rush of magic as we blinked out of my bedroom and reappeared outside the restaurant. It was the same place I had visited with Lucifer when Morgan Le Fay had interrupted our lunch.

I turned to Marcel, capturing his lips with mine before pulling away with a wobbly tilt to my lips. "Thank you."

He flashed a warm smile and told me, "Enjoy your lunch with Sasha. Text me when you're done and I'll come get you." With that, he blinked out of sight, leaving me standing in front of the restaurant.

Pulling open the door, I spotted Sasha almost immediately seated near a window. Her posture was slightly rigid as she looked at her menu. I made my way over to her, and she looked up, a tentative smile flashing over her face as I settled into the seat across from her.

Fuck, the awkwardness between us was palpable. Sasha glanced at the table. "I ordered you tea and a glass of water. I hope that's okay."

"Yeah, that's perfect, thank you," I replied. She nodded her acknowledgment. We fell into silence again, the kind that's heavy with things unsaid. Picking up my menu, I pretended to pour over it, knowing that I was going to order the same thing I always did. It gave me something to do with my hands.

That distraction only lasted so long before she set her menu down and I mirrored the movement. The pregnant pause just carried on. I fidgeted with my napkin, trying to find something to break the uncomfortable quiet.

Finally, I spoke up, "How has the adjustment been for you?"

Sasha took a deep breath, her eyes flickering away as if searching for the right words. "It's been. . . . challenging. Being in the veil for so long did things to me."

"What do you mean?" I had known there would be consequences, but Sienna hadn't mentioned anything. To be fair, she barely mentioned Sasha to me at all unless I asked.

She hesitated for a moment before continuing, "I see the dead now. At first, I thought I was hallucinating, but I went to Señora, and she confirmed it. They're real spirits."

I felt a jolt of surprise. "Wow, that is . . . wow."

Sasha snorted softly, her expression a mix of frustration and resignation. "Yeah, it's been a lot. Especially being in a city where millions of people died at once. It's like I'm constantly surrounded by them."

The thought of Katherine crossed my mind briefly, but I dismissed it. I couldn't afford to let myself obsess over my sister wandering the veil. For my own sanity, I had to focus on the here and now.

Sasha continued, "I've also been having these awful nightmares and dealing with a lot of anxiety. Señora gave me some herb blends to help, but she said the seeing ghosts part isn't really fixable. The herbs help keep me calmer, which helps some since it seems like the spirits mostly show up when my emotions are all over the place."

I nodded, feeling a pang of sympathy for her struggles. "I'm really sorry you're going through all of this," I said genuinely.

Sasha gave a small, shrugging smile. "It's better than the alternative."

The silence returned, still laden with the weight of our unspoken thoughts. I sipped my tea, the warmth comforting against the cool of my anxiety. I couldn't think of anything else to say that didn't address the elephant stomping around the room.

After several long minutes of us both sipping our drinks and looking everywhere but at each other, the waitress finally arrived, breaking some of the tension that had settled over our table. With a warm, practiced smile, she took our orders. But that reprieve only lasted so long. As soon as the waitress left, the quiet returned, wrapping around me like a noose.

Sasha broke it after a moment. "I wanted to say it was really nice of you to give Mist a chance to work with Sienna at the women's shelters. It's been great seeing her start to take on more responsibility."

I couldn't help but smile genuinely at her words. "Mist has grown so much," I said. "She just keeps proving herself every day. It's been amazing watching her come into her own. I gave her my old apartment because I figured it would be the best scenario that lets her have a little more independence while still being close to Hallie and the Señora."

Hallie had been happy to have her 'angel' so close to her these last few weeks and Sienna appreciated the big-sister-like role Mist took with Hallie. It made a world of difference for the single mom, but also for Hallie and Mist's relationship. All of the kids were growing rapidly still, each looking around eight or nine now.

Sasha's face lit up with a soft grin. She was missing the edge that made her, well, her. "It was a good solution."

The conversation lulled again, leaving us both in our thoughts. Then Sasha took a deep breath, and I saw her expression shift, growing more serious. "I invited you to lunch because I wanted to let you know that I won't get between you and August. I know you completed your aurae bond and—I'm happy for you."

"I'm so sorry." I searched for more words and just as I

opened my mouth again to explain how things had ended up, Sasha cut me off.

"There's no reason to be sorry," she said firmly. "I know you, Nat, and you don't have a selfish bone in your body. If there had been any chance that relationship was meant for me, you'd have never pursued it. Death changes a person." My heart lurched when I heard her echo the same sentiment Kat had shared before she'd died. Sasha thankfully didn't notice, and she carried on in her explanation. "Drifting through the veil gave me a lot of perspective about my life and what I want for it. I realized that pining and chasing after someone who doesn't want me isn't how I wanted to live. And I don't want to ruin the relationships I value over someone who was never truly mine."

Her words hit me with a weight I hadn't expected. I struggled to find the right response, my emotions a tangled mess. "I value our friendship so much," I finally managed to say, my voice thick with emotion. "I've missed being in your life."

Sasha's expression softened. "I missed you too," she said quietly, her voice trembling just slightly.

At that moment, the waitress returned with our food. She placed it in front of us with a friendly smile and then disappeared again. The silence that followed was more comfortable, filled with the soft clinking of cutlery. The tension between Sasha and me had eased some in the wake of her admission.

After a few moments, Sasha put her knife and fork down and fixed her eyes on me. "I do have one ask, though, if you'll indulge me," she began softly. I lifted an eyebrow and motioned for her to continue. "Will you cut the thread between me and August?"

I almost choked.

"I may have the Eye but I don't like using it unless I have to," I said carefully, my voice trembling slightly. "It feels like playing god . . . but I can't fault you for wanting the separation. Are you sure about this?"

Sasha nodded firmly, her expression unwavering. "I know it's a lot to ask," she said, swallowing hard. "But I'm sure. I can't live with this empty ache and still find a way to move on. I accepted the bond on my end and that can't be undone. I am truly happy you have each other. I do mean that. But still having the rejected bond makes it impossible to get over August, even though that's all I actually want at this point. I just—I want the freedom to find my person." She reached across the table and clasped my hand in hers. "Please."

I could see the resolve in her eyes, and my own heart ached for her. "Okay, I'll do it."

"Would you be comfortable doing it now?" she asked eagerly, her green eyes lighting up. "I don't want to wait any longer."

"If you're ready," I said slowly. "Do you want to come to the bathroom with me? Do it in private so no one watches?"

Sasha nodded, and we stood together, making our way to the ladies room. Once inside, I locked the door behind us. I had gotten more and more used to the Eye, to the point that I had started to see the world again without focusing on the threads connected to everyone. It had made going out far less stressful.

"Okay, so full disclosure, I have no idea if this is going to hurt. I've never cut bonds between anyone except, well, you know," I told her as I materialized the shears.

She simply nodded standing still with bated breath. I analyzed her, focusing on the crossing threads tying her to the world around us. My eyes tracked the delicate, intertwining strands until I spotted a thin, fraying thread that I instinctively knew was Sasha's connection to August. I reached out, knowing I probably looked crazy right now as I pinched the thread between my fingers. Bringing the scissors up, I lined them against the thread. I didn't ask her again as I carefully snipped it.

The thread disintegrated and Sasha gasped, her breath catching in her throat. She clutched her chest and bent at the waist. I grabbed her shoulders, panicking instantly.

Had I made a mistake? Was this the result of playing with fate?

"Are you okay?" As soon as the words left my lips, I flinched. Of course she wasn't okay. She was bent at the waist and gasping for breath. I gently rubbed her back, trying to soothe the pain I caused.

Slowly, Sasha straightened, and a real smile spread across her face. Something I wasn't sure I'd ever truly seen. Tears glazed over her eyes, and she pulled me into a hug, something she rarely did, and her voice was filled with emotion as she spoke.

"I'm free."

EPILOGUE 1
SASHA

Five months later...

The May breeze fluttered through the trees, carrying with it the promise of summer and a hint of the flowers that bloomed along the sidewalk. I strolled down the street, letting the gentle wind tousle my hair. Today was one of those rare, perfect days when the world felt just right; when I'd woken up knowing I'd had no nightmares and there weren't any specters hanging out in the corners of my vision.

Since being stuck in the veil and essentially dead, having my body snatched, my body actually dying, and then being resurrected all over again, life had been one hard thing after the other. But today was going to be a good day. I just knew it.

I was headed to grab a cup of coffee before meeting Piper for the conference with the faction leaders. The fallout from the death of the last black witch had left a gaping hole in the supernatural community that everyone seemed desperate to fill. It was a constant juggling act trying to keep everyone's peace. But for now, a little caffeine was my only priority.

Lost in thought, I wandered into the coffee shop, my eyes fixed on my phone. My feet were moving forward without really paying attention to my surroundings and I didn't see the guy walking in time to avoid the collision. My body crashed into a hard wall and strong hands grasped my arms, tingles exploding where the pads of his fingers touched my skin.

I looked up and into the most mesmerizing pair of hazel eyes I'd ever seen. They were warm and inviting, with flecks of brown and black that seemed to dance in the sunlight filtering through the shop's window. The man's face was chiseled, with a strong jawline and a hint of stubble that made him look ruggedly handsome. His dark brown hair was a tousled mess of tight curls.

He was fucking gorgeous.

Shit, I internally cursed after a suspended moment. I was definitely staring.

"Sorry about that," I mumbled, trying to regain my composure.

He took a moment to rake his gaze over me, and I could feel the heat rise in my cheeks. There was something undeniably magnetic about him, something that made my heart race and my thoughts scatter. I had dropped my phone in my surprise, and he bent down to pick it up, his movements smooth and graceful. When he handed it back to me, our fingers brushed, and a jolt of electricity shot up my arm.

"No problem at all," he said, his voice deep and rich. "I'm Finn."

"Sasha," I replied, still feeling a bit flustered. "Nice to meet you."

He flashed a charming smile that made my knees weak. "Can I buy you a coffee, Sasha?"

I hesitated for a moment, then nodded. "Sure."

We walked to the counter together, and as we waited in line, I couldn't help but notice the subtle aura of otherworldliness about him. His presence was magnetic, and I could tell he was some kind of supernatural, though I couldn't quite place it.

"So, Sasha, what is it that you do?" he asked while they made our drinks.

"I work with Piper Fallon and Nathalie Le Fay," I answered, momentarily wondering if that was going to be the end of our interactions. If hearing the names of the two most powerful people in the city would turn him off . . .

"I've met Nathalie a few times," he said, nodding in appreciation. "Good lady. I really appreciate what she does for the city. What they both do, really."

I smiled, and there was no way I could hide how happy it made me that he'd said that.

"What about you, Finn?" I asked. "What is it that you do?

"Construction," he said, tilting his head side to side. "Well, acquisitions and construction, if I'm being entirely honest."

"Oh? What does that mean?"

"I acquire abandoned buildings around New Chicago and work to restore them. Some are for affordable housing, others are retail. Some of them had horrible back stories, and those just get leveled to the ground and rebuilt into something that just makes the city . . . I don't know . . . better. No one needs a reminder of what happened in some of these places." He paused when the barista was ready for us to order.

There was a quiet confidence about him and the more we talked, the more intrigued I became. By the time we reached the counter and he paid for my coffee, I had to admit that I was embarrassingly captivated by this stranger.

"Is that how you met Nathalie?" I asked as we waited for our drink to be made. "Buying buildings?"

He nodded. "It is. She's helped me find a few. I just finished a new one on the east side of town. Old vampire den. Nasty place. Burned to the ground."

I had an idea of where he was talking about, but I didn't plan on sharing that just yet. "What is it now?"

"Group home for foster kids and orphans," he said, smiling proudly. "I grew up in one, so this was a little close to the heart. I'm on the board, so this one is going to be significantly better than what I had."

"I'm an orphan too," I said softly. "I'm . . . happy to hear you did that. Built a place for them where they can be safe. The city needs more of that."

He grinned, nudging me gently with his elbow like we were old friends. "If you're working with Nathalie Le Fay and Piper Fallon, you're doing it too. I know the changes they've made. It's why I want to stay in New Chicago. I wanted to be part of it."

"Thanks." I blushed at the compliment and soft touch. *Gods*, I must have looked like a love-struck teenager. I couldn't stop grinning like a fool. I had to look like a complete weirdo. We grabbed our drinks and headed outside, the warmth of the coffee cups contrasting with the cool breeze.

"So, I do have a site I need to oversee today," Finn said, as we walked towards the corner of the street, "but would it be overstepping to say that I really want to see you again?"

"No. I feel the same way." I flashed him a genuine smile. I was used to being seductive and getting my way with any man, but this one felt different somehow. Less like a game of attraction and more *real*. He made me nervous and fidgety in the best way possible.

"Good, what about this evening? Dinner, my place. I'll cook." I grimaced at that.

"Sadly, I have a very...involved job, working with Piper. I'm pretty booked up until next week." I thought about it for a second before adding, "But I do have a family dinner on Sunday, if you want to go with me?"

"Family dinner, huh?" Finn said, his eyebrows raising. "You're inviting me to meet your family already?" I would have felt embarrassed if not for the amused light in his eyes.

I laughed. "If you're brave enough. My twin sister is likely to be a bit much . . ." That was putting it mildly.

Sienna would be fucking ecstatic and planning a bonding ceremony before the end of the night.

"I'm not scared of meeting your family," he quipped with a smirk. "What's the worst that could happen?" Knowing my chosen people? Just about anything could happen, but I didn't want to actually scare him off.

Besides, we were on a good six-month streak of nothing bad happening so far.

"I've gotta warn you my family is pretty eclectic. I hope you can handle them. But if you can't . . . well, it's better to know now."

"Your doubt wounds me, Sasha," he retorted, clutching his chest dramatically before chuckling. "I'm positive that I will love them and more importantly, they'll love me."

I laughed and it didn't sound like the bitter wake that it had for years. Even to my own ears it was softer. More hopeful. "You sound sure about that."

"I am." He gave me an appraising look before his eyes met mine again. "What's your number? If this work schedule of yours eases up at all, I'd love to have you over —or meet you somewhere—one day before then. If not, Sunday's a date." He winked.

Butterflies took flight in my stomach. *Oh.* That was new. "Absolutely."

We exchanged numbers quickly before we both admitted that we'd both walked slightly in the wrong direction. "A few extra steps never hurt anyone," Finn declared with an easy shrug. "Besides, if I hadn't walked with you, I'd have never won you over enough for that date."

"You won me over in the coffee shop," I admitted, surprised I'd just said it out loud. "So, I'll see you next Sunday, then?"

"Sunday," he confirmed. We hesitated for a second longer neither of us wanting to walk away before he tucked a stray lock of her behind my ear and said, "I'll see you soon, Sasha."

With that, he turned and walked away. I watched him go for several moments, feeling a smile spread across my face.

As I turned to head toward where I was meeting Piper, I couldn't shake the feeling that something had shifted. I had been right about this being a good day. It was *more* than that. Like . . . fate. Somewhere deep down in my lonely heart, I had this iron-clad assurance, even though it made no sense. I shouldn't be able to know after one chance meeting.

But I did.

It was finally my turn.

EPILOGUE 11
NATHALIE

I leaned forward in my chair, fingers steepled beneath my chin as I listened to the ever-present debate between my others. In the months that followed my encounter with The Morrigan, my loci had slowly returned to normal. Or some version of it.

Ann and Bad Nat fought on ninety percent of issues. The Warden was often the tiebreaker. And Rage, well she was going by a new name these days.

Passion.

In the wake of the destruction of the memory loci, she and I had sat down and had a heart-to-heart. That was when she first broached the subject of a name change. I'd been more than happy to agree if it would help ease some of the underlying tension between us.

Over the past six months, she'd matured a lot, finally growing up to meet the age that the rest of my loci, minus the embodiment of my childhood innocence, was at. She still had time to grow, and I knew that was partially my fault considering I was still unlearning years of repressing myself. But already she'd hit young adulthood, looking very similar to how I did around twenty years old.

"Cookies are ready," Caretaker called out from the kitchen. Little ran into the room carrying a plate of seasonal sugar cookies with colored eggs on them while Caretaker followed behind with seven small cups of milk.

The lack of an eighth still hurt, but I didn't dwell on that.

Bad Nat sneered in disgust at the wholesome sight, dropping her boots from the tabletop to the floor one at a time. "You have shitty Easter cookies, and we don't even celebrate Easter—but no whiskey?" she grumbled.

Just as Caretaker started to respond, the atmosphere shifted. Lucifer materialized in the room. He'd gotten really good at slipping in and out of loci, but we had learned that he couldn't access it if I wasn't mentally inside. His eyes swept across the scene, and a mischievous grin spread across his face.

"I'm with Bad Nat, whiskey would be an excellent addition—"

I groaned, rubbing my temple. "Lucifer, we've talked about this."

"What? I'm just saying—"

"Nothing, you were saying nothing."

He pressed his lips together in a pout, but it wasn't very effective when his eyes twinkled with mirth. "Very well. Is my favorite Nat back yet?"

The sudden shift in energy took the playful

atmosphere away as we all exchanged glances. So much for ignoring that pang in my chest.

"Peace hasn't returned," I said quietly.

"Give it time, Prime," Bad Nat said, moving to stand. She snatched a cookie off the plate while they were still hot and bit into it. She was still chewing when she added, "Of all the things that you lost, peace takes the longest to return."

"I know," I sighed, scrubbing a hand over my face.

"I didn't want to say anything until I was sure . . ." Caretaker began, shifting side to side, her fuzzy slippers squeaking slightly. "I check the greenhouse every day. Keep the plants watered. Talk to them. You know . . . It's what Peace would want. When I went out there this morning, the door was locked."

Everyone at the table stilled.

That could only mean one thing.

"Well, well, my little witch has healed from the events last winter, after all. We should celebrate. The six of us," he said, smirking and waggling his eyebrows.

Bad Nat swatted him on the back of the head as she walked by.

"Hey! What was that for?"

"Play stupid games, win stupid prizes," she called over her shoulder as she rounded the corner.

The Warden sighed. "I'm with her on this one."

"Me too," Caretaker added.

"Oh, come on," Lucifer said. "Ann, what about you? I know you're secretly in love with me—"

"Nope," Ann pushed away from the table. "I'm opting out of this escapade. He's all yours, Prime."

I laughed lightly under my breath while Lucifer stood there looking put out at the rejection of my others. "How many times do I have to tell you, we're not having an org—group activities?" I switched last second with a glance at Little. "These are all me. That's weird."

"Oh come on," he said. "It'll be like touching yourself while I watch. Nothing we haven't done before—"

"Lucifer!" I admonished, glancing over at Little who stared up at him with innocent eyes.

"Right, my bad." He crouched down in front of her and patted her head. "Sorry about that."

"What is—"

"Anddddd we're going," I said standing up. Lucifer took my hand and tugged me toward the door. As we stepped through, my body gained awareness, the loci drifting away.

I opened my eyes, finding myself back in the familiar surroundings of my room. Marcel leaned against the door watching me with bemused eyes. Lucifer was perched casually in front of me, a smirk still playing at the corners of his lips.

"You always shoot down my ideas for the loci."

"Because all of them involve fucking several versions of me," I responded with a roll of my eyes climbing off of my bed and heading to Marcel. "Something you're shameless about in front of Little, I might add."

"I wish I could see inside your mind," Marcel commented.

"So he can join the nonexistent orgy," Bad Nat responded with a snort.

I led the two of them down the stairs and into the dining room. "I don't know why," I told Marcel. "It's not like I'd let you fuck them either."

Marcel grimaced. "That's not why."

"Oh?" I prompted as we stepped into the dining room. "Then why do you wish you could enter the loci?"

"Because the level of eidetic memory you possess fascinates me." That was . . . very Marcel, actually. He was the intellectual among my men. It didn't surprise me that he'd find the way my mind works interesting.

Looking up from setting the table, August added, "Not everything is about fucking with some of us. I'd love to see inside that mind of yours because I want to know everything about you."

A blush crept up my cheeks as I walked over to him. August looped an arm around my waist and brought me in for a kiss. Lucifer scoffed.

"I'm not *all* about fucking. I'm just saying we should celebrate the return of Peace."

August paused his breath mingling with mine and a slow smile crept across his face. "Peace is back?"

I bit my lip and nodded. "Sort of. She's there, she's just hiding. I don't think she's ready to come out yet."

While it made me a little sad, I could also understand it. Of all my others, the one that needed the most time to herself was Peace, and the greenhouse brought her that.

"You have no idea how happy I am to hear that, sunling." His whispered words had goosebumps trailing over my skin. We kissed. Softly, at first, but it gradually deepened. I was starting to get carried away when the doorbell rang. August and I pulled apart, both breathless.

"I'll get it," Marcel said, leaving the room.

The sound of my niece and nephew greeted me as the twins bolted inside, shrieks of laughter following in their wake. Piper and Ronan followed after, with Marcel bringing up the rear.

"Can I just say again how much I love that you took over hosting family dinners?" Piper said as we all headed for the dining room. "Not making dinner for a small circus is the best part of my Sundays."

I laughed and said, "I have more help, so I don't mind."

The doorbell sounded again, and this time August went to get it since Marcel and Ronan were already locked into a conversion. Piper and the others settled in at the bar as I went into the fridge and grabbed two pitchers of peach lemonade. I came out and set them on the long island as Hallie, Mist, Anders, and Sienna entered the main area. Of course, Hallie was at Orson's side in an instant, her face lighting up with a smile as the two of them began talking excitedly.

The children, now appearing around eleven years old, had grown so much. Orson and Hallie remained the best of friends, their bond as strong as ever. Sienna had come to accept that Hallie's bond with Orson would evolve naturally, regardless of her influence. Honor, on the other hand, was in the midst of a sassy rebellious phase. Well, that's what Piper liked to say. I'm pretty sure Honor *was* a sassy rebellious phase. Her attitude was sharp and her magic wild. It made for an interesting combination on the best of days.

As I scanned the room, I realized Sasha was missing. Since cutting the bond with August, she'd stopped avoiding me, and while the first family dinner was decidedly more awkward than the ones that followed, by now we'd all gotten used to our new normal.

"Where's Sasha?"

"She'll be along," Sienna said vaguely, a smile playing on her lips. I narrowed my eyes, getting ready to grill her when the doorbell rang again.

"I suppose it's my turn," Lucifer said, exiting the room to get it.

Every eye turned toward the entrance as a deep, distinctly male voice sounded from the foyer. My lips parted. Could it be . . .

Sasha entered a second later with a tall dark-haired man I recognized from some business transactions. Their hands were clasped, and she was smiling widely up at him as she made introductions with Lucifer.

My gaze snapped back to Sienna. "They're holding hands . . . Am I seeing things?" I asked quietly. "Or did Sasha just bring Finn Clarke to a family dinner?"

"You're not seeing things," Sienna replied. Her smile was nearly as big as mine.

"Sasha," Piper called out from where she sat casually inclined against the island bar. "Who's this?"

She was absolutely glowing as she said, "Everyone, meet Finn. Finn, this is my family."

My heart squeezed as a round of greetings and pleasantries were exchanged. I used my magic to materialize an extra chair next to Sasha's usual place. She gave me a grateful smile and I grinned back at her widely.

August, Lucifer, and Marcel busied themselves in the kitchen, quickly coming back out, each carrying a large, covered dishes to be served family style. Piper was not kidding; feeding a house of supernaturals was like cooking for a small circus, but I loved it. And having three extra sets of hands helped.

I walked back into the kitchen to grab the last few things, and Mist fell into step beside me, holding a covered plate. She stopped at the island counter. I grabbed potholders to pull my last dish out of the oven. Holding a large casserole pan, I nodded my head toward her plate.

"What's that?"

Her pride was evident as she set them down. "I've been working on my baking," she said with a shy smile. She pulled off the covering and my heart swelled with pride as I observed her cookies. They looked perfectly edible, not a single one burned. I reached down to pluck one off the plate and took a bite.

"Oh my gods . . . these are so *good*," I said around a mouthful of butterscotch shortbread. I wrapped an arm around her shoulders and pulled her in for a quick hug. "You've come so far, Mist. You should be proud."

I was talking about more than just the cookies and she knew it.

She nodded and then chewed at her lip before flashing me a look of hesitation mixed with excitement. "I've been thinking," she began, "I feel like I've improved a lot these last few months. My training with the Señora is really coming along and for the first time I think I have a good grip on my powers."

I nodded along. "I agree, you really have."

"Right . . ." She fidgeted with the edge of the plate. "So I was wondering . . . I heard you were looking, or considering—gosh I'm messing this all up." A light red tinged her cheeks with embarrassment. "Forget I asked—"

"Nope," I gripped her tighter, not letting her flee back to the dining room. "What's the question?"

Mist took a deep breath and then the words came pouring out, like a dam had broken. "I overheard Sasha and Sienna talking about you wanting to hire another personal assistant and I was thinking maybe I could do it?" She flinched. "I mean, if you're open to it, I'd really like the job. The apartment has been great and I'm really thankful for all that you've done for me. It's just. . . I want to do something with my life. Help people. I don't think I could be Piper's assistant. Too much of what she does is still triggering for me. But I was thinking maybe you might have a spot . . ."

My heart melted a little. This beautiful, broken girl was so strong. She'd never know how proud of her I was, even if I told her every day. "I think that's a great idea. Why don't you hang around after dinner and we can talk about what kind of work you're envisioning?"

Mist's eyes lit up. "I would love that."

I gave her another small squeeze before letting go.

"Of course. Now come on. I wanna watch Sasha with her new man," I whispered conspiratorially with a wink. She laughed lightly before turning and leading the way back to the dining room.

Dinner came and went like the breeze. By the end of it, Finn had us all convinced he was a godsend. I knew he was a good egg from the few times we'd done business together. He wanted to improve the lives of the people who lived in our city, and he cared about others. What wasn't to like? It was obvious from her smile that he made her happier than I'd seen in a long time. And, from the way he gazed at her, he was just as obsessed as she was.

When everyone was stuffed and wandering back toward the living room, I saw my opportunity to get her alone.

"Hey," Sasha glanced at me with a knowing look.

"Hey," she said.

"You have a second?"

"Sure," she said as we both made our way toward the patio door. We stepped outside but left the doors open. Chatter filtered through, hushed by the night air of summer.

"So, Finn Clarke?" I said, grinning wide. "Both a

charmer and handsome. Anything else?" She threw her head back with a laugh.

"Funny. Kind. Considerate. Thoughtful." She smiled wistfully at the scene unfolding in the living room. Finn seemed to sense her eyes on him and turned to give her a playful wink before resuming his conversation with Anders and August. "All the things."

"How long have you been together?"

Sasha's face lit up with a secretive smile. "You're going to think I'm crazy."

I raised an eyebrow. "I'm with three men. Try me."

Sasha laughed. "Touche. We've only been together a week."

I blinked. "Only a week? I was positive you'd been keeping him secret for months the way you guys acted around each other."

Her smile widened. "Only a week."

I stared at her for a second and then I spotted it. She had a new thread connecting to her. I gasped, my hands instinctively covering my mouth in excitement. "He's an aurae bond for you, isn't he?"

Sasha's eyes sparkled as she confirmed with a broad grin. "Yeah, he is. We ran into each other at a coffee shop on Tuesday and have been talking since. It was sudden, but when you know, you know."

I glanced towards the kitchen door, thinking about the three men who held my heart and soul in their hands.

Looking back at Sasha, I nodded. "You know what, you're totally right. When you know, you know."

Finn walked over and extended a hand. "I hope you don't mind terribly if I cut in on girl time. I'm missing my date."

I could have melted into an ooey gooey puddle right there and he wasn't even my beau. "Of course," I said, all but shoving her toward him. Sasha laughed, the husky sound washing over me as she left the porch.

I stayed a little longer, watching their interactions as a group. All of them. The loves of my life. My best friend and her mate. Anders. Sasha. Sienna. Mist. Hallie and Orson and Honor. They smiled and laughed, love and happiness filling the room. Those were the faces of the people that mattered to me most. My found family. I'd do anything for them. Everything was right in the world. We'd fought like hell and made it to the other side. But there was one person's happiness I couldn't confirm. I just had to hope.

I leaned back against the railing, forearms braced on either side. Whispering to no one but myself, I said the words out loud, wishing it would be enough so I could let go. "Kat, if you're out there, I hope you got your happily ever after. I love you. I miss you. But I hope you found everything you were looking for."

I didn't expect an answer. Still, I sighed in silence. Then a dark blue wisp of magic danced in the corner of my vision, and it made me catch my breath. A distant laugh followed, one that I'd know anywhere.

It sounded happy. Free.

Tears pricked my eyes. "Kat?"

This time no answer came, but the night settled

around me like a warm blanket because I knew in my heart that she was happy too.

The End.

Thank you for reading PREMONITION OF PEACE! We hope you enjoyed Nat's story.

If you'd like read an exclusive sneak peek of Nat and Lucifer's Meet Cute scene, go here!

Beneath the Cursed Veil is a fast-paced fae romantasy with tropes such as: touch her and die, one-bed, and enemies to lovers.

"Beneath The Cursed Veil is a super fast paced fantasy with multiple POV's and tons of plot twists. It's an enthralling story that kept me on the edge of my seat. The MMC is absolutely swoon worthy and once his possessive nature kicked in, honey I was drooling! It had me laughing at times and tense with anticipation at others. I did not want it to end. I thoroughly enjoyed this book and can't wait for the continuation of this story." - Alisha Cook, *Goodreads*

About Beneath the Cursed Veil

My captor, my enemy, and my fated mate.

I'm the best bounty hunter in the business. I find lost artifacts that people would kill to possess. I'm also broke. When a notorious leprechaun offers me a job I can't refuse, I realize too late I'm not hunting an object.

The contract was simple; steal the prince, escape unseen.

Spoiler alert: I failed. Horribly.

The moment I step into the fae kingdom beyond the veil, I feel it—someone watching me. Waiting for me.

King Vareck.

He's nothing like I imagined—fierce, unyielding, and as cursed as the frozen lands of Faerie. An ice-cold ruler whose very presence bends the room to his will. He shouldn't care about a thief like me, but we have one thing in common.

Vareck is more than just a king—he's the man who has haunted my dreams for years.

And apparently, I've been in his too.

The difference?

He's been searching the nine realms for me, and I never thought he was real.

Now that he's found me, he has no intention of letting me go.

Beneath the Cursed Veil is sarcastically funny, fantasy romance novel with steam. This is book one in the Faeted Seasons: Winter duet.

START BENEATH THE CURSED VEIL NOW

You can subscribe to our newsletter at https://kelandaurelia.kit.com/subscribe.

Acknowledgments

Nathalie threw us for a loop so many times. She was never meant to have a poly relationship, but apparently we didn't know her as well as we thought. August burst onto the page in book one and their chemistry was not planned. Every time we thought we knew the direction this story would go, Nat changed course. For this final installment, we ended up fully plotting this book . . . and it *STILL* took turns we were not expecting.

So here we are. The finale.

We couldn't have done it without the support of the author community. Just as Nat leans on her friends—her found family—we lean on ours. Heather Hildenbrand, Annie Anderson, Heather Renee... you all know how special you are to us. This would be so much harder without you in our lives. To Becca Syme and Skye Warren . . . you have taught us so much. Your brilliance and knowledge are invaluable, and we are so grateful you share it with us all.

To our children. We love you. Always.

To Mr. Jane, for being TMFS and holding down the fort during two conferences and the edits that never ended, all while you were slammed and being a badass at work. I appreciate you.

And finally, a thank you to our readers for following Nathalie's journey. We hope you feel the love as we all say goodbye to New Chicago.

Until next time,
Aurelia & Kel